ALSO BY ERICA ROSE EBERHART

Tarnished (Book One of the Elder Tree Trilogy)

DIMINISHED

DIMINISHED
THE ELDER TREE TRILOGY
BOOK TWO

ERICA ROSE EBERHART

This is a work of fiction. All of the characters, organizations, and events portrayed in this novel are either products of the author's imagination or are used fictitiously.

Published in the United States by Creative James Media.

DIMINISHED. Copyright © 2025 by Erica Rose Eberhart. All rights reserved. Printed in the United States of America. For information, address Creative James Media, 9150 Fort Smallwood Road, Pasadena, MD 21122.

www.creativejamesmedia.com

978-1-965648-09-4 (hardback)

First U.S. Edition 2025

AUTHOR'S NOTE

Diminished is a high fantasy that shows the events preceding war. As is often true with life, particularly when on the brink of conflict, this story is not always happy. There are moments of bliss and accomplishment, but there is also figurative and literal darkness. I promise this trilogy will come to a happy ending—we just have to travel through the dark to reach the light.

With that, dear reader, please take care and know this novel contains the following: depictions of fantasy violence (sword fights, arrow strikes, etc.); death of parental figures and death of a loved one; discussion of torture and murder, escalating violence and fantasy genocide; talk of superior race and social persecution; female oppression and marital abuse; body horror/transformation including descriptions of blood, burning, injuries, and scars; light spice/sex; complicated parent-child relationships; discussion of self-harm; and depictions of anxiety and panic attacks.

As always, if you are sensitive to any of these areas, please take care. Only you can best decide what you can handle.

*For those who choke on the fire within:
let it be wild and free.*

PRONUNCIATION GUIDE

Many of the names of places and people are influenced from Gaelic, Scandinavian, German, and English pronunciations, but some variances from those languages of our world may defer to the world of Visennore.

People
Ailith: *Ay-l-ith*
Caitriona: *Kah-tree-nah*
Greer: *Gh-rear*
Barden: *Bar-den*
Isla: *Eye-lah*
Kayl: *K-ale*
Cearny: *Kear-knee*
Róisín: *Ro-sheen*
Ceenear: *See-near*
Raum: *R-ah-mm*
Onora: *Oh-no-rah*
Niveem: *Nive-ee-m*
Shad: *Ch-add*
Malcolm: *Mm-al-come*
Lachlan: *Lack-lan*

Places
Visennore: *V-iss-en-nor*
Wimleigh: *Whim-lee*
Braewick: *Brr-aye-wick*
Ulla Syrmin: *Ooo-la Sear-min*
Invarlwen: *In-varl-when*
Mazgate: *Mah-zz-gate*
Avorkaz: *Ah-vore-kah-zz*
Beaslig: *Bees-ll-ig*
Caermythlin: *Care-myth-lynn*
Umberfend: *Uhm-burr-fend*
Ätbënas: *Hau-t-beh-nah-ss*

Caitriona Gablaigh. Art by Luxury Banshee

Caitriona's Dragon. Art by Olesya Tivuel Kolpakova

CHAPTER ONE

GREER

The gong of bells sent finches skyward and past the open window of the queen's chamber; their wings on the wind whispered of dead souls whilst the bells pealed again. Deep and hollow, their ring vibrated through the bones of the bell masters whose callused hands pulled on the thick ropes to make the bronze chimes herald in the evening. They declared to the entire city the day was done. The funeral rites could begin.

Queen Greer, the ruler of Wimleigh Queendom for nearly two years, was drawn from her writing pad by the sound. Her focus on notes and figures, a world of paperwork she hadn't quite expected to contend with when she received the crown, could finally be placed aside as she met the gaze of the royal guard waiting across from her. The serious young woman stood at attention by the interior door of the room and gave the queen a single nod. Greer placed her quill into its holder and stood. They had only a few minutes to catch up.

The internal stairwell reserved for secret movement of the royal family provided their quickest route to the guard yard which sat in the inner ward between the castle and the servant homes built into the outer ward. The stairwell was cool, but the ever-present humidity leaked through the slivers of windows they passed as they rushed down the stone steps. In the height of summer, the sun lingered in the sky longer, but the valley was already filling with shadows. With the sun going to rest, its burning heat loosened its grip on the city, whilst memories of the beating rays still rose from the castle's stones. With light fading, the grieving family could at last do what they deemed proper.

As Ailith opened the door to the yard, the percussion of drumbeats indicated the proceedings had already begun. Greer hesitated, her stomach knotting and a jolt of concern expanded to her limbs.

"You aren't late," Ailith reassured, her voice soft despite that they were alone. Greer gave the guard a concerned look but found Ailith's expression one of gentle sincerity. She even offered her queen a small smile before directing her gaze elsewhere.

Ailith MacCree took over many duties in Barden's absence and Greer was surprised daily by how much she mirrored the senior guard. Just a year into working for the royal guard and in close proximity to Greer, Ailith could read her moods and thoughts almost as well as Barden. She appreciated this in her moments of uncertainty, like now as she hovered in the doorway to the stairs and found that taking the next step into the yard was harder to do than expected.

Greer pulled the hood of her summer cloak over her blonde hair and brushed her hands down the simple tunic and pants royal guards wore, all borrowed from Ailith specifically for this outing. She once had similar uniforms, but they were discarded when she became queen under her mother's orders.

"A queen doesn't have to dress like a guard. She's the *queen*," her mother declared shortly after Greer's crowning. Greer had sat miserably as her mother dropped the well-worn uniform into the eager flames in the hearth of her room. Nearly two years later and Greer still clutched at her bitterness for it all. While she quickly had pants and shirts made to match her sovereign role, it was necessary she blend in for this outing. It was one thing to legalize magic again, another for the queen to be seen at previously-outlawed funeral rites steeped in what once was banned.

"Do I look alright?" It was startling to feel so hesitant to enter the yard; every inch of the castle grounds was hers since birth and never once was she reluctant to go into the area, at least not until now.

Ailith pressed her fingers to her lips as she shifted back. The guard was close to Greer's height with skin browned from the summer sun. The ripples of scars over her right arm stood out, but that didn't stop the guard from rolling up the sleeves of her shirt as she worked in the stifling rooms of the castle. After a moment of consideration, Ailith reached forward to adjust Greer's hood, her fingers light and quick. "You look like any other guard; no one will know. Just don't let your hood fall back."

They crossed the yard alone, past training lanes, wooden beams with hack marks from swords and dented bullseyes. It was a place often filled with training bodies, a place where both Greer and Ailith spent hours and left their sweat and blood behind to mix in the dirt. The emptiness made Greer's uncertainty grow. Dust kicked up from their boots to coat their dark leather and turn it pale. They weaved their way through the yard, silent beyond their footsteps, and past a training post where a small bird sat. Twisting its head, it watched Greer with knowing. A death bringer. When they flew, the black and white feather markings on their underside looked like floating skulls, while their heads had red caps as if they were dipped in blood. Some said their red caps were due to their plunging into dying bodies to drink the souls of the dead, but Greer knew that wasn't true. The sight of the bird made Greer choke, and she turned away to focus on the homes they walked toward with determination to ignore the existence of the creature.

Like shadowy witnesses, many of the guard homes stood quiet and dark as their inhabitants clustered outside of one in particular. It wasn't a miraculous or special home. The clay and stone outer walls were similar to the rest of the dwellings lining the first rampart, a listless color of earth with the greenery of vines growing on the walls. The small windows of the two-story structure glowed brightly against the darkening world. What occurred inside the dwelling, however, drew a group of interested fellows who clustered near the windows and open door. Their murmurs were low against the persistent beat of the drum but provided an additional vibrating hum beneath each beat.

Greer glanced over her shoulder again. Ailith followed close behind and waved her forward.

"Go." Ailith directed Greer with ease few other guards were capable of. The rest were all professional, but Ailith was part of the inner circle and her manner exhibited that. She flashed a reassuring smile, her teeth bright in the gloom. "I'll be outside waiting."

Breathing deeply, Greer rolled her shoulders and stood tall to step amongst those outside the home. The crowd was made of guards; guards who worked for her family for generations, longer than Greer was alive. There were younger guards, too; people she witnessed train and even received their pledges for devoted service. With barely a glance at their queen, the group parted, making a clear path forward. Perhaps her outfit didn't allow as much discretion as she hoped.

The mourners nodded, but continued to speak amongst themselves, unbothered by her arrival which eased some of the tension from Greer's shoulders. She was their boss, yes, but in this instant, she wasn't their concern. They were here for the first funeral rites since their banning many years ago for a guard they had an abundance of respect for. Greer was honored to receive an invitation from the grieving family to attend.

Barden's family.

There was never a time Greer didn't know the Willstrung family. Shaw, Barden's father, led the royal guard until Barden was born. He quit on the spot; his attention turned to training youths who hoped to become royal guards themselves. He didn't want to lose his life on a field, not when he had a child to care for. It was something Greer's father was bitter about until his death. There was never any dispute: Shaw was the best royal guard and having him leave to become a trainer wasn't just a loss to Cearny, but the entire kingdom. Greer, however, had found it sweet Shaw gave up such a desired position because he wanted to ensure his longevity for his family; it was one of many views that differed from her father's.

The royal guard benefited from Shaw's instruction with the next graduating classes more skilled than previous. When Barden came of age, Shaw taught him, and a few years later, Greer too. Not a single royal guard hadn't worked with Shaw at some point, it was what made his sudden death so hard for the entirety of the castle. All the worse for Barden.

Greer stepped into Shaw's home where his wife Rowan and his three daughters still lived. Gazes lifted to take in the queen at the doorstep which spurred shuffling bodies as they made room. The house's interior was heavy with the scent of melted beeswax and herbs, and glowed with the yellow light of candles. They sat on every available surface with dying flowers nestled at their bases; the melted wax was long, bumpy strands that hardened over the petals and off the edge of tables. Greer was told it was tradition to light candles in the home of the person who passed and keep them lit until the body left the residence. The light provided a pathway forward for the soul, so it may return to its family and body if it was chased away in the fearful moments before death.

Upon the dining table just beyond the door lay Shaw's body, still, cold, and with pale skin. His brown hair was flushed with gray, and smile lines carved along his eyes and cheeks. He seemed to only be asleep, his expression one of rest, if not for the pallor of his skin.

Would Barden look similar when he was older?

She searched the room until her gaze connected with only his. Brown stubble shown against his face, articulating the curve of his clenched jaw. His auburn hair hung loose with wavy strands hanging into his eyes that rose to meet Greer's. He visibly relaxed as his lips softened and his shoulders dropped. A brief shadow of a smile crossed his face and his eyes glistened, bringing out their blue while the skin beneath was shadowed from both lack of sleep and sadness. He turned his hand, exposing the paleness of his palm, and signaled Greer to come to his side.

Greer stepped further into the room; her hands held together as she tried to make herself small while she searched for a path forward. Her eyes passed over the remaining Willstrungs. Rowan stood at the head of the table, bent over her husband's face as she gently wiped it with a thick golden syrup—honey—and Barden's sisters placed reeds; grasses; small, red bog fruit; and yellow, pink, and white swamp flowers betwixt Shaw's body and the sheet he rested upon. Guards thirty years Greer's senior stood at the corners of the table, their hands at their sides and their gazes down while Barden's family worked.

As Greer circled the table, squeezing past mourners, she considered the last time she saw Barden a few days prior, yet the space in time felt infinite. She never went long without interacting with him.

"May I attend the rites?" Greer had asked when he requested leave for the funeral. She hadn't known what his answer would be. It wasn't until adulthood during one night of their travels that Barden confessed his family practiced the old ways and honored the magical creatures of the world. At the time, the very act was illegal, but Greer held the knowledge tightly against her chest. A secret cherished and never revealed—not until it was safe.

Her father would have sentenced Barden's parents to death, Barden would have lost his role in the guard if not his head, and his sisters would have been thrown to the streets if not killed as well. It had been a risk for him to tell her and all the more important to hide the knowledge away.

Her father's hatred of the old ways made her uncertain of Barden's answer, but she was selfishly pleased when Barden's red-rimmed eyes brightened, if only for a moment. He nodded then pulled his gaze from Greer's, seemingly shy as he said softly, his voice rough with unshed tears, "That would mean the world to me."

Now a few days later, his shyness was gone. He focused on his parents as his mother hummed quietly, bringing Greer to the present as she stepped beside Barden. It was rhythmic, akin to waves of the shore, rushing forward before drifting away. Each Willstrung began humming too. The vibration filled the house and spilled through the windows to pass over guards clustering in the yard. Guttural, groaning murmurs became low singing that rose in volume from nearly all present.

Greer took in the song with wide eyes; it was unfamiliar, and she was one of the few who did not join. It was a welcome surprise that the old practices never quite died amongst the men who followed the king's orders. They sang with pride and their children standing at their side knew the lyrics as well. How often did the guards sing these songs in the privacy of their homes, away from the judgmental ears of Cearny and his closest supporters? It thrilled Greer to think they all maintained secret practices for so long. It also served as a reminder that what she set forth to do—to lead her country to accept magic practices and creatures once more—would find resonance in more than she hoped.

Rowan tilted her head back, drawing Greer's attention to the matriarch of the family, and closed her eyes as she clutched her chest. Her fingers were desperate, scratching at the fabric of her dress as if to pry her heart from there. Rowan's lips parted to release a singing cry. It was as if her soul would fall into her hands due to the depths of her sorrows, all conveyed in her keening. The vibration of her voice caught Greer's throat, urging her to join although she didn't know the song's words. In the end, she still understood the language. There is no barrier when it comes to words of loss. She cared for Shaw too, after all. He was strong and determined, stern yet soft. She strove to make him proud when he taught her, and thrilled when he complimented her growing skills, something she never experienced from her own father.

A deep hum rose beside Greer, drawing her attention away from Rowan. Barden sang, taking the place of his mother in the silence that followed her cry. Greer sucked in a breath. In Barden's exposure of grief and the sound of his voice, low and rhythmic, she saw him anew. His eyes remained on Shaw and tears shimmered in their blue gaze. He stepped back from the table as his song ended and slipped his hand into Greer's along the way to pull her with him. His siblings also stepped back, leaving the four men at the corners and his mother at the head. The men reached forward to take the ends of the sheet and pull it tightly to lift the body. They shifted and with the mournful song's beat, moved toward the door.

One by one, Barden's younger siblings followed the men, and Greer took an uneasy step backwards to give room.

"Stay with me." Barden's breath was hot against her cheek as he bowed his head toward her.

She nodded and realized her hand remained in his. Greer couldn't speak, the display of their heartache filled her chest and made it tight. When her own father died, there was never this number of tears. Perhaps from some of his devoted personnel, although Greer never noticed, and certainly not from those expected. Her mother remained blank, her emotions carefully held back; Caitriona remained asleep, exhausted by the curse that tore her body apart and then brought it back together; and Greer felt nothing but boiling rage.

For the Gablaigh family, tradition called for the heir to keep vigil of the dead monarch the night prior to their burial. Locked in the room with his corpse, Greer was expected to seek wisdom and mourn her father as he had done with his before. But instead, Greer sat in a corner avoiding the corpse at all costs.

What wisdom could she seek from a man with so much blood on his hands? What could she learn from him other than hatred and distrust? What could be absorbed since she was the one who drove her sword into her father's gut and witnessed the glow of life seep from his eyes? An act she knew, over a year later, she would do again if given the chance?

Barden shifted on his feet, his hand solidly holding Greer's as he stepped forward and followed the trail of people leaving the little house. Greer studied the tears moving freely down his cheeks, following the paths forged by those that came before. Looking at his heartbreak displayed so honestly, she wondered with a different type of heartbreak, what must it be like to have loved and been loved by your father?

She found her breath caught between her teeth when he turned to her, their movement slowed by the exodus of people. "Is this alright?" His grip tightened on her hand.

"Always." Greer squeezed his hand back.

Physical touch was all part of the job. He was viewed as the valiant protector of the queen, although she held her own in a fight. Often, he reached to help her on steps or touched her back as she passed before him through a door. This was somehow different in the way he looked at her, in the delicate way he held her hand, and the close proximity they kept to one another.

As they neared the doorway, one of the older guards who retired years before bowed, snapping Greer out of her drifting thoughts as Barden led her away. Barden's touch was nothing, just par for the course.

Fresh air and the continued murmur of people greeted them outside the home. The chatter was louder and hung in the humid air, as if being indoors forced those within to hold their tongue and stew in their thoughts until they could release them to the night sky. The mourners climbed onto carts and horses, others seemed determined to walk, and the shuffle of bodies felt startling after the stillness inside.

A cart rolled to the doorway and the four men gently placed Shaw's body upon it and covered him with the ends of the cloth. Rowan climbed to the front row of seats for the cart; her gaze lingered on the form of her husband before she settled beside the driver. Two of Barden's sisters sat in the second row. Another cart arrived behind the first, and Barden's remaining sister climbed on the back, leaving the front row free.

"I'll drive the cart," Barden told the driver, another guard, who stepped off with a nod and receded into the crowd. Barden looked behind him, his gaze falling on Greer and for a moment, as he took in a slow breath, she could see how much he struggled to maintain his composure. A ripple expanded over his face, and he appeared suddenly younger. A boy afraid, lost, sad and in need of his father.

Barden let go of her hand as he reached for the edge of the cart. The tip of his tongue passed over his lips before he looked at Greer again. "You're welcome to ride with me. But I understand if you prefer to ride with your guards."

Beyond the mourners and carts was Ailith with another guard at her side, Paul. Beside Paul, Greer's horse with an attendant holding the reins waited. She made a pointed look at the cart and gave a nod. Ailith raised her chin and murmured something to Paul who bowed his head toward the attendant. The boy turned away, taking her horse with him as the two guards moved into the line behind Barden's cart.

Greer turned to Barden. Their eyes met and it sparked a tingling in Greer's throat and down her chest.

"So long as you want me here, I'm here." Greer's voice was quiet, that nervous feeling when she left the castle still a curled thing in her chest and drowning her volume, but it faded slightly under Barden's expression.

A ghost of a smile on his face was there and gone before he helped her onto the cart. The warmth of his body pressed into her side as the cart lurched forward. It kept Greer's back straight and her gaze ahead. Mourners who hadn't mounted horses or carts parted to let them through and they began the sad journey ahead.

They passed through the wards and gatehouse, before spilling into the city—a solid procession weaving through the main street toward the southern road that left the valley and curved toward the marshes. The lower marshes, the closest to Braewick, were an hour of consistent travel by horse.

Once beyond the ramparts, the scent of the city rose in the warm summer air: wood smoke, urine, stale beer, and cooked meats. Citizens still making their way home stepped aside and their reactions mirrored the variety of political beliefs Greer quickly came to understand. Some watched with interest, others bowed their heads and placed their hands against their chests with the sign of respect, and a few glared and spat at the ground. Greer studied the reaction of her people around the edge of her hood. It wasn't surprising; since legalizing magic and naming her half-dragon sister the heir to the throne, practice of the old ways rose while those who hated magic became a stronger voice all together. The agitation it brought was festering and soon to burst, but that was a problem for later.

Greer shifted on the cart and noted her guards remained close, their backs straight and gazes forward. Beyond were older men who worked with Shaw, and further on, the young guards who trained under him. The ride to the swamps continued in relative silence beside the creak of the cartwheels, the snuffle of Ailith's horse and the rhythmic footfall of people and horses alike.

They moved along the coastal road, the travel slowed by those walking until they reached an area where the ground flattened. Beyond, pools of swamp water glimmered against the half-moon's glow and small lights blinked to life as the drowning dukes turned their attention to the group. The mourners slowed to a stop and Greer pulled the hood of her cloak down. People fanned out in the tall summer grasses, the night bugs shrill in the settled night, and the lapping water speech of the drowning dukes heightened as they moved closer to shore.

The four men lifted Shaw's body from the cart and kept the cloth-wrapped body elevated as they moved to the edge of the shore with Rowan following close behind. Others gathered, holding aloft lit lanterns that highlighted their surroundings and sharpened shadows as they cast a warm glow over the group and made tears stand out against cheeks like glittering dew.

"Follow me," Barden instructed, his voice low and for Greer's ears only. They joined the rest of the Willstrungs on the water's edge.

Ignoring the bite of bugs, Greer narrowed her eyes to study the glimmering lights in the water.

"The dukes." Greer released the air she held in her chest.

"We've drawn them here," Barden explained.

Once upon a time, all guards and kings were brought here as their final resting place. Greer's great grandfather was the last king placed into the waters before it was banned by his son—her grandfather, Donal. She wondered if all the time that passed felt long to the dukes, or if the decades were only a blink of the eye. How did they judge time when it was meaningless to them?

Rowan sang again; a long, sorrowful wail filled with pain and ending with a hollow *ohhh* that leaked into the night and silenced the bugs. Greer's brow knit with question and Barden stepped close, filling her nostrils with the scent of him; a mix of sweat and wood, and a spice he often crushed against his clothes.

"The guides will carry him to the water's edge and place him there. We'll watch to see if the dukes accept the offering. He's old, so they won't change him into a duke fit for battle, but if we're lucky and they find him honorable, they'll bring him to the depths of the water where he'll rest."

"Why wouldn't they make him into a duke who can fight in battle?" She turned back to the water. Some of the dukes were close enough she could make out their faces. Human-like if Greer didn't study them too much. Maybe they were even recognizable by their relatives, if any were present. The wetness of their skin shone in the firelight, their teeth were too sharp, and ripples of gills ran along the sides of their necks before disappearing behind their ears. They could kill a man within seconds of entering the water, but long ago they used to rise and become a fearsome army. The dukes' acceptance was an honor but becoming one, even greater. "He was the best guard and served for so long."

"That's exactly why," Barden continued. "To my understanding they only accept young warriors into their ranks, those who haven't completed their earthly work. For men like my father, they'll be similar to the dukes in body so they exist beneath the waters, but they won't come to fight. They've earned their eternal rest."

The glittering eyes of the dukes broke apart as they spread and swam closer to shore. The waters were shallow along the edges of the pools but no one knew just how deep they went. No one was willing to find out; to step into the water was to welcome the dukes' rage in all instances but this.

As the dukes neared the shore, they paused, their eyes attentive as they looked at the men holding Shaw. Rowan continued to sing, her voice loud and singular in the night as the men stepped into the water. Greer sucked in a breath and grew tense as she expected the dukes to attack.

But the dukes remained motionless, allowing the men to move further into the water where the dark liquid lapped at their knees as they stopped to lower Shaw. Water seeped into the sheet, surrounding Shaw's body. The reeds, fruits and flowers found their way beyond the sheet to float as bright spots against the inky dark water. Rowan stood behind Shaw, singing as the men let him go and returned to solid ground. Shaw floated briefly with the parting gifts of his children framing his form before he began to slowly sink.

The dukes moved forward.

In the dim light of the lanterns, they appeared even more youthful. They emerged, climbing to their feet but never leaving their watery home entirely. Their clothing—various guard uniforms of Wimleigh and kingdoms that no longer existed—were tattered and water-logged, but their skin glistened in shades of gray and green. Old war wounds were open, but no blood oozed out, whatever magic that made them exist preserved the marks. They studied Rowan long enough for Greer to slowly breathe in, then stepped with sturdy legs best used for swimming to circle Shaw in silence. They reached for him, guiding his body through the water as they sank down in deeper pools where other dukes waited.

Rowan stopped singing. The clicks and slurps of the dukes, the language only they knew, became the only sound. Turning their glowing gazes back to the crowd, they waited.

"What—" Greer began but Barden stepped forward, dropping Greer's hand.

Immediately she felt the loss of his warm palm, but it was quickly forgotten as his voice tumbled out, his deep guttural wail of song vibrated through the air and made Greer's chest ache. He sang in another language, but the meaning was clear all the same: *Here is my father, I give him to you, please let him rest.*

Greer closed her eyes. The disdain for her own father still coated her tongue as an awful aftertaste. She wrestled in the darkness of night with the disgust she felt when looking at his corpse, at the sense of freedom she felt when she saw him lying in that cold room over a year before; she never would have thought to sing out the same wishes. He hadn't deserved them.

A loud splash forced Greer's eyes open; the dukes hit the water with the palms of their hands, making droplets glisten in the air prior to slipping beneath and vanishing from sight—Shaw's body disappeared along with them.

"They accepted him." Barden's voice cracked. His body bent forward; the strength gone. He hastily wiped his eyes and made fists with his hands as he studied the water. His voice was barely above a whisper. "They found him honorable."

"Of course, they would." Greer reached forward, slipping her hand over Barden's and pressing her fingers through his. His fist came loose, his fingers spreading and she held tight. Gently pulling his arm toward her, she encouraged him to turn away from the scene and sought out his gaze. The pain on his face made her heart ache in a million places. "Barden, he was one of the most honorable men I've ever known."

One by one, people began to leave. Those who walked already turned away, making as quick a time back to the city. Other carts turned, the horses eager for their barns and feed. Rowan and Barden's sisters loaded onto their carts, and Ailith and Paul, lingering toward the back of the crowd, moved to the side as they kept a quiet eye on the proceedings.

The hour was growing late, the summer bugs that only sang in the deepest corners of the night filled the marsh. Barden guided Greer to their cart and helped her to her seat as she thought of her bed and was glad she would soon greet it.

Ailith moved closer and nodded a brief greeting to Greer before reaching forward to touch Barden's shoulder. "I'm sorry. For what little time I had with him, it was clear he was a wonderful man."

Barden smiled, although it didn't reach his eyes. "Thank you, I know."

"Is there anything you need from me or Paul?" Ailith lobbed this question towards Greer.

"When we return to the castle—" Greer's voice was lost by a singular screech that overwhelmed the landscape.

Another shriek came from a further corner of the marsh water, followed by other screams whilst dukes' glowing eyes reappeared one by one. Soon all screamed in unison. Spiderwebs spread over the glass of what lanterns remained. The hands of observers covered ears and horses kicked, their ears going back as they shook their heads from the sound. Their whinnies were lost, overpowered by the screech of the dukes. Greer clenched her teeth and curled her back away. Barden's hands fell upon her, pulling her against his chest, one arm wrapped over her head in an attempt to protect her ears.

Then it stopped. As suddenly as it started, it stopped and the waters where the glowing gaze of the dukes remained grew still. Ailith's horse backed away and stomped its feet with discomfort. Paul's ran out of the lantern's light.

"What—what was that?" Greer sat up as Barden's hands fell from her.

He stared at the water as a trickle of blood leaked from one ear. Licking his lips, he sat down, his free hand having held the reins through the torrent of sound. With a flick, he pulled the horses from their discomfort and urged them to move. His brow furrowed and he didn't look back at the water as he directed the cart toward the city.

"It was a warning from the dukes. There's death ahead."

CHAPTER TWO

Caitriona

A month prior, the night Shaw was sent to the dukes, Ailith reiterated what happened as she faced Caitriona. They sat upon Caitriona's bed with their knees touching as Ailith described the screamed warning the dukes gave. All the while a pit formed in Caitriona's stomach, rising until it wedged itself between her heart and her ribs, and made every beat full of suffering. She felt ill at ease with a sense of discomfort like the rising of hairs on one's neck during a lightning storm. No one living ever heard the dukes give such a warning and Caitriona felt it stemmed from true knowing.

Since returning from her respite in the Endless Mountains, all was peaceful in Wimleigh Queendom. Greer called off advances against the Mazgate Dominion and sent a peace treaty that Jace Hergrew, the steward of the dominion, signed. There appeared to be no threats and they were not at war. With each week, the guards and castle staff relaxed a little more. The threat seemed to pass, maybe the dukes were wrong. But the older guards who were educated on the myths of the dukes made clear this was not the promised death of any one individual, but many. Now Ailith was leaving and Greer as well, traveling beyond the valley to Stormhaven for a fortnight while Caitriona was left behind and forced into the role she never really thought she would experience: the acting steward of Wimleigh Queendom while the monarch traveled. A nerve-wracking task on its own if it wasn't for the fact she would oversee the Day of Royal Greeting.

The day Greer and Ailith were scheduled to leave, before the sun fully rose, Caitriona slipped to Greer's room to give her goodbyes. It was in its normal state of disarray; dresses discarded onto the unmade bed, papers covered the table beside the window, maps and crossed-out notes sat beside candles that had melted to misery. Caitriona stood in the center of the room, wringing her hands as Greer darted from her wardrobe to open drawers.

After a few moments, Caitriona conveyed her dread. "Must you take everyone with you? Must you leave me with no one? I have no idea what I'm doing, I have no training."

Greer frowned before her dresser as she pulled her riding gloves on. "I think you have a lot less faith in yourself than you should. You've a lifetime of learning, and you're empathetic. You're likely one of the best people to do the Day of Royal Greeting."

"Why are you putting those on?" A voice chirped from the doorway, drawing their attention. "And why won't you let the servants clean your room?"

Their mother stepped in, somehow appearing younger since becoming a widow, as if the weight of being the former king's wife slipped from her and recovered a rare jewel. She was already dressed in her day gown, her hair delicately braided back from her face and exposing the slight curving point of her ears. Her neck and fingers glittered with jewels and the early morning light made her green eyes sparkle as she looked over the room. She must have been awake for hours.

Greer paused, her lips tightening into a line. "My riding gloves?"

"Yes. You'll ride in the royal carriage," their mother continued, stepping before Greer and looking her outfit over. Her nose wrinkled with judgment before she reached to fidget with Greer's collar. "You're the queen, you can't ride horseback to a royal event. You shouldn't wear your riding clothes either. You must be presentable. More presentable than the state of your room."

"Luckily, the queendom can't witness the state of my room. You know I'd rather clean my own mess. Demanding the servants do everything was Father's tendency, never mine," Greer replied, pulling back and rubbing her collar. "Anyway, I'm going to change into a dress before we arrive. We have to camp in the marshes for a night before reaching Stormhaven."

"You're still leaving here are you not? The people of Braewick matter just as much as those in Stormhaven. Actually, they matter even more. If you anger them enough, they're right at your doorstep so it's best to put on a proper front. You need to give a show as you leave the valley and to do that, you need to be in a carriage."

"Father always rode out on horseback," Caitriona offered, trying to come to her sister's defense. While she was upset Greer was leaving and taking Ailith with her, the unspoken bond to stand united against their parents remained.

"He was involved in so many battles I'm not surprised you don't remember, but for royal calls he rode in the carriage, as your sister should." Róisín looked over her shoulder at Caitriona. Pausing her administrations to Greer, she turned to face her youngest daughter. "You should wear something more fitting as well, not a simple dress like that. You're expected on the parapet walk to see your sister off, it's a presentation for the people, not just bidding farewell. Both of you hop to it, get dressed, the procession is in an hour."

Their mother left the room as quickly as she entered. A bustle of fabric and glint of jewels, leaving the pair to stare at the empty space between them.

"See?" Greer said. "I'm *not* leaving you alone. Mother will guide you through the Day of Royal Greeting."

Caitriona's shoulders dropped and Greer's face softened.

"I know, you'd rather Ailith be here."

"And *you*," Caitriona admitted. "The both of you."

"How come?" Greer's tone wasn't judgmental, but soft with genuine curiosity. She pulled off her riding gloves and tossed them to her dresser before approaching her wardrobe once more.

"I worry I can't do this without the both of you. I've never ... I've never interacted with the people before. I always wanted to. I was always desperate to join you when you did things like this with Father, but now it's different." Caitriona stepped to the dressing table where Greer's hair pins and combs were laid out. Her fingertips traced over the pearls inlaid in the metal of the pins and the cuts of diamonds glittering from the early morning light. She lifted her gaze to the looking glass above the table and her frown deepened.

Caitriona believed she was pretty once. Round, pale cheeks. Large blue eyes. Deep red hair she inherited from her mother. Her reflection was nothing like the appearance she once had. Her hair had become an unnatural gold, the blue of her eyes had faded to a yellow hue, and four horns sprouted from her skull to curl backwards. That was just what was visible. Even in the summer heat she wore dresses that covered her shoulders so no one could see the glimmering scales covering them. It was the only part she could hide away from the world.

At first, when her hair became gold, she embraced the change. She thought it magic. The problem was that it *was* magic, a dark magic, and now she was trapped with the remnants of a curse displayed for all to see. A constant reminder of what was done to her.

While Greer went through great efforts to legalize magic use and stop the immediate killing of magic creatures, Caitriona wasn't convinced all of Wimleigh Queendom were willing to accept the heir as a half-dragon woman.

In the mirror's reflection, Greer pulled a traveling dress free and turned to Caitriona. She paused; her face sympathetic as the dress dropped from her hands.

"Mother will be there," Greer repeated as she crossed the floor and gripped Caitriona's arms from behind. She leaned down to rest her chin on Caitriona's shoulder. "She's well-versed in all that needs to be done. She'll guide you. And the guards remaining here are good people; they'll protect you. I know you're nervous, but I also know you're completely capable of this. And you need to start taking on more roles within the household as my heir."

Caitriona leaned against Greer's chest, tilting her head to the side as she couldn't risk her horns nicking Greer. Studying their reflection in the looking glass, she realized they both changed in the last year. Greer's skin was less sun kissed than before she became queen. Beforehand, she was often outdoors practicing in the guard yard or running errands for their father, and her tanned skin brought out the honey tones in her otherwise brown eyes, but now she was inside nearly as much as Caitriona.

"I'm also worried." Caitriona's eyes widened with her confession. Her reflection mirrored her look of concern. "I'm worried about what the dukes did. From what the guards said and what I've read in our history books, their warning is something to be taken seriously."

Greer's eyebrows rose and a distance formed in her eyes. Caitriona saw this look pass over her sister's face more than once; it was typical when she tucked emotions away and secured her mask to perform her birthright. After all, emotions had no place beneath a crown.

"We have no solid proof that's a sign of death. We only have tales from old men and the singular historic text in the castle you found that mentions the dukes. Even if it's a sign of death, there's no tales indicating how soon. A month has passed and everything is fine. I'll see if the Stormhaven elders have additional books that may give us better guidance." Greer embraced Caitriona tightly and kissed her cheek. "I'll be home before the next full moon, and so will Ailith."

But that was just the thing, Caitriona's soul was tied to Greer and her heart to Ailith. Between the two of them, she felt safe. She felt whole. Between both of them, she found she was more accepting of the dragon-like girl she was. She forgot herself when she was with them; she forgot what she had become. Between both of them, she didn't despise herself as much. What would she do without them by her side?

Hours later, upon the parapet walk of Braewick Castle's curtain wall, which was wide enough for protection from both weaponry and people, a line of royal guards stood at attention. Recent graduates, eager to follow every order, were stepping into their role as a fleet created specifically for the heir to the throne. As the sun rose, the humidity thick and indicating another warm day with a possibility for storms as summer continued its hold over the valley, the guards were joined by two figures in regal gowns who stood like flames against their gray and green wardrobes. Princess Caitriona first crossed the parapet walk to the gatehouse overlooking the main thoroughfare. Placing her hands upon stones that still held the coolness from the previous night, she looked down the city's main road and felt her gut twist into a knot.

A yell pulled Caitriona's attention to the street below, now filled with morning sun. A guard signaled to open the gates. The heavy wooden doors slowly swung back and the metal gates pulled upward.

Her mother stepped beside her, not a hair out of place despite the heavy, wet air.

Curious townspeople gathered along the roadway. For many, it was their first opportunity to see their new ruler up close. They waited and spoke to one another while keeping their gazes on the gate. The rumble of horseshoes against cobblestones quickly drowned their chatter as a series of guards issued onto the street. Caitriona leaned forward, squinting down at the tops of heads until she spotted Ailith riding Onyx, the large, black horse they acquired from Avorkaz.

The sight of Ailith made Caitriona's chest tight, the ball that formed a month prior grew in size. She was being unreasonable; hadn't Caitriona just come home a year before after abandoning Ailith? Who was she to be so bitter over Ailith going away?

She thought of Ailith's excitement when she burst into Caitriona's room after receiving news she would go. Many nights, although not all, Ailith slipped into Caitriona's room after the evening meal. They rarely saw one another during the daylight hours, beside days that Ailith was free from work, so they met after sunset and devoured their time together as if starved.

"Can you believe it?" Ailith had exclaimed. "Greer wants me to go as a top guard. I'll be equal to Barden, at least almost. He's still the top of it all, but I'll be in the same room as him. Where Greer goes, Barden goes. I'll overhear discussions and Greer said afterward, she reviews everything with Barden and the other top guards to see if they have any personal insight."

She was pulling her boots off and her brown hair hung loose over her face until she looked up. Caitriona saw Ailith's gleeful smile.

Ailith's bright excitement was like a flash of heat near a fire, and the flames of her joy nearly brought tears to Caitriona's eyes. Ailith always dreamt of traveling and doing more, and she nearly lost it all helping Caitriona when the curse began to consume her. Her dreams were now coming to fruition; how could Caitriona be both gleeful for Ailith yet so bitterly sad?

"I only wish I could take you with me," Ailith breathed, tossing her boots to the side and working at the thin, cloth shirt she wore during the summer months. As she rolled the sleeves up, Caitriona's eyes landed on the scars remaining on Ailith's arm. The familiar disgust with herself returned like a flame roaring to life. Blinking, she forced her gaze away and returned it to Ailith's.

"The coast was certainly beautiful," Caitriona admitted. "You'll enjoy being there again."

"It's where everything I thought about you changed." Ailith rose to her feet and crossed the stone floor to Caitriona at the edge of her bed. Ailith gently ran her fingers through Caitriona's hair, over the curve of Caitriona's horns, then down to cup Caitriona's cheeks. Caitriona stilled, tasting sourness on her tongue at the idea of anyone—including Ailith—touching her horns. Ailith smiled, clearly oblivious to her internal struggle. "That moment when we danced on the beach? That moment started it all. If I'm to be in Stormhaven, I'd rather you by my side."

She leaned forward, kissing Caitriona and pressing their bodies together, and Caitriona felt her heart surge with love. No matter Caitriona's appearance, Ailith still offered love and Caitriona greedily consumed it. She thought, at times, that perhaps she didn't deserve Ailith's adoration. Ailith's scars were a constant reminder of that. She hurt Ailith, after all. It was accidental, but it still happened, and Caitriona's shame was like hot coals pressed against her heart. But when she thought it was better to let Ailith go, she quickly doused the idea and gathered her all the closer. How could she let go of someone who loved her despite what she became?

Ailith never flinched at the sight of Caitriona, not like her mother did. She didn't turn her gaze away, not like most of the staff within the castle. In moments of privacy, they barely kept away from each other. In moments of publicity, they were tethered to each other by gazes and quick, hidden, passing touches as they fought to maintain professionalism in their roles.

With Ailith gone, and Greer as well, no one was left behind to remind Caitriona she was still herself, even if she looked different. Even if the memories of her dragon form blasting fire upon the castle lived in their minds, they didn't make it apparent like everyone else did.

Now upon the curtain, feeling the heat of the sun as she watched Ailith move out with the other guards, Caitriona felt a piece of herself detach and follow down the main thoroughfare. Raising her hand, she waved and Ailith returned the gesture before turning away. Caitriona considered calling out and asking Ailith to come back but knew she never would make such a request because Ailith *would* turn around. She'd return to Caitriona in a heartbeat, and Caitriona couldn't live with the knowledge that she took this chance from her.

The carriage bearing Greer rumbled out next, black and sleek with the kingdom's crest painted on the side. The windows were busy with curtains and Greer was hidden within. The wheels were loud against the cobblestone, likely reflecting the grumbling the sovereign made from within.

"She's going to hate being in that carriage," Róisín observed.

"She'll get out and ride her horse the moment they're out of sight from Braewick City," Caitriona replied. Her mother sighed.

"I could never control her." Róisín shook her head. "She's always been so strong willed."

"I think that's the perfect attribute for a queen, don't you?" Caitriona's smirk spread into a smile. She looked back at the procession and watched her heart ride away. Ailith waved at a cluster of little girls standing along the road edge; they jumped with excitement and waved back. Caitriona could spot their grins all the way from the curtain. "Are you ready for the Day of Grievances?"

"Day of Grievances?"

"Ailith said it's what the commoners call the Day of Royal Greeting."

Róisín coughed and Caitriona glanced at her, surprised to see the queen mother with a twinkle in her eye and a smile on her lips. "That's actually quite an accurate name. There certainly are plenty of grievances shared."

"I'm dreading it," Caitriona admitted. "I can only fathom what they'll say."

"Greer's project to build the new castle on the valley hills, this castle being converted to a school." Róisín ticked off on her fingers, her rings reflecting the sunlight. "Often enough there's some quarrel about one neighbor or another. Usually over cattle or wives or both. There are *always* complaints about taxes."

"What about magic? People aren't unanimously thrilled Greer allowed magic again and they'll come to the castle to complain about that to the two people in the royal family who are paintings of magic."

Below the procession moved beyond the castle's curtain and the large doors closed, the gate lowered. Some of the crowd dispersed, while others loitered, either looking at the procession or at the curtain where Caitriona and Róisín stood.

"People may surprise you." Róisín reached forward and brushed Caitriona's loose hair from her shoulder. It was a gentle gesture, loving, but Caitriona still noticed Róisín's gaze never lifted higher than making eye contact. She always avoided looking at Caitriona's horns. "Many of the most outspoken men will be silenced by simply walking through the castle doors. They'll become too nervous to speak poorly about the kingdom, particularly if they are facing us."

"I certainly hope you're right." Caitriona folded her arms onto the stone's edge and watched the procession curve out of sight. The thick, summer breeze stirred her hair, lifting strands into the air and tangling them with her horns. Above, the sun beat down now that it fully crested the valley hills and made everything feel too hot. She felt the heat on her hair and horns and she wished, not for the first time, that there was magic that could properly make them disappear for good. She asked the fae of the Endless Mountains and according to them, there was no such thing. She'd have to look like this when she faced the people. "I wish she put off this trip to Stormhaven another week so she could attend this."

Róisín stepped forward and mirrored Caitriona's pose, leaning against the stone and looking down the road. "She could have, with minor inconvenience for those she's meeting with in Stormhaven, but she opted not to. She thinks you're ready for this."

Caitriona frowned. From the corner of her gaze there was movement, and her eyes met a man standing on the side of the road a stone's throw from the castle gates. He gritted his teeth and rolled his shoulder. Lifting his hand, he twisted his torso before launching something hard in Caitriona's direction. Despite being so high, despite knowing it wouldn't hit her, Caitriona couldn't help the gasp that escaped her mouth. She stepped back as fruit splattered against the stone below, dripping down and coloring the gray stones with red pulp.

Looking at the man, Caitriona found him staring with disgust. He pursed his lips and spat on the ground, before they curled upward into a vicious smile, one filled with disgusting enjoyment when Caitriona's jaw dropped. A ripple of laughter reached her ears, and the man glanced over his shoulder. A group of people stood behind him, all wearing similar expressions of judgmental disgust. They continued to laugh as Caitriona's eyes burned.

"Come along, Caitriona," Róisín said coolly, reaching to gently pull her daughter back from the wall. Róisín looked at a nearby guard and nodded. He moved to a ladder leading to the ground level by the gate. Other guards called and already one of the spare doorways into the city was thrust open with guards moving toward the man. Caitriona watched, her jaw still hanging and her vision swimming with unshed tears. Róisín's grip on her shoulders tightened. "There's no need for us to remain here. Your sister is off and we have events to prepare for. Ignore them."

CHAPTER THREE

RÓISÍN

Thirty Years Prior

The wind blew her hair into her face and Róisín gave a frustrated sigh as she brushed the long, red locks backward once more. With another gust, it returned to covering her face and Róisín leaned against a boulder as she pulled free a ribbon to tie her waist-length hair back at the nape of her neck.

"You're going to get caught," a voice cautioned.

"When have I ever been caught?" Róisín replied, dropping her hands to grasp the rock ledge and pivot. Tilting her head to one side, she smiled. It was a quick, mischievous thing—that's how Nanny, the caretaker of the orphanage, described her grin. Róisín was known to sneak about, whether to steal a bakery pastry, watch the neighbors fight, or listen in on Nanny speaking to potential adoptive parents, she was always seeking out *something*. Scrambling along the rockface of the swelling earth amongst pines and brush was easy in comparison.

Kayl's lips tugged down into a frown. Her smile usually triggered one of his own but not this time. "I don't trust him. He's Donal's son. If he catches us up here, he'll send his guards to fetch and question us."

"We're completely hidden, Kayl. And just because Donal is a tyrant doesn't mean his child is one," Róisín chirped. "I hate the idea that all children are the exact replica of their parents. Can you fathom that?"

"Just because you'd never leave your children like your father left you—" Kayl said as he slowly inched along the rock ledge to crouch beside Róisín. He kept his eyes down, his voice low while concentrating on his footsteps and his hold on the rocks. "—doesn't mean that applies to everyone. I've heard Cearny's going to be the perfect king to replace Donal. I don't think that's the compliment you think it is."

"*Pfft*," Róisín huffed and turned her attention back to the road. She didn't have much to say in response to the comment about her own father. All she knew about him was summarized into a sentence: her mother loved him but the moment she was with child he abandoned them both, never to be seen again. He was human, leaving Róisín with less pointed ears than her fae mother's. He also left her with a mother who forever wondered if the man that abandoned them would return. Leave it to Kayl to figure she had personal stake in her father's disappearance, like his absence hurt her in any way, when the real victim was always her mother and the longing looks she gave the sea from the house they lived in.

Scratching at the point of one of her ears, she sniffed and pushed back the recollections of her father and mother to focus on the view before her. Below and far enough away that their faces were obscured, traveled the crown prince and his band of soldiers. Earlier that morning, the crow caws declared the royal party was moving near the village. Róisín left shortly after, wanting to see their movement herself, and Kayl begrudgingly agreed to go with her.

The crows hadn't prepared Róisín for the sight of the party. Chainmail glinted in the sun, and showing brightly against the fading landscape was Wimleigh Kingdom's banner with the deepest green and gold thread detailing the Elder Tree. At the head of the procession was a man, broad shouldered and head held high. His blond hair fell to his shoulders and the crown he wore glinted in the sunlight. He was impressive, even from their far distance.

"Why would he wear a crown while riding?" Kayl murmured as he leaned forward and pressed his shoulder against Róisín's.

"I don't know why royals do the things they do." Róisín stretched her neck, trying to get a better angle around the brush they hid behind. "Diplomacy? Pride?"

"Probably pride."

Róisín looked at Kayl whose frown hadn't dissipated. His dislike of the crown was so great it wafted off him to color the hillside in shadow and wilt late season flowers. It brought a bitter taste to Róisín's tongue that dribbled down her throat and turned her stomach. Róisín lifted her hand with nails lined with dirt, the pads of her fingers rough from baking and sewing and whatever else Nanny needed her to do, and reached for Kayl. Kayl's stiff shoulders immediately relaxed under her palm and her smile turned to something of kindness when he looked at her. "We confirmed he's headed this way, so let's go home."

It was still morning as they scrambled down the hillside and made their way through the game trails toward home. A far quicker route than taking the roads the procession was on. The closer Kayl got, the lighter he walked, and the more often Róisín's commentary encouraged him to smile, which in turn made her all the happier. The further from the prince Róisín got, the more her mind churned and detailed her plans became. An idea was always there, but now it was set into motion, she just needed a few other things to go right before she took the next step.

As they walked, she considered what she knew: King Donal was a monster, a king who thrived off the blood he spilt and built his kingdom on the bones of his own people. His father, Róisín was told, was never like him. He was kind and loved his people, whether or not they possessed magic. But Donal was the opposite. When Donal was crowned he outlawed magic, decreed the old religions could no longer be practiced, and magical creatures were a target to kill, rather than creatures to honor and respect.

Rumor spread that Donal sent his son to visit Wimleigh Kingdom towns to ensure citizens were following these orders. It was only a matter of time until Cearny came to Caermythlin and that time was now. Cearny was young, still figuring out his power, and with the steady determination that Róisín was known for, she suspected he just needed gentle guidance to realize his father's hatred of magic was a mismarked thing. Magic wasn't frightening, it wasn't dangerous, but something as wonderful and delightfully unique as people who had a talent for singing or carpentry. It was a substance knit into the very fabric of existence, something that touched all living creatures, and it wasn't scary. Cearny only needed to learn.

Caermythlin was small, at least from Róisín's minor experience with the world. She'd only traveled to Gil'dathon once in her life after her mother died, and it was a foggy memory at best as her grief was too great. She recalled buildings rising far above her which made her head dizzy, and tight streets with little room for movement. Comparatively, Caermythlin was spacious. Each little house stood ground level, with a handful reaching two floors, but all had gardens and yards filled with growing vegetables and chickens. The orphanage was near the center of town, pressed against a growth of pines that whispered magic in the early winter months they found themselves in. It was a house of joy, a place of sorrow, but above all a home of loving chaos normally caused by the hands of the smallest children and occasionally tricks thought up by Róisín herself when she was particularly bored. But it was her second home after she lost the one she lived in with her mother and like any late adolescent, the walls were too close, the ceiling too low. Her self-importance, her goals, her desires and dreams were too great for the thin walls. She and Kayl were too old to be claimed by a family, and so they worked for Nanny in exchange for the continued roof over their heads. After so many years, she felt her limbs would grow out the windows and doors from its tightness. There wasn't enough space between the many orphans who arrived from all over the kingdom and her lofty ideas.

"I'm going to leave Caermythlin, I think," Róisín declared after they returned to the orphanage. They were gone so short a time they returned to their chores of changing the straw for the chickens without notice.

"You say that every season." He dropped a straw bale at her feet and turned to grab hold of the bucket of old straw.

"But I think I'll do it this time." Róisín took the pitchfork and stabbed at the bale, breaking it up as chickens pecked at her feet. She stewed over this idea for months but now it was a thing bursting in her mind and ready to take flight. "With the prince traveling to the western coast, I think this is my chance."

"And what are you going to do with the prince, Ro?" Kayl stopped, turning fully to her.

Róisín straightened her back, gripping the fork with both hands as she looked directly at Kayl. It was time to be out with it. "I'm going to marry him."

Kayl stared at Róisín, his right eyelid giving a slight twitch. "You're an idiot."

"No, listen, I have it figured out and I've been considering this for a while—"

"You're absolutely insane."

"If he comes to Caermythlin, we'll *have* to meet him. It happens in every town he travels to. The citizens line up and meet their future king. He has to interact with the people, doesn't he? So, I'll make sure to put myself front and center. I'll be sweet to him, I'll try and attract him, and if he likes me maybe I can convince him to legalize magic again."

Kayl let out a puff of air and moved closer, shaking his head and keeping his gaze on his best friend.

Róisín stabbed the bale once more as she continued. "Then when Donal dies and he becomes king, magic can be practiced again and this ridiculous removal of it will be reversed. People can share their histories, their beliefs, and not worry about punishment."

"And what are you going to do about these?" Kayl flicked Róisín's ear in a quick movement unseen by her eyes, his magic always ready to be used and as natural to him as breathing.

"Ah, stop!" She reached to her ear and felt the cartilage that extended into a point. It wasn't as obvious as people with two fae parents, but her fae ancestry from her mother was still apparent, as it was for Kayl.

"One look at you and he'll know what you are. Why would he even give you the time of day?"

Róisín clenched her jaw and narrowed her eyes as she leaned forward and pushed her magic energy outward. A silent spell, something made from her pure spunk and desire. Her determination and pride tugged at the tips of her ears, making them burn until they shrunk into a curve similar to the non-fae. "I may not have as much magic as you, but I can pull this off easily enough."

Kayl rolled his eyes and stepped away, returning to his chores. Róisín let him go, surprised by how well the conversation had gone. Kayl was never one immediately sold by her ideas, and she knew he'd come around. The most important part was that this phase of her plan —telling Kayl and testing the boundaries of her magic to appear more human—was a success.

The following morning, as the world grew light, crows alerted the town of Cearny's approach. Róisín heard their cries and rolled over. Grasping the ledge of the window beside her bed, she looked to the snow-heavy skies and watched the crows' dark forms dart towards the deep woods where creatures and witches lived.

"Róisín, gather the girls!" Nanny yelled as she rushed into the room and hastily lit candles. The older woman's gray hair stuck out in a frizz, her apron crooked, and Róisín knew by her state that this would be a morning to hurry. "Kayl! Gather the boys! The prince is coming!"

Frenzied movements overtook the previously quiet orphanage. Róisín rushed to scrub clean the faces of little ones and run combs through their tangled locks. Despite the chaos, she maintained a sense of calm. When she and Kayl spotted the prince, they suspected he would reach their town by daybreak, and she was sure to plan accordingly. She bathed the night before and braided her hair carefully so when she pulled the ties free, her red hair fell in fire-filled waves to the small of her back. Pausing at the lone looking glass in the hall, she pinched her cheeks and forced her pointed ears to their human curve, grimacing as they burned while they shrunk. Her best dress hugged her body tightly, clinging to every curve, and the collar came a touch too low on her budding chest. She needed a new dress to fit her still-developing womanly form, but such things were rarely available at the orphanage. It would have to do.

She was the last outside, moving down the pathway to stand in line behind the youngest girls. She shook her hair back, earning a glance from Kayl who already stood with the fleet of younger boys before him. Leaning close, he whispered. "You're not planning to do anything, are you?"

Kayl looked her over, his expression unreadable. Róisín ran her hands over her skirts and lifted her chin. Gazing down the road past the breath curling from the open mouths of chattering townsfolk in the cold morning air to where the procession appeared, she licked her lips. "Nothing I haven't already shared with you."

Kayl followed her gaze with his storm-filled eyes, his shoulders hunched, and his hands turned to fists at his side. She could taste it again, his upset that lifted off him and radiated through the group. It made the children uneasy, their feet shuffling in the frost-lined leaf litter. Adults clutched their shawls and cloaks more tightly and side-eyed one another. A dog whimpered and slunk back to his home. Kayl always hated the royal family. Always. And everyone could feel it.

When he arrived in Caermythlin as a child, he had screaming fits in the middle of the night, crying out about knights and crowns, kings and tyrants. It haunted him still and Róisín knew that; she knew with every mention of the royal family, he hurt. His pain was always a physical thing descending upon anyone who dared to draw close. But in this, she could find a way to make things better. She'd improve their situation, their very lives, by getting into the thick of things with Cearny. She had enough spunk and determination to pull it off. And then, maybe finally, Kayl wouldn't raise his hackles at the sight of the golden prince traveling down the street. Maybe then he would finally relax and be free of his nightmares, and they could live happily.

All the same, she reached for Kayl's hand and gripped it tightly behind the folds of their winter cloaks. His hand quivered against hers but slowly stilled as she looked at the prince and put on her prettiest smile.

He wore the finery expected of a royal. Thick fabric entwined with golden thread similar to the banner his men carried. His blonde hair was still loose, his dark eyes emotionless as he took in the townspeople lining the street, and his beard was clipped short and tidy. Now up close, Róisín saw the glittering gold crown on his head in greater detail. It was simple, but its simplicity still displayed elegance. With all his refinery, it seemed he would dip himself in gold if he could.

As he drew close, Róisín stood straight and lifted her hand to brush her hair behind her ear. It was a soft movement, one made with delicate passing that implied she didn't know the appearance she had, nor the power it wielded. She blinked, looking shyly at the ground before gazing upward through her lashes. It worked, his gaze fell on her and locked with her green eyes. The world seemed to hold its breath.

She had him, just as she hoped.

It became an affair for the ages. The poor orphaned girl who caught the eye of the future king was a romance meant for stories told to little girls before sending them to bed; a way to cause citizens to see a softer, kinder side of the prince.

All of Caermythlin was in on it, a mutual decision made without any spoken word. No one commented on Róisín's ears now appearing human. No one mentioned her long dead fae mother. Instead, the town supported her with force. A new dress was gifted to Róisín, as well as scented oils for her hair. She was relieved of chores at the orphanage, so she had more time to spend with the prince as he visited. All understood the importance of this pairing. They weren't oblivious to the stories that preceded Cearny's arrival; of towns that crumbled under the pressure of his sword, destroyed because they dared to be different and refused to change. Even his presence now was a threat, but he only seemed interested in a few days' rest before continuing further up the western coast, and there was no mention of banning the fae who lived there or destroying the statues to old gods and monsters.

He wasn't kind, Róisín knew that, but he was kind to her once she gathered enough of his attention to draw him away from his guards and into the private spaces of Caermythlin.

"May I take your hand?" he requested softly; his brown eyes dark in the winter light.

"Of course, my king." Róisín lifted her pale hand and smiled as his large palm touched hers and his long fingers wrapped around her delicate digits.

"I wouldn't want you to slip on the path." His grip was strong as they walked amongst the trees into the hills where the ground climbed upward toward the mountains where the mist lay. Her destination was where a large tree grew.

"Imagine the embarrassment if I slipped on this path and twisted my ankle." Róisín's laugh wasn't entirely natural; she made it more feminine, higher in tone, and softer in volume. An act, like everything else. "I walk this path almost daily. The town would laugh at my clumsiness."

"I'd carry you straight away to my healer." Cearny's hand tightened around hers, almost to a point of discomfort. "You'd receive the best care and none of your neighbors would be the wiser."

Róisín's gaze met Cearny's and they paused beneath a snow-covered pine. She offered one of her most flirtatious half-smiles and the coloring of his cheeks indicated it found its mark. Letting out a soft breath, she pulled her gaze away and nodded ahead where the path ended beneath a tree not much larger than the rest yet obviously cared for with coins and ribbons hanging from its branches.

"There it is, our tree."

Cearny turned and nodded. "An Elder Tree of sorts, I suppose."

"Most of our town has been born here and will likely die here. They're unable to travel to the Elder Tree in your city, so they make do with this one. We pray here and send our wishes. We have celebrations for the seasons ... or rather, we did. We've adhered to your outlawing of such practices, but they were innocent in nature and quite lovely, I promise you."

He wasn't a terribly thoughtful person, Róisín found, but he furrowed his brow with deep concentration as Róisín spoke of the wonders of her little town—magic included. She could see him consider it all and he didn't turn away, didn't brush her off, didn't condemn them all to death.

He came back for more.

He listened.

He stayed.

He fell into the grip of her plan.

And perhaps, if she was truly honest with herself, she fell into him as well. His attention was something she craved and there was a spark of undeniable pleasure from his hungry gaze when at last he pressed his palms against her waist and his lips to hers.

But nothing gained comes without loss. Kayl drifted from her, further and further with each day. He lingered in the shadows of the orphanage, busying himself with the boys he was tasked to help Nanny look after. When Róisín returned with a blush in her cheeks, the cold making the tip of her nose turn pink, and the scent of Cearny still on her skin, Kayl pulled away even further.

"Won't you speak to me?" Róisín asked in the shadows of the hall after the younger ones were asleep. "I feel like I haven't seen you at all in the last fortnight."

"You haven't." Kayl's voice was gruff with disappointment. "Because you've been with him."

"It's for our benefit, Kayl." Róisín reached forward to touch his shoulder. How often had she touched him? He was as familiar to her as she was familiar with herself. They were like one soul split apart and placed in different bodies. The polar opposites of one another and yet undeniably tied together. She held his pain and he carried her joy. At least, that was what Róisín always thought. She questioned if her perception was correct as Kayl stepped back and pulled away. His gray eyes held the shadows of the hall but something else made her stomach turn.

"It's for *your* benefit, Ro," he uttered and Róisín felt the hairs on her neck rise. There was ice in his voice that she was unfamiliar with. She lowered his hand, silent as he continued. "You've always talked about leaving Caermythlin and traveling the world. This is just a way to get that while you lie to yourself that it's for some brave reason. You understand how awful the royal family is, don't you? Donal would happily put our heads on a spike, and Cearny would be the one wielding the ax. If he saw you for what you are, for *who* you are, he'd kill you and spit on your body."

"But what if I can get him to understand magic isn't a threat? Kayl, just for a moment, try to picture how this could benefit us. *All* of us. Imagine if we didn't have to hide who we were or practice our gifts in private."

He chewed on his bottom lip and looked toward the boys' room. Róisín nearly repeated herself after he paused for so long but he at last broke his silence. "You're already half gone. You've already made your decision."

"Kayl, let me try, let me see how far I can get. If it doesn't work out, I'll come back to Caermythlin and you can say you told me so. But if I *can* be the secret weapon, if I can get into the kingdom and convince him to not follow in the footsteps of his father, it'll all be worth it, don't you think?"

"Will it be worth it to lose everything in the process? There's that risk too, Ro, and you know it. You could lose everything. You could lose us. You could lose *yourself*. Are you willing?"

"Kayl ..." She sighed. Frustration spread in her chest and made her tingle with unease. His emotions were a storm of betrayal, jealousy and sadness scratching at her skin and coating her teeth.

"The worst of it all is you've fallen in love with him, and you won't admit it, not even to yourself, but it's plain to see."

Róisín's jaw dropped but he didn't wait for her reply. He turned and retreated into the boys' room without another word. Róisín was alone in the hall, her cheeks hot with emotion and the whisper of winter's wind easing through the drafty windows her only company.

Cearny left, their lives continued, and the ice between her and Kayl began to thaw until Cearny returned a month later and with him, a cold snap. Everything iced over. The streams, the water troughs, and even deep breaths brought a swell of frost to one's throat. But worst of all was the coldness from Kayl when he saw Cearny request Róisín's hand in marriage outside the orphanage door.

People called it a whirlwind romance.

Róisín called it a success.

She always heard things moved quickly with royalty, but she didn't care. Kayl was wrong, she wasn't in love, not very much. She had a plan and hastily jotted ingredients on a piece of paper she sewed into her dress's hem. All the ingredients necessary to concoct spells to aid achieving her dreams. She'd do it in the name of her dead mother, in the name of the people in Caermythlin who hid in their homes—afraid to expose their pointed ears to Cearny's directed sight—and in particular for Kayl.

"You don't understand," she pleaded as she folded her summer cloak and tucked it into her bag. She turned, her heart physically pulling toward Kayl's form. He stood at the foot of her little bed, his hands gripping the footboard and his expression pinched in anguish. "Nothing's going to change if we stay in this village. We can't just sit here like waiting ducks, hoping the king will take kindly to our magic. We need to do more, and I *can* do more. I can convince him magic is good, and I can save our kind."

"But you haven't the faintest idea how evil that family is," Kayl pleaded, following Róisín as she weaved her way out of the orphanage. "I've seen it, I've seen what they do to our kind. I saw it done to my parents."

Róisín hesitated. It was so rare that Kayl spoke of his parents. Whenever he did, she would listen. But this time it didn't stop her. "That's King Donal's doing. Cearny's different. I'll work on him so he'll be better once he's king."

"They won't listen to you; you're nothing to them."

Róisín spun on her heel, facing Kayl directly with fire flashing in her eyes. "I may be nothing now, Kayl. But I'll be a great *something* and I'll prove you wrong. I'll end the line of Gablaigh men's terror and make something wonderful grow in its place. Just watch."

CHAPTER FOUR

A̲ɪʟɪᴛʜ

Ailith expected the smell of horses, sweaty bodies, tough ground for sleeping and campfire meals like other excursions they did before and Barden promised for the future. She expected the elation from traveling, nerves for the task, and homesickness for her family and Caitriona. She expected exhaustion by the constant interaction with other guards and discomfort of her royal guard uniforms that were made from fabric that felt itchy against her skin. What she hadn't expected was finding herself trapped in the queen's carriage beside Barden on the final day of their journey while Greer ran through notes. She hadn't expected to stop an hour from Stormhaven's limits to be kicked out of the carriage, a clean uniform tossed into her arms and her horse's reins handed over.

"Is this normal?" Ailith murmured to Barden riding beside her. A row of guards led the procession with Greer's carriage following. She and Barden followed the carriage, and behind were carts bearing supplies and additional guarded protection.

He raised an eyebrow with question, making Ailith roll her eyes. "The meetings in the carriage for half of the ride, the new wardrobe, Greer being so ... nervous."

Barden pressed his lips together in thought, his gaze returning to the road where the scattering of homes grew in number. Ailith spent nearly every day with Barden since joining the guard, she knew his expression wasn't one of unknowing. He had the answer but was always protective of how much he shared about Greer, even to Ailith.

"She's always more comfortable in the muck of things with a sword and her boots. Even when she held court while Cearny was alive, it was on her own turf. He'd leave and she did her duty in her home. But this is different, she's going to a city she hasn't visited very often and taking up discussions with people she's never met before, all to clean up after her father's mistakes."

"She holds a lot of guilt regarding it all." Since the curse was fulfilled and Ailith was granted a position with the royal guard, she grew closer to Greer by proximity through duty and family gossip as Caitriona's partner. While Greer was serious, thoughtfully sincere, and a quick-witted woman, she was also steadfastly devoted to those she loved. Her sister and Barden stood above them all—even if Greer wouldn't admit her adoration for her head guard, it was plain to see—and not far behind was her desire to help her queendom. She wanted to do right by them, and she felt legalizing magic achieved that.

Ailith's new position provided housing within the castle barricades with her parents and their aide, Gwen. All three still did business within the city and they came home with gossip. For all they heard, there was a mix of emotions regarding magic's return. Betrayal being the primary one. Ailith assumed people felt betrayed that Greer went back on what Cearny promised—a queendom with equal playing fields, where magic was wiped out and all humans coexisted without any magical aids—but the betrayal came instead from families and neighbors only now discovering people they knew kept their magic a secret all this time.

Having witnessed Caitriona's body twist and turn, ripple, swell, and break from its human keep to become a dragon was proof enough of magic's power. Cearny did a plentiful job making magic appear as a frightening, dangerous thing. It *was* dangerous if used as a weapon; just as dangerous as a cannon or sword. But magic was also beneficial; the fact Ailith endured nights in freezing temperatures without harm through the aid of potions, and magic makers like Isla and May helped heal her burns from the dragon's flame with potions and salves were all proof. Yet people in Braewick were shocked to find their neighbors or parents practicing magic and worshiping lost traditions.

Now they entered Stormhaven with a political acknowledgement of how much damage the previous two kings caused. Greer's very presence admitted the former two generations in her family were wrong and showed her effort to be better. She hoped to gain further knowledge of all that was lost: the histories, stories, religions, languages, and culture. For some, it was a source of embarrassment. But Ailith found herself all the more impressed by her queen. It took a lot for someone to admit the errors of their relatives, even more to approach those harmed with hope to fix what was broken.

"You're doing that thing." Barden pulled Ailith from her thoughts, allowing the city to swell back into focus. "Where you frown extra hard and don't seem to see what's before you because you're chewing on your shirt cuff. What else is on your mind?"

"What's ahead? This is all new to me and I'm worried about messing up."

"And that's why we have rooms beside one another," Barden said with a gleam, his smile dazzling despite the skin around his eyes still appearing pink and raw. Ailith had been selfishly worried Barden wouldn't go on this trip due to his father's death. While a month passed since the funeral, Ailith wasn't certain Barden was ready to travel—she knew she wouldn't be if she were in his place—and she hadn't pressured him to go. Greer reminded him constantly he could back out as well. Ailith hoped he'd go anyway, and sure enough, he was insistent that returning to work was what he needed.

His warmth pushed her to smile. Since his father died, there were rare moments where he seemed happy, but this appeared genuine. The corners of his eyes creased, and his blue eyes sparked. Always soaking up the emotions around her, Ailith found her own mood improved to see Barden like himself again.

He was a handsome man, which said a lot since Ailith never found men attractive. Still, she saw his beauty and his personality was bright. Ailith understood Greer's attraction to him. When Ailith joined the royal guard, he took her under his wing, determined to get her up to speed quickly. She was already trained in weapons but politics and protocols with the royal family were all new to her. The burns to her dominant arm also held her back. Still, he diligently taught her how to use her weapons with her left arm as her right healed. When they would hit a wall with her training, he brought his father in and listened to his advice. Many times, Ailith felt he was as eager to learn as much as she. He was like that with everyone though. Selfless, patient, and ensuring he performed his job to the extent of his ability; just like his father.

Now he nudged her shoulder before straightening on his saddle. The sun reflected off the chest plate he wore. "Don't worry, I've got your back on what to do."

Barden kept his word, directing Ailith after they arrived with pointed looks and nods. Greer received flowers from onlookers and scholars alike before the trio retreated into their rooms. Ailith was given yet another change of clothing and sighed with relief. It wasn't the standard royal guard uniform but something lighter and more akin to the cloth she preferred.

"Thank you, Cait." Her voice was barely a whisper as she embraced the light shirt to her chest. She had complained on numerous occasions about the itchiness of the guard uniform and how she yearned for her favorite fabric—one she had multiple shirts made in—and none else. It had to have been Caitriona who got the simple shirts packed in her wardrobe.

Still, she found it funny that while the royal family had trunks full of clothes for travel, the multiple wardrobe changes extended to guards.

Standing before a looking glass over a wash basin, Ailith fidgeted with her hair. It hung loose, clinging to her skin in the hot air and covering the ripple of fading scars on her neck. It also distracted from the scar along her cheek.

Since receiving her injuries, Ailith learned people couldn't help but stare. Their eyes wouldn't meet hers, lowering as they concentrated on her skin, thinking it over, wondering if they should ask questions about it. She didn't have to be told their thoughts; it was too clear on their faces.

Ailith understood the desire not to make eye contact. With strangers, it made her skin crawl. But she knew this wasn't that. They studied her as if she was a curious creature, and she was thrilled to point out their behavior.

"Is there something you're looking at?" Ailith would ask, her voice bland of emotions. She carefully kept her face blank even while the person blinked and stepped away—always away—as their cheeks colored.

"Oh, nothing. Forgive me," they always replied. A lie and an apology wrapped into a pretty response. By this point, she was shocked if they said anything else.

Rolling her shirt sleeves up, she exposed her forearms and paused from the sight of scarring down her right arm. It was a continuation of what occurred on her neck but with substantially more damage. The skin was often tight, and some areas were sensitive to changes in temperature. The scars formed ridges similar to the hills and mountains she traveled over with Caitriona. After Caitriona's dragon form burned her nearly two years ago, almost all range of motion returned to her arm, but the scarring would always remain.

Her injuries always drew further stares from people. Their eyes flicked from Ailith's arm to her neck then up to her cheek, tracking the injuries she wore as further questions developed behind their gaze and they considered whether to ask.

Ailith pulled her shirt sleeves down, not wanting to draw looks from any of the Stormhaven folk. But it was hot, this close to the sea the humidity was somehow worse than in the valley and it brought constant discomfort. The cloth of her sleeve stuck to her scars and irritated them immediately. *Enough of this.* She rolled the sleeves back up. Even her favorite cloth had its downsides, or perhaps it was just the humidity. *There. Perfect. Let them stare.*

She braided her hair quickly, exposing her neck and instantly feeling the air cool her sweaty skin. For her, her scars were proof of the trials she endured and what she survived. They were a part of her story. She was proud of them. She wasn't chosen to sit in meetings with Greer only to worry if her scars made others uncomfortable. They could grapple with their discomfort on their own.

A knock sounded at the door, drawing Ailith away to find Barden waiting, clean from the ride and sporting an outfit similar to Ailith's.

"We'll go and retrieve Greer from her room," Barden explained as they walked down the marble hall, their footsteps echoing off the floor. The amount of stone somehow made the interior of the building cooler and Ailith wanted to linger. "Every time Greer's set to go somewhere, I'll debrief you beforehand. For today, we're expected to escort her to this meeting. You're there as a confidant. I am as well, but also as protection. Greer hates involving the elders of Braewick because they're too like her father, so she chose us. There are other guards whose sole focus is to protect, so we may do our own tasks. When it comes to the meetings with the elders themselves, you're expected to partake—leave searching for threats to the other guards. Greer wants your input on the discussion from the perspective of a person who grew up in Braewick City, so it's essential you follow along."

They reached the double doors to the royal suite and turned toward one another. Her hands were sticky with sweat and her breathing quick. She hated her nerves. Ailith swallowed. "Got it."

Barden brushed the arms of his top before looking at Ailith and patting errant hairs down on her head. The gesture calmed her slightly; he was like this since Ailith joined the royal guard. Barden consistently took the role of what Ailith assumed an elder brother was to be. Teasing but protective, friendly but quick to call her out. While Ailith spent so much of her life guarded and unwilling to accept the attention of anyone else beside her parents, she couldn't help but thrive over his calm and sincere instruction.

"Chin up, you'll be fine. Now here we go." Barden turned to the door, barely knocking before it flew open with a whirlwind of air. Greer burst from her room in a chaos of cloth.

"The humidity is *awful* with this fabric." Greer tugged at the clinging sleeves of her dress. Ailith smirked, she knew the humidity was the culprit of Greer's discomfort. Greer's face was flushed and Ailith bet her hands were sweaty too. The queen kept many of her opinions close to her chest but her hatred of heat was something she shared freely and often. "And my hair is seemingly expanding from my head. Between the heat and the bugs, I hate summer. To think we still have weeks left of this weather."

"I doubt the elders will notice." Barden reached behind Greer and closed the doors to her room. "They have hair growing out of their ears, after all."

Greer shook her head, but a smile appeared on her face. Her gaze moved on to Ailith and she paused, the smile softening but not disappearing.

"You look good. Are you ready?"

The nerves rushed through Ailith again and left her feeling filled with lightning. But she smiled. "As I'll ever be."

"Don't be nervous."

Ailith wasn't sure if Greer was speaking to her or herself.

They moved through halls and up staircases, the moist air and heat climbing with each floor until they reached a large room in a tower with open windows overlooking red and brown roof tiles. Further out, the sea glittered in sunlight. The humidity was still a wet weight, but the breeze moved freely and allowed a small reprieve.

The elders waited by seats surrounding a long table. They wore maroon robes that appeared heavy for the weather, yet their skin was untouched with sweat. Ailith looked over Greer and Barden, even the additional Wimleigh royal guards, and all their skin gleamed with moisture. Perhaps the people of Stormhaven were just used to it.

"Please, have a seat." Hollan, the apparent leader of the group, swung his hand out to present the only unclaimed chairs. They all faced the open windows, as well as the breeze; it was a gift more than Hollan likely realized.

"Thank you." Greer smiled, her gaze connecting with the elders. Ailith didn't know how she could maintain eye contact with such unflinching ease. Barden pulled out Greer's chair and helped her into her seat.

"Your seat, miss," another elder said, looking directly at Ailith and offering the chair beside Greer. Ailith stood more upright and shuffled her way around Barden to her seat. While Greer fluffed out her skirts, her entire countenance that of regal tidiness, Ailith tried to pull her own chair out with as little sound as possible. She sat down, her hands fidgeting in her lap beneath the table and eyes cast down on the smooth wood until Greer's voice drew her gaze upward.

"Thank you for accepting my request to join you in Stormhaven."

Greer's smile was dazzling. Her queenly behavior firmly in place. Ailith always marveled at Greer's ability to switch it on and off. She could slip into this performance with ease but then, the moment she could drop it, she returned to herself. A less dazzling version of royalty, but a personality that still left Ailith watching and abundantly impressed. Greer leaned forward, gently touching Hollan's hand. "Or, as I hope, we may begin calling your gorgeous city Gil'dathon. That's the original name of the city, is it not?"

The elders' brows rose and smiles formed as they glanced back and forth at one another. "Yes, Gil'dathon is the proper name. Although we do enjoy Stormhaven; quite the compliment that seafarers may find a haven here."

"My father forced that name upon the city," Greer cut in, her voice clear as a bell and her eyes meeting each of the elders' gazes with unflinching sincerity. "You don't have to maintain that name if you don't want to. I'll leave the choice to you and the city. Perhaps a vote is beneficial? We'll adhere to whichever name your people prefer. But the main point is that between my father and grandfather, much was taken from the people here. We all know what their actions were doing. They were trying to wipe away your cultures and beliefs. They tossed it away due to their blindness to the beauty in difference. In my sister's relations with fae in the Elder Mountains—rather, Invarlwen—we learned the proper name for this city, but I admit we know very little else because of a loss of records and history."

"Yes, you mentioned in your correspondences your royal library was ransacked prior to your crowning," an elder pointed out gravely as others shook their heads with disappointment.

"Worse than that," Greer said. "It appears my father had an active role in destroying the material a little at a time beginning years ago, before I was old enough to have much knowledge of it. I'm not sure how long since many of the pieces were destroyed, or what we had beforehand. I only have vague memories of our library having more tomes than it currently does. He was determined to wipe any opportunity for self-learned knowledge from our city. It's why I humbly request any information you can provide."

"Unfortunately, many of Gil'dathon's historic texts were destroyed when we joined Wimleigh. The libraries burned and the effigies of those we worship destroyed."

Greer's shoulders dropped; her disappointment apparent but the sternness in her brow conveyed the news wasn't a surprise. Everyone knew how ruthless Cearny and his father were, although Cearny always took it to the next level. Ailith was more surprised he allowed the elders to live amongst his destruction of the libraries.

Greer drew her fingertips over the table and tapped her nails, the room silent for the moment beyond the *thunk, thunk, thunk* reflecting the beat of Ailith's heart.

"Are there no people who remember the old ways? Or those who hid books? I ask of you all to teach me what you can, but I understand my request is quite the burden and my family has given you enough weight to carry. I want to learn. I want to do better. If you have any materials I may read privately while I'm here, I'd greatly appreciate it."

The men exchanged looks as a steward stepped into the room, releasing the quiet hold the discussion had on them. Tension in spines and shoulders diminished, breaths held back were released, and Hollan's face, serious at first, relaxed.

"Ah!" Hollan waved the steward further into the room. "May you bring along some tea? Enough for everyone at the table?"

The steward nodded before bowing and stepping out of the room without uttering a word. As the door closed, silence returned. The elders gazed at Greer, their lips drawn beneath heavy mustaches and bearded chins. Ailith felt herself mentally receding, wishing she could blend into the wood of her seat. What information could she provide them? How could she be of any benefit? She went to a small city school, a single room used as a classroom where they were taught to read and write but not much else. She never traveled beyond the city boundaries beside the woods between the castle walls and the growing fields where she foraged food until she took up Greer's job offer to sneak Caitriona beyond the valley. She barely heard the names of these other cities, let alone any historical context, until just the last two years. It was her first opportunity to see other cultures and people beside those she grew up around. The politics of the queendom and others was beyond her understanding. She had a lofty position now, but in the end, she knew little.

Ailith swallowed her discomfort and immediately regretted the movement. Choking on her own spit, she terrifyingly drew the attention of everyone in the room. Barden's eyes widened, one of Greer's eyebrows raised, and the elders looked with surprise. Lurching forward in her seat, she covered her mouth.

"Sorry," she croaked as she attempted to clear her throat.

Hollan's eyes settled on Ailith and didn't pull away. *Elder Tree, let me die now.*

His eyes held a twinkle as he looked her over; his gaze passed over her hair and arms, barely flicking over her scars, before settling on her face. This was different from the people who studied her scars as something to judge and wonder. This was the observance of someone just remembering Ailith was there and growing curious about her. Ailith fought the urge to look away.

"I've heard of you, my dear," Hollan said, leaning slightly in his chair toward her. His eyes were unmoving, meeting Ailith's gaze without flinching which made her all the more uncomfortable. She pressed her back against her chair. "You're the guard who traveled with Princess Caitriona, correct?"

Ailith froze, her gaze slipped to the side, searching out Greer for help. The queen nodded.

She looked back at Hollan. "Yes."

"You traveled through the continent in search of a cure for her curse, but before that, you were a child of Braewick City, were you not? Forgive me if I misunderstand, but from what I've learned, it isn't typical for children of the city to become a royal guard, is it?"

This time Ailith looked at Barden. He came from a line of guards. It was true most royal guards received their title due to heritage. City guards—those who dealt with petty grievances at the border walls and checked the gates—were built up by city inhabitants. Every few years, one or two city guard graduates were given the honor to proceed to royal guard training, but it was rare.

Ailith's voice was softer than she intended, "You—you're correct."

"And you received your position due to helping Princess Caitriona?"

Hollan continued, his voice clear and sincere. Ailith swallowed. She knew what he was doing, he had the answers to his own question, but he wanted to hear Ailith admit these things.

Her eyes flicked to Greer; Ailith couldn't read her expression. Perhaps Hollan wanted to see how freely Ailith admitted the favoritism of the royal guard. He was testing how much of a tether Greer had on her subjects.

But Greer conveyed no emotion and Barden stared ahead, not meeting her eyes. Taking a deep breath, Ailith looked back at Hollan.

"Yes," she said, trying to convey confidence despite not knowing if she was putting her foot in her mouth. "I proved my strengths through helping Princess Caitriona. Queen Greer was very kind in allowing me to step into a recently vacated spot within the royal guard."

"Have you learned anything from joining the royal guard?" He appeared hungry as he spoke and leaned forward, craving her response.

"I've been taught many things. I'm better at a sword and bow, and I've learned more about the dwellings of the queendom, too."

He shook his head, although his expression wasn't one of upset. "No, what I mean to ask is have you learned more than you were taught in the city? Have you learned more about how your country is ruled and do you see the difference our queen is making?"

Ailith blinked. Her answer could fill a day. Her entire world changed in the last two years. Beforehand, she was starving and slowly working herself to death. When she wasn't working, she worried over finances and her parents' care. Magic was something to fear, something to hate, and an item of advantage for people while she and others killed themselves to survive. But Cearny caused her struggle and her father's disability. Her grievances festered and spread to the distrust of the entire royal family. She viewed them as lofty, rich snobs with little understanding of how hard it was in any class lower than themselves.

But through her travels, she realized Cearny was a separate being from his family. His greed and hatred filled him whole and controlled his every decision. He was so overtaken by it all, he was even willing to kill his own child for exhibiting magic.

So much of Ailith's perspective changed since she returned to the queendom and was offered her job with the royal guard, more than could be conveyed with a simple response.

"What I've learned through working in the guard is that my queen is trying to right the wrongs of her heritage. I've learned she's honest to her people. There's no difference in stories told amongst the people of the city and what Greer's doing. She's upfront and following through on her word."

Hollan smiled and leaned into his chair before returning his attention to Greer. "We have books we can bring to your room. You're welcome to read through them and we can offer a transcriber to copy over any materials you feel are beneficial for Wimleigh Queendom. Understandably, we'd rather not give you our copies directly."

Greer's stern, queenly mask slipped off and a smile appeared. Ailith always found it amazing how much Greer changed when she smiled. Her statue-like, stern expression, filled with an air one could find warmth in, and she was nothing but serious expectation melted away. Both Gablaigh sisters were like the sunshine peeking through clouds when they were happy, and it had the power similar to sunshine to soften even the coldest hearts.

"Completely understandable. That would be wonderful. I hope you understand how much I appreciate your willingness to share. I'll make good work of the time I have here and read all I can."

The doorway opened again, and the steward stepped into the room, the tea he was requested to procure missing.

"I apologize for the inconvenience." The steward looked between the elders and Greer; his brow wrinkled with something like upset. "There's an urgent call for Queen Greer and the guards. A messenger's arrived and insists on speaking to all three."

Greer stared at the steward. Her hands gripping the ends of the chair's armrest the only sign that this news was unnerving and a surprise. Barden stepped to her chair, one hand gently brushing over her shoulder to her back as he gestured to pull the chair from the table. Ailith glanced between the pair, feeling the air change and the energy shift, like the start of rain preluding a storm.

"My queen," he said softly, snapping Greer out of it. She allowed him to pull the chair back and accepted his hand as she got to her feet.

"I'm sorry, gentleman," Greer declared. Ailith rose to her feet too, cringing as her chair scraped across the floor with a whining sound. "But I suspect we should see what this is about. I'll return shortly, if that's alright?"

"Our sovereign is a busy woman," Hollan said with a chuckle. "Go ahead, do what must be done."

The steward silently escorted the trio down a flight of stairs to a hall with royal guards standing outside another much less marvelous meeting room with shuttered windows. Greer maintained her composer although Ailith could see the corners of her eyes narrowing slightly and the slightest frown tugging at her lips.

"Is it clear?" Barden asked and they immediately stood at attention.

"Just the woman who requested the queen."

"She has no weapons, we checked."

Barden exchanged a look with Greer and moved to the door, pushing it open and stepping in ahead of her.

"What is it?" Greer followed. "Why have I been called away?"

A figure at the table wearing a summer cloak leaned forward upon Greer's entrance, her gnarled hand rested on her knee as she pushed to her feet with some difficulty. The steward stepped from the room and closed the door, leaving Barden, Greer, and Ailith inside.

Barden's hand rested on the hilt of his sword as he angled himself before Greer. Ailith stepped to Greer's exposed side, eyes locked on the figure as it reached to pull its cloak free.

"I wish I could see the three of you on better terms," a familiar voice croaked, "and I do apologize for interrupting your important meetings. Heavens knows we certainly need as many peace talks as we can get in these times."

Ailith released a breath, every sparking nerve in her body relaxed as she stepped forward, a small smile began to appear on her lips.

"Who are you?" Greer asked, her tone cautious. She didn't recognize the voice, that much was clear, and Ailith couldn't help but let out a small laugh.

"After all I've done, you don't recognize me?" The figure exposed her face and freed the mass of gray curls from the hood. "I mean, I understand, I suppose. The last time you saw me, you just killed your father—quite the good thing to do, I might add. He certainly had it coming, the bastard. You girls and Róisín are all much better off without having him darken your doorways and destroying families with his silly conquests. It's a shame you're left to deal with his mistakes though."

Greer gasped and Barden's shoulders dropped, the grip on the hilt of his sword going slack as Ailith moved forward to embrace the elderly woman.

"Isla." Ailith was unable to hold back the relief mixed eloquently with slight horror for how blunt their visitor could be. "Why are you here?"

Isla smiled, leaning into Ailith's embrace before gently gripping Ailith's shoulders. She looked at Ailith with bright eyes, clearer than any elderly eyes Ailith ever saw, as if she still had decades of living ahead of her.

"I truly *am* sorry to bother you three," she repeated before giving Greer her full attention. "But I fear I come with dreadful news."

CHAPTER FIVE

RÓISÍN

Sixteen Years Prior

The room was flooded with so much red Róisín was convinced her dreams would drip with crimson for the remainder of her life. Pieces of cloth used to try and stop Caitriona's bleeding were discarded on the bed and fallen to the floor; remnants of the awful moments just after the dragon attack when Róisín thought she surely would die on the spot and follow her youngest daughter to wherever she had gone. Amidst the scraps of red was the gray of Caitriona's burnt gown, outlining her pale white skin like offerings left to a corpse. They nearly were until Caitriona was restored.

Róisín stood with still quivering hands beside her sleeping daughter returned to life. She was entirely present for all the horror, but now her mind detached and became a distant thing from the world, as if she was held back and forced to view everything from detachment. Two thoughts turned over her mind again and again.

Her youngest child died.

Her youngest child was brought back.

Her youngest child *died* and was *brought back*.

Silently, she reached into the bucket of clean rags. Dipping the cloth in a pail of water she held in her other hand, Róisín cleaned Caitriona's arms and legs. The little girl didn't react to the cold water or Róisín's gentle touches, but her chest still rose and fell.

Her youngest child died and was brought back.

Her senses were overloaded and she couldn't process anything beyond what occurred in stunted moments, waves of horror she knew came and went quickly yet felt painfully slow.

How did we get to this place? Róisín thought before images burned in her skull from the last few hours returned in flashes.

The shaking of the castle, the attack of the dragon, the fires, and the collapsing structure. The bells, so many damned bells, ringing and ringing to call citizen workers to aid. The terror of Greer, crying and frantically running to Róisín, followed by relief to find one daughter safe. The fear she felt, holding Greer's hand tight as she ran to the nursery, screaming that Caitriona was in there with hope any guard or servant would hear and help.

When the door opened, smoke funneled out. The pictures of the horror repeated themselves.

Fire.

Rubble.

The tattered little girl found beneath a table.

The scent of charred lumber and cloth, and burned skin and blood clung to the fabric of Caitriona's dress.

"May we bring her to my room?" Róisín asked a servant, cutting off the imagery that flicked in her mind. The words physically hurt to say, her throat raw from screaming, but she couldn't remain in this tiny room with bloodied sheets and sulfur in the air. "And retrieve a nightgown for the princess? I doubt there's anything of Caitriona's that survived the blaze, but we have outgrown gowns of Greer's. Search her room."

Even transitioning from room-to-room Róisín's mind was a floating presence, not quite part of the world and switching to mindless movements as she followed the men carrying Caitriona. She witnessed her body moving, she saw the passing of familiar halls and her room, but she wasn't present to experience it. Quietly, she worked to dress Caitriona in a soft nightgown faded with age. Her movements were as gentle as when Caitriona was a milk drunk infant and filthy, and Róisín didn't want to rouse the sleeping babe while replacing her diaper. She brushed her hair, pausing over and over to ensure the girl continued breathing, and tucked a stuffed toy into the crook of the girl's arm. It wasn't one of Caitriona's favorites, but all those had gone with the blaze.

When Greer entered the room after changing from her own bloodied and dusty gown, Róisín felt herself pulled back into her body again. Suddenly conscious of her surroundings and her firstborn clinging to her skirts as she cried, a sense of duty clicked into place. She could be separate from the world while tending to her sleeping daughter, but her presence was necessary for her eldest.

"Oh, sweet lark." Róisín sank to the floor and cupped Greer's cheeks in her hands. "It's over, we're safe."

"But Caitriona," Greer wept as she wrapped her arms around her mother. The tip of her nose was as red as her eyes from crying. "She was hurt so badly."

"She was," Róisín admitted, even though admitting it hurt. "But she's all better now. She's only sleeping. Such an event would tire anyone. Come, come see your sister. She's better now."

Greer rushed to Róisín's bedside and looked Caitriona over. She touched her hands, brushed hair away from her cheek, and repositioned the toy. The mother hen, many of the servants said, as Greer was always quick to care for Caitriona. The mother wolf, Róisín silently corrected, because she knew Greer was just as protective of the girl as Róisín. She knew Greer had teeth and used them without pause.

"Come now, let's get into bed," Róisín offered. The day was spent and there was nothing else to do. All Róisín wanted was to be surrounded by the two most important things in her world.

Silently, they crawled into the giant bed that Róisín rarely shared. They bookended the little girl. Greer snuggled against Caitriona's little body and rested her cheek on Caitriona's shoulder. Róisín pulled a blanket over all three of them and curled along the headboard, keeping her face close to both.

In the quiet of the room, she softly sang songs in her mother's language. Róisín had very few memories of her, but she could recall the songs and through their lyrics, her mother became clear in her mind again. Tall and thin with pointed ears and eyes like starlight. She sang the lyrics of her people repeatedly by her only child's demand, and now Róisín sang them to her own children like a whisper. In this her heritage remained alive. Songs of creatures in the great Northern Wood, of castles on mountains, and magic trees with roots covering the world. The song was a prayer to the girls, quietly kept, because she knew the language and magic of it all wasn't allowed by her husband. There was enough to sow distrust between him and Róisín since they married and today surely pulled them apart to the furthest expanse they ever felt.

Róisín hoped to meet Kayl earlier that day. When she received his letter requesting an audience to discuss the further outlawing of magic, she knew it would cause a fight with Cearny, but she didn't care. She hadn't realized how much she missed her old life until she saw his familiar handwriting and she responded with a formal invitation to the castle. She said she would change the world for the better and thus far had made very little movement in that effort. Maybe this would be a turning point.

Over a decade passed since she left her village, over a decade since she lost Kayl's constant presence, and she eagerly awaited the chance to feel like herself again—if only for a little while—and tell him at last that he was right.

She prepared for them to meet. She would introduce her children to her childhood friend and she dared to be excited. Instead, she screamed for him whilst the dragon spewed fire over her home. Her voice penetrated the walls of the castle and found its way down the halls as she called for his aid in a frightened spell to save her youngest child.

After Caitriona was confirmed alive, her hair regrown, her skin unmarked, he lingered in the room, awkward and shy. Róisín felt similarly and surely would have behaved the same had she not been so focused on Caitriona. Shock took her energy and left her an exhausted shell that sat like a statue.

Cearny hadn't come; Cearny *wouldn't* come, but Kayl sat in a seat on the other side of the bed, watching Róisín over the rise and fall of the toddler's chest who lay between them.

A decade had passed and he still came when she called for him.

It wasn't surprising she could depend on him, but it was a reminder of what her life became after she gave up her home. A reminder of what she gave up without a second thought and only missed after she realized it was gone and unobtainable.

"She may remember a little of what happened," Kayl admitted, knowing Róisín's focus was only on her child and she was in no mood for other topics. He always read her moods and understood what she had energy for, just as much as once she could taste his temperament in the wind. Róisín had forgotten but having him there before her brought it all back. His presence brought much of *herself* back. They had an entirely shared life before she set her eyes on the castle and briefly thought her love and determination could change the world. "She shouldn't remember the pain, at the very least."

"You're spent," Róisín murmured and Kayl met her gaze. He smiled and Róisín's eyes filled with tears. There were slight creases at the corners that hadn't been there previously. So many years passed since they were last together. His brows rose at the sight of her tears and he gave a small, shy shrug.

"I'll recover."

"What if you need magic?" Róisín persisted.

"Am I not safe here?"

They looked at one another knowing the answer and what Kayl gave —*who* he gave it for. Kayl was passionate about those he cared for but he wasn't one seeking to rescue people he didn't know. He spent his magic for Róisín and Róisín only.

"I'm going to have one of my personal guards stationed outside your room for the night," Róisín offered. Kayl nodded.

"I suspect that'll be wise." He wasn't a fool. He knew who Róisín married and for a moment she wondered how he would react if he knew just how terrible Cearny was. He called it, he knew that she would be nothing and he warned her. She didn't listen, she was a fool, but he wouldn't point that out.

He left shortly after and Róisín's focus shifted to her daughters. Róisín planned to visit Kayl secretly the following morning to discuss why he came, but also to thank him again. Yet that was not to be. When morning dawned and Etta arrived to tend to Greer and help bathe

Caitriona, she also delivered news that didn't entirely surprise Róisín yet left her hurting and worried all the same.

"I saw him set off in the carriage just after dawn," Etta admitted as she brushed Greer's hair. She looked to Róisín and concern wrinkled her brow. "I heard the king sent him off."

Róisín looked out her window to the gardens of the castle full of boulders and stone that fell in the attack. A heaviness settled in her gut as she spotted Cearny. She never claimed to know everything, but she did know both Cearny and Kayl well enough to realize her old friend would not leave so suddenly of his own free will.

Róisín remained in her room through the day, checking on Caitriona and tending to Greer whose upset from the attack rapidly became clearer. She was frightened to leave her mother's side, only daring to separate from her should Etta come into the room with food or bath water, but even then, she kept a cautious eye trained on her mother and Caitriona, as if having them in her sights would keep them there.

Róisín understood her firstborn's fears, she also wanted to cry and jump at sounds. She wanted to cling to the folds of Caitriona's nightgown to make sure she was truly and wholly there. But she was a queen as well as a mother, such displays of fear weren't allowed. She had to swallow them back and put on a face of knowledge, understanding and calm.

Yes, a dragon attacked; yes, half the castle was ruined; yes, the nursery was destroyed; yes, Caitriona was burned and killed, but she was healed and alive. She had to look at the bright side and what mattered most in the end was her children.

It was near noon two days later that Cearny darkened her doorway. Greer was reading a book to Róisín in the chair between the bed and the large windows. Caitriona continued sleeping on Róisín's bed and Greer only agreed because the chair was an arm's length from her little sister. They just began a second story when Cearny threw open Róisín's doors and stormed in, the air rushing forward from the movement and tinged with bitterness. Barely a glance at Caitriona caused his lip to curl in disgust before he observed Greer, his heir, and snarled as she leaned into Róisín's side.

"Enough of this," he spat, moving swiftly across the floor and grabbing the book from Róisín's hands. He threw it over his shoulder, sending it sliding along the stone; its spine flailing and pages folding. His dark eyes flashed while turning his attention to Greer. "Do you want to be seen as a coward? As pathetic? Enough of this childish behavior."

Greer cringed, pressing her body against Róisín's side, her brown eyes large as she stared at her father.

"Caitriona was hurt," Greer stated with a sternness in her voice that made Róisín's heart ache. Her sweet girl, forever—rightfully—afraid of her father, yet willing to talk back.

Cearny looked down at Caitriona then back at Greer. "The first true lesson you must learn if you'll be queen is you *never* let personal matters like this cause you to run and hide. That's weakness and I'll have none of it. Get up, you need to witness the work it takes to repair a kingdom after an attack."

He grabbed Greer's arm, tugging her roughly off Róisín's chair and pulled her toward the door. Greer stumbled, trying to catch her balance as she looked wildly from Róisín to Caitriona, her little arms reaching for her mother. Róisín wanted to reach for her as well and snatch her back, but she continued to sit with her hands at her side. If she reached for Greer, it would threaten them all. Even as the first look of betrayal crossed Greer's face by Róisín's lack of action before Cearny pushed her into the hall, Róisín continued to sit. Cearny nearly followed before seemingly thinking better of it. There was enough time for Greer to turn, her face painted with confusion, before he closed the door and lurched toward Róisín. His gaze was steady, refusing so much as to look at his youngest child; angry ocean waves were more friendly than his expression.

"I *know* how she was brought back," he snarled; each word seemed sour on his tongue. "The entire castle is buzzing with the news and the blatant display of the very magic I've outlawed. You're lucky I don't toss her out of the kingdom. Perhaps to the Mazgate Dominion, I hear they accept magical filth who left Braewick."

"She isn't magic," Róisín said softly, internally fighting the rising panic in her body.

"She's *made* from magic." Spittle flew from Cearny's mouth as his brown gaze flashed. His words were thrown at her with a yell and rang through her head. "The very breaths she takes are by magic. Her *life* is by magic. And you allowed that man entrance to our home, you asked that man for help, *you* did this to our daughter. You tainted her."

Róisín blinked, her mouth working but words not coming out until she gathered herself. "She *died*. What else would you have me do?"

Cearny stared and raised a single, blond eyebrow. Róisín's gut dropped. She feared this, that Cearny would rather his daughter dead than brought back by magic. But she hoped, for once, her terrible assumption of him was wrong.

He left in silence, the scent of his disgust heavy in the air and draping over the room in a cloud of hate. Róisín fell back against her chair, defeated and empty, an all-too-common feeling after interacting with her husband. But as Greer's cries echoed in the hall, growing fainter by the moment as she was surely dragged away, something else formed in Róisín's breast: a simmering rage. So hot and fast she nearly missed Caitriona's sudden stirring from the bed.

Caitriona's gasp drew Róisín back to the room and she fell from the chair, reaching rapidly to run her hand over Caitriona's forehead. The girl slept on, but her breaths came quicker and her skin felt hot to the touch. The scent of sulfur easing from between her lips made Róisín grow cold.

"Caitriona?" Róisín whispered as she pulled the strings of Caitriona's nightgown, opening the top half and exposing the girl's shoulders. The light through the window glanced off Caitriona's damp skin, wet from sweat, and there was a glimmer of something unnatural. Róisín blinked, leaning back as Caitriona's skin began to steam. The girl moaned, moving her head, her eyes opening slightly to reveal a golden glow.

"No!" She saw enough magic work in her time. She witnessed Kayl bring Caitriona to life just days before and it didn't look like this. It didn't *feel* like this. Her skin itched, prickled by energy beyond her control, and Róisín was on her feet searching the room for a foe that wasn't there.

"No, don't do this!" She spoke to the air, hoping he heard. He was the only one she knew powerful enough. She didn't know what would cause this change, but it was him. *Must* have been him.

Caitriona cried in her sleep and Róisín's mouth grew dry. Rubbing her hands together, she attempted to wake her long dormant magic. She used it so sparingly, only to cover the shape of her ears, that it was sluggish to respond. She never had the patience to learn proper wielding of her gifts and her regret stabbed her heart.

"Please, please don't," she begged the air as she sank beside Caitriona and took her daughter's small hands into her own, ignoring the heat on her palms and fingers where blisters formed. Pushing her weak magic into her daughter's hands, she attempted to shove away whatever was consuming her but Caitriona's skin only burned Róisín's hands further. She sucked in her breath, holding it as she watched her daughter until the tension broke. Caitriona grew still, sighing with smoke issuing from her mouth. Róisín stared, the pricking of her skin lessening, and she knew whatever curse thrust upon Caitriona was complete.

CHAPTER SIX

Caitriona

Caitriona shifted on the high throne; a seat she was never permitted upon until now. To her right sat her mother, prim and proper, her gaze set before her. Standing along the walls of the great hall, as well as behind the thrones, were royal guards. They kept stony expressions as they focused on the line of citizens extending down the entirety of the hall and out the doors, their serious manner casting a stillness in the room whilst all held their breaths.

A guard informed Caitriona that citizens began gathering the night prior. The idea they waited through the humid night air with biting bugs buzzing around made her increasingly uncomfortable. Was this normal? Did this happen in past years? Or were citizens particularly eager to share their commentary with the royal family? Even if she wasn't ready, the citizens seemed eager for their day of grievance.

Caitriona sucked in a slow, long breath before letting it ease out. Her nerves were at war with her mind, rattling in her body and making her tense. Even her hands quivered as she held the arms of the chair. Beside her, her mother displayed a comfortable air of professionalism; it was a stark comparison to Caitriona's jittering aura.

Róisín's red hair was parted at the center of her head and braided back elaborately, placing her pointed ears of her half-fae origin on display. Caitriona was still growing used to her mother's appearance, because she once had the curved human ears Caitriona and Greer shared. But upon Cearny's death, Róisín shed the minor magic she used that made her ears appear more rounded—the first change of many.

Caitriona was never oblivious to the fact that relations between her parents were strained and her mother's change in demeanor seemed to prove that. Her queenly attitude remained, but in many ways, she was more open. Since Cearny's death, Róisín chatted with Caitriona and Greer more than she had in years, she touched their cheeks and kissed their foreheads. Greer told Caitriona their mother once had no issue displaying that she was full of love, but it changed after the dragon attack when they were little. Caitriona wondered how much was true change, or if Róisín hid it all and was now free to be herself since she was no longer married to a man who hated everything different from himself—including his wife.

"You'll have to open the Day of Royal Greeting," her mother said, glancing at Caitriona and holding her gaze with a calm, resolute expression. Caitriona fought the urge to visibly deflate at the mere mention of it. Her mother witnessed all of this in the past, although she didn't run it herself, she still had more experience than Caitriona. But this was her job as heir and there was no getting out of it. Róisín gestured to the waiting people. "Do so loudly with a clear, authoritative voice. You know how to go about this, and I'll be here the entirety of it."

Caitriona gave a single nod and returned her attention to the crowd. Swallowing, she inched forward on her chair and cleared her throat, drawing further stares from the gathering people. With all eyes on her, she was forced to stand. The citizens looked at her with obvious curiosity and judgment, making her nerves jolt in her spine, but she settled her attention on her guards who, at the very least, were professional and kind to her.

"Welcome, all." Her hands were hot and sweating. The back of her dress stuck to her skin. "I appreciate you've come to speak with me today and are understanding that I'm filling in for my sister. I hope you all are comfortable sharing with me your concerns with the kingdom. I have a scribe noting all you say so we may present it to Queen Greer when she returns. As we have before, my guards will direct you forward and allow you to speak your mind. Do understand, time is limited and they will move you on so the next citizen may speak."

Turning to the guards and scribe, Caitriona flashed a brief smile. "Ready?"

All seemed to brace themselves. Backs straightened, quills posed, and for a glimmering moment, Caitriona felt confident this would go alright. Then the first two speakers who already glowered at Caitriona stepped forward. Her hope turned sour and dropped to the bottom of her belly.

Sinking into her seat, there was a stirring in her stomach; the dragon, smelling a threat, woke. Sometimes Caitriona felt like herself in body and spirit; but other times the beast she was forced to become was still too close at hand. It was most frequently woken by intense feelings: fear, lust, and anger. She wasn't surprised to feel it grow aware, only frustrated that it hadn't vanished from her entirely since she last felt it. Caitriona forced a pleasant smile at the approaching pair. "Sir, ma'am, you may proceed."

They were dressed in well-worn clothes and their skin scrubbed clean. The man looked Caitriona over, a sweeping gesture from foot to head with his gaze lingering above her eyes. His lip curled as he took in her horns.

Sometimes, although rarely, Caitriona forgot they were there. Then someone's gaze lifted upward and the horns' weight bore down. She could sense every inch of them. The way her skin ended just beyond her temples, her hair stopped growing, and the sharp bones protruded upward and curled towards the heavens. At times, the edge where her skin and horns met itched and in the early months after she sprouted them, she'd scratch the area until she bled, desperate in her self-disgust to be rid of them.

The man hissed, pulling his gaze away and Caitriona remained still, fighting the urge to look to her mother for help. A ruler didn't seek help from those beneath her station, at least that was what her father told Greer. She was the heir to the throne and her mother was only that—her mother—which was a different type of odd. How could you be married to a ruler one moment and discarded as only the mother of a ruler the next? They were both in awkward places, pushed there by expectation and tradition and little else. She wondered if the citizens could sense the oddness of it all. By the expression on the man, he certainly sensed something.

"We wanted to speak about the magic," he said.

"How it's been made ... *legal*," the woman added as if the very word caused a terrible taste on her tongue.

"Has there been an issue?"

"Yes," the woman replied quickly, clearly offended Caitriona would question her as if the answer was obvious. "It's the fact it's legal. Your kind freely exist in our realm. You do as you please and surpass the rest of us. Your kind cheat and make your lives better with an unfair advantage."

"Do you have specific examples?" Caitriona attempted to keep her voice even. The dragon was fully awake now and clouding her vision as heat rose within her. The scent of sulfuric smoke felt heavy on her tongue and nausea brought saliva to her mouth.

"Well, there's you to begin with." The man practically snarled. Spittle coated his lips as he spoke and stepped closer. A guard nearby moved his hand to the hilt of his sword and the man paused before stepping back. "You attacked the city and now sit as heir to the throne. You're a half-dragon creature, you aren't human. You don't deserve this position. You—"

"*Sir.*" Róisín's voice was clear and cool, ringing through the hall and immediately silencing him. "You're coming dangerously close to defamation. Did Princess Caitriona kill anyone in her attack on the city?"

The man began tripping over his words until his wife stepped forward, putting her arm out to stop her husband with eyes hot as iron in flame. "The *king*."

"Alas, you've been misinformed." Róisín sounded more sorrowful than she portrayed in private. It was something else Caitriona learned—how good of an actress her mother was as she faked sadness over the loss of her husband. It seemed that way for most within the castle, herself included. They all put on a face that displayed the depth of sorrow but secretly, they found they didn't particularly miss the king. It was the lack of missing that bothered Caitriona the most. She felt nothing, just an emptiness, and if she searched through that space that lacked emotion she would find anger, hurt, and disappointment collecting dust in the corners. All feelings that she felt because this was her father, a half of her, and he never loved her and wanted her dead.

Most of those who liked him quickly left when Greer legalized magic so now all that remained were actors of grief. That didn't stop his supporters from within the city from voicing their pain.

"A misfired arrow from a guard struck the king during the dragon attack. It went straight to his heart, killing him instantly. The guard was immediately dealt with for such a grievous error. So, do you have another example of how magic has wronged you personally?"

If they shared this story enough times, perhaps it would make it true. It was months after her awakening before she was told the truth of what happened—that Greer killed their father herself—but it was something mentioned only once and never discussed again. Caitriona had to sluggishly remind herself that his death was by murder and not by accident. She also reminded herself that most would feel some type of emotion over losing their father, but she seemed unable to. While she wasn't present for her father's death and much of that time was a foggy memory, she still clearly recalled the look in her father's eye as he tried to kill her. But like her mother, she supposed, she felt some relief and only in that relief did she find any guilt.

"If it hadn't been for the very presence of your daughter as a dragon, the king wouldn't have been struck by that arrow. If it hadn't been for your half-fae heritage, your daughter wouldn't have become a dragon," the man continued, finding his voice again, full of venom and anger.

"While magic certainly can be used for wrong—as is evident with my daughter because she was cursed and *that* was why she became a dragon beyond her control—magic does serve a greater purpose by giving us advantages to things we don't have. Had magic been legal when the king was struck by the arrow, perhaps he would've survived. We could have tended to his wounds and he would still be here with us. But it wasn't. And so, he was lost to this world and us all."

The couple blinked, as the words appeared to permeate their skulls and sink in. Never mind the fact magic was primarily used for little tricks and minor aids for illness and injury. Helping the wound stop bleeding, yes, that could have been done. Chasing off infection, too. But the cut into the king's torso with Greer's sword and the force behind its plunge into his stomach and organs was nothing magic could patch. Bringing someone back to life fully healed of their killing injuries was something incredibly rare, only performed by the very few people possessing the most magical of gifts. It was why what Kayl did for Caitriona was felt by magic users through the kingdom; it was also why he was capable of cursing her, because that level of magic made him bound to her in a strange, invisible way. But the citizens didn't know that. They never would. Not that Greer was imposing laws to prevent them from learning, but that it was something not often shared. And if anything was made clear, it was that those with hatred in their hearts for anything they considered 'other' rarely found desire to learn what they didn't understand.

Caitriona looked at her mother. What Róisín shared was enough. They didn't want to risk sharing too much.

"I apologize magic has hurt you." Caitriona returned her attention to the couple, blindly searching for words to calm and allow them to feel heard. "We'll take note of your complaint and report back to the queen."

The couple stared at Caitriona, then the wife's eyes changed, as if everything the royal pair said to them was at last absorbed but became soup along the way, a mix of things rather than a series of facts. A flash of anger returned as her gaze sharpened. Her expression of disgust was something Caitriona only ever saw her father give. She realized now, through her change and his death, how often he kept his face blank when she was around, but his look turned to revulsion if he thought she couldn't see. The gloom in his eye, the wrinkle of his lips—wet from biting back whatever dislike he was ready to spew, the reddening of his skin and hunch of his shoulder that left him radiating with the stench of his loathing. Hatred had a way of making people look ugly and this woman was foul.

The dragon nestled in Caitriona's breast rose its head. It sensed Caitriona bracing herself for whatever words were coming next. Fire licked the inside of Caitriona's throat, and she pressed her lips together, worried the flicker of flame would be seen behind her teeth.

"In truth," the woman began, "We wanted to see with our own eyes the atrocity sitting on the throne. King Cearny would roll in his grave if he knew. Whether or not Greer is queen, to think you're next in line is horrendous and disgusting. Your kind will surely bring the downfall of this kingdom."

They turned without another word and walked away. Róisín nodded to a guard who went after them. Their informal behavior and not calling Greer by her title was enough for a fine, but Caitriona wasn't so sure they'd face punishment for all they said about her.

She took the moment to lean back in her seat and close her eyes. The couple hadn't even reached their full time, but enough was said to leave Caitriona feeling like she would burst into flame, or into a dragon's form. For the first time, she wished for her dragon's wings to fly to the sky and go far away from here.

"Calm yourself," Róisín whispered. "Never let them see you affected by what they say or claim. A reaction is as good as a confession."

Caitriona took a deep breath, swallowing back smoke and sulfur as everything burned within her. The dragon urged, *begged*, for release.

Let me free, it seemed to say. *Let me stretch out my wings and claws. Let me swoop down the hall. Let me pluck those hateful people from the ground and fly high into the sky. Oh! The terror they would feel! And I could revel in it. I could find joy in their suffering.*

A part of Caitriona wanted to let the dragon out, but she knew it wouldn't do any good.

You can't teach them that they're wrong, that I'm not a scourge on this kingdom, if you do exactly what they expect you to, she told the dragon. *You can't prove them right.*

Looking down at her lap to straighten her skirt she ground her jaw. Her nails gained a glossy gold sheen and lengthened like claws. Caitriona spoke through clenched teeth: "*The dragon.*"

"Tell it to back away," Róisín continued to keep her voice low. "Remind it, and yourself, *you* are the one in control. Tell it to wait until you truly need the dragon to rise. Not now over hateful people."

But the hateful people continued to come. One after another, anger filled the hall with spitting fury as citizens of the city complained about magic, the discovery of neighbors who long-hid their abilities, the worship of old gods and fae, and in particular, the fact the queen found it alright to allow a half-fae and half-dragon woman to sit upon the throne and take their complaints. That Caitriona dared show her face rather than disappear into seclusion was enough to have seven citizens frothing at the mouth.

Others had legitimate concerns about taxes, building projects, areas with high theft, and neighborly squabbles; some expressed their adoration for the changes, they appreciated all Greer did thus far and were happy to see Caitriona finally stepping into the limelight. Some spoke warmly, gently, but expressed worries about the appearance of magic, and unexpected consequences: magic users would retaliate against their foes, that there would be an uneasiness amongst neighbors, that those who disliked magic would torment those who did.

But primarily, overabundantly, there was hatred. Rage. General unease and distrust for Róisín and Caitriona, separately and together, and by day's end when the sun slipped behind the hills, Caitriona was exhausted from holding the dragon back and forcing her face to remain blank and sincere.

"Once the sun has set," Róisín whispered between rotations from one group to another. "You'll be free to go. I've requested your dinner brought to your room. You'll be able to express your feelings freely there. *Privately*."

"I don't even know if I'll make it that far. I don't know if my room can contain it all," Caitriona adjusted her position to appear ready to offer her full attention to the hooded couple walking down the aisle toward them. Thankfully, the last people on the line.

"Princess," a voice said softly from behind. She glanced up to find the handsome, tan face of Paul. His green eyes met hers as he leaned over the back of her chair. He worked as a royal guard for a few years, led by Barden when Greer was still the heir. Upon her crowning, she continued to have Paul train under her with more expectations before transferring him to lead Caitriona's personal protection effective the moment Greer left for travel. "These two aren't from Braewick but demand to see you. They were willing to wait until all the citizens had gone through."

"Not citizens?" Caitriona asked, confused, but internally rejoicing that she was done speaking to those who lived in the city.

"They came armed but allowed us to take their weapons. They have accents I don't recognize but they wouldn't say who they were."

"Do you know what they want?"

"They said they know you, and it's necessary to withhold their news until they're before you."

Caitriona looked at the couple, a man and woman from what she could see. Both had their faces hidden from the hoods of the green cloaks they wore. Caitriona's eyes narrowed as she recognized the delicate stitchwork of the tunics peeking from beneath the light cloaks. Fae designs, she was certain of it after having spent nearly a year living in Ulla Syrmin. The female form stepped forward and Caitriona leaned toward them. "Thank you, Paul. You may return to your position."

"Princess Caitriona, Queen Mother Róisín." The clear, smooth and instantly recognizable voice made Caitriona's eyes bulge. "Thank you for seeing us."

"What—" Róisín began, turning to Caitriona with confusion as the couple reached to their hoods and pulled them back, exposing their fair faces and stirring a small smile on Caitriona's lips. Finally, friends rather than foes.

"Ceenear and Raum." The dragon eased off, the heat of fire quenched, and tension was finally gone from her shoulders. "What are you doing here?"

Raum, usually joyful and rarely without a glint of humor in his eye, was far from his normal temper and Caitriona's smile suddenly felt too eager. He stepped forward and maintained eye contact, never once glancing at the horns on her head.

"We come bearing news," he started. "Queen Onora has died. Her husband, King Malcolm, has taken claim to the throne and declared his first act: a declaration of war against Wimleigh Queendom."

The air rushed from Caitriona's chest, the dragon silent, and her vision tunneled rapidly. "*What?*"

"We were beyond the mist when word came. Isla reached us with a message from Niveem and we were instructed to tell you immediately. Isla said your sister wasn't here but would find her to convey the news."

"She's in Stormhaven," Caitriona said faintly, the feeling coming back to her body, the shock still there but her sight broadening. "She's gone for weeks. She only just left a few days ago."

Ceenear and Raum looked at one another.

"Is he about to attack? Should we raise the alarms?" Caitriona asked, getting to her feet and triggering every guard within the room. They stood straighter, their swords at the ready, their bodies moving a step closer and all of them with rapt attention.

"We hope it won't be soon," Ceenear said. "She only just passed, they still have to bury her, but King Malcom is ..."

"Aggressive," Raum added. "He's power hungry and has long disliked non-magic users, particularly your father. If he attacks as soon as possible, I imagine it won't be for a few weeks, at the very least. But I advise your sister return home because he certainly isn't one to wait if given the choice."

Róisín got to her feet, her face stern as she looked from the people to Caitriona. "You know these two? You trust them?"

"They're who cared for me when I was in the Endless Mountains," Caitriona said. "I trust them with my life."

"You have magic," Raum said, looking at Róisín. "I know you're part fae. I saw your magic shimmer as I walked down the hall. If you can, use your gifts to see if there are lies in this room. Read our thoughts if you're able."

Róisín's jaw set tightly, her eyes narrowing, and for a moment Caitriona was convinced Róisín would promptly kick Ceenear and Raum out of the castle entirely, but then her features softened. "Caitriona, we need to immediately alert Greer that we received this message and she must return."

"I have Ailith's crow," Caitriona offered. "I'll send her a letter. Crowley flies quicker than our fastest rider."

"We have a speaking stone and so does Isla." Ceenear patted the side of the bag she wore slung over her shoulder. "We can message Greer directly so long as you have something belonging to her person."

"Of course, I'll take something from her room. We'll message her promptly then, but we must also make provisions while being wise not to cause panic within the city. We'll begin by closing the castle gates and adding additional guards to the parapets." Caitriona turned toward her guards. "Go, send word, but do not pass this information to anyone beyond other guards. Ensure the castle is safely secured so we may figure out what to do next. Now, Ceenear, Raum, may you follow me?"

CHAPTER SEVEN

GREER

"You traveled all this way?" Ailith sat at the table, stretching out her legs while observing the old woman. Her stressed exterior had calmed—if only Greer could feel similarly.

"Gil'dathon isn't far from my home." Isla shifted on her chair between Ailith and Barden. Crossing one leg over another with some effort, she rubbed her ankle and relaxed into the seat. "Niveem reached out with the message and requested I find Ceenear and Raum. They were beyond the mist, on our side of the land, and Ceenear was guarding Raum while he inspected the borders. I sent them to Braewick to forewarn your sister and scried to find you three."

Greer remained standing. Her exasperation from the humidity and this unwelcome news felt like she was rubbed against splintered wood; the sharp pricks stabbed her skin and irritated her thoroughly.

"How do you know this is true?" Greer blurted, unable to handle these finer degrees of chit-chat and wanting the brunt of the information so she may begin figuring out a step forward. "How do you know the fae queen's dead? You weren't within the mountains, nor was Ceenear or Raum. How can you trust this message you received from Niveem?"

Isla leaned to the side and reached into the folds of her skirt to pull a glittering stone free. "Niveem spoke to me through this and we can speak to her again if you'd like. But I trust Niveem. I've known her for decades and she's a wise ruler over her city, but also loyal to her queen. She's masterfully talented and discreet. For all the time Ailith and Caitriona spent in the mountains, very few knew about it, even less during the time Caitriona returned.

"Niveem suspected something foul was afoot for some time. The queen grew ill, Niveem visited but left feeling all the more uncertain. Then messages she sent to Queen Onora were unanswered, visits she's requested denied. In part, it's why she sent Ceenear and Raum out of the mountains on such a simple errand, so she could have fae beyond the mist in case something went wrong.

"But all that aside, you should be asking about *Malcolm*, the self-proclaimed king."

Greer's eyes narrowed. She only encountered Isla a few times, enough to know the woman said whatever she pleased. If it wasn't directed at Greer, she would have appreciated this behavior more, but this instance only irritated Greer's already frazzled nerves.

A war was proclaimed against *her* kingdom and she, the monarch, was not at home.

"Yes," Greer spoke through gritted teeth. "What *of* Malcolm? The fae kingdom's never been a point of conquest for Wimleigh Queendom. My father didn't even know it existed and there's no mention of Invarlwen in any of our history books. If they ever interacted with those who make up Wimleigh now, it's been generations since that time. I only learned of it from Caitriona's travels. Why should Malcolm care to battle Wimleigh? Does he recognize no one in Wimleigh realizes his kingdom exists?"

"He's always been a man of desire. Your father would've hated him for being fae, but I suspect he would've found an equal in Malcolm, if only through their greed. You see, Queen Onora was never meant for the throne. Her brother ruled, and he forced her to marry Malcolm years ago. When her brother died childless, Onora was crowned. But Malcolm always craved more power. He hated being king consort, he wanted full ability to make decisions. For years, he attempted to push the fae kingdom's power beyond the mist, for years he wanted to retaliate over Cearny's destruction of fae people, but Onora always quickly denied him this. The mist provided protection, the fae of Wimleigh Queendom were always welcome to go through it, and those in Invarlwen were comfortable. The fae wanted for nothing, they didn't have to worry about a war or conquest on their land, there was no reason."

"And now Onora is dead," Ailith whispered.

Isla nodded gravely. "Odd, as she was still quite young. There was word she grew rather sick over recent months which is unusual as Invarlwen has many good healers. Then she was simply ... gone. Barely a week passed before Malcolm called leaders of various cities to the castle for his crowning. Niveem attended, thinking she would see Onora's burial, but it didn't occur. When she returned, she admitted something felt off beyond the obvious. The tone of the kingdom's seat had changed."

Greer blinked. Even with her father's death, she waited a year for her people to mourn before accepting the crown. *She* hadn't mourned very much, she spent her time battling increasing anxiety for the task before her as queen and the constant feeling her father's ghost was near, ready to strike, despite that she saw to it he was buried beneath the damp earth. "Is that standard?"

Isla turned her gaze to Greer and shook her head. "While the fae are different in many ways to you, and Onora's politics different from your father's, the tradition of allowing a period of mourning was a similarity shared. Proper protocol calls for a burial prior to the crowning, too. His rushed attempt to crown himself and be done with the queen hasn't particularly won him many favors."

"What have the fae said?" Barden leaned his elbows against the table edge. He had nearly as much interaction with Isla as Greer, but—ever the good communicator—was asking the right questions.

"I suppose it's much the same reaction as your people with the allowance of magic," Isla said, cracking her fingers one by one. "Your people aren't solidly sold on the idea of magic returning to Wimleigh, are they?"

Greer frowned, her shoulders dropping. "Not particularly. It depends on where you ask. Stormhaven—*Gil'dathon*, I mean—has readily accepted magic because it's a city built on it. The Umberfend Marshlands are too broad, the homes too scattered, to make a general consensus. There were once towns within the marsh that worshiped the dukes, but they disbanded when magic was made illegal and their worship not allowed—if people still lived there, I suspect they would've supported magic. Braewick City, however, hasn't allowed magic for much longer and there are ... mixed reactions at best."

"Exactly," Isla said. "And that's much of what is occurring with the fae. I'm certain it was the same when your grandfather originally banned magic. People were upset with the change, but those most devoted to the sovereign followed. Slowly that behavior spread, whether by changes of heart or violence."

"Is Malcolm threatening the fae?" Ailith asked.

"Enough that Niveem felt it unwise to travel beyond the mist herself. Enough that she warned Raum and Ceenear not to return."

"Then it's good they've gone to Braewick." Greer began to pace, unable to stand still any longer. Her body craved action. "They have safety within our castle until it's safe for them to return. You helped Caitriona so much, you've helped *me*, and I owe that to you."

"What are we going to do though?" Ailith asked, turning toward Greer. Her brows were furrowed and while her voice remained even, Greer saw the clear distress in her brown eyes. "When your father was battling the Mazgate Dominion it was always so far and away. It was a war that went on for years. I ... I don't know what happens when a war is declared. What do *we* do?"

"Ensure the queen is safe," Barden replied, drawing their attention to him. He sat upright, stepping into his role as the lead guard with ease. "Which she is. Then we return to Braewick City. It's a shame we've only just arrived; I doubt the horses will be ready to go until tomorrow. But we're closer than the mountains are and we'll get back as quickly as we can. We'll ready the troops, ensure the city is safe, and then ... wait."

"For what?" Ailith asked, her voice soft.

Greer turned to the table, taking a deep breath to remind herself her chest could expand despite how tight it was becoming.

"We wait for the official declaration of war, which may come by messenger from the Endless Mountains. A letter of some sort. But considering Malcolm likely assumes we're unknowing of his kingdom, if I understand correctly—" Greer's focus narrowed on an indent in the table, her fingertips tingling and the numbness spreading. "He may simply attack. The element of surprise. But we need to prepare for all possibilities."

"So, we just wait?" Ailith asked.

Greer couldn't meet her eyes. She focused on the dent of the table and the way the shadows and shine of light warped in its curve as her heart rate grew and thundered in her ears. Beyond the room, there was the caw of gulls, but it was similar to taunting laughter.

"Yes," Barden's voice was sorrowful. Greer tried to focus on the conversation as the tingling reached up her arms like ants crawling over her. At the corner of her vision, she saw movement, something shifting, there and gone again. Looking at the shadowed part of the room, it was empty, but she could have sworn she saw her father hunched there. His red face displayed a smirk of delightful success.

What? he asked from the corner of her sight, his tone taunting. *Did you think ruling a kingdom would be so easy?*

"But there's another option ..." Isla's voice came suddenly but it sounded far away, buried under the rush of Greer's pulse in her ears and the echoing laughter of her father. "Most of the fae aren't behind this declaration of war. They've lived a quiet life and have never been threatened before. They feel it's dangerous to draw attention, to let your kingdom know they exist. They could go against Malcolm, I suspect, but they can't unless there is an alternative. Someone else that they can crown as ruler of the kingdom. But right now, the only available alternative to Malcom is his son, Shad."

"I thought the queen had two sons?" Ailith asked. Greer glanced at the young guard, focusing on her for a moment while trying to will her throat to open and allow her to breathe with more ease. "When I was there with Caitriona, Raum and Lumia told us stories about the royals. They said there was a rumor Onora had a child before marrying Malcolm. Then together they had Shad."

"Shad may not even be the queen's," Isla continued. "Her first child, Lachlan, did in fact exist. He was secreted away when he was still a wee thing and taken beyond the mist. Very few knew of his existence though. Technically, he has the right to the throne over Malcom and Shad both. There's been some rumor Shad came from another relationship or perhaps came with Malcolm when he married the queen. All in all, there's the chance Shad may not be Onora's blood-related child.

"Perhaps, and I say this as only a possibility and not in any way a direction, if you find Lachlan and get him to side with you, you may be able to take on Malcolm and have a better justification for it. The fae of the mountains will more than likely support you as you'd be fighting to return the land to the rightful king."

The thundering in Greer's ears reached a fever pitch before becoming a solid ringing. Her chest felt tight, and invisible hands gripped her ribs and applied pressure. Her neck felt hot against the confines of her dress and she was certain she was breaking out in hives. But these words brought her attention upward and she stared at Isla for a moment, meeting the witch's gaze without flinching. "The rightful king?"

"The rightful *fae* king, and a wonderful way to show you truly stand by your words that you want those with and without magic united rather than enemies," Isla replied, her mouth turning up into a smile.

Greer collided with the doors to her room, nearly breaking them off their hinges as they swung inward then back closed behind her. The force of her impact startled a pair of doves sitting on the sill of her open window, sending them to the blue skies with quivering, shrill calls.

She left the meeting room after requesting Isla travel to Braewick City with them. The old witch gratefully agreed and Greer could barely stop herself from running out the room. Instead, she walked briskly and purposefully. Head held high, lips pressed together, she didn't want anyone to suspect anything was amiss, that *she* was amiss. Yet Barden wasn't far behind, her constant shadow, and she spared him the look she gave to everyone else, one that could freeze the very soul of any innocent who got in her way.

All along the hall her father flicked through shadows, laughing as he darted along the edge of her vision. His voice wiggled down her ears to squirm into her head and fill it whole:

You're going to crumble over this.

You aren't built to be queen.

You already have blood on your hands from murdering me and it will only grow worse. It will fill your throat and consume you whole.

This is your destiny.

With the wooden door closing behind her, Greer finally found herself alone. Her chest heaved from the effort to breathe as she reached for the pin in her hair and pulled it out, allowing her long blonde locks to fall loose before she threw the pin across the room with a cry. Her eyes burned as the silver piece struck the wood of her headboard and quivered where it lodged itself.

She wasn't the queen of steel and intent she portrayed herself as.

The click of the door handle sent Greer's attention spinning to find Barden peeking in. With quiet steps, he entered the room and pressed the door closed behind him before adding the lock for good measure.

"Are you alright?" he asked as he turned. Greer quivered in the center of the room. Her hair fell over her shoulders in tangles, stirred by the breeze and bringing forth the scent of her bath oils—lavender and lilac, a scent she loved but would forever associate with this awful moment.

His three words were nearly her undoing. Already, the pressure in her chest grew and her breaths came quicker.

Cearny continued to taunt from the shadows, *Murderer. And to think I was your first. Imagine how many more people will die by your hand now that there's war.*

"Where's Ailith?" Greer quickly asked. When she left the room, only Barden followed her and she hadn't the mind to ask about the girl.

"With Isla. The elders offered her a place to rest for the night and Ailith volunteered to get her settled. The elders know, by the way. I spoke with them and conveyed your sorrow over having to cut the visit short. I explained there's a dire emergency within Braewick that needs your immediate attention. They're already working on copies of the books and plan to send them as soon as they're done, they insisted I let you know."

Greer let out a withheld breath that sounded more like a hiss as she turned on her heel toward the windows. Outside, beyond the room where the walls felt like they were quickly closing in on her, the sky was a perfect shade of blue and birds flitted through the air. The scent of roses and rich herbs rose with the heat of the day and floated through her open window. It would be beautiful if Greer wasn't panicking. But for now, it served as something to hold onto.

Murderer, Cearny hissed.

Greer forced a single breath in.

Killer.

She breathed out. The scents, it was necessary that she focus on the summer scents.

"Should I have not said anything to the elders?" Barden asked hesitantly, his voice close, and his body nearby. She could always sense him, even without seeing him.

Greer shook her head, the movement a jolt, and raised her hand to her mouth as her teeth quickly worried at the skin along her thumbnail. She considered all before her: she was a queen now, not just the head of the royal guard. If there was a declaration of war on her kingdom, all those who entered the fray were her responsibility, their lives were in her hands.

And when they die, it's your fault.

"What am I going to do, Barden?" Greer dropped her hand from her lips, feeling the sting of pulled skin along her fingernail and the heat of fresh blood. The instant reminder that she wasn't only her emotions, but a human body as well. But that was part of the problem, wasn't it? Her emotions were contained in her body and they were too great to be captive within flesh. They needed to expand, explode, and they had no way out. She was swelling like a corpse, filled with the gas of all the awful things her father whispered in her ear.

She couldn't look at Barden, not yet. She didn't want to risk him seeing the guilt crushing her. "If I'm killed, Caitriona is queen. It's the last thing she wants. She's too young, she doesn't have enough experience. Did you see how terrified she was when we left? I can only imagine the things said to her when she met with the citizens. And Ailith's still young. She can't be in a battle. What about Paul? He's just rising in the guard. All of these children fill the ranks, they can't handle a war."

"Those children are adults," Barden reasoned, his voice growing clearer as he came closer to Greer. "You trusted Ailith with Caitriona's life and the seriousness of this is no different. Caitriona, Ailith, Paul, they're older than you were when you fought your first battle. You were barely eighteen."

"It doesn't mean they should have to do the same," Greer whispered. "They shouldn't have to face the same horrors I did, and I don't want to be the reason their lives are made short."

"What's this about?" Barden asked. He stood behind her, but didn't touch her. He remained still, waiting for her reply, or some motion clarifying what she wanted.

"I wasn't even seeking a war, yet a war found me, and all of those in the guard will surely see death, and the blood is on my hands," Greer began. Her throat started to close, and her vision narrowed. She held out her hand, the edge of her nail creased with blood until it swelled and dripped over. "Sometimes I think my father cursed me in his final moments. That he wished I suffer as much as possible. That he's getting his way."

Her terror swelled and overtook her in a rush. Her vision was fuzzy, as if looking through a fog, and the world became off kilter. Her muscles spasmed as she choked on air. Barden's face appeared before her, his eyes concerned and brow furrowed. He reached for her and gently pressed the palm of his hands to her cheeks while his lips moved. Greer gasped, blinking rapidly as her hand patted over her heart. She pulled at the fabric of her dress, trying to get air to her chest to chase away the rapid beating as she focused on Barden's face and strained to hear his voice through the cotton filling her ears.

His lips moved, a repetitive motion, and finally the sluggish churn of Greer's brain recognized the movement on his lips. She saw him speak this a million times; her name, he was saying her name, over and over he called her back, pulled her down, tethered her to him and yanked her from the grasp of her panic.

Greer.

Greer.

"*Greer,*" he repeated, her name finally finding its way to her ears.

She gasped, a true breath filling her lungs and with it came the barely held back wave of emotions. Her eyes burned, but she clenched them closed, refusing to cry as Barden stepped forward and enveloped Greer into his arms. She didn't even have the command over that as a few betraying tears leaked from her eyes.

He held her, filling her nose with his scent of herbs that tied her to the world and gave her focus. He held her, instructing her when to breathe in and out until she finally felt her heart return to normal. The world became fully present again and Cearny's taunting face vanished from sight, and still Barden held her.

CHAPTER EIGHT

RÓISÍN

Sixteen Years Prior

F ire tells the truth. It was something Róisín's mother taught her as a child before she faded away and was lost to time. A memorized lesson coating the interior of her mind, now rubbed to life after collecting dust for decades, and the clarity of her mother's instructions pushed Róisín into action. There was more to the teachings.

Ash exposed secrets and smoke revealed reality, you only had to know how to feed the flame and ask the right questions. You only needed certain provisions.

After Greer was dragged from her room, after Caitriona was overwhelmed with the scent of a curse, Róisín waited. She gave it a few days of being tactfully well-behaved so Cearny would back off and stupidly believe she was no longer a threat and once more under his thumb. After a week had passed since the dragon's attack, she waited until the sun sank behind the valley ridges before leaving Etta to sit with Caitriona.

With a cloak hood pulled up and the shadows turning the landscape to a hushed shade of silver-blue, she moved swiftly to the gardens, avoiding the rubble from the partially destroyed castle and did not make eye contact with anyone who passed. With the castle so recently hit and the dragon's body still in the northern fields where men reportedly prepared to hack at its corpse, there was enough chaos to pass with very little notice. At least, that was what she thought.

"You should have a guard with you," a voice called from behind. Ice shot up her spine and she stopped moving, her back straightened. Turning on her heel, relief flooded her.

"You won't tell Cearny?" Róisín asked Shaw. He was a tall, broad man some years Róisín's senior with auburn hair and bright green eyes. It was years since she saw him regularly, but she held a soft spot for the man. He was always kind to his wife and fought for his family. It was something Cearny struggled to understand, the selfless decisions others made often confused him.

Still, she knew Shaw well enough, even if their interactions had grown rare.

He smiled shyly. "Not if you let me go wherever you're going."

"I don't want to draw any attention," Róisín cautioned and Shaw shrugged slightly in response. He rolled his gaze to the castle walls where guards were silhouetted against the fading light in the sky.

"You won't, not if you have me with you," Shaw replied. "Now why are you headed to the back garden door?"

"If you're coming along with me, I'm sure you'll find out."

The garden door was somewhat a poorly kept secret. It was an easy way to pass through the castle walls with minimal sight of the watchtowers. It was something the royal family used to visit the Elder Tree and leave the castle without drawing attention from citizens. A mass of thorny rose bushes grew along the back entrance, keeping the door generally hidden from view, and on the other side sprawled the forest surrounding the Elder Tree. Cearny's ancestors planted prickly bushes against the walls, with the thickest beside the garden door, but anyone who passed knew that going around one bush, down the wall, and behind a boulder allowed for a clear enough path with little injury. The door stayed locked, with only two keys in existence. One for the sovereign, and one for the heir. Luckily, Greer was too young to have use of the key just yet.

Together, Shaw and Róisín moved silently through the area as crickets sang.

"This isn't a long visit beyond the wall, is it?" Shaw kept his rumbling voice low, his footsteps discreet.

"I only need to go to the grassy opening beneath the Elder Tree," Róisín said, making quick footwork to reach her destination. Amongst the bushes and lofty branches of the trees, night was already falling and the crisp scent of autumn was thick. For a moment, Róisín feared she ran out of time, but the glade was brighter and while the first frost was threateningly close, it had yet to strike. What light remained in the sky shown down through a part in the branches of the tree and highlighted what she needed beneath.

"I shouldn't be long," Róisín murmured as she moved into the grassy opening and dropped to her knees. "Just alert me if anyone's coming."

She felt Shaw's eyes on her, but ignored him, there was only so much time she could be away from Caitriona who still hadn't woken.

It took her a moment, her fingers tracing over the grass until she found the little tufts of greenery complete with dainty flowers. Their petals were white, yellow, and purple with tiny streaks like starlight. She only found these flowers beneath the small tree they worshiped in Caermythlin and here beneath the Elder Tree. They bloomed after the last frost in spring and died promptly upon the first frost of autumn, and they didn't survive in sunshine, only the shade of the magic trees.

Snapping the flowers and leaves at the base of the stems, she left the roots in the earth as she gathered the plant quickly. Stuffing them into the folds of her cloak, she took as many as possible until the glade seemed empty as darkness fully settled in.

Standing, she turned and found Shaw staring at the flowers in the folds of her cloak. Slowly, he raised one eyebrow.

He knew.

Shaw sniffed and rolled his shoulders, yawning as he looked to the heavens. "Well then, my queen. It's growing late, are you ready to return home?"

A tension released from her spine that she hadn't realized was there. She swallowed and gave a solitary nod.

After they made their way through the garden gate and crossed the greenery toward the castle door, they paused as Shaw turned to face her.

"Well, I'm off to sup with my wife," Shaw said with a smile. Now they were only two acquaintances chatting in the gardens, ignoring the destruction around them, nothing more.

"How's Rowan?" Róisín asked, leaning into the act of accidental meeting.

"Wonderful, our fourth child is on the way and she's kept quite busy with the first three." Shaw smiled, not acting at all this time. His pride for his family left Róisín wishing for something in her husband she knew she would never have. When things were still new, she thought there was a chance to have this experience with Cearny, but she was wrong about that as she was with much more.

Was this what other relationships were like? Did love actually exist? She thought it did one day, years ago, but now ... It was so rare she was met with kindness by men that when one happened to give her any, she couldn't help but feel her heart broaden and a small crush develop.

"What are their names, again?" Róisín questioned, drawing close to the doorway of the castle and finding she didn't want to end their chat yet. She needed a moment of pleasurable conversation from someone who wanted to hear from her, who asked questions and listened to her replies.

She shuffled through her memories of the various guards, having tried her best to know little gems of their lives. It was easier with Shaw, considering it upset Cearny so much that Shaw left the guard for family life. At first Cearny refused to let Shaw step down from service, but Shaw was smart and threatened to leave completely. Like most men, Cearny had some respect for another man, so he allowed the compromise, although it still vexed him. "Holly and ... Posey ...?"

"And Barden," Shaw replied. "Barden is my first. Then Holly and Posey. Barden will begin training for the royal guard soon, you know."

Róisín smiled and found it was genuine. "You must be proud."

"How could I not?" Shaw's smile brightened the entire garden. "And your daughter will train soon too, won't she?"

"A few more years. She's already eager for your teachings."

Shaw beamed as he stepped forward and pulled open the door for her. "And your youngest? How is she?"

"Better with every day, thank you." What happened to Caitriona was no secret amongst the staff and royal guards of the castle but Róisín still didn't want to risk speaking of it too much for fear word would get back to Cearny. He made it abundantly clear they were to pretend nothing happened at all, whatever that meant. So Róisín took to saying Caitriona was fine, healthy, and happy as always. She didn't share the finer details. No, no one knew beyond herself, Greer, Etta and Cearny. All Róisín could offer was a smile and look that she hoped conveyed more than her words.

Shaw gave a nod of understanding and stepped aside as Róisín stepped into the hall.

"Have a good night, my queen. And—" He glanced at the bundle in her arms and gave her a wink. "I hope you see whatever you're looking for."

IN HER ROOM, CAITRIONA CONTINUED TO SLEEP. ETTA LEFT to tend to Greer, and Róisín remained seated by the window waiting for moonrise. The look of knowing on Shaw's face was still clear in her mind. With eyebright flowers pressing beneath the padding of her bed, slowly being crushed by its weight, Róisín had all she needed. She only had to wait a while longer as the castle grew quiet, the staff and people off to bed. The moon climbed higher and shone brightly through Róisín's window, it was a comforting, watchful presence.

She snuffed out her candles, moving through the room by moonlight to her cold fireplace. Pushing logs inside, setting them just right, she paused to retrieve the eyebright from under the mattress where Caitriona slept. Tucking them amongst the logs, she lit a match and set them aflame as she settled onto the cold stone floor before the hearth. The flame licked at the logs before catching the eyebright, forcing them to sputter and curl under the heat. It was best to work with dried herbs and flowers, allowing them to catch fire all the quicker, but Róisín didn't have enough time to let the flowers dry. She needed to know what happened and she needed to know immediately.

The festering heat of Caitriona's skin hadn't happened since that night when sulfur was strong on her breath. To the best of Róisín's abilities, the girl was healthy and fine, but she wasn't a fool, she knew a curse when she saw it.

As the fire grew, she leaned forward, cupping her hands in the billowing smoke. Feeling the heat burn her skin, she brushed the smokey air towards her and took deep breaths, smelling the wood with the twinge of earth burning throughout. The eyebright smoke burned her eyes and coated her tongue, tasting like regret and dysfunction. She sat back and looked to the ceiling. This only worked with the smoke of eyebright flowers and familiarity of someone she knew and loved. It wasn't a spell capable of following those unfamiliar to her. Would not being close to someone anymore destroy her chances? There was only one way to find out.

"Show me what I don't know," she requested the smoke. "Show me what happened to my daughter Caitriona."

The flames leaped in the hearth, eating away her words and making them into substance. The smoke curled forward, finding Róisín's mouth and choking her throat. She gasped and raised her hand. Her fingers crawled against her neck as she tried to find air, but only the blue smoke of the eyebright filled her lungs and seeped into her body, taking her from the room and thrusting her into another place within the palace walls days before.

Kayl rapidly packed and glanced nervously over his shoulder at the guards darkening the doorway of the room he stayed in.

"I'm moving as quickly as I can," he said. The guards continued to glower and said nothing.

The scene shifted and Kayl walked to a carriage with the same guards close behind. He looked toward the castle with a frown before stepping in. The door slammed closed behind him. The carriage jolted forward, moving quickly with a line of guards following on horseback.

She shifted on the wind and settled on the castle's curtain where Cearny stood.

"What can I do for you, my king?" a voice called. A guard stepped forward with eager eyes. Róisín recognized him as a newer guard who always made her ill at ease. His blind devotion to the king was desperate, and Cearny's constant overlooking of the man, leaving him on the fringes of everything, made it all the more embarrassing.

"Watch who converses with the queen," Cearny said. He was like a statue watching Kayl's carriage move through the city. "She's not to know what's happening with that miscreant."

The man smiled, his lips cracked and face moist with sweat. Ian, that was his name, and Róisín immediately took note to avoid him at all costs.

"May I ask what your plans are?"

Cearny rubbed his chin and didn't pull his gaze away from the city. "The queen needs a reminder of her place in my kingdom. That man's too much of a temptation for her, he steers her too far off the path of respect for my authority, and he's brought magic to my home. I'm ensuring he understands magic has no place in my kingdom, and through this, Róisín will understand her position a little more clearly. She must be silent, she mustn't touch magic again, and she must not befriend those folk. Two birds killed with one stone."

The scene shifted and a sound of rage fell from Róisín's mouth as she took to the wind. She wanted to know more of Cearny's thoughts, but that wasn't what she asked the vision to provide and it insisted she discover the truth through different methods.

She was thrust inside Kayl's carriage. He sat in the corner, clutching his bag to his chest and tapping his foot impatiently. He appeared more exhausted than when he entered the carriage with wrinkled clothes, shadowed eyes and stubble on his cheeks. Time passed, although she wasn't sure how much.

The curtains were pulled down. Róisín wasn't sure if it was Kayl's doing or the guards. Suddenly, the carriage jutted to a stop and the door flew open, a guard's hand reached in and grabbed Kayl, pulling him out roughly despite his protests.

He was thrust to the ground and his belongings spilled from his arms as he caught himself. He attempted to speak but his words were caught behind his lips before a guard grabbed hold of his head and forced him to look forward. The vision moved Róisín again, placing her behind Kayl so she saw what he did. A scene, a horror, a killing of Caermythlin.

Róisín's childhood home, the town that accepted her as their own after her mother died. She lived with other children who lost their parents to illness or unspeakable things in a building that should be standing but seemed missing amongst the rubble. Róisín still dreamt of the few traumatized children crying in their sleep at night of men who came into their homes with blades shining and anger in their eyes.

When she met Kayl at barely seven years old, she found him crying, tucked away and hidden from everyone a short time after his arrival at the orphanage. It was there they became friends with determination to protect one another through it all—the heartbreak of losing their families and homes, the terror of the unknown, and the loneliness of being left behind. It was also there she broke his trust and his heart.

But now the town she left so many years before was in ruin. What buildings still stood were blackened crisps pointing to the sky. Smoke rose while bloodied corpses littered the ground. The trees looked odd against such a ruined landscape, standing out amongst the rubble with faded green leaves and shadows shifting beneath. Kayl cried out as he lifted a shaking hand toward the trees, and Róisín realized the shadows were swinging bodies hung from its limbs.

The only place she ever felt truly at home was completely destroyed and all its people dead.

The guards stepped forward, murmuring something Róisín couldn't make out beyond Kayl's cries. A flash of a blade caught in the sunlight, and Kayl's sobs turned to screams as the tips of his pointed, half-fae ears were cut away. The guard tossed the tips into the grass, laughing as they stepped back and turned without another word to mount their horses for home.

Kayl sat upon the bloodied earth, unseeing the guards retreat as he clutched his ears and cried over the sight of his town he so fiercely loved. Róisín sank to the ground beside him, unable to interact with anything in the vision but feeling as if her heart was being tugged from her chest.

The scene shifted. The sun moved westward and Róisín stood on the ruined doorstep of the orphanage. Kayl picked through the rubble, blood dried along his neck and face, and he paused before a small corpse.

Róisín felt the strength in her deplete. She turned away, unable to look. The sight of the child reminded her too much of her own daughter being pulled from her nursery just days before.

"A curse," Kayl murmured. He sniffed loudly and wiped his nose with the back of his hand, snot glistened on his skin in the poor light and the ash in the air immediately clung to the moisture there. "So that you may suffer as well when you believe you're at your safest.

"A curse." His voice grew confident, and his rage reached the heavens. He stumbled forward and out of the doorway, moving through Róisín and making her gasp as he stepped onto the street. The pressure grew rapidly as the air changed and developed a taste of iron. The hairs on Róisín's arms rose and she felt the urge to flee from the sparking feel of Kayl's gathering magic. Nothing that happened in the vision could hurt her, and she had to see it through, she had to hear what he was sure to say.

Kayl paused at the main road, turning his attention toward the west. He stared down the very road Róisín took when she left Caermythlin, beyond the low-lying hills of the Endless Mountains to where Braewick Valley lay. His bitter laugh fell from him like a torrent. When they were children Róisín delighted in making him laugh, but this was different. This was broken. This was the laughter of someone actively changing into something she didn't recognize.

The air continued becoming ferrous and thick. Róisín followed him, daring to step before him and look into his bloodshot eyes. The veins under his pale skin stood out and shifted from pink to red to black.

"King Cearny," he yelled, "*I curse you*! That your daughter will be the very beast you are most proud of. That your daughter will be your death. That you will suffer knowing those most close to you, those who share your blood, will see to your end."

Everything expanded into sound and light. An explosion that sent Róisín backward and thrusted her into her body where she gasped on the floor of her bedroom.

Rolling over, she vomited. Black bile splattered across her dress and ran down her chin. Wiping her mouth with the back of her hand, the gesture immediately brought Kayl to mind. She looked at the flames, dying now, with tears in her eyes. Hours had passed; the moonlight shifted and left Caitriona in glowing light. Róisín studied her from the floor, a sob building in her chest and releasing. So loud she nearly missed another sound, soft but penetrating. A sound any mother was trained to hear.

The whimper of her child.

Róisín was on her feet and across the floor in a moment, falling beside her bed and running her hands over Caitriona's face. Ash marks covered her cheeks and brow from Róisín's hurried fingers, but it didn't matter because Caitriona's eyes finally opened. Blue, but with a shimmer beneath that Róisín saw before.

What had Cearny said the other night? His eyes bright with rage and damning words like poison-tipped daggers. That she was to blame? For once, he was correct. *She* did this by asking for Kayl's help. *She* allowed him to come close enough for Cearny to set sights on him. And now, all suffered. Her home was lost, her people dead, her friend turned to something other, and all would hurt because of it, particularly the innocent. Like her daughters. Her sweet, caring Greer, and Caitriona, her cursed child.

CHAPTER NINE

Caitriona

War approached like a gathering storm. Dark and thunderous in the west, it made skin prickle with energy and strengthening terror, and Caitriona was left waiting for the lightning to hit.

After Ceenear and Raum's arrival, everything was rushed. There was no time for her to calm down from being verbally assaulted by the citizens of Braewick City; no time to eat her dinner in silence; no time to get her bearings before she was brought into the meeting room with her mother, Ceenear, and Raum. When her mother called for council, as exhausted as she was, she knew it was necessary to meet and figure out steps forward.

"We can speak to Greer through this," Ceenear explained, leaning over the table to place a glittering stone in the center. "Isla may already be in Gil'dathon."

"Did you pass by Greer on Wimleigh Way?" Caitriona asked as she sat at the head of the table, feeling odd taking Greer's place—her father's place—but having already received a stern lecture from her mother when she first took one of the other seats.

"We must have been passing ships in the night," Raum said. There were shadows under his eyes, his lips pale, the exhaustion of his expedition—or perhaps carrying the weight of the news they brought forth—a clear shroud over his being. "We stayed a night along the road at a home of fae-folk. Their party may have passed us then. We attempted to contact Niveem or Lumia but were unable to reach them."

Caitriona frowned. Niveem was the sweet, appointed lead of Ulla Syrmin, the mountain peak where she recovered from the curse. Lumia was Raum's partner; the silence from both seemed odd and left a sick feeling in Caitriona's belly.

"How does the stone work?" Róisín nodded to the table, her arms crossed over her chest. "I've heard of such stones, but I've never seen one."

"Do you have something of Greer's?" Ceenear asked, resting her hands upon the edge of the table patiently. Caitriona offered Greer's preferred quill.

"She uses it to write personal letters," Caitriona said. "I have items she gave me as well, if that doesn't work."

"This is fine." Ceenear placed the quill next to the glittering stone. Covering the stone with her hand and closing her eyes, she began. The air shimmered about her with magic at work as Ceenear forced energy into the stone. When she pulled her hand away, the rock cracked, chipped, then began vibrating on top of the quill until it bounced with such aggression it fell apart, breaking into a fine sandy grain that covered the quill. For a moment, all was still, then the material stirred, swirling in the air by an invisible breeze until it formed what looked like Greer.

Caitriona's eyes widened and she leaned forward. "Greer?"

The figure turned its head and looked at Caitriona with a frown. The grains shifted, and what still sat on the table tumbled to form another face.

"Just, place the rock on the table. Stop touching it!" Isla's voice came pouring forth.

Greer's figure dropped something invisible and shrank back. Her frown still plain on her face and hands on her hips for a moment as she studied something. Then her expression softened into surprise and finally, happiness. "Cait?"

"Oh, Ree," Caitriona sighed and all at once she felt she could fall apart in a way she hadn't realized she wanted to. "Isla's with you? So, you know what's going on?"

Greer's sandy figure nodded. "We're already packing our supplies and preparing to return to Braewick. Isla arrived a few hours ago, just after us. The horses must rest before we leave, but we're trying to make it back to Braewick as quickly as possible."

"What do I do?" Caitriona asked, wishing her voice didn't convey how scared she was. Her mother, off to the side, gave Caitriona a look. She ignored it, certain it was of disapproval. She wasn't before the populace anymore; her emotions were safe with those present.

"Ensure there's additional forces at the city gates and the watchtowers," Greer began.

"Already done. What next?" Caitriona replied and Greer's expression softened.

"Then you've done all you have to for the time being." Greer's tone was comforting and enough to be her undoing. Caitriona felt her eyes burn. "We're hatching together a plan. Get your rest, when we return we'll have a meeting to discuss our next steps forward."

"Alright." Caitriona forced her shoulders to relax. "And Ailith? Is she ...?"

"She's preparing to ride with Barden, otherwise I'd let her say hello. She's excited to see you."

Caitriona grinned. "I'm excited to see her too. *And* you. Soon, okay?"

"As soon as possible," Greer said with a smile before the grains collapsed and began vibrating back together to form the sparkling rock from before.

They disbanded quickly. Raum and Ceenear escorted to guest rooms while Caitriona and Róisín turned in the direction of the staircase to the royal family's private chambers. They walked side by side in silence with Paul following Caitriona a few steps behind. Her mother explained that in threat of war, it was best to always keep a guard nearby. Róisín nodded at servants as they went until the halls eventually grew empty beside the few guards on duty near the entrance of the private quarters.

"The other woman," Róisín broke her silence, drawing Caitriona's attention just as they reached her bedroom door. "The one who told Greer to sit the stone down. She seems familiar."

"Isla," Caitriona offered. "She's the witch that lives in the woods just south of the Endless Mountains. The one who helped us when Ailith was injured. She was here, at least that's what Greer and Ailith told me. She came back to the castle with them when I was ..."

She felt her cheeks grow warm with embarrassment and suddenly it was impossible to meet her mother's cool green gaze. "Anyway, you likely met her, although briefly. She didn't linger."

There was a stretch of silence that lasted long enough for Caitriona to look at her mother. The queen studied the shadows of the hall with her brow knit while her concentration remained elsewhere. She was so swept up in something else that she startled when Caitriona gently touched her arm.

"She just reminds me of someone," Róisín said with an air of exhaustion as she returned Caitriona's gesture and steered her toward her room. Paul stepped aside, taking position by Caitriona's door. "Now, go get rest. You've had a long day."

Caitriona reached for the handle, glad to finally go to the privacy of her room, only to pause.

"Mother?" She turned to find Róisín hadn't moved, as if she waited to ensure her youngest was tucked away in her bed. Caitriona frowned; her mother always was particularly protective of Caitriona but there was a different energy about Róisín she couldn't quite pinpoint. "Do you think I did alright earlier today? Before Raum and Ceenear arrived?"

The line between Róisín's brow softened, the hard edge of cut emeralds that were her eyes shown in the low light turned into pools of green. She stepped forward, her fingers brushing over the curve of Caitriona's cheek and alighting on her shoulder. "Darling girl, you did better than most kings when faced with that type of behavior. Please don't take it to heart. What they all said was awful yet you handled it with grace. But I want you to know that none of it's true. You aren't a disgrace, and you aren't evil."

"I felt like I was about to turn into a dragon again," Caitriona admitted in a pained whisper. The tears that threatened to release all day suddenly flooded her eyes, burning hot. "I felt so threatened and in so much danger, I wasn't sure I was going to last."

"But you *did*." Róisín stepped forward to cup Caitriona's cheeks in her hands. She directed Caitriona's face to turn and face her own. "You're stronger than you realize. You've survived a dragon's attack and a curse. Now you've survived the misguided judgments of hateful people. Give yourself the credit you deserve. Now go, get in your room, and rest. When Greer returns, well, I doubt we'll have a quiet evening for quite some time."

With a brief kiss on Caitriona's cheek, Róisín stepped away and moved down the dim hall, giving a snap of her fingers which drew out additional guards who were hidden in the shadows. "Watch the princess's door, please. There is a growing threat to the castle, and she must have a guard present at all times."

Caitriona met Paul's gaze as two guards stepped forward. "You should go home and see your husband. You've been working since before daybreak."

Paul looked at the two guards and Róisín's retreating form with uncertainty, but there were shadows under his eyes. He was likely up longer than Caitriona.

"I'll see you tomorrow?" she offered. "I'll be fine here."

"There's two of us, Paul. You've got to rest," one of the guards reassured and Paul's exhaustion finally descended upon him like a cloak.

"Alright, see you in the morning, princess." He flashed a smile and gave a quick bow. With a final pat to the shoulders of the new guards, he turned and left the hall. Caitriona gave the new guards a tight-lipped smile and dip of her head before entering her room. Locking the door behind her she released a long-withheld breath before sinking onto her bed.

She lay there, going over the scenes of the day before remembering her mother sent her evening meal to her room. Sure enough, it sat on her table near the fireplace. Not bothering to call any of her ladies to help her undress, Caitriona climbed to her feet and began to peel off her gown. She desired privacy and silence above all else.

Caitriona made her way to the plates of food that were disappointingly cold with a trail of discarded fabric behind her. Her gold eyes glanced to the lock on her door and back to the food before she gently lifted the steel plate of chicken and biscuits into her hands and transferred it to the edge of the fire to warm back up.

When the curse was completed nearly two years ago and she woke in her human form, she absconded to Ulla Syrmin where she rested and received lessons from the fae on how to control the tides of magic that now seemed permanently a part of her. She met with more fae than she could count and had them all inspect her body, her magic, and her trauma over and over. She could make and control flames and see magic at work, but beyond that she wasn't sure what she could do. Based on the feelings of heat across her skin and smoke that appeared from her mouth in times of upset, her caretakers suspected she could still shift into a dragon, but Caitriona was terrified to even try. Since returning home, she shied away from use of her abilities, wishing instead the physical display of what happened to her would vanish if she refused to use them.

It didn't happen.

The horns were still there, as well as the scales on her shoulders, her eyes remained a shade of gold, and moments like the previous many hours reminded her that a dragon still resided within.

Caitriona stepped before her looking glass and continued pulling off the layers of clothing until she stood naked with fabric covering the floor around her bare feet. She stared intently at the curve of her hips and breasts, more obvious in the last two years as she entered her twenties. Her skin was pale like moonlight and previously unblemished. Now however, there was a mixture of scales and scars. Funny that her scales glittered from the firelight and candles and were more noticeable than her scars. She scratched at them, feeling them poke under her nails. At a particularly low point in her recovery, she pulled the scales from her shoulders, ripping them off one by one. Despite the pain and blood, she picked at them every night, but scales only grew back. She also had scarring from arrows that struck her dragon form. The scars were fading, but even as they disappeared, they remained etched permanently in her mind. The arrows were shot by her own father and there was nothing she could do to remove the emotional scars he created.

When her hair initially became gold, she liked it. She even found her golden eyes fascinating, but now they were only part of the gruesome package watching her from the mirror. The words of citizens came back to her; a monster, a half-dragon creature, and an embarrassment to the crown. No matter what her mother said, she couldn't help but hear them and find herself wounded.

Now with war threateningly close, Caitriona wondered if she would lose control due to it all and slip away into herself only to watch the dragon take hold. Perhaps she could help her sister in that way … but quickly she brushed the idea away and moved to her wardrobe, pulling free a gown to sleep in for the night that tied tightly at her throat. She wouldn't bring more shame to her family by becoming the literal monster the citizens were so certain she was.

Greer arrived two days later after sunset, rushing into the castle hall with Barden and Ailith close on her heels, and Isla drifting behind at a substantially slower pace. Uncaring of who saw, Caitriona ran to quickly embrace her sister before colliding with Ailith, wrapping her arms tightly around the guard, and savoring the smell of summer grass and wood smoke on her hair as she buried her face into her neck.

"I wasn't even gone for half the time that was planned," Ailith laughed, although she held Caitriona as tightly as she to her. Caitriona pulled back and Ailith studied her expression, the laugh tapering off as she grew serious. "How was the day of grievances?"

"Very much full of grievance," Caitriona said as Ailith brushed her hair back and tucked it behind her ear.

"Cait, Ailith!" Greer called, "Come, we need to meet immediately. I already have a guard retrieving Ceenear and Raum."

Greer waved them forward impatiently before turning on her heel to stride down the hall, her riding boots leaving a trail of dust behind. The pair exchanged a glance.

"She's been really straight forward since the night we got the news," Ailith kept her voice low as they followed Greer toward the war room.

"She seemed stressed when we arrived in Stormhaven but after Isla showed up and told us what happened, she seemed ..."

Ailith shook her head, her brow furrowing. "I don't know Greer from *before*," she began, referencing Caitriona's curse and Greer killing their father. "But when we searched for you after the curse took hold, she seemed to handle everything ... better?"

"I know what you mean," Caitriona whispered. "I've seen it too."

"It's only going to get worse now, isn't it?"

"Her oddness? Maybe. She's always been good with stress, at least she used to be."

Caitriona watched the back of Greer's head a number of paces down the hall and frowned. Greer always was serious and secure, so determined and capable, and Caitriona knew her sister was still all those things. But something shifted after the curse ran its course. She was still herself, and yet a shadow seemed ever-present, lurking behind Greer's shoulder.

Near the portion of the castle Caitriona destroyed as a dragon was the war room. She avoided it at all costs, not wanting to see the destruction she created with her own hand—or claw. But her mind didn't allow that. Sometimes, early in the morning when she was restless in her bed, she saw murky images of her time as a dragon. She could still recall the warmth of Ailith's presence, suddenly small beside her. Ailith felt light, warm, and so delicate; and Caitriona remembered the hurt from the arrows plunging into her chest.

If she allowed herself to enter the darker rooms of her memory, the shadowed places she avoided most, she found her father there. Murder on his face and loathing in his eyes as he raised his crossbow, directing the point of the arrow toward her heart. The memories often woke her, thrusting her into her day because she was unwilling to go back to sleep with fear of re-entering them and remembering more.

It was hard even now to ignore the lingering memories as they moved down the hall and saw portions blocked off. Builders worked every day on the area and the bones of the structure were intact, a roof in place, but finer details still had to go up. Her footsteps slowed and the expanse between she and Greer grew. Ailith touched Caitriona's hand, urging her forward and angling herself to block the view of the unfinished hall beyond until Caitriona entered the war room.

"Alright, please take your seats," Greer called, charging forward to the queen's chair and pushing it aside to stand before the table with a large map covering the entirety of it. Róisín slipped easily into a seat near Greer, and Barden sat to Greer's left. Isla pushed by and settled beside Róisín who gave the witch a curious glance.

Caitriona lingered in the doorway with Ailith's warm hand slipping into hers. She calmed briefly, the dragon in her gut settling and nearly sleepy with Ailith's comforting presence returned, while Caitriona looked at the table and hesitated to take a seat. Greer raised her eyebrows, giving a pointed look at the seat opposite her at the end of the table. Dutifully, Caitriona headed there with Ailith sitting beside her. Ceenear and Raum moved quietly and sat beside Isla, looking serious if a little uncomfortable.

"Thank you for joining me," Greer began, pressing her fingertips along the edge of the table. "As you all know, the queen of Invarlwen has died and her husband, Malcolm, declared himself king. Now war is upon Wimleigh Queendom with Malcolm at the head of it. Communication with those in the fae realm seems impossible. Messages sent are not responded to or received, is that correct?"

"We've attempted to send messages," Ceenear began. "But they're going unanswered."

"And who are you reaching out to?"

"Niveem, the leader of our mountainside."

"And Lumia," Raum cut in. He licked his lips, clear concern on his face. "She's my partner. We've always stayed in contact when I've traveled but my calls have been unanswered."

"Oh, Raum," Ailith whispered, drawing his attention. Caitriona reached forward and touched his hand. He lowered his gaze to the table and said nothing more.

"We cannot pass the mist which surrounds the Endless Mountains without harm to ourselves, as we intend harm toward the king, yes?"

Greer continued, receiving nods in response. It was a magic barrier that the fae kingdom had—a magic mist that lay at the base of the mountain range and would lead to the death of anyone who passed it with intention to harm. "Alright, my first plan of action is to place lookouts along the edges of the marsh with hope that should Malcolm's people move forward to attack, we can meet him within the marsh, rather than in the valley."

Ailith glanced at Caitriona then leaned forward, her lips parting before Róisín spoke first. "What about the dukes?"

Greer looked at Barden. "Go ahead."

"It's with hope they'll rise and aid us." Barden addressed the room as he stood from his chair. "While many have heard the tales of the dukes rising to aid kings in past battles, my family, and many who follow the old ways, have documentation that such has happened. Family histories, written in journals and song books, of our own ancestors who served the royal guard generations ago have risen from Umberfend Marsh to form a secondary army and serve the current sovereign of the land they once lived on. There's a chance they'll do it again, and if they do, our people will be safe to pass over the marshlands. The dukes will understand they are not a threat and aid them in battle, while still dragging the opposing forces beneath the waters. Beyond that, if they don't help, perhaps Malcolm's men may fall victim to the dukes as they protect their waters."

"We've heard of creatures in the marsh waters," Raum said. "But it's a story told to children. Something to keep them from being tempted to leave the mist."

"We've a better understanding of the marshlands," Greer added. "We can use that to our benefit but that's only if we know they're advancing with enough time and we're able to draw them toward Umberfend."

"With people stationed along the roads, we should be able to see beforehand," Barden offered.

"There are also magical ways, traps that set off alerts so the castle knows there's movement," Isla said with a grin, drawing a look from Róisín.

Caitriona fidgeted with the skirts of her dress, rubbing the fabric between her fingers repeatedly before she gathered enough courage to speak what plagued her. "The dukes predicted death. So, is that all we can expect? Malcom will bring his men forward to fight and we enter just a constant state of war until one topples the other? What end are we striving for?"

Greer looked at Caitriona, her face frozen for a moment as she studied her, then a small hint of a smile curled the corner of her lips. She nodded as if agreeing to something only she knew and her broadening smile seemed to confirm a decision made while Caitriona was left feeling greater unease. "An excellent question and we have a plan. We obviously don't want to fight the fae and will only do so if they attempt to attack us. We aren't seeking any war. But Malcolm sounds problematic at best, particularly since he's already declared war within days of obtaining the crown. In the long term, even if he doesn't attack soon, he's a danger to the safety of our kingdom and so, with Isla's help, we've the beginning stages of a strategy. That's where Ceenear and Raum hopefully come in."

"What do you need of us?" Ceenear asked, her gray eyes reflected the candles in the room as she looked amongst her human neighbors.

"We're going to try and find Lachlan, the lost prince and true king to Invarlwen," Greer announced, leaning back from the table and standing straight. She grasped her hands before her and slowly looked over her audience as if taking in their reactions. "While we prepare for battle, I'm going to send a group to find him before Malcom can. Isla, please share what you know."

Isla gripped the edge of the table and lifted her chin. "When Lachlan was born, Onora was set to marry Malcolm only a short time later. While she wasn't queen at that point, something compelled her to seek out safety for Lachlan and send him away from the kingdom. She had Niveem bring the babe to a town beyond the Northern Wood in the Mazgate Dominion prior to Malcolm's arrival. The town he was sent to is one where people worship magic and those with greatest gifts study and train. It's there he was raised. I've never been to the town, nor have I met the boy. I've never spoken to him, but I was given this knowledge by Niveem and Onora should anything happen to them: he exists and he's placed there somewhere in that region. Now Onora is dead and Niveem doesn't answer our calls which is not normal for her. It feels like time to release this knowledge.

"It's unclear how many know these details. I kept my end of the bargain by speaking this information to no one until now, but information has obviously leaked out. Ailith knew of Lachlan, even his name from Lumia and Raum—"

Raum sat upright and looked at Isla sheepishly. "It was just rumors. Lumia told me about it and I assumed she learned it from Niveem. It's always been fun, courtly gossip, nothing more."

Isla bowed her head. "All to say, we must assume Malcom will know where the boy is located soon, if not already."

Greer leaned against the table and turned her attention to the two fae. "With all of this, we hope you'll help us. The both of you. Your knowledge and magic could make all the difference."

"The last message we received from Niveem, she requested we do anything to stop Malcolm," Raum admitted, his voice soft, the normal joking cadence Caitriona had grown used to gone. "Very few of the fae like Malcolm. With him in power, it's ... concerning. The silence from beyond the mist admittedly made me all the more worried. All this to say you have our full support."

Raum leaned back in his chair, looking at Ceenear who sat straight backed and composed. "Yes, you have our support and our word."

Greer nodded, tapping her hand on the edge of the table once before looking at Caitriona. "Caitriona, I've a task for you as well."

Caitriona sat up in her seat, suddenly nervous. "I'll do anything."

"I want you to lead the search party to find Lachlan and ensure his safety. You'll be the representative for the crown. Ceenear, Raum, and Ailith will go with you. If you find him in the Mazgate Dominion, I hope you'll convince him to return to Braewick so we may work together and ensure we can return him to the role that's his birthright."

All eyes at the table turned toward Caitriona and she felt herself shrink back. "Me? Are you sure?"

Greer smiled and placed her hands on her hips. "You're the first person I thought to take on this role. You leave in two days' time."

CHAPTER TEN

A̲ɪʟɪᴛʜ

A̲ilith was rarely one for comedy, yet she couldn't ignore the humor—albeit dark—that things were so different and yet, the same. Rather than greet the incoming autumn as she did when she took the task of sneaking Caitriona from the kingdom two years before, summer insisted on its presence. It clung to her skin and clothing, and made any movement uncomfortable as Ailith gathered her pack once more. It was the middle of the season and the weather urged for laziness. Afternoon naps and swimming in lakes were meant to be a priority, not traveling.

The sun rose earlier in the summer, long before people stirred, yet Ailith's household was already up and dressed. Once her items were ready to go, the sunshine was already over the ridge and shining into the valley.

Cari, Ailith's mother, placed a hand on her shoulder. "You have all your things?" Her palm traveled along to Ailith's hair to stroke it gently. Ailith felt her heart grow, the familiar ache of leaving and not knowing when she'd return filled her whole.

"Yes," Ailith murmured, tying her sleeping pack to the bottom of her bag and ensuring the ropes were secure. "I got everything together last night; I'm just making sure I didn't forget anything."

"I made pastries," Gwen yelled, rushing from her bedroom and hopping on one foot as she slipped her shoes on. "They're in the cupboard. I made enough for everyone. Take them with you, you can have them as you walk."

The offer was a reminder of how far they had come. From foraging for nuts and herbs that kept them from starving to not having to worry about the cost of food. Ailith and her family struggled making ends meet for the majority of her life; however, since Greer came to power, things became substantially better for the MacCree family. With the money received for Ailith's task, Cari saw castle physicians who crafted delicate glasses to broaden her vision, allowing her to continue doing her previous work as a seamstress, but this time for the royal household. Ailith's father, Taren, was also content teaching budding stone masons and developing plans for the reconstruction of the castle, as well as building the new castle Greer wanted on the western valley ridge. Carpenters of the castle created a wheeled seat Gwen pushed Taren in when his pain prevented him from walking, giving him more independence than in nearly two decades, and a small ramp was built against their doorstep so he had easy access getting in and out.

Located in royal guard housing, concerns of deteriorating roofs, or not enough food in the winter, were no longer something the MacCree family worried over. Gwen took care of Ailith's parents, keeping the house tidy, and making meals in exchange for a place to live and clothing to wear. She settled into the role, developing an entire social circle with other guards' family members and going so far as to flirt with the librarian, Callan. It left Ailith torn. Grateful, of course, for her family's health, but she knew many former neighbors within the southern ward of the city who worked hard and still struggled.

The problems existing while Ailith was a city guard still remained; prices were high, the winter was long, and the threat of war made the feeling of unrelenting weight worse. Ailith was all the more determined to help things settle so Greer would have the power to do what she owed her people: change the kingdom so her citizens didn't feel they were constantly standing on a precipice.

"Another mysterious quest," her father grinned when she announced she was leaving.

"Yes, but this time it's not entirely a secret," Ailith corrected. This time, the royal family knew what was happening and they weren't on the run from guards of their own land.

This time, Ailith didn't have a price on her head.

"Stay well." Ailith stepped through the door, her bag over her shoulder and wrapped pastries clutched in her hand. "I'll be home as soon as possible and send messages frequently. Find Barden if you want a check-in. All my letters will go to him."

"There will be no finding me," a voice spoke. Barden stood in the sunshine, the beams bringing out the red in his auburn hair. With one hand on his hip and the other clutching a sword in a holster, he looked oddly casual. "Any updates I have, I'll come tell your family as soon as possible. If that's alright with you, Cari and Taren."

Ailith's mother softened; she adored Barden from the moment he escorted Ailith's parents out of the city to keep them safe from Cearny's rage after the king realized it was Ailith who snuck Caitriona from the kingdom. Afterward, Barden became a frequent visitor to their home while training Ailith. "You're always welcome here, you know."

"We appreciate your looking after us," Taren called as Gwen pushed him to the doorway in his rolling chair.

"And while I know you'll all be safe," Ailith added, glancing from Barden to her parents. "Still, *stay safe*."

"Always, under *his* care," Cari teased. Barden even blushed. Ailith would never let him live it down.

Cari grabbed hold of Ailith and squeezed her tight. Taren came next, his embrace stronger than it had been for years and Ailith sighed into his hug before stepping away.

"Thank you for the breakfast," she called to Gwen who pushed Taren forward. Her parents waved and Ailith did the painful thing of walking away once more. She didn't look back; it would hurt too much if she did.

"You ready for this?" Barden asked, side butting her with his arm holding the sword.

Ailith raised her brows. "I suppose so. It seems more straightforward than before. We know Lachlan's somewhere in the Mazgate Dominion. We don't have Cearny or a curse to worry about. But I still feel uneasy."

"That's due to the threat of it all." Barden matched Ailith's pace as they moved through the dusty yard of the inner ward and past varied training devices before climbing steps toward the great hall. "At least in my experience, whenever we were sent to find key information, or do something specifically tied to one of Cearny's battles, I felt pressure and fear."

Ailith nodded, shifting her bag to her shoulders as they reached the top of the stairs. The idea of war, of being in one, frightened Ailith. She wasn't oblivious to what war did to people. Not just the physical wounds but the emotional toll as well. "I think that's it. I want to do this right, to find a way out of this before there's any bloodshed."

"Wait." Barden touched Ailith's hand before she stepped out of the stairwell and into the promenade leading to the grand hall entrance. He held out the sword. "I want to give you this. I had it made. A proper sword for your size rather than the borrowed ones."

"Barden," Ailith whispered, eyes going wide as she looked over the blade and decorated handle with carvings of what looked like scales. Since joining the royal guard, she worked with borrowed swords and never her own. It was common to measure royal guards for their own specialized sword at some point, but Ailith never got around to doing it. Even still, the swords were often plain, simple things. There was an extra cost to personalize them. "Barden, this is *gorgeous*. This had to cost you so much gold."

Barden shrugged. "A little, but nothing to worry yourself over. The crown covered the sword, but I took the liberty of paying for the extra work."

Ailith lifted the blade from Barden's hand. She brushed the tip of her fingers over the carved scales on the grip. The guard of the sword came to curved tips. It was beautiful and recognizable. "Like Cait's horns—"

"And the scales of a dragon," Barden said softly. They looked at the blade in silence for a moment before Barden pressed his hand on Ailith's shoulder. Bending forward, he leveled his gaze with hers. "I know Caitriona's struggling with what the curse did to her, and I suspect she'll continue to, which is worrisome, but understandable. But I also worry for you. You're entirely capable, I know this, but I don't want you to get caught up in comparison."

Ailith raised an eyebrow and shook her head. He was right, Caitriona had a certain disgust for herself Ailith wished would go away, but worrying about herself was something Ailith did less frequently. "I don't understand."

"This is your first trip solo beyond following Greer around," Barden continued, his voice soft and not judgmental. "You're entering a land filled with magic users, and your group excels at it. You, just like myself, lack magical abilities. But you've your own smart senses and are quick to read people. Use that. Remember, you helped to conquer the curse, you helped bring Caitriona back with your brain and your heart. There could be times you won't be able to use this sword. Remember the power you wield is internal above anything else."

Ailith held Barden's blue-eyed gaze for a moment before giving a slow nod.

"Thank you, Barden." She gripped the sword and held it out to feel the weight of it in her hand. "It's beautiful and if anything, this will remind me of all *your* teachings."

Barden grinned and patted Ailith's shoulder. "Good, now go, your team's waiting to depart."

Ailith stepped away but found her feet could go no further. Turning back to Barden, she embraced him tightly, unable to vocalize the rush of appreciation she had for him. For a moment, she felt her cheeks grow hot with embarrassment as he didn't return the gesture, but then his strong arms gently came around her, embracing her back.

"Good luck and I'll see you soon," he said softly in her ear before letting go.

AILITH RODE ONYX, HER TRUSTED STEED, BEYOND BRAEWICK Valley once more. A large black work horse meant for the fields but significantly too handsome—at least in Ailith's opinion—to do anything other than be a royal representative horse for a well-meaning royal guard. Since Onyx was so large, Ailith carried the brunt of their supplies, while Ceenear, Raum and Caitriona rode on smaller horses.

Crowley, the crow Isla gifted Ailith shortly after Caitriona's curse completed, followed along as a dot overhead. Since he came into her life, Crowley quickly became inseparable from Ailith unless she requested him to remain by Caitriona's side—then again, Caitriona was the only other person Crowley was willing to stay with. He'd carry any necessary correspondence to Barden, and having his shadow pass over was a welcome sort of comfort, because wherever she went, he followed. Most times.

The foursome left as the city began to stir. They rode to the western gate in silence, the roads relatively empty, and those who woke early enough had a chance to squint and judge Caitriona as she rode by. It made Ailith's grip on her reins tighten. Ailith knew the city's running commentary. For many, they found Caitriona a source of odd interest—terrifying, disgusting, or curious. She was a spectacle, which was the last thing the already self-conscious princess needed.

By nightfall, the horned princess riding her horse from the city with two fae would be top gossip and secretly Ailith was glad they'd be gone. Gossip always had a way of finding itself into the castle one way or another, and Ailith was certain Caitriona would catch wind of the wagging tongues.

Riding over the valley hills, they turned onto the Umberfend road, traveling north toward the post. The marshland's waters glinted silver in the early morning sun, still of movement as the drowning dukes rested beneath. They were never very active during the day; would they still rise if a battle happened by daylight? Or were they only helpful at night? The thought brought a chill to the back of Ailith's neck.

Passing where Shaw's body was released, Ailith shifted on her saddle with discomfort, recalling the warning screams from a month before. All the better they traveled during the day, because Ailith wasn't sure she wanted to see if they would scream again.

"Have you heard from Lumia yet?" Caitriona asked near midday. Raum was relatively quiet the entire morning, his bright mood subdued since they last were all together.

He shook his head, the sweat on his brow glinting in the sun. "No answer. She's been different. She visited Onora prior to her getting sick and again after she became ill. She was sent there, you know. Sent to the queen to help calm her because whatever sickness took her, it left her anxious and paranoid. She came home and hasn't been the same ever since."

"It must have been traumatic to see your queen in such a state," Ailith said. Lumia was able to sense feelings of others and with touch or close proximity, she could change the emotions. She could take someone's fear and calm them, making them feel relaxed and at ease. While she likely provided comfort to her queen, she would have been able to feel all of Onora's true feelings as she drew closer to death.

Ailith couldn't comprehend how upsetting it could be to lose a sovereign that you liked, though she liked to think she could sympathize. She hated Cearny and was glad he was dead. She never wished Greer spared him. But with Greer her queen, her feelings for her sovereign changed. She wouldn't want to witness Greer in the position Onora had been in.

"It makes me all the more worried. I didn't want to leave Ulla Syrmin. I wanted to stay with Lumia, to make sure she was alright. And now her silence ..."

"There's silence from everyone," Ceenear cut in. Her voice was calm, but her tone was serious and commanding Raum to listen. "I know you're concerned she's ignoring you or unwell, but Niveem herself said it was better for us to remain away. They're likely being cautious and not responding. Who knows what power Malcolm wields."

They returned to an uneasy quiet. The threat of war nestled into Ailith's heart as a thing heavy with tears that would surely shed in the future.

By early evening, they arrived at the post. The sky clear of any clouds and relieving Ailith's growing unease of surprise thunderstorms that could greet her in the night.

The difference between her first time at the Umberfend outpost to this encounter was night and day. Within Wimleigh Queendom, they were discreet in traveling only because Caitriona was now the heir to the throne, and her appearance well known enough to draw the stares and whispers of patrons.

"We have a meeting room," the bartender said as they paid for lodging. He was the broad, half-fae man working when Ailith and Caitriona came through before, but this time Ailith greeted him without fear of being found. "It's through the kitchen and in the back. A meeting space of sorts. Queen Greer works there if she and her guards come through. We can serve meals there if you'd prefer not to draw much attention."

Ailith glanced at the people around them, nearly all human and stared pointedly at Ceenear, Raum and Caitriona. "That's actually preferred." Ailith reached into her coin purse. "Do I have to pay extra?"

The man waved her away. "For the crown it's on the house."

He led the group through the kitchen area and into a room with a single window overlooking an apple tree and the marshes beyond. "I can bring the evening meal once it's ready."

"That'd be excellent, thank you," Caitriona replied, her voice soft as her gold eyes met his. He blushed and nodded before backing from the room and closing the door.

"So, we have some privacy; that's good." Raum pulled out a seat and dropped into it, tilting it to balance on the back legs with a sigh of contentment. It appeared his concerns from earlier in the day lifted slightly once they were at the inn, as if the forward movement in their journey was a comfort. Ailith understood, it felt better than sitting around waiting for something to happen.

"We should discuss our way forward," Ceenear said, taking her own seat across from Raum. "The attention we've drawn on the road to this post, and in particular in the pub, is concerning."

"Do you think the people of the Mazgate Dominion will notice though?" Ailith asked as she too sat down at the end of the table to keep her eye on the door and window. Caitriona circled the table to gaze out the window. "They're magic-accepting."

"It's because of me," Caitriona said. "There aren't many people who look like me. They'll know immediately who I am and I doubt they'll be pleased to see the sister of Wimleigh's queen; particularly since Greer only called off the conquest against Avorkaz last year."

"Oh." Ailith looked at Caitriona. She was used to Caitriona's appearance, having inspected every bit of her body over nights shared together. She memorized every curve and scale, even the arch of her horns. She knew what people in Braewick City said, but she often tied that to their general dislike of magic. Caitriona being viewed as a potential threat was an idea she hadn't considered for the Mazgate Dominion and immediately she felt a flush of embarrassment over her lack of foresight. They'd have to find a way to slip into the city, a way to know where to go and what to do that would be the safest going forward. Suddenly, a thought popped into Ailith's mind and she brightened.

"Perhaps we can go to May and Declan's home," Ailith suggested, drawing Caitriona's attention. "They live on the outer walls of the city in the hamlet Greenbriar; we'd have to pass where they live to reach the main gates. Maybe they'll have guidance, or they can help us get around the city and closer to the Northern Wood."

"Maybe they'll have a better idea where this town is that Lachlan lives in," Caitriona wondered. Ailith glanced at their travel partners and smiled.

"May and Declan helped us before. They send creams to help my burns. I've written them letters for the last year. I'll send Crowley out to see if they'll welcome us; we'll likely have an answer beforehand."

"You trust them?" Ceenear asked, her face serious.

"Entirely." Ailith pulled her writing supplies from her bag. Quickly, she scrawled a request that they visit on her note paper sized to fit Crowley and not weigh him down. Leaving the paper so the ink would dry, she turned and opened the room's window. Leaning out to call for Crowley, she noticed a dark movement in the branches of the apple tree and discovered the black bird there.

"Haven't you anything better to do than wait for us?" she teased her black-feathered friend. He croaked before gliding down to the shaded grass outside the window. "We have a letter for you to bring to May and Declan. Can you do that? I have a whole bag of nuts; you can have a handful as a reward."

Crowley stretched his wings and gave two lazy flaps to make the jump from the ground to the windowsill, and tapped at Ailith's hand, pausing to tilt his head to one side and stare at her expectantly before tapping her hand again.

"Fine, I'll give you some nuts now," Ailith sighed dramatically, turning to retrieve the treat bag.

"Here, Crowley." Caitriona rolled the scrap of paper Ailith wrote on. Pulling a string from the pocket of her riding pants, she held it for the crow. "May I tie this to your foot?"

The crow clucked and hopped at the window in seeming agreement and stood resolutely as Caitriona worked fast to tie the paper to his leg.

"Count this as the first half of your payment." Ailith dumped a handful of nuts on the sill. "I'll give you more when you come back. Follow the roads, Crowley. You've been there before."

He made quick work of the nuts before giving a loud croak and taking to the air, flying away just as a knock came to the door.

"Food!" Raum declared with a clap of his hands, jumping to his feet to go to the door. Ailith turned back from the window and stepped beside Caitriona. She slipped her hand around Caitriona's waist and studied the princess's expression.

"Are you alright?" she whispered, ignoring the clatter of dishes as Raum placed them on the table and the murmur of Ceenear accepting glasses of summer wine.

Caitriona watched the interaction before her. A line appeared between her brows, not unsimilar to her sister, and the corner of her lip turned down slightly. Ailith wanted to kiss it but took note of that spot for later.

"This is the first time I've traveled since everything," she said. "I mean, other than to Ulla Syrmin. For some reason, I assumed it would feel different, that traveling this road with you would be a reminder of how far *we've* come, but instead, all I'm doing is reliving who I was back then and how that person is gone."

Ailith's shoulders dropped, her grasp around Caitriona's waist tightening. "We've just left," Ailith began, keeping her voice quiet and private. "Give it a day or two. It felt strange for me to leave Braewick to travel to Stormhaven. It'll take you some time too."

Caitriona didn't respond but allowed Ailith to pull her closer. In the end, Ailith knew there was nothing she could say to shake the princess from the self-hatred she felt. Ailith despised it, she disliked watching the person she loved have so much self-loathing. To Ailith, Caitriona was beautiful. Whether with red hair and blue eyes, or golden, dragon-like aspects. That wasn't something she could convince Caitriona of; it was something she had to wait for the princess to realize on her own. But she'd be there when the moment came, whenever it would be.

CHAPTER ELEVEN

Caitriona

In the secret place just before dawn, where birds still nesting on branches were the only witnesses to the strongest of emotions, Caitriona found her first bit of excitement for the trip before them. Between overanalyzing others' perceptions of her—concern for her kingdom on the brink of war, and the slight anxiety traveling to the Mazgate Dominion brought after her last visit ended in fire and transformation—the previous day was taxing. The group ate a heavy meal before splitting to rest in separate rooms with plans to continue north through the former war lands shortly after dawn.

Caitriona watched the sky grow light gray from the single bed in the room she and Ailith shared. The birds who made small, cautious chirps from their places of rest began to sing with full lungs of joy for the approaching day. Caitriona listened as Ailith continued sleeping undisturbed. It was peaceful, but the softness of morning left Caitriona's emotions laid bare. Returning to the Umberfend post left an ache in her heart she hadn't expected, but her newfound freedom and the purpose she was given made her core a little lighter.

Rolling toward Ailith, she nudged her to wake with a kiss to her cheek, relishing the warmth of Ailith's skin under her lips and saying what was expected of her, versus what she desperately desired. "We should get up and eat something. The sun's going to rise soon."

Ailith grunted in response before rolling toward Caitriona and wrapping her arms tightly around the princess. Caitriona's cheeks grew hot. Ailith as always knew Caitriona's desires: to stay right there and enjoy the moment. The day was already beginning on a good note.

"Alright," Ailith spoke into the curve of Caitriona's neck, making goosebumps rise along her skin. There was a pause as they settled against one another, savoring each other's scent and the feel of their loose hair tangling and falling over cheeks and the curve of shoulders. When Ailith's eyes fully opened, Caitriona knew their alone time was over.

"Let's get moving."

They ate and purchased loaves of bread, dried meat and fruits from the post's kitchen, and replenished their skeins of water. As the last of the cool night air evaporated and was replaced by building heat, they mounted their horses to continue northward.

"I'm not going to lie," Ailith admitted as they moved at a steady but slow pace. She twirled a flower between her fingers before tucking it into her hair—a little gift Caitriona had slipped to her that was plucked from the field beside the outpost. "It was a lot more pleasurable traveling in autumn."

"I'll take snow over this," Raum complained from behind. "In winter you can layer. In the summer, there's only so much you can discard before you run out of options."

"This is only a little bit of heat." Ceenear glanced over her shoulder at the rest of the party. She tied her long braids into a large bun on the top of her head, exposing her neck which already shone with sweat. "I've traveled in all kinds of weather and this is certainly not the hottest I've experienced."

A caw sounded overhead, drawing their attention to the blue sky.

"Crowley! Finally!" Ailith waved as a black spot circled down to materialize into the shape of a crow. He swooped down with another caw to land on Ailith's outstretched arm. "Oh, and you've brought a letter too."

"And?" Caitriona asked, moving her horse beside Onyx as Ailith unrolled the scrap of paper. Crowley hopped off Ailith's arm and balanced on the bags tied to Onyx's back, he croaked and pecked Ailith's bag of nuts, impatient to get his reward. "What does it say?"

"Wait a moment, Crowley, won't you?" Ailith gave the bird a pet on his head before unfurling the letter. Her brown eyes darted over the writing as a smile grew on her face. "Declan and May are happy to help us. They gave directions to their home."

They continued traveling, growing sweatier and more tired as they went. The landscape changed as it curved further from the hills leading to Braewick Valley, north of the marshlands with spotted pools, into a place flat and barren. The landscape was broken by tree stumps, rubble of destroyed homes, and littered with snapped wheels and horse skeletons—remnants of Cearny's war. Caitriona frowned at a mound of rusted, forgotten weapons. Her sister fought here. Many people from both sides died here.

Her stomach turned.

"I never realized how expansive the battle grounds for Avorkaz were," Caitriona murmured, the back of her throat growing tight as her mouth filled with saliva.

"Nor did I." Ailith leaned close to grasp Caitriona's hand. Her eyes were large, the sunshine bringing out the various browns of chocolate and old leaves. Ailith's next words were quiet and only for her. "Cait, keep your eyes ahead."

"He managed this war for years, right?" Raum asked, looking from side to side as they moved. The roadway had fresh wheel and horse tracks, the purpose of the pathway returning to constant use now that a battle wasn't being waged on it. But the remnants of the death her father brought to the land would stain the region for years. The soil was rotten and dead. How could anyone rebuild here?

"Yes, it went on for ages and with very little movement in my father's favor."

"I wonder how he handled it. He had no magic makers on his side, right?"

Caitriona nodded. Swallowing back queasiness in her gut and dutifully keeping her eyes on the road. "My sister came here a few times and then eventually refused. It caused a great fight between them. She was so angry. He kept insisting she go and she refused over and over. She said our father was a cheat and doing awful things that broke any sense of fairness in war."

Was war ever fair? It was something Caitriona always wondered but felt she would be scolded if she asked. How could she ask when she lived in a castle built off the money and blood gathered through war? The answer seemed to be around her in the fabric, the carved stone, and each jewel in every crown. War was fair for those who won and a disaster to those who lost.

"Do you know what upset your sister so much?" Ceenear asked. Caitriona took a moment before continuing.

"This area used to be deeply wooded and he destroyed all the trees. With it went more than just lumber, but food and jobs. I think he had spies poisoning Mazgate Dominion crops, as well as crops outside their city walls. He poisoned Avorkazian water too. He worked to destroy the forces from the very base of their creation. My sister said there was more, but she never really shared that with me. But knowing my father ... he truly didn't care. Anything was possible if it meant he could win. Everything was fair game."

"And yet he never overtook Avorkaz," Raum said.

"That's due to their magic," Caitriona pointed out. "At times I feel our technology could work so well with the cures magic makers provide. While so many of the healers in Braewick provide physical aid to the injured, there isn't much that happens internally. Potions made from herbs toed the line to my father's outlaw of magic, but those things help. The knowledge of magic makers combined with physical medicine could do so much. Under my father's law, people prayed over the injured for divine intervention from the Elder Tree. A comfort, surely. I've prayed there myself. But prayer only goes so far. At times, there must be action. So, while my father did awful things and injured many, Avorkaz had a way to heal their people. Ways to stop fevers and disease from within. I think that was an advantage my father never considered."

They slept in a field overnight. An area seemingly untouched by the war where grasses grew thick and tall, and summer flowers dotted the landscape. Herbs growing in the field released their scent as they packed down the grass to make a place for sleeping. With two grouse roasting over a glowing fire, Caitriona settled beside the flames while Ailith wrote to Barden. Her hair was highlighted by the light and Caitriona was suddenly, without warning, transported to their early travel when her magic released and all that was hidden was exposed. In that moment, Caitriona feared all would be lost; that Ailith would return her to her father and her hopes were destroyed. She had that feeling again, a sickness in her soul that spread through her body and filled her head.

"I'll send Crowley now. He makes his best time when he's able to fly at night," Ailith commented as she wiped her quill in the grass and tightened the jar of ink. Her gaze met Caitriona's and she blinked. Leaning back slightly, surprise drifted over her expression, but then she smiled in a way that quenched some of Caitriona's ill feelings. And yet, she couldn't quite shake it.

She slept beside Ailith in the field, the guard drifting off quickly and leaving Caitriona to stare at the stars. Rolling onto her side, she wrapped her arms around Ailith's waist and trailed her fingertips along the exposed skin there. She smiled into Ailith's hair when she heard Ailith suck in a breath of air. Nuzzling the back of her neck as Ailith shifted into Caitriona's embrace, she closed her eyes. When her powers were new, she never would have guessed her future would be there beneath the star strewn sky with the spark of reciprocated feelings in her embrace. The world rushed toward the oblivion of suffering, but at least she held her emotions in her hand and knew she was loved. Her heart settled and at last she drifted to sleep.

By late afternoon the following day, they arrived in Greenbriar. The small farming hamlet was scattered on the southern side of Avorkaz's wall. Beyond the main road, standing along a grove of trees, stood the little house the note detailed as Declan and May's.

After they left their horses at Declan and May's barn, Ailith led the group to the front door and knocked, hearing a crash within and May yelling for Declan before the door pulled back.

"Ailith!" May said with a toothy grin. "At long last, child. Come in!"

One by one, the group eased through the doorway and stood awkwardly in the entryway of the cluttered house. May's eyes lingered over Caitriona, setting her cheeks ablaze.

"Oh, sweet girl," May said after a moment as she grasped Caitriona's hand. "That curse did quite the number on you, didn't it? This won't do if you're traveling through Avorkaz. You stick out like a sore thumb. You too, Ailith. Both of your reputations precede you and Avorkaz is still a bit *sensitive* toward Braewick royals."

Caitriona frowned at Ailith who only smiled with encouragement. "I'll admit, it's part of the reason we wanted to see you. Can you help us?"

"Potion work as always," May replied, patting Caitriona's hand. "Not a healing type, but something to push the brinks of reality. I'll work on it while Declan makes you a proper Mazgate dinner."

Declan served rich sausages covered in a dark gravy with potatoes. Hot and steaming, it wasn't necessarily a meal fit for the heat of the summer evening, but after riding for so long, their stomachs growled with interest.

"This is the best meal I've ever eaten," Raum whispered as he shoveled another forkful into his mouth.

"You say that with every meal," Ceenear said, although her plate was noticeably empty of food after she consumed it at rapid speed.

"A man who knows what he likes," Declan added with a smile. "There are so many ridiculous things to deal with in life, so many sorrows, if food brings you joy then all the better, don't you think?"

"Really, Declan," Ailith spoke from behind her hand, her mouth filled with food. "You're quite skilled in the kitchen."

"Less so with needles." Declan waved his fork in Ailith's direction. "I'm glad you got healing ointments for the cut on your face, you can barely spot the scar."

"The ointments have done wonders for all of it." Ailith smiled. She shifted her right elbow to show her arm, the candlelight catching the shine of her burned skin. "They've helped me heal so much."

Caitriona busied herself with moving food from one place to

another when a wrinkled hand covered with freckles from many years in the sunshine reached forward and touched her own.

"Let's get your mind off things for a minute, follow me. We can give a potion to change your appearance a try."

The back room of the little house was filled with herbs and bottles. Plants hung from the ceiling in clusters to dry steadily throughout the heat of the summer, and a small window towards the back lent enough dying light that bottles were illuminated by their browns, greens, purples, and blues. It was nearly vibrating with magic, a colorful shimmer glowed over every item and seemed to expel from May herself.

"Sweet girl," May said as she closed the door behind them. "You carry an awful heavy weight of sadness, don't you?"

Caitriona pressed her lips together and looked around the room. "I wouldn't say sadness ..."

"You're sad," May pointed out as she turned to the shelf of jars. "You blame a lot of things on yourself, as if it's your own doing. The guilt you carry is jarring."

Caitriona crossed her arms over her chest and frowned. "Can you explain the potion you're giving Ailith and me a little more?"

May studied her for a moment before giving a small shrug. "Right now, we'll work on something small and brief, in case we need to alter it additionally before you leave tomorrow. A potion to change your appearance. You'll still be yourself, but you'll look like yourself from *before* the curse. The horns will go away, your eyes will be blue, your hair red, but I'm also going to make your ears pointed—like your fae friends —because it makes more sense for four fae to travel together."

Caitriona immediately felt a surge of excitement at the idea of removing the horns from her head. "Will they just be glamoured? Will the horns still exist but be invisible?"

May shook her head as she moved to a counter where a bowl already sat with a glittering substance inside. "They'll vanish and you won't feel them. Your pointed ears will feel like your own ears. It'll be a bit of a transformation, something similar to when the curse took you but on a much smaller scale. It may be uncomfortable to lose the horns or have your ears grow to points, it always is when something changes and you're no longer the true representation of yourself."

"And Ailith?"

"Pointed ears for her too. She isn't as well known, so I feel we can get away without doing much more to her appearance." May smiled as she studied Caitriona for a moment. A roar of laughter eased into the room from the rest of the group but neither reacted. "Will that be alright with you? I understand the sensations could be similar to what happened and I wouldn't want to—"

"Please," Caitriona cut in. Hating the desperation in her voice. "Please just give me the potion."

May pressed her lips together but didn't say anything, instead turning to mix the dark liquid and pouring it into a cup. She fished out a spoon from a drawer and held it up to the dying light before filling it whole and offering it to Caitriona. "Just drink it like you would any liquid and if I mixed the components correctly, the change will be immediate."

Caitriona took the spoon and plunged it into her mouth, immediately fighting a gagging sensation over the foul taste that coated her tongue and flooded her senses. She swallowed, feeling the liquid drain sluggishly down her throat, like a soured syrup determined to take its time and linger for as long as possible. She felt it drop to her stomach and immediately, her organs tingled. The sensation spread rapidly like a wave flooding her body, rushing to waken every nerve, every vessel. Then came the pain.

When Caitriona turned into a dragon, she thought the pain would kill her. At one point, she hoped it did so she would be put out of her misery. Blind with agony, the world turned white and so hot, she no longer existed because the pain was everything. She was a thing possessed, not recalling anything she did, forgetting Ailith was there entirely. As the curse took hold, her body broke as it created new bones, stretched others, grew new skin and created a never-ending fire within her body that could not be quenched. All she was exploded into something large and powerful when she was otherwise small and meek. But the pain of May's potion in comparison was, gratefully, only passing. A headache, pressure, and an itching of her skin, like a fierce fever rash, there and gone again. She closed her eyes as they ached and when she opened them May was smiling.

"It looks good enough to me." May offered a looking glass. Caitriona found her face in the reflection. Her old face, her old body, *her*. Blue eyes, red hair, no horns or scales. Her ears were pointed as May said they'd be, but Caitriona couldn't pull her gaze from the reflection of the top of her head. Cautiously, she reached and patted her hair, only feeling her skull and no boney horns.

A laugh escaped her lips, the girl in the looking glass smiled and her cheeks gained color. "How long will this last again?"

May lifted the cup. "This is the rest of your dose to keep this appearance going until tomorrow evening. Drink three spoonfuls and it'll last a full day. Alternatively, you take a spoonful with each meal. I'd recommend drinking it at night, personally, so if there's any brief return to yourself it may be hidden in the night. You shouldn't linger in Avorkaz long so I'll make enough to last you during your time there."

Caitriona grinned and accepted the mug, drinking it entirely despite the awful taste. "Is it possible to continue this potion beyond our travels? Maybe I can just use this to be myself again?"

May's lips pressed together and her eyes appeared sad. Rubbing Caitriona's arm, she took a deep breath. "Go, show your friends, and get Ailith so we can test her potion too."

It wasn't a no, and for that Caitriona was grateful and clung to hope. This could be it; this could be the way she became herself again.

Caitriona rushed into the living space and stood before the table, drawing a double take from Ailith which reddened Caitriona's cheeks. She felt elated, alive, and like Ailith was looking at her the same way she had when they traveled together before the curse took her. Their bodies came together, bumping drunkenly into one another despite not having anything to drink, as Caitriona led Ailith to the back room where May waited.

"Drink up," she said as she offered Ailith a similar mug.

Ailith accepted it. "Will it hurt?"

"Only when you turn into something other than yourself does it hurt," May stated. "Growing your ears to a point—it'll hurt. But when they return to normal you won't feel a thing."

Ailith tipped the cup back, swallowing the potion without another word.

"Ah, I see what you mean." She passed her cup over then touched the tips of her ears that grew red and irritated as they pushed upwards so the curve stretched to a point similar to Raum and Ceenear's. "I'm surprised such a small change can cause pain."

May shrugged and placed an arm behind both girls' backs as she led them from the room. "Being something you aren't comes with a price."

Ailith left shortly after to leave out food for Crowley who'd likely return to them by morning. They'd sleep in the loft of the barn for the night with fresh air cooling them before they continued into Avorkaz the following day. Leaving Ceenear and Raum with Declan and May, Caitriona wandered from the little house down a dirt path toward the barn, the late day bugs loud and the air cooling.

"With those ears, you look like you could be Raum's sister," Caitriona teased as she leaned her hip against the barn's doorframe. Ailith looked up from her bag and smiled, her fae ears poking out from her loose hair.

"Don't tell him that, he already teases me enough."

"You do your own amount of teasing too." Caitriona stepped into the barn and lowered herself onto a hay bale beside her. Ailith studied her, her brows wrinkled with consideration.

"You look happy."

"I *am* happy," Caitriona admitted. "I ... I look like myself again. I don't have those awful horns anymore. My hair's normal, my eyes too."

"I like your horns," Ailith replied softly. She looked at the top of Caitriona's head as her brow wrinkled. "And your eyes, *and* your hair."

"Come on, Ailith," Caitriona began, increasingly exasperated. She was lying, surely. She was trying to keep Caitriona's feelings from being hurt. How could Ailith *like* anything about what she became? "Would you rather the golden, dragon version of myself or this version? The person I was before the curse."

Ailith tilted her head to one side, she considered Caitriona in a way that made Caitriona uneasy. She was truly looking at her, truly considering what Caitriona asked in that unnerving way that Ailith sometimes did when she took things so literally. But it was also when Ailith was the most truthful. Caitriona held her breath and forced herself to remain still. Slowly, Ailith shook her head. Her hand reached out, and her fingers ran through Caitriona's hair and along her curved scalp that was free of horns. "Cait, I'd take whatever version I could get. I'd rather have one than none. Both versions of you are special and beautiful to me. They're you, through and through, and I love *you*."

Caitriona didn't agree, but she chose to focus on the positive moment at hand and brush aside the conversation. She didn't want to linger over discussion of her dragon-like appearance. Leaning forward, Caitriona pressed her lips against Ailith's. Ailith's hands moved through her hair as Caitriona shifted, her mouth leaving a trail of kisses along Ailith's jaw, the scar on her cheek, and to her neck.

"Let's make the best of this time," Caitriona murmured, her teeth against Ailith's ear as her knee pressed between Ailith's legs. "We don't know how often we'll be alone after this."

Ailith pulled back, her lips curling into a smirk before she looked toward their horses in the stalls beyond.

"Okay, I guess I can show you the loft where we'll spend the night. We can roll out our sleep packs—"

"Get things set up before it's too late."

"Make sure it's all comfortable ..."

Caitriona slipped her fingers along Ailith's waist, her glee making her drunk with lust. Ailith's lips parted, eyebrows raising with surprise as Caitriona's fingers tugged at Ailith's belt. Caitriona stood and pulled Ailith with her. Hands slipping to Caitriona's hips, Ailith backed toward the ladder for the loft, unable, it seemed, to keep her hands to herself. Just like Caitriona liked it.

"Alright then, show me," Caitriona whispered, pulling away just long enough for Ailith to ascend the ladder with Caitriona close behind.

CHAPTER TWELVE

GREER

The absence of Caitriona left Greer uneasy; the emotional flashback to Caitriona's search for a cure to her magic was still fresh and nestled in Greer's mind. The memory could overwhelm her if she let it, but she chose to do what she always did and ignore the emotions. She kept herself busy, immediately calling for a special bell that would ring should the form of a gold dragon appear on the horizon. It was a plan already in place but with Caitriona not around, she could finally implement it and have it hung above the castle walls.

"If Cait changes and approaches the castle, we'll sound this warning," she explained to the top royal guards. "It's a shriller bell, different than the warning bell for attacks. You must ensure the guards on the parapets and towers understand this bell means to proceed with caution. We do not shoot to kill the dragon; we only shoot to injure it if it threatens the city or castle."

"How do you know the dragon's friendly?" an older guard asked, one of the few who worked for Cearny and revealed he practiced the old ways when magic was allowed again. He could have retired when Cearny died but opted to continue in his position, bolstered by the freedom to practice magic.

Greer looked the men over and met Barden's gaze last. "We don't. But those with magic who understand transformation and curses better than I have good faith that if she were to become a dragon again, she'll have her mind. So, we can only hope that's true."

What she didn't say was she planned these protections well in advance. She waited for an opportunity to install the bell and perform drills when Caitriona wasn't present. Even still, Greer felt taking these precautions was a betrayal to her sister.

It also was a poor bandage to the wound of her worry. A distraction, a sense of being productive and active in the face of danger, and it didn't work. Her discomfort doubled as she turned to her southern-facing study window overlooking the city. The blazing sun shone down and despite the heat, wisps of smoke rose from rooftops; food still needed to cook and blacksmiths had work to do, nothing stopped for the heat. Nothing stopped for war, at least not yet.

"How do I tell them what's coming?" Greer wondered out loud. She was alone for the moment, escaping the gathering elders who gave their two bronze pieces of advice seemingly forever, and ignoring the endless maps Greer stared at with hope they would reveal some message of what her next steps would be.

How did she grapple with an impending war when she wasn't expected to know the war was even happening?

A door creaked open but she remained at the window looking over the city, *her* city. She was content to cling to whatever moments of peace they still had. While she didn't want to be bothered, the sound of boots crossing the floor, a cadence Greer memorized, allowed her to relax at last.

"Is someone looking for me?" Greer didn't turn.

"Not yet." Barden stepped beside her and looked out the window as well, his shirt sleeve close enough to brush against Greer's arm.

"Good," Greer said. Silence spilled into the room, rapidly surrounding them and stuffing their mouths, trapping any further speech from escaping which was exactly what Greer wanted. The world became too loud since her coronation, and she felt her father was at fault for that. He was at fault for most things, really.

While Cearny was alive, he threw instructions and demands at Greer, rarely allowing her to think for herself except when she traveled from the castle on some errand or to fight in a battle. Then she *could* think, then she was the one giving instructions, but it was so rarely done in the castle. Her brain was numbed, trained to shut off and wait for Cearny to bark an order. If he only gave her some leverage, perhaps she wouldn't freeze in this moment. If she had experience making decisions, she wouldn't be overwhelmed by everyone asking her what to do next. If he allowed her to come up with her own plans or ideas and run it by him, maybe she'd have an answer of what to do now. If they had a partnership, a loving relationship overall, maybe she would be better prepared.

Maybe she would have even hesitated before killing him.

All my work destroyed, she could almost hear him say from the corner of the room. Arms crossed over his chest with spittle clung to his beard as he snarled at her. *All because you're too weak to simply attack the kingdom. You aren't supposed to know they're going to spring a war on you, but* they *don't know that* you *know their existence.*

Greer waved her hand as if brushing an insect away, hoping to rid herself of the haunting spectacle of her father. She turned her attention toward Barden. He was something present, solid, and would allow her to fully return to the world rather than drift in the haunted halls of her mind.

He looked down at her, immediately responding to her movements and met her gaze. He could destroy every one of her torments with his smile. He could free her from everything that plagued her with his voice. He could undo all of her troubles with his touch. Greer smiled, a secret thing she shared with so few.

"Do you think we'll have enough time for a sparring match?" Greer asked, watching Barden's entire essence brighten and spark.

"If we slip out and don't tell anyone where you're going, I'm certain we do," Barden replied and Greer's smile grew.

He reached forward, his fingers trailing down her arm before entwining with hers. His grip tightened, arm pulled, and he began to lead. He was the only person Greer allowed to take lead, and she relished in the break from decisions as they turned to the door and rushed into the maze of the castle.

More than once when they were young, they slipped from trainings or lessons to spar in secret passages or corners of the garden. As they grew older, it was Barden's persistent offering when the world grew too heavy for Greer's shoulders. Before she was crowned, it was a nearly weekly outing, but now it was rare to slip away.

"Where should we go?" Barden asked, pulling open a door. Greer willingly followed him as they escaped into the staff halls.

"The garden." Greer laughed. "Let's get out in the day and away from the heat of the stones!"

Greer never tried her hand at growing plants, but she loved the brightness of the garden all the same. In the summer, it was at its most wild stage with roses and puffy clusters of delicate blossoms reaching heights as tall as the top of door frames. The pathways became tunnels in some places, thick with flowers and vines.

Amongst a corridor created by wooden beams, the pair pulled out their blades beneath purple cascading flowers and heart-shaped leaves. They were hidden under the greenery and away from curious eyes from the castle windows or the parapet walk.

"Come now, I know you can do better than that," Barden laughed after Greer tried to knock him off his feet straight away. She always went for the most embarrassing of blunders on her opponents' behalf, her taste for competition flaring to see her partner fall flat on their back. But Barden knew her tricks, having experienced them all over and over in the training yard.

"I *could* do better than this if I wasn't in this bastard of a dress!" Greer grinned. She repositioned her feet and took her stance, using one hand to gather her skirts and bundle them under her arm, leaving her to raise her sword with only one hand as she readied for Barden's move.

"Even when you were allowed to don your royal guard wardrobe," Barden teased, thrusting his sword forward and turning quickly to knock Greer's blade to the side. "I was still better."

"Not all of us had the best swordsman of the land training us since we could walk," Greer said but her swing went wide, her sword dropping as her eyes grew with embarrassment. She saw the flicker of pain in Barden's face and heat rushed to her own. "Oh, Barden, I'm sorry. I shouldn't have brought up your father."

Barden lowered his sword; his tongue ran over his lips briefly before he looked away. Silently, he returned the sword into its holder. The sparring was over. "It's alright. I don't want to *never* speak of him, it's just … it's hard at the moment. Because to mention him, even for the briefest time, I think he's with us, and then I realize I'm only fooling myself. Each day the expanse between the time he was here and a part of my life, to the time he's been gone, grows. Each day I'm further from when he last knew me."

Greer lowered her blade, her breath coming quickly from the heat and the layers of fabric in her dress. "I feel that way too sometimes. When my father's name is brought up, for a second I forget he's gone. Then it rushes back."

Barden's brow furrowed. He turned, a mixture of emotion on his face. He didn't like Cearny. His loyalty was always with Greer, and because of her hurt, sorrow colored his features. "Sometimes I forget we both lost our fathers. I'm sorry."

Greer shook her head, stepping closer as she waved away Barden's apology. "Similar situations yet they're completely different. You shouldn't be sorry; my father was an awful man. A criminal mastermind allowed to rule a kingdom."

"But that's why I'm sorry," Barden replied, mirroring Greer's movements to step forward, the distance between them shrinking. "Greer, you've gone through a lot these last two years. I know everyone has understandably paid attention to Caitriona and what's on her mind. And they should, what she suffered was awful. But I often feel your experiences are forgotten, even by yourself."

Greer's cheeks grew hot and her eyes stung. Embarrassed by the display of emotion, she attempted to turn, to find interest in the flowers or distraction in the leaves, but Barden's hand caught her face. His thumb pressed against her chin, his feather-light fingers curled along her jawline, all warm and soothing. She sucked in her breath.

"Greer." His voice held a sigh of something long hidden, something he nourished in his heart and grasped tightly until he could finally, cautiously, set it free to the wild world when she was most accepting to receive it. She knew it had been there, and she fostered much of the same emotion, but duty was always first. Duty to her country, her people, her family. She couldn't deny his voice exposed her feelings, pried them open and undid her carefully constructed walls that stood around her heart. A quiver rushed down to Greer's core as she looked into his blue eyes.

Birds cried in the bushes and took to the sky as Greer's lips parted. She often wondered about fate, and fate always seemed to play a strange role in her life. She was fated to kill her father; the curse saw to that. She was fated to become queen. She felt fated to know Barden as they always were paired off and worked so well together. She wondered, not for the first time, what if she was fated to know *all* of him? And the world, or her queendom at the very least, was fated to keep her on her toes the very moment she decided to shift her priorities. Her queendom reminded her of her duty and that love came last.

Her queendom began to shake.

It was the quiver Greer felt, but this time all the greater and not caused by her heart churning back to life. Rising and spreading and moving from below. A shaking that came from the earth and spread upward to take hold of every plant and building and person. Greer grasped Barden's arms. Whatever was about to happen slipped away into the air with the fleeing birds. Their moment gone.

"What ...?" Greer asked, looking at the ground and her surroundings. The arches above swayed and purple petals fell around them.

"I don't know." Barden pulled Greer closer as the shaking grew, as if the ground wanted to throw them into the air like a dog with a flea. A growing hum and a distant groan mixing with cries of people made Greer's mind fall backwards in time. The dragon that attacked when she was a child, and just before when her sister was transformed and set fire to the castle itself, this was similar to those moments. But that was different, the destruction came from above while this was from below. Deep and dark, a movement that was older than angry kings and cursed princesses.

Time slowed as the world lost control and tantrumed from a trigger no man could fathom. Greer lost her semblance of time, the shaking felt like it lasted for hours when perhaps it was only minutes. They held fast to one another, moving from the overhang of purple flowers and into the opening beside a fountain whose water sloshed back and forth like the sea in a powerful storm. Barden curled his spine, bending to tuck Greer against his body as his arms wrapped around her, tightening his hold of her while pebbles and broken stone slipped from the walls surrounding the garden. His palm pressed against her head and pushed her to his chest with his wild heartbeat filling her ears. Greer squeezed her eyes closed, allowing herself a moment to give into her fear as everything shook, and then it stopped as suddenly as it began. At last, the ground grew still.

"What was that?" The castle appeared relatively unharmed. The sky, previously blue, turned hazy as smoke and dust rose. Everything was silent. The lack of birds and sound of people became a quiet ricocheting in Greer's chest.

"My father used to tell stories about giants who walked the land, making it shake and quiver." Barden squatted beside the fountain, studying the water that spilled over the edge and onto their shoes moments before. "He said it was just stories, giants never existed, but the earth has been known to shake in that way. It's passed though, look at the stillness of the water."

"I—" Greer glanced at the fountain but turned her attention back to the castle. "I don't know what to do."

"We'll figure it out." Barden squeezed Greer's shoulders, his hands remaining there afterward and briefly, Greer allowed herself to relax against him. "You're safe, that's my priority, and I need to continue to ensure your safety."

"We need to check on everyone," Greer murmured, looking at the haze gathering in the air. "I fear the city's in ruin."

It was a delicate affair, moving to the castle and creeping inside. Barden was on high alert, taking his task seriously and not allowing Greer to move forward on her own until he ensured the area was safe. Luckily, the castle sustained little damage beside the areas already under construction, but as Greer feared, the city suffered the most. Smoke rose from homes, different this time and black with flame and items burning that were never meant to.

"Every fire must be put out," Róisín stated after they gathered into the war room.

"We also need to gather what destruction was created by the quakes and how many people are injured," Greer said.

"It'll show quick aid and compassion, which you have in abundance. Good idea," Róisín replied and Greer felt something twinge in her heart. Her mother looked at her with warmth and yet, all Greer found herself capable of was looking to Barden. There was no time for feelings.

Greer kept her face blank as she looked at the guard. "Call for those in the city guard who aren't already stationed at the gates or working. Tell them they need to help. They must go house to house to take count of fires, structural problems, and any injuries."

Barden nodded and closed the door to the room behind him as he slipped out. Greer looked at her mother and Isla, who sat across from her. Her father always kept a much larger inner circle. It was filled with stuffy old men who were still around, trying to control her by making too many suggestions that sounded more like demands. Greer hadn't quite figured out who her circle was, not yet, and with Caitriona and Ailith gone it seemed substantially smaller.

"Do either of you have suggestions of what we should do with the injured? We'll call the healers of the city, but should we bring in magic healers as well?"

"If there aren't many injured, I'd stick to the traditional healers," Róisín began. "There's no need to upset those who're already frustrated with magic's allowance."

"You could also bring the magic healers though," Isla offered, her eyes daring as she pointedly looked at Róisín. "Don't announce it, just have them there to prepare cocktails of healing ointments and liquid magic. You may change the minds of some of the injured if they find themselves healed and realize it was done through magic."

Róisín looked at Isla, her eyes narrowing. Ever since Greer returned to Braewick with Isla, Róisín kept studying the old woman with a sense of unease and annoyance. Each time Isla gave advice, the look from her mother intensified.

Greer pushed forward, trying to distract her mother from studying

Isla. "Do either of you understand why this happened? We've never had the ground shake like this before."

Isla perked at this. "There's stories of giants—"

"Barden said as much. They don't exist, do they? Do we have to prepare for giants?"

Isla shook her head. "Oh, they died out generations ago. No, this came from the earth. I've only read of this happening before but I've never experienced it myself either. There's stories of what can cause it, but to me, it felt like an expanse of magic. Like a discharge."

"Is it an attack?" Róisín questioned.

Isla's brows furrowed. "I don't believe so. The magic was released, it's gone. Like it swelled and exploded and is lost to the world. I believe it passed but we may yet see where it was expelled from."

Greer tilted her head back, grinding her jaw as she considered the repercussions of this with those in the city already frustrated by magic. Now magic was destroying their homes.

In the privacy of the war room as they fell quiet, with no one else present, Róisín took the opportunity presented to her while Greer worried. The queen mother leaned forward in her seat and studied Isla intensely.

"I *know* you," Róisín said softly. "Isla ..."

Isla's eyes sparked and she leaned back in her seat, knitting her hands together on the table before her with an air of satisfaction. "Yes, I believe you do."

"You once went by another name." Róisín's eyes slowly widened.

"And I was much younger." Isla laughed. She leaned forward, her smile like a cat about to pounce on an oblivious bird. "My age has finally caught up to me. I think that's likely the reason you haven't quite placed me all this time, Róisín. I wasn't as wrinkled nor my hair as gray thirty years ago."

Her gray hair began to grow darker, black that came from her roots and dripped to the tips as it smoothed out into long, wavy tresses. Her wrinkles smoothed, the spots from sunshine vanishing, and her complexion evened out. Before their eyes, Isla's age melted away and she became someone middle aged.

"*Maeve*," Róisín whispered. "You trained Kayl. You taught him how to use his magic."

"You as well when you first arrived in Caermythlin. Do you not remember?"

Slowly, Isla's age returned, growing over her and making the years come within seconds. Róisín's jaw hung. "I went to one, two lessons at the most. I haven't seen you since I left—"

"Yes, in pursuit of the king's heart and to change the world. It didn't work out quite as you planned, but in a way you still were successful. It just took longer, didn't it?"

Róisín's eyes flashed; stubborn defenses raised that Greer always saw color her mother's expression with her father, yet her mother never acted upon. She was free to do anything now, and Greer found she didn't want to know entirely what her mother was capable of. That was a discovery best for another day.

"Is this the time?" Greer sighed. "Our queendom just suffered a devastating blow. We need to focus on our people."

Róisín looked at Greer and deflated, her focus returning to the present. "Follow Isla's lead. She's right. This is a good way to present magic as a benefit to our society, but don't announce it. Just have them work behind the scenes."

Greer nodded as she rose to her feet and looked between the two women. Isla always struck her as a mysterious age, possibly older than time, but she hadn't much of an opportunity to know her beyond her brief time with the woman when they were looking for Caitriona and again on the return trip from Stormhaven. She was a curious entity, and the revelation Isla knew her mother as a child was tempting. But Greer's city came first.

"Gather the healers from the castle," Greer requested from Paul, who stood outside the door as she left her mother and Isla behind. She kept the young guard in her own unit while Caitriona was gone from the city. "Tell them all healing is allowed, magic included, but any magic must be done quietly and out of sight. We don't want there to be an uproar when we should focus on healing anyone who's injured."

"Yes, your grace," Paul replied with a nod before going down the hall.

Greer moved through the castle and past hustling servants gathering linens to create a healing encampment below the castle walls. Turning for the parapet walkway, Greer moved into the summer heat once more. This time alone, other than the remaining guards standing on the parapet along the curtain wall and keeping an eye on the proceedings below, she approached the gatehouse to look down upon the city. Her closest view to it all, close enough to hear.

The royal and city guards alike led injured people to sit in haphazard rows on the street and the courtyard-like space before the castle entrance. The chatter of voices became a stream of noise, nothing clear from Greer's position as she looked at the cityscape itself. She nearly slipped into a blank state, staring before her, resting her mind briefly before trying to figure out the next steps forward when a word pricked her ear. It came again, heightened, shrill. Someone screaming.

Below, Barden and another guard directed a group of injured people forward but the woman whose hand clutched Barden's arm was screaming accusations, pointing around her as she continued ranting.

"The *magic* did this," she snarled. "You welcomed it here and magic has come, quaking the land and destroying our homes. This is all the result of *your* magic."

"You've cursed us!" Another voice yelled, a man who spotted Greer and stood separately from the growing crowd. "You allowed magic to suit your *own* needs and desires. You allowed magic for your *sister*. You're condemning us to death!"

A number of voices rose in agreement and more faces turned toward Greer, Barden's being one of them. Others yelled their complaints, their anger, their rage. It wasn't the words she heard, shrill in all the chaos, but their message was all the same. *She* was to blame after all, she welcomed magic back in.

A screech came from above, the sound from before. Overpowering the ambush of negativity, dark spots flashed past Greer. Red caps, skulls on the wind, they were quick and hurried as they sped by, stirring Greer's blonde hair with their movement. Ten years, if Greer wagered correctly. Ten years since Cearny made a great display on the front steps of the castle to an audience of his people as he dipped the metal cages filled with death-bringers into hot oil, silencing their shrill calls in an instant.

But this time there would be no oil. The birds were permitted to fly freely through the square below and down the streets to households where the injured still lay. Their calls repeatedly declaring the future: "*Die, die, die!*"

Complaints stumbled in throats, replaced by cries of fear as people batted away the death bringers. Some guards joined in, swinging their blades as they attempted to kill the small birds before they could eat the souls of any who died.

Still proving my point, her father taunted, *you aren't built to be queen.*

The strength in Greer's legs slowly fell out from her. Her throat closed in as the world became smaller and smaller.

What quaint symbolism of what your rule will be remembered for, Cearny commented. *Die, die, die, everyone will die.*

Barden's eyes locked on her. He moved forward, attempting to push through the desperate crowd like trudging through deep snow. A death-bringer darted at his face, its wings flapping erratically and he slapped it away as Greer sank to her knees and disappeared behind the wall, her panic a fist in her throat.

Spit plopped on the ground beside her as Cearny stepped forward, gesturing beyond the wall as he spoke. *Already your people suffer. Their very souls are being sucked up, sipped upon by those birds you allowed entrance.*

He squatted beside Greer and Greer forced herself to look at her father. This close, she smelt death lingering on him and could see into the gaping wound in his stomach from her sword. Maggots squirmed there, feasting on the wound and falling to the ground by her prone form. This close, she saw him for what he was: a dead thing filled with disgust and vile thoughts.

He leaned forward until his lips nearly touched her ear. Frost spread over her skin as he whispered, *Killer.*

"I know," she blurted with what air could wheeze its way through her closing throat. "I know I'm a killer."

Ten years since Cearny killed the death bringers, but it hadn't been ten years since they were last seen in the city. While there had been one in the guard yard at Shaw's funeral, Greer saw one before that.

Nearly two years prior she sat in the darkened corners of the hall where her father's body lay, slightly drunk off mead she snuck in with her—the only thing she could rely on to get her through that dreadful night—and up in the rafter she saw a death bringer. She never stopped it, never batted it away as it flit near her father, but she did release it from a window before her watch ended.

CHAPTER THIRTEEN

RÓISÍN

Sixteen Years Prior

T he library was a balm to Róisín's soul. When she first came to Braewick City, it was her own private kingdom where both Cearny and Donal—her father-in-law—rarely went. Amongst the shelves of books, she could drop the mask she always wore. She could rid herself of her minor magic and feel the tips of her ears again—it was the one remaining thing she had of her mother. She was allowed to smile and laugh at humorous poetry, and daydream of a different life. She escaped the gossip and expectations of her in the royal world. She was free.

When Greer and Caitriona were infants, they slept against her breast as she read them stories. When they were toddlers, they played seeking games amongst the shelves and watched snowflakes fall onto the gardens beyond its windows. She pretended they too were free.

The librarian, Henri, even became Róisín's friend.

"Another book of poetry was delivered, Queen Róisín," Henri greeted many times. It was rarely a hello, but an offering of escape within onion-skin pages. "Another book with stories I think your girls would enjoy."

It was a cordial, quiet type of friendship. She brought him sweet pastries and he gave her epic poems. It was an even distribution that spoke of their respect for one another. Róisín found her day always brightened after interacting with him. He was the only person within the castle who didn't have any expectations of her.

Once, when she thought Henri wasn't there, he surprised her. Bustling around a column they both jumped and his eyes darted to the side and took in her pointed ears. There was a breath where they looked at one another and recognized the information he now held. Róisín opened her mouth and before she could speak, Henri hurried away. He never mentioned her ears.

After Caitriona woke from the curse, Róisín waited another week before feeling she could safely leave Etta alone with the girl—who gratefully remembered nothing—and take to the halls of the castle by herself. Cearny had war meetings every afternoon, making it possible for Róisín to visit the library, less so to escape her daily life, but now with a specific purpose.

"Henri, I hope you can provide me with every book on magic you have," Róisín requested, her voice quiet despite no one else being present. Sometimes Greer and her tutors came to the library, but it was rare anyone else did. She and Henri often joked they were the only two in the whole of the castle who liked to read.

Róisín assumed when she met Cearny, he was well-read, but he could barely figure out how to hold a book, let alone read one. A waste of time, he told Róisín years before. He didn't even want the library, it was something his father insisted on maintaining, but it was a good place to store maps and he admitted to needing those.

Róisín's question, however, made Henri's eyebrows rise. For all her interest in books, she never requested ones on magic. He stepped back to look toward the door of the library, as well as the one hidden behind a half-empty case that led through the secret stairways and halls for the royal family.

"The king would be displeased if he knew you were looking at them," Henri replied with a frown.

"So, he *has* kept such books."

"His father did, just in case there was reason to study them if magic makers rose against the kingdom. But Cearny's banned anyone reading them."

Róisín leaned forward over the table. "Then we mustn't tell him."

Henri's frown continued, his unease obvious, but as he sighed Róisín knew she won. Without another word, he waved Róisín forward, beckoning her around the half wall and tables that separated the map room from the rest of the library.

"If you're going to read these texts, I ask you to agree to these terms," Henri said as he moved past tables covered in maps to the darkest corner of the library. "You won't take the books from this area. If the king or any of his men come in, shove the books away and behave as if you were just passing through, or you snooped through them without my aid. I'm not falling victim to Cearny's rage. I know nothing about this. If they ask me, I'll deny it all."

"I agree completely," Róisín said quickly. She stepped forward and reached for Henri's hand, taking it in her own and squeezing it tightly. "I swear on my children's lives that if I'm caught, I'll say it was my own doing. In fact, I have an addition to your terms: if I'm to look at these books, it should be when you aren't here."

"Even better," Henri said with a sigh, turning his hand over in Róisín's and gripping hers tightly in return. "I have maps to bring to the king shortly after the mid-day meals. You can read these books then."

"And I'll leave the moment you return."

The two paused, studying one another. Róisín, to see if the deal struck home for Henri and he was willing to work with her. Henri, to see if the queen was absolutely serious. In the end, he briefly nodded and silently pointed to a low shelf with dusty books before walking away.

"I have an errand to run and will be back in a half hour," he called over his shoulders.

"Thank you!" Róisín watched Henri disappear around the corner and out the door. Once it closed with a solid *thunk*, Róisín sank to the floor and pulled free the first of the books and opened it on her lap.

She did this for only a fortnight; going to the library and consuming as much as she could each day for an hour while Cearny had his war room meetings and Henri waited with the king in case Cearny requested additional materials. No one ever entered the library. Etta reported no one came to Caitriona's room to ask for the queen either, but she never once assumed the arrangements would be long lasting.

After the first heavy snowfall covered the land, Róisín slipped away from Caitriona's room and made her quick descent to the library. When she opened the library door, she found Henri still there. She hadn't seen the librarian since they made their deal and the sight of him made her pause in the doorway.

"Queen Róisín, what can I do for you?" Henri asked brightly. Róisín glanced about, not seeing anyone present, before stepping further in and closing the door behind her.

"Henri, how are you?" She cautiously moved toward the table between the stacks and maps where Henri stood.

"Quite good. I'm about to bring a few maps to the war room, though I'm glad I caught you." He stepped back from the table and waved Róisín around. She followed silently, back straight and her face blank, masking her confusion and pretending she knew what was going on. "I wanted to show you the great progress we've had with King Cearny's request to remove the books. It's been quite a bit of work since this morning, but I think it's coming along just fine."

There in the shadows of the map room was the shelf with all the magic books Róisín poured over for the last month, now empty beside finger swipes through the bits of dirt and dust.

Henri turned to Róisín; his expression sympathetic. The hand he placed on Róisín's shoulder conveyed his obvious sadness despite his words. "I hope the smoke from the book burning isn't reaching your room. I requested they burn them on the far side of the castle to avoid the bedrooms."

Róisín stared at Henri and let her mask slip to expose all her frustration. Sadness colored her face and she felt she could weep. Henri remained silent, but his grip on her shoulder tensed for a moment while their gazes met. He understood. He felt it too.

Swallowing, Róisín stepped away, patted her cheek and touched the skin below her eyes to ensure no tears escaped. Licking her lips, she looked back to Henri.

"I'm quite impressed by the speed of their work," Róisín stated, keeping her voice serious and unwavering. "And thank you for having the fire moved away from the rooms. We aren't receiving any smoke which is quite good, I wouldn't want it to upset Princess Caitriona."

Moments later Róisín burst into her room and rushed to her bed, pushing the heavy mattress back to expose little papers she wrote remedies and ingredients on. Pulling them free, she scanned her tiny writing, committing all she could to memory before thrusting them into the flames of her hearth. She didn't move. She refused to turn away until she witnessed the papers curl and burn, turning into unrecognizable ash. Only then was it safe.

When a knock came to her doorway, her body tensed. Glancing hastily at the fire, she rubbed her hands on the skirts of her gown and studied the ashes to find the paper had burned thoroughly.

"A letter for the queen," a young messenger said when she opened the door. He held forth a piece of tattered paper with haphazard writing upon it.

"Thank you," Róisín replied, taking the letter and closing the door tightly. Pressing her back to it, she frowned at the scrawl declaring "Queen Róisín of Wimleigh Kingdom." It was familiar, but she couldn't pinpoint how.

Ripping off the wax on the back and unfolding the paper, Róisín received the second shock of the past hour when she saw Kayl's signature. That was why she recognized the handwriting, it was his, and yet there was something peculiar about it. Something off.

The last time she saw Kayl in her vision, Róisín suspected she knew exactly what was off and felt the expanse of her sorrow and guilt crash over her again. Her people, her home, all gone, and she left behind and unable to do anything about it. In Kayl's shaking handwriting, he made clear that what she saw with her spell work was true.

I've determined the fate of your family, as you've determined the fate of mine, Kayl wrote. *You lied for your success, for your greed, and I've turned a blind eye from it. I still trusted you. And yet your husband killed for joy. Your husband has destroyed the life you could have had in every way. <u>You've destroyed it too</u>. Understand this: your child will be the one to take it away, and in the end you will know you are the creator of your own suffering.*

Róisín lowered the letter and her head fell back against the door. She breathed in the scent of the wood smoke and counted to ten as she looked at her room. It was filled with the finest fabrics and the most beautifully carved wooden furniture in the land. The walls were bursting with art and her wardrobe held gowns in every color. It was a dream for many and yet she wanted none of it.

If she could, she would take both her girls and find a village like Caermythlin. She would raise them there. A simple life where she would work as a cook—she was so good at baking before she met Cearny—and they could live in a little room above a shop. Her girls would grow up and marry simple farmers who treated them well. They would have an abundance of children and know happiness. But she knew none of it was possible. Cearny would hunt them down and have her throat if she even made it so far as getting the girls out of the castle and beyond the valley hills. No one would stand between him and his heir. If she were to go, she couldn't take Greer with her, and she wasn't willing to abandon her firstborn.

Kayl always made accurate observations when it came to Róisín. He was the only person alive who knew her first dream was to live in a little flat above a bakery. When they were children and teens, it was like he could read her mind—perhaps he could—but he always figured out her plans and her heart. Just seeing her observe Cearny from afar all those years ago, when Róisín developed her plan, he knew she was up to something. He knew the heart of her desires, even though he felt it wasn't worth the risk. No matter how foolish her plan, nor how much he loved her, he had no qualms in calling out her more ridiculous ideas. He understood, he always understood.

But in this he was incorrect. He assumed she was oblivious to all that occurred, but he was wrong. In the end, she already knew *she* was the creator of her own suffering.

CHAPTER FOURTEEN

Caitriona

The four made it through Avorkaz's gates early the next morning. No one paid any mind to four fae traveling by horse, leaving them unbothered and safe. When asked the reason for their visit, the tale that they were going through the Northern Wood in search of a fae settlement only caused a raised eyebrow or two. By noon they arrived on the northern edge of the city where buildings became only a few stories high with yards in between and the dark pine forest stood tall to the north, threatening and overwhelming.

"So that's it?" The color drained from Ailith's face.

"That's it," Ceenear said. "For all the places I've been, that damn forest is the one I hate the most."

"How often have you come here?"

Ceenear's expression was grave. "Only once. It was more than enough."

"Did you ever make it through the forest and to the northern coast?"

Ceenear shook her head. Her full lips were turned downward, and her gaze weary as she stared beyond her as if she didn't trust it.

"If it's so dangerous, why do people pass through?"

"Few actually pass through for the northern coast. Their priority is the forest itself since the forest south of the border was destroyed. They use this forest to collect lumber, but it's severely restricted. People have to obtain permits to even enter or go with a registered guide like the hunters because there are so many creatures that kill swiftly and without pause. The pelts of the creatures are also rare and extremely expensive, and there's numerous magical properties that can be harvested within. The town on the coast, that's something I've heard of only rarely and with little detail."

"Why did you come here?" Ailith asked.

Ceenear rolled her shoulders. "I was searching for a fae who left Ulla Syrmin. He was depressed for some time. His family was in a panic when they found a note saying he left. I attempted to track him down. He was last seen in Avorkaz, but said to have gone into the woods. He never came out and we never found him."

Ailith frowned and looked at Catriona with obvious unease.

"Do you know where the monster hunters are?" Caitriona asked. May made it quite clear they needed one to escort them through the forest. It was too dangerous to go it alone, they needed a guide. Declan described a series of small cabins along the city's edge where the hunters lived, awaiting job opportunities for those who decided to pass through the trees of the Northern Wood for whatever reason.

From the edge of the city, they looked down a hillside of a small valley. Ceenear scanned the houses before pointing to the west. "That cluster of homes is what we're looking for."

If there were any hunters left.

Each building stood empty. Door after door was unanswered. Standing before the fifth, a small hut with a wild garden and trinkets hanging off the simple fence, Caitriona felt a building sense of dread. If there wasn't a hunter to hire, what would they do? Go forward on their own with hope to fend for themselves? Meander the forest for who knew how long until they found this mysterious town?

"Last chance," Ailith announced as she handed Onyx's reins to Ceenear. "I'll try this time."

"I'll come with you." Caitriona passed her reins to Raum. They traipsed along the overgrown path to the front door and knocked.

Half expecting it to go unanswered, Caitriona jumped when the door pulled open. A woman Greer's age leaned out. Her black hair hung loose and fell into her dark eyes that darted between the two of them. Her lip curled with clear judgment. "Yes?"

"Uh," Ailith blurted and looked at Caitriona then back to the woman. "We're hoping we can hire a monster hunter? We're trying to travel through the Northern Wood to the coast and back, and we were told it's safer to hire a hunter."

The woman's eyes narrowed before she held the door open and stepped aside silently. Exchanging a look again, Caitriona and Ailith stepped in.

The little house was tidy and relatively empty. A loaf of bread and summer apple sat on the table, a bed in the corner was neatly made, and a hearth with burning embers was centered with a teapot nestled in it. The walls were impressive, lined with various swords and daggers, and Ailith's eyes went wide as she looked them over.

The woman, however, continued to stand in silence as she studied them.

"We can pay you," Caitriona blurted out. "We can pay whatever your fees are. We have a large horse with us as well that can fit two; I can ride it and you can borrow mine if you don't have one—"

"You aren't taking your horses into the forest," the woman said, placing her hands on her wide hips as she studied them with a look of obvious judgment, her dark eyes lined with thick, dark lashes and a poisonous feel. She was shorter than Caitriona and much broader; her curves made obvious with the tight riding pants and vest she wore. Her dark hair was straight besides a curve at the tips, and Caitriona stared at her beauty, despite the scowl.

"Why can't we take our horses?" Ailith turned her attention to the woman. "I'm Ailith by the way and this ..." Ailith looked at Caitriona and paused, realizing her mistake in offering her name too easily. There were plenty of Ailiths and a number of Caitrionas but together was too much of a risk for recognition.

"Lumia," Caitriona offered with a smile, hoping Lumia wouldn't mind having her name used—even if she knew. Raum still hadn't been able to get in touch with the pale-faced fae despite trying every morning and evening, and sometimes at noon. "What's your name?"

"Fiana."

Silence. They looked at one another, Caitriona and Ailith shifted with mild discomfort while Fiana stared them down.

"So ..." Ailith broke the quiet and offered a smile. "Can you help us?"

"You don't have an accent from the Mazgate Dominion," Fiana pointed out, making Ailith immediately frown. "You, I can't figure your accent out. It reminds me a little bit of the coastal accent from down south, but you, Lumia." Fiana flicked her gaze back to Caitriona. "Your accent reminds me of Braewick."

"She had a Braewick mother," Ailith continued, "who was her primary caregiver growing up."

"Can she not speak for herself?"

"She's my ..." Caitriona began then found herself stumbling over the words. "She ... she can speak for me. We're a package deal. And she's right. My mother raised me, she escaped Braewick."

Fiana sniffed, then turned away. She walked to her fireplace and pulled a cord hanging from the ceiling before sitting down at her table and eating as if they weren't still waiting for some type of conclusion to their meeting. Caitriona looked at Ailith, who shrugged before stepping forward, her boot making a low clunk on the hardwood floor of the little home.

"So, can you do it?" Ailith stood a foot away from Fiana, looking at her with quiet intensity. The hunter ignored her and ripped a piece of bread from the loaf with her teeth. "Look, we'll pay you. But you're the last hunter house—unless there's more we haven't visited. But if you don't help us, we either have to wait to go or go without a hunter, and both options aren't possible for us."

Fiana paused and looked up at Ailith, her cheeks bulging with food. "Sorry," she grumbled, "I'm busy."

Ailith bit her lower lip, her shoulders growing tense. "Look, this is incredibly important. We need to go through the woods. We're looking for a town. A fae town we've heard is north of the woods itself along the coast. We need to find it as soon as possible and we can't without help."

"Can't help." Fiana took another bite of her food. "Good luck though."

Ailith gave an exasperated sigh and dropped her hands to her sides as she spun on her heel and looked at Caitriona with desperation.

"It's alright," Caitriona replied, waving Ailith forward to entwine her hand in hers. "We'll figure this out."

Fiana continued eating, although her eyes flicked to take in the sight of the two women holding each other's hands. She sniffed, returning her focus to her food and after long enough time passed it appeared she was finished speaking to them. Caitriona and Ailith slipped out, both staring at their feet with disappointment.

"Uh, excuse me?" Raum called from the foot of the path. Caitriona looked up and froze. Ailith reached for the hilt of her sword, ready to draw it. Ceenear and Raum stood side by side with their hands tied behind their back, surrounded by Avorkazian guards. "The uh ..."

He turned his chin upward, seeming to point at them. Caitriona looked at Ailith, her jaw dropping to see her ears with their normal curve. Her hands flew to the top of her head, and sure enough her four horns pushed through her skin, parted her hair, and curled upwards. Running her hand down her braided hair, it was unsurprisingly gold.

"Your eyes too," Ailith whispered. Caitriona's eyes burned with tears from surprise that the magic was undone but also, primarily, embarrassment. Ailith shook her head. "It wasn't like this inside the hunter's house. It must've happened while we were walking the path."

"You're under arrest," a guard announced as he separated from the group and moved toward them with another following. Both had their swords drawn and Ailith tightened her grip on her hilt.

"What for?" Ailith asked.

Two guards that remained behind with Raum and Ceenear shook their heads. The leader advanced down the path with a laugh. "For threats to the Mazgate Dominion and endangering its people."

Caitriona sat in a furnished room. Having been told the rest of her party was split and scattered in the cells of Avorkaz's city center, she was on edge. They left her there long enough that the sun shifted. Its beams fell on the floor through the single window and inched across the dark wood, highlighting the dust floating in the light.

Her stomach growled. They were likely coming close to the evening meal.

The weight of iron-bound shackles dug into her skin and rubbed against her wrist bones. The fae told her iron was a good way to keep magic from escaping a person. She stretched her fingers, and leaned forward to allow them to swim in the dying sunlight as she concentrated.

The dragon in her belly stirred to life in the moments after their arrest and nearly burst from her when she was dragged away from Ailith. Ailith kicked and cursed and bit the hand of one of the guards while she was brought through a gated door and down dark steps. Raum and Ceenear were led down separate stairs, both wearing iron cuffs as well but with much less fight in them.

So enraged was the dragon, Caitriona felt ready to explode when she was brought to this simple yet furnished room. She sat in silence while waiting for someone to return, to explain what she had done wrong and allow her a chance to speak for herself. But the dragon was pacing through her core and she was close to spitting fire.

If you let me out, I could break down the walls, I could fly free.

Caitriona ignored the dragon. She turned her wrist, exposing her palm to the sunlight and watched the skin of her hands pool with sweat that steamed then flickered: a spark, a firelight on burning oil.

Yes.

It grew from there, this fire she made in the palm of her hand, rising upward and covering her hand which ached from change. Her nails thickened into claws; the skin of her fingers glittered from golden scales.

It feels good, doesn't it?

She could easily burn the room down and set everyone ablaze who dared take, or worse, hurt the people she loved.

"It does." Caitriona's voice was small, barely a whisper, as she confessed this deepest and most awful secret. She stretched her fingers, watching fire lick over each digit. It was there even still, the dragon, smoking from the mouth and making her skin hot, but she had a role to play if she wanted to ensure her party was kept safe. Releasing the little bit of flame allowed the dragon to back down for now. "Maybe someday you can be free."

A knock came to the door, and she clenched her hand into a fist, the flame disappearing into a poof of smoke. The door swung open without waiting for her answer—a guise of manners when really they still held the upper hand—and a pair of guards looked at her with unease. "You're to come with us."

The hall was filled with shadow, unwelcoming but cool, yet the room she was brought to had a large window showing the sun over Avorkaz. A man with dark eyes and hair, and a well-groomed beard, waited at a table. He immediately got to his feet and bowed. "Princess Caitriona. My apologies."

The guards unclasped the iron cuffs before returning to their position by the doors. Caitriona rubbed at her wrists as she took in the room before setting her sights on the man. She hadn't the faintest idea who he was.

"Why did you arrest my friends and me?"

"I believe the guards said *for endangering my people*," he said. Caitriona frowned as she realized who he was. Jace Hergrew, the steward of Avorkaz.

"We haven't done *anything* to your people. We just arrived to Avorkaz this morning."

"But you and your human guard have sported potions making yourselves appear fae. You've intentionally hidden yourself from detection."

"Apparently not well enough."

Jace's eyes narrowed.

Caitriona's palms grew hot. "We didn't want something like this to happen when we were only passing through."

"And why are you passing through?" Jace asked as he propped a foot on the seat of a chair and leaned an elbow upon it. "Why does Wimleigh Queendom's heir need to pass through my city with two fae and her guard?"

Caitriona studied the man. He wasn't much older than she and, to her understanding, thrust into the role at an exceptionally young age. To her understanding, he was well loved and after years of being in the position much more comfortable with the role than Greer was with being queen. He already saw wars as a leader, after all.

She wondered what it was like, ruling while her father fought the city in an attempt to seize control. He very well could have years of resentment for her family—not that he would be the first. It seemed to be a common enough sentiment.

With nothing else to lose, she figured honesty was the best approach. "We're looking for someone, someone to aid my sister. Wimleigh Queendom has been told that we'll be attacked."

"Ah, yes, the Invarlwen war," Jace replied, dropping his leg off the chair and circling the table to the hearth at the end of the room which lay dormant of flame.

"You know of it?"

"The new king asked me to send guards to his aid some weeks ago."

Caitriona's heart tightened. Jace turned back to Caitriona and tilted his head to one side. His eyes were bright and calculated. "You're worried I said yes."

Caitriona really didn't like this man, and she made no effort to hide her distaste from her face.

He smirked. "Don't worry, I told him we wouldn't help. We've had our fair share of battles in recent years. We don't want to be involved in another war with Wimleigh."

"So, there's no sense in asking you to help us, is there?"

His teasing expression melted into a smile that wasn't unkind. "I'm sorry, princess. I'm not going to help your cause. You do understand, don't you?"

Caitriona laughed, a short, bitter thing. "After all my father did to your people? Of course, I understand. Probably better than you even realize. I wouldn't want anything to do with us either."

This surprised Jace and the guards standing by the door shifted uneasily.

"You're not what I expected," Jace admitted. It was there, just a flicker at the corner of his jaw, the start of a smile. "Although I suppose you weren't what your father expected either."

Caitriona smiled, but it wasn't kind. It was something of her father's making, the smile of someone who knew her entire existence disappointed her parent. "That's the thing, I think he expected me to be exactly who I am and that was half the problem. If you can't provide guards to help my sister's cause, can you let me and my party go so we may continue searching for those willing to lend aid?"

Jace looked Caitriona over, his face curious and studious, as if committing Caitriona to memory as something new, something unexpected. He nodded slowly. "Only if you tell me who you seek in the Northern Wood."

It only took a moment of consideration before she quietly said, but not with fear or shame, only simple determination. "Lachlan, the rightful heir to the Invarlwen throne."

CAITRIONA WAS LEFT IN THE ROOM WITH JACE AND THE guards while a messenger retrieved the rest of her party and their belongings. The two settled at the table, an uneasy truce between them as they attempted to speak casually but found themselves too curious of the other to keep prying questions away.

"No one has seen you for years," Jace admitted. "But how you appeared after you became a dragon, that news spread rather rapidly."

Caitriona felt her cheeks burn and smoke fill her nostrils. She took in a long breath, comforting the dragon and urging it to rest. Despite her upset by Jace's comment, she didn't believe they were in any true danger.

"Beforehand I was nothing worth noticing by the gossip of the land. Now I'm something my father would have hated, which is a win or a loss for many, depending on what side they stand on."

"And what side do you stand on, princess?"

"The side that doesn't want there to be a war with the fae. The side that only wants to undo the hatred my father and grandfather created."

The door burst open and Ailith was pushed through, cursing at the guards and with a bruise already appearing on her brow.

"Bastard," Ailith hissed at the guard who undid her cuffs and stepped from the room. Ceenear and Raum followed with iron still on their wrists. Those leading the fae undid the iron and disappeared without a word.

"Ailith!" Caitriona shot up from her seat and Ailith spun, eyes going wide.

"Well, if he told me he was bringing me to you, I wouldn't have punched him," Ailith replied as she circled the table, crashing into Caitriona and embracing her hard.

"Sorry about that," Jace replied serenely from his seat.

"Your guards are right bastards." Ceenear gave a smile filled with venom, her wardrobe smudged with dirt. "Perhaps if you're going to place us in holding cells for a few hours only to have us rejoin the princess later, you could tell us next time?"

Jace waved her words away as he got to his feet, turning to Caitriona and giving her another bow. "Princess, my apologies to you and your group for interrupting your mission. When you entered Fiana's cabin she alerted our guards. Your illusions dropped from passing through her garden, exposing your true self. We wanted to ensure you all were simply traveling through and held no real danger to us."

Caitriona held his dark gaze for a moment before turning to Ailith, Raum and Ceenear. "You're alright?"

"Just a bit bruised," Raum sighed, rubbing at his wrists where the iron cuffs were taken off. Ailith remained silent, her gaze on Jace and hand tight in Caitriona's.

Caitriona turned back to Jace. "What have you done with our supplies?"

"It should be waiting outside the door. Your potions included. I'd recommend taking the potion again to hide how you look before you leave the building. You *are* quite ... noticeable."

The dragon grew restless in Caitriona's belly and she took a slow breath to calm it.

"Thank you, Jace," she said through clenched teeth. "We'll be out of your hair as quickly as possible."

"Best of luck," Jace replied as they began to shuffle from the room. "By the way, I think it's Ätbënas you're looking for. It's a town on the northern end of the woods where a group of highly powerful fae live. You might find your prince there."

"I'm grateful for your help. By the way—" Caitriona stopped in the doorway and turned to Jace with a smile. "I appreciate you don't find us dangerous. We'd *never* hurt a person of Avorkaz, not without reason."

The cold hearth behind Jace sparked and a fire whooshed to life, filling the area with a flash of heat and making Jace jump forward.

"Also, the iron did nothing for my own gifts. You'll have to do better next time." Caitriona smiled before stepping fully out of the room, her gold eyes glowing. "Goodbye."

In the bowels of the building, Ailith and Caitriona clinked together the glass of their potion bottles before pouring out the required amount onto separate spoons. Drinking the sour mixture, Caitriona groaned from the discomfort. Opening her eyes, she found her gold hair red again, her shoulders free of scales and the horns gone.

"I'm surprised it hurts so much," Caitriona murmured. "Although it's nothing compared to becoming a dragon."

"May said it would," Ailith commented and pushed the stoppers back into the bottles. She glanced at Caitriona shyly, a flicker of guilt in her eyes. "She said changing into something you're not hurts. That's what this is."

Ailith slipped by, heading down the hall toward where Avorkaz guards prepared their steeds. Ceenear gave a sympathetic smile and followed Ailith with Raum patting Caitriona's shoulder and doing the same. Caitriona remained for a moment, realizing at last the implication and the certainty of all she hated and feared. She could never return to the girl she was before the curse took hold; it was simply something that was not herself any longer.

I've been trying to make you realize that, the dragon sighed, or was it only her own voice, her own thoughts—a part of her she had not yet accepted? *I am you and you are me.*

On their horses in uneasy silence, they rode onto Avorkaz' busy streets to find Fiana standing before them, arms crossed over her busty chest, a bow on her back and a sword at her side.

"If you want to go into the Northern Wood, you're going to have to put those beasts into a stall first so they don't attract every creature there," she said. Her gaze moved to each person but rested on Caitriona the longest. She raised one dark eyebrow. "We can head out on foot immediately after ... if you pay up first."

CHAPTER FIFTEEN

Ailith

A ilith wasn't in the best of moods when they entered the woods. Their capture by Avorkazian guards and the way they discarded her because she didn't have magic made her sensitive and bitter. While Raum and Ceenear had iron bands clamped to their wrists before being pushed into iron cages, Ailith was kicked into the lower levels of the jail. The floor was coated with mud and other substances, people were filthy and ill, and only one low-lit lantern gave light to the disgusting hall. She fought back, yet the guards still taunted her.

"She's magicless, she can't do too much harm." One laughed as he closed the jail cell door and left her in the muck. "Why would the queen think you could guard the princess? You're weak. Then again, I suppose the queen doesn't have any magic either."

The memory made Ailith's hands stiff from tightening them into fists.

With her pack on her back and Barden's gifted sword gripped in her hand, they set into the woods on foot, and Ailith tried to leave the memory in Avorkaz. Fiana urged their silence and Ailith reveled in it. Better to be grumpy and lurk over her feelings quietly than forced to move past it all.

Only a few feet into the trees, the thick foliage made it substantially darker. "You all need to understand creatures are *everywhere* in this wood," Fiana cautioned as she led them forward. "They rarely leave the trees but just stepping within, it's not uncommon to greet a creature looking for your blood."

They continued forward, somehow avoiding the creatures Fiana declared salivated over their very presence, until sunset grew close and the woods managed to grow even more foreboding as the air dampened and the temperature dropped. Fiana started a protective circle as the group laid out their packs. Ailith rested on her belly as she blew sparks to flame on the pile of sticks and firewood she gathered—Caitriona hadn't offered to make fire and Ailith couldn't bring herself to ask. They were all quiet, focused on their end-of-day settling of packs, cleaning of weapons, and preparation to eat. It made the noises of the woods all the more heightened.

Something snapped and it wasn't the crackle of flame eating away at wood. A sigh, hiss, and the ruffle of leaves. Everyone grew still. Ailith lifted her head, looking over the fire just starting to catch. Then the ground breathed, rising upward until it burst like a cyst and half a dozen partly rotten creatures pulled themselves from the rocks and dirt, their groans echoing off the dense trees around them.

"Undead!" Fiana yelled, dropping her bag of salt and pulling her sword free. "Everyone, up!"

The undead's bodies which appeared mostly human were held together by rotting flesh and ooze dripping from the rips of their skin that sizzled as they came in contact with the unfinished protective circle. They groaned and gasped as a mixture of rotting gas and air eased through their broken windpipes and parted lips, or whatever was left of their mouths, as they moved.

Ailith pushed off the ground and into a crouch as the multiple undead rushed toward the encampment. Everyone leapt to their feet and moved forward, and she was separated by the growing flames. Reaching behind her for the handle of her sword, she tried to lift it ... and it didn't move. A weight pressed down on the blade, drawing Ailith's attention. She stifled a scream as the leering, rotting face of an undead swung toward her as its foot slipped along the blade's smooth surface.

Ailith gripped the handle with both hands and pulled, sending the undead stumbling backwards as she rose to her full height. Lifting the blade and swinging it to the side, she prepared to strike the creature but pain exploded in her shoulder. Ailith screamed as something bit down hard. A sharpness, heat, and the tearing of flesh made worse with the rot and vomit-smelling hot breath overcoming her.

Twisting on her feet, she couldn't help another cry as the teeth tore away. An undead stumbled as she moved, blood—her blood—coating its jaw. She swung her sword and her blade finally found its mark, connecting with the undead's neck and nearly severing its head from the body.

The blade stuck. The other undead moved in.

"Ailith, step back!" Fiana yelled.

"My sword's stuck!"

She kicked her foot forward, pressing her boot into the chest of the undead and pushing as she tugged. It broke free as her heel sank into its rotting chest. She swung her sword again, cleaving the head off entirely, but there was little room for recovery.

Another undead grabbed her arm. Beyond in the woods, darkened by the growing firelight, two more shambled forward. They were surrounded.

Minutes passed as Ailith was forced into a dizzying dance with one undead after another. Ceenear brought one down, Raum another, and Fiana was a force killing them with dusts and potions, blades and bow. But they kept coming, focusing on Ailith entirely as she tried to fight them off.

When her sword pulled free from another undead, her swing went wide, the tip bumping over something that gasped from behind. They were surrounding her, growing in number, and Ailith felt desperation clawing at her insides.

"They keep coming!" Ailith yelled, stumbling backwards and nearly falling on her rear, the gasp a fleeting thing to her awareness.

A flash of heat passed Ailith in such a rush, Ailith found herself covering her face. Fire exploded, catching onto the remaining undead. They panicked, flailing their arms and stumbling blindly as they attempted to put themselves out, but it was enough of a distraction for Fiana to rush forward, cutting each of their heads off with her sword while Ailith stood to the side.

"I could have helped," Ailith pointed out as she pressed her palms into her knees and attempted to catch her breath.

"They were surrounding you." Fiana immediately cleaned off her blade and stepped over the discarded bodies. "We cleared out the ones on the other side of the fire, but we had to get rid of those too. They're attracted to you like a moth to a flame."

"I wonder why." Raum stepped forward with a spare piece of fabric he held out to Ailith.

She was covered in blood and not sure how much of it was her own. By the pain in her shoulder where the undead bit her, she was sure a good amount was hers. She wiped the blood off her face and hands, hiding her embarrassment in the fibers of the cloth.

"It's because she doesn't have magic," Fiana replied. She looked from Raum to Ailith and offered a shrug. "Easy target."

Ailith closed her eyes, the sting of Fiana's words making her jaw tight.

"Are you alright?" Caitriona jogged to Ailith's side, taking the already-dirty cloth from Ailith's hands and tossing it into the fire. With a flourish of her hand, the scent of flowered oils always rubbed into Caitriona's clothing rose in the air as she produced a new cloth to press against Ailith's wounds.

"I'm okay, I think."

Caitriona's eyes glowed gold despite the potion still being active. Unaware, she pulled Ailith's collar to look at the bite on her shoulder. Ailith remained still, allowing Caitriona to fuss over her, as she stared into Caitriona's golden gaze.

"It was good seeing you use your gifts."

Caitriona frowned. "It's necessary here in the woods."

"You used it in Avorkaz too, I could tell," Ailith pressed. They so rarely discussed Caitriona's abilities. Caitriona never allowed it; she rarely used her gifts and if there was ever the semblance of gold glowing from her eyes she was quick to deny it. If Ailith brought it up, Caitriona would brush it off, but Ailith knew it was a discussion they had to have at some point or another. With her free hand, Ailith brushed her fingertips over Caitriona's waist. "I just wanted to point it out, to tell you I'm glad to see you're using them."

Caitriona glanced at Ailith then looked toward Fiana. "Is she going to be okay? She was bit by one of them."

"Just a bite." Fiana stepped closer to look. "Treat it like a bite from a person. Clean it, don't let it get infected. Undead are made from magic users, not from each other."

"So, someone just left a bunch of undead in the woods for travelers to come across?" Raum asked.

"These woods don't go by common sense or the expected," Ceenear said as she came forward with a healer's kit. "They may not have been placed here; they may have come here on their own. For some reason, magic creatures seem attracted to this place."

Ailith couldn't help but look at Caitriona when Ceenear said this, her lover still avoided Ailith's eye as the glow in Caitriona's returned to the potion-made blue. She gripped her left arm with her hand and shifted from Ailith, but it only drew her attention more. Caitriona's white shirt sleeve had blood on it. "What happened to you?"

Caitriona's cheeks reddened. "The tip of your sword caught my arm. It's just a nick, that's all."

Ailith's gut dropped, her nerves firing off in her face as embarrassment heated. She drew the undead to the camp, they found her an easy target, and she came out of it having injured the very person she was meant to protect.

"Cait, I'm so sorry."

"It's nothing; I'll be fine. Let's get you patched up." She got to her feet and walked away, going to her bag to pull out supplies to tend to Ailith's wound.

"Should we just travel through the night?" Ailith turned to Fiana, trying to ignore the simultaneous urge to run after Caitriona and beg forgiveness despite her reassurance. "Keep moving so we can get out of the woods quicker and rest during the day?"

"They're more active at night," Fiana continued as she plucked her bag of salt from the ground. "But if we rest while they're active, I can put the protective circle around us so they don't bother us. You can't do that if you're walking."

She began to fix the outer edge of the circle as Ailith continued cleaning herself off and Ceenear administered healing ointments.

"I'll take first watch. One of you can take a watch towards the end of the night and all you have to do is wake me when you've made the morning meal," Fiana said as she laid out her sleeping pad and sat down on the edge with her bow.

"I can take the first watch," Ailith volunteered. She sat on the edge of her own quilt, using the extra water Fiana encouraged them to bring to wash the blood off her shirt. They didn't need creatures drawn by the scent of her blood, too.

Fiana turned and eyed Ailith. "I think you should rest."

Pressing her lips together tightly, Ailith returned to scrubbing her shirt and ignoring the sympathetic smile Ceenear offered from opposite the fire.

"She hates me," Ailith whispered as Caitriona settled beside her. Her sleeve was pulled up, her arm wrapped and the blood gone. Ailith bit the inside of her lip.

"She doesn't hate you," Caitriona replied. "At least, I don't think she does. I think she has an understanding of the woods better than any of us and knows what to do to ensure we don't get killed."

"Cait ..."

Caitriona's gaze met Ailith's then looked down at her arm. "I'm *fine*, Ailith. I swear to you. Let's talk about something else?"

Ailith squeezed her shirt, then draped it over a log close to the fire to dry. "Remember when we looked for Kayl and I kept wondering if I was fit for the mission?"

Caitriona frowned. "You're fit for this mission, Ailith. Even more now. You have greater experience; you can wield your own sword and dagger with both hands with ease. Many guards only do it with their dominant hand. You've proven yourself already, don't get in your head that you aren't ready for this task."

Returning to her mat, Ailith stretched her legs and laid down behind Caitriona who sat at the edge of her own mat. Curling her arm around Caitriona's waist, Ailith ran her hands over Caitriona's thigh.

"Sorry. It's tough when you can't wield some type of magic and you're the only one who managed to get bit."

Caitriona brushed her fingertips along Ailith's jaw and smiled. "I love you, you know that, right?"

"Always," Ailith replied, the very words lifting her mood.

"Then believe me when I say you're talking yourself down. Now sit up and eat your dinner."

Ailith did as she was told, although she still felt embarrassed. Despite smiling, despite joking with Raum, despite kissing Caitriona and teasing her with trailing fingers when no one was looking before they parted for the night, mild concern frequented Ailith's mind as she laid down to rest. If she was back in Braewick and had the gift of foresight, she would have wished at the Elder Tree for sudden magic powers. She would have asked May to give her a potion that did more than grow her ears into points. She would have wished for some type of advantage. After all, the weakest link made the entire chain frail, and she didn't want to bring her team down.

THE ATTACK OF THE UNDEAD WASN'T A STANDALONE experience. By the following day, a cockatrice crashed through the trees with little warning. It towered over the group, double Raum's height as its chicken-like head broke tree limbs off, forcing them to scatter while its giant talons scraped the ground.

A memory flashed into Ailith's mind of years before. A cockatrice approached the city walls while she was stationed at the northern gate. She called the royal hunters and remained at the gate—as was her assigned task—but was forced to witness the royal hunters die, one after another, by the creature's quick movements and lethal breath—

She grabbed Caitriona's hand, pulling her back as the cockatrice stretched its skin-like wings. "It breathes poisonous gas," she rushed to explain.

The creature stretched its neck and bellowed, a screeching caw that made Ailith's very bones shiver. Its sharp beak jutted forward and nearly knocked Raum's sword from his hand. Fiana dug into one of her many pockets, pulling free a vial of liquid she poured into her mouth before lifting the single torch they carried and spitting into it, making a ball of fire blast forward into the air and sending the cockatrice stumbling backwards towards Ailith and Caitriona.

The cockatrice's serpentine tail swung out, catching Ailith's legs and sending her into the air, her sword knocked from her hand as she spun head over foot. She crashed amongst the ferns with the air forced from her chest.

It screeched at the rest of the party, kicking its barbed feet outward and throwing Fiana and Raum into the ferns before it turned and focused on Ailith. Each footstep was earth shaking and Ailith gasped, trying to gain back breath so she could fight back. So she could do anything.

It puffed its feather-covered chest and released a green-tinged breath of air. Gas. Throwing her arm over her mouth and nose, Ailith desperately sucked in a strangled breath to fill her lungs, then clamped her mouth shut. She lay prone on the ground, the cockatrice staring down at her. There was no escape.

No escape but through flame. Caitriona showered fire onto the creature, making it rear back, close enough to Ceenear, who slashed the tendons of its legs. It collapsed onto the ground and narrowly missed Ailith's body. It flailed; its sharp beak reaching out mindlessly as it tried to strike while its wings flapped. Caitriona's flames continued, roasting the beast and sending it swiftly to its death.

Fiana and Raum were both bleeding. Ailith lay on the ground, watching as the cockatrice's gas slowly dissipated before she heaved to her feet. Brushing leaves and dirt off her clothing, she found her sword and moved toward the camp. What good was the training she received in Braewick if it didn't prepare her for creatures? What good would she be on a battlefield facing fae who could just as easily turn into things with talons and claws? But maybe it wasn't the training at all. Maybe it was just her.

As Ailith patched Raum's wound, the blow to her ego softened a little bit. At least the cockatrice didn't draw her blood.

They moved through the thick forest quickly, avoiding interacting with the plants growing thick along the path due to the risk of undead nestled beneath or other creatures that could lurk. They stuck to the trampled pathway of previous hunters and their parties. In some areas, they found stumps of trees that were cut for lumber. In others, Fiana made them pause as she gathered odd looking mushrooms and different plants.

"I need to make my spells one way or another," she pointed out.

"What is your magic exactly?" Ceenear asked as she held open Fiana's bag while the hunter dropped more fungus inside.

"I haven't any magic. Not like your lot," Fiana said, glancing at Ceenear. "I'm like Ailith."

Ailith blinked with surprise. "How? You've made protective, magic circles, and use powders and liquids on creatures."

"I don't have any magic," Fiana repeated as she brushed off the knees of her pants. "I can't make something out of nothing. I can't turn into someone else with some power from within; I can't read auras just by looking at someone; I can't make fire in the palm of my hand. What I know is magic creatures. I know their strengths and weaknesses. I also know a ton of recipes, all different brews. There's magic in what I create, but it's not from me, it stems from ingredients. If you're determined to say I have magic, let it be that my magic is knowledge."

"That's why they aren't attracted to you." Ailith's shoulders dropped. "They can sense the magical ingredients."

"Exactly. You and I are the same, we only have different skill sets."

As the day grew closer to evening, the woods thinned and creatures began to disappear. When they entered the woods, Crowley flew away, determined to find his own path to the coastal town of Ätbënas, but an annoyed caw came from a clearing ahead.

"That's him." Ailith smiled, picking up pace with Fiana to catch up.

"That crow? How can you tell his call from others?"

"I know his call," Ailith said. "You spend enough time with them, you'll be able to tell the difference."

As they stepped through the clearing, temporarily blinded by the brightness of the open area, a black shadow passed over. Ailith grinned, waving at Crowley overhead before reaching into her bag for nuts.

"Ailith." Caitriona touched Ailith's shoulder and redirected her attention from the sky to the ground. They stood on a ridge that funneled down to a stream that curved along before widening to an inlet for the northern sea. Along its edge stood gray structures with grassy roofs covered in wildflowers.

"Well," Fiana said with a voice Ailith hadn't heard from her before. Something soft and filled with marvel. "Welcome all to Ätbënas."

CHAPTER SIXTEEN

RÓISÍN

Sixteen Years Prior

A long time ago, Róisín was filled with youthful determination and marveled at her self-confessed cleverness.

She thought when the first guards of Wimleigh Kingdom came through her town, she could outsmart Prince Cearny and King Donal.

She assumed if she hid her slightly pointed ears and made sure to be as presentable as her town's supply of cloth and her meager sewing lessons allowed, she'd grab their interest.

She believed if she married Prince Cearny, she could convince him not all magic was bad, that both magic users and those without could live together in harmony.

She viewed herself as smart.

She learned she was actually a fool.

Kayl knew; he tried to explain this to Róisín but she didn't listen. She still recalled his wounded expression, his hand outstretched as he tried to touch her shoulder and get her to stop and listen, but she spun away with her pack of clothing as she readied to leave with the crown prince.

It was the last time she saw Kayl. She left him standing there, his brow wrinkled with unspoken rage and his eyes filled with unshed tears. He hadn't come out of the orphanage as she handed her pack over to a carrier and stepped into the carriage. She looked for his face in the crowd of well-wishers, hoping to see him one last time, but he wasn't there. He always was softer than her, more prone to strong emotions, and she comforted him when he was lost to his feelings, but not that time. And in his disappearance, she felt the first true wedge between them that grew with each passing second and every traveled mile.

She left with Prince Cearny, her fae ancestry hidden, and she lied through her teeth to get in his bed. Oh, she was glad to be gone from that town. She convinced herself as much. She dropped her small-town dreams like petals: no longer did she yearn to see the eastern sea (she dreamt of it regularly), no longer did she enjoy baking since she had her own fleet of castle cooks (she often would visit the kitchens and watch them at work, craving to step in and help); everything was perfect and all she dreamt of! Of course, this was what she wanted. Of course.

She finally felt a sense of control and power to be in the monster's lair and make progress on her plans. That, at least, was a true feeling amidst her falsehoods. She lied to Cearny, declaring her hometown could provide so little for her. She lied that she always yearned to be rescued. She wanted to see more of the world, this was true, but leaving the town wasn't a rescue. It was a means to a specific end. Still, the lies came. She repeatedly mentioned how kind he was to provide a way for her escape. She told Cearny he saved her, and he listened with hungry attention. Only those who loved themselves a little too much had this type of hunger, and she fed him compliments by the spoonful to satiate his appetite. Once he seemed completely in her grasp, she slipped in the dialogue that she hoped would bring freedom to Caermythlin.

Did he know magic could give him a streak of luck on the battlefield?

Did he know magic could relieve him of his tooth ache?

How about the stories of the magical creatures of the land, that they could perhaps stand by his side and for his cause?

But quickly, she realized she wasn't as clever as she thought. He didn't care about magic-made luck, his pride wouldn't allow that. He didn't wonder about the healing elements of magic. He wanted nothing to do with magical creatures. All in all, he grew bored of such discussion.

As soon as they were wed, it wasn't just boredom but aggressive hatred when she attempted to bring up magic.

"I endured your chatter about this before," he snarled, snatching his hand from hers only days after they married beneath the Elder Tree. "I won't permit it anymore. Keep talk of those wicked creatures and selfish practices out of my home."

And when she attempted to bring up magic again, foolishly in front of King Donal who always seemed enraptured by Róisín and quick to agree with her, it was Donal who told Cearny to beat such talk from her. A lifetime later and delicate scars from the leather strap still lined her back.

She lost.

Kayl was right; she was nothing to them. Nothing until she became pregnant after multiple failed attempts to perform her queenly duty. For nine blissful months she was protected. For nine months Donal made sure Cearny stayed in line and catered to Róisín. For nine months she thought, perhaps, she had a second chance to appeal to Cearny's nature, and then she had Greer.

Greer, her fierce-eyed little girl who wasn't the boy Cearny desired but would be raised to take the throne all the same. Greer, who took half of Róisín's heart with her when she was birthed into the world.

After the birth, Cearny no longer doted after Róisín. She served her purpose by providing him an heir, so he left her alone. Róisín didn't quite care. Her focus was on her daughter, and she knew anything that upset Cearny could put her own life in danger and a child needed her mother, whether or not she was trained to rule a land.

After Greer was born, Donal also seemed to change. He became fiercer and crueler.

"Move aside," he growled at Etta one morning.

Róisín was feeding Greer against everyone's wishes. They had wet nurses for that, didn't she understand? But it was one aspect she was determined to maintain herself. She held the small babe against her chest, her finger held out, gripped tightly by the small infant's hand whilst she drank. Róisín felt her insides tug downward and heal with each sip and she marveled at the simple magic of the human body. Donal's sudden appearance pulled her from that revelry and left her blinking with confusion.

Although Etta was hired for the specific task of being a nursemaid, she became a stand-in mother of sorts, helping Róisín learn the ins and outs of reading a baby's cues and taking care of her own healing body. Etta guided Róisín through the process, giving quiet commentary of how to bring down the flow of milk, ways to position Greer, and how to trigger the best burps. Róisín loved Etta for it, and found she was finally, at last, happy.

That was the first strike as Donal walked in: Róisín wasn't using the servants as they were meant to be used and doing a low-ranking activity like feeding one's child. His lip curled as he stared down at them.

"Put the babe on your bed, I need to inspect her."

Róisín felt her stomach drop. Anyone with less training, with less control, would appear distressed. But she held it together, looking emotionless as she pulled Greer from her breast and laid her down. Unsatisfied to be taken from her meal, Greer immediately began to fuss, her face turning pink as her cries made Róisín's breasts leak.

Donal leaned over the baby and pulled at her limbs while roughly searching her body over.

"Your majesty, that could hurt the babe," Etta attempted but Donal's glare silenced her.

"Is there something you're looking for?" Róisín asked, her voice light and sweet as she closed the front of her dress.

Donal lifted his face, his brow risen, and he paused his movements as if for emphasis. As if the answer was so clear. "Fae marks."

"Oh." Róisín remained in her chair, frozen, unable to move as she watched the man handle her daughter. There was no such thing as fae marks, other than wings or pointed ears—neither of which Greer possessed—but that didn't stop the threat Donal presented. He didn't know of Róisín's ancestry. She wore her glamor to cover the points of her ears and never spoke of her mother beyond that she died when Róisín was young. Yet, Donal suspected.

When Greer was three months old, Donal no longer suspected, he knew. Etta rushed into Róisín's room one night in a panic. While Etta was still Greer's nursemaid by title, she was so much more to Róisín: a pair of eyes to let Róisín know of anything amiss.

"There's a prisoner," Etta whispered. "Some older woman from Caermythlin. She was caught on the roads to Sage Hill trying to poison the king's guards. They brought her here for questioning and they've done awful things to her. But in doing so, she called for you, begged for your aid. She asked why the king hates magic makers so much when the future queen is herself part-fae."

Etta's words faded from existence, the world turned into a blurry tunnel and Róisín's heart hammered in her throat. She waited for retaliation, for the king's guards to collect her and throw her into jail, but nothing happened. He stared at her over family meals as if to taunt her to place a toe out of line. This simply would not do. She tossed aside any hope of convincing Donal and Cearny of magic's wonderful uses. She had to go another route and do so quickly before Donal decided he actually wanted to act on his information.

When the king suddenly fell ill, Róisín was the picture of perfection. She attended the king's bedside, pushing the healers from the room so she could bathe the king and ensure he retained his pride. She spoon fed him soup, urging his silence so he maintained his strength. His voice was gone, as was his mobility, and all that remained was a knowing look in his eyes as he glared at Róisín, forced to obey her commands, a puppet that she created.

Cearny was oblivious. He was glad Róisín showed such grace in caring for his dying father. He was never there when Donal was awake; had he seen the look in Donal's eyes he would've known. But each time he had availability in his busy schedule to visit his father, he arrived to find Róisín sitting beside his bed.

"Oh, he's just fallen asleep," Róisín would say with a sigh, running her hands over the quilt that kept Donal warm. "He wakes for such brief periods now."

When Donal finally succumbed to whatever illness he had, the entire city looked to the new king, but during Donal's funeral, their eyes fell on their queen. The city was in a tizzy, all discussing how beautiful Róisín was as she sat with her back straight in the carriage behind the one bearing Donal's body. Her tears fell silently, her gaze straight forward, and many of the citizens who hadn't cried over the loss of the king, couldn't help but weep when they saw her outward display of sadness.

They didn't know that she wept because if she had the chance, she would have killed Cearny too. But Greer was only a toddler, far too young to have the crown thrust upon her. She had to wait, she had to bide her time until Greer was old enough to rule.

With Donal out of the way, they lived as a family of three in tense silence. Róisín behaved, not wanting to threaten her or Greer's safety, and life continued. Despite tension between herself and Cearny, he still found use for her. But once he impregnated her again, providing the expected spare to his dynasty, he stopped touching her. Róisín was fine with that.

Now things had changed and his words released fear in Róisín's soul. Was ten too young to become queen? Probably. But the threat on Caitriona had Róisín frightened, so she resorted to her old ways that she kept carefully hidden since Cearny became king. Greer would still have her mother and Caitriona would have her life if Cearny happened to lose his. Róisín would raise both girls to grow compassion towards magic makers and creatures alike, she would change the course of the kingdom. She was too late to save Caermythlin, but perhaps she could save other towns like her own.

In the bustling kitchen which was separate from the main halls of the castle, a busy place with rich scents of various foods being prepared, Róisín watched the chaotic dance of meal preparation before forcing everyone to leave.

"I want to prepare the king a treat to celebrate his great and successful conquest over the dragon," Róisín announced with a kind smile as she waved the cooks out. "How many kings can say they've killed a dragon? Not many anymore, that's for certain. He has all he needs in the world, but I hope my baking skills will suffice nonetheless."

She reached forward, stopping a young cook who just began working the kitchens from leaving. "Would you mind keeping an eye at the door? I wouldn't want the king's surprise ruined. I'll be sure to mention how much of a help you were to your superiors when I'm through."

With the girl watching the door, Róisín worked quickly to make the meat pies Cearny so loved. Rich with sausages, apples and herbs, the heavy flavors masked the addition of the poisonous flowers she cooked within. When she was courting Cearny, she made these pies—without the flowers, but Róisín hadn't cooked since becoming queen. These meat pies were perhaps the loveliest she ever made.

"You aren't permitted to cook in here," a gravelly voice announced from the doorway as Róisín plated the pie. "You're putting off dinner for the entire castle."

Róisín turned, eyes wide and a smile plastered on her face. The girl stood beside the king looking sheepish and pale, her gaze lowered and head hanging down. She could only imagine what Cearny said to her when the poor thing tried to stop him from entering. "Oh, Cearny, what a pleasant surprise and just in time. I made you a gift."

Cearny raised a golden brow and stepped forward, sniffing the air like a dog and running a hand over his stomach. "Meat pies?"

"Your favorite." Róisín smiled as she lifted the plate and held it out. "I wanted to treat you since you've unveiled the dragon's head. It's such a testament to your strength as a leader. I know that a meat pie is very little to show my pride, but I hope you'll enjoy it all the same."

Cearny breathed in the scent, his eyes sparkling and Róisín felt the tightness in her spine relax. He reminded her of the pigs in Caermythlin when they caught the scent of their dinner, their noses wet and their eyes eager for the slop. He lifted his gaze, meeting her own directly, and smiled as he took the plate into his hands.

"Girl? Kitchen girl?" he called without turning, his gaze unmoving from Róisín. The hungry, foolish look he often wore faded into something more poisonous. Like a viper waiting in the grass. The girl started where she stood in the doorway and rushed forward, keeping her eyes low even as she stepped beside the king.

"Yes, my king?" she whispered.

"I want you to eat this pie."

Róisín's smile froze on her face, everything about her becoming a mask as she attempted not to give herself away. The girl cautiously stepped forward, confused by the request. Cearny looked at her, his voice coming out as a scream despite that she stood only a foot away. "*Eat the pie!*"

She made quick work whilst Cearny continued studying Róisín and Róisín held unflinching eye contact with him.

"It's quite delicious, my queen," the girl whispered. Bits of crumbs covered her lips which she wiped clean with the back of her hand. A small burp escaped after she ate half. "I am quite full."

"You'll eat the entire thing," Cearny demanded, his gaze unshaking as a smile slowly spread over his face. Róisín's began to fade as she stared at it; his yellowed, crooked teeth became closer to a snarl by the minute.

And the girl, the poor girl who only just began in the kitchens; the girl who so happily obeyed Róisín's request, continued to eat until the pie was gone. The foam didn't take long to begin falling from her mouth and choking her airways. Róisín didn't move as the girl stumbled forward, a hand desperately reaching for Róisín, seeking help that wouldn't come. She gurgled, a pathetic sound that nearly undid Róisín's mask before collapsing between the king and queen.

"I know your tricks, *witch*," Cearny hissed, taking one step forward, his foot falling onto the girl's body. He was close enough that the scent of his spoiled breath filled Róisín's lungs. "I know you were behind my father's death. You thought you covered your tracks but you aren't that smart; I have eyes everywhere."

Róisín remained silent, her lips pressed together to prevent herself from saying anything to ruin her further.

Cearny leaned closer, the last of the kitchen girl's dying breath pressing out of her lungs in a hush under the weight of his boot. "Bake me something again and I'll feed it to Caitriona while you watch. Do anything else out of line, and I'll have her killed."

He stepped back and dropped the empty tray onto the body of the girl, leaving a trail of crumbs over her still breast and speckling the foam that clung to her lips. He let out a short breath, something like a laugh before leaving Róisín with the mess she created.

CHAPTER SEVENTEEN

A̧ɪʟɪᴛʜ

At a distance, the small town appeared quiet, peaceful, and Ailith immediately felt out of place. Everything seemed clean and tidy, and she was filthy with sweat from the multiple encounters with various creatures of the Northern Wood. Ailith's arms were marked with scratches and healing scabs, her hair slick from days of not washing, and her nails crusted with dirt. Compared to the manicured gardens and white stone paths surrounding them, she was a smear. Maybe they had a bath house.

"Perhaps we take our potions again?" Caitriona looked at Ailith with unease. While substantially less injured than Ailith, Caitriona's hair was a mess and dirt smudged on her skin and clothes. Ailith pulled her pack off her shoulder, ready to fish the potion out, but Fiana stilled Ailith's hand.

"These are some of the most powerful magic makers in the entire world. They'll see right through your potions. Save it for later."

Fiana stepped forward with Ceenear and Raum following closely.

"Here we go," Caitriona whispered as she took Ailith's hand. They moved towards Ätbënas with hope.

"Do either of you know what he looks like?" Ailith asked. They wandered down the main path of the town with the oppression of silence making them speak quietly, as if in a place of worship. It was silent, not a soul in sight, but the markings of people were present by the wisps of wood smoke coming from chimneys, the scent of cooked fish, and a soft singing echoing from further within. "How are we going to know when we find him?"

"We can ask," Ceenear said with a smile. Now back in a place full of magic makers and not being actively arrested at the same time, Ceenear relaxed. Her quiet, observant personality returned. "But if he's anything like his mother, he may have red hair. Tall and thin. She had the most sparkling eyes I've seen of anyone. As if her magic was so great, universes were created in her gaze."

"I'm sorry." Ailith reached for Ceenear's shoulder and Raum's arm. "You both lost your queen and she sounds like someone who you could miss."

Toward Ätbënas's edge where buildings tapered off and the land separated to allow view of the sea, an amphitheater faced the water. Rows of empty seats faced the shore and along it, a group sang to the tides in robes the color of the landscape. Grays like the stones and waters whose chill took life before drowning could, whites and tans like the sand Ailith and Caitriona danced upon in Stormhaven, and dark greens like the shadows in the Northern Wood with its creatures within. They lingered in the back, waiting for the singing to end.

It was in a language similar to what Ailith heard when she visited the fae, but the meaning felt obvious in the song. It reminded her briefly of what Barden and his family sang when they buried Shaw. Another language she didn't know, but the meaning was still painful. Bringing to life emotions most brushed aside, unwilling to encounter because of the discomfort it brought. The lyrics were mournful, heavy with tears not yet shed.

"They're singing about someone who died," Ailith whispered.

Raum looked down at Ailith. "How did you know?"

She shook her head and gestured toward the people. "Isn't it obvious? It's so sad and final."

The crowd of people listening to those singing was vastly uneven.

Anytime she saw some type of performance—granted most were done by Cearny as he put on a display of killing magic creatures—the audience outnumbered the performers. But this time it was the opposite. Five figures in the audience, besides her party, compared to the thirty or so singers.

"I think that's him." Ailith pointed to the center of the attendees. A figure in green, bookended by four figures in gray robes.

Raum shifted closer to her. "Go on ..."

"They're singing something mournful to that group. But look at the person in the middle, he's slouched. He's not sitting upright. His head keeps bowing forward, as if he's lowering his gaze. His hands keep moving to his face. He's upset."

"The song is about death," Ceenear softly said. "About someone who died and it's their prayer that their magic, their energy is released to the world and left to pass through all."

Caitriona sunk onto an empty seat. "It has to be Lachlan."

They waited for the singing to end while waves crashed along the shore, taking the lyrics of the song as the sea dragged back out. When they silenced, the spell relinquished. People began moving, figures greeted one another before exiting, but all paused before the person in green.

"I suppose we should try and speak to him," Caitriona said, her fingers fidgeting with her hair nervously.

"Better now than never." Fiana took a seat in the back of the amphitheater and put her feet onto the row before her. "Remember, you pay me by the day."

Caitriona straightened her shirt and brushed her braid behind her back, her expression determined as she turned away. She moved past robed figures down the main aisle with determined steps. They drifted out of the area, a few glancing at Caitriona as she walked by, but didn't show any clear interest. Ailith jumped to her feet and stepped over Fiana's extended legs to catch up.

"Excuse me," Caitriona called, her voice soft and shy as she reached the figure in green as Ailith came up behind her. "Hello there. I'm sorry to bother you, but I've come quite a long way and I'm looking for someone."

The green-robed figure turned and Ailith knew the moment she saw him it was Lachlan. His eyes were a whirlpool of every shade in the ocean and sky, at all points of the day, all colors at once yet separate. His hair had red but was closer to blond. He was tall, thin, and his face clean of any hair and pink around his bloodshot eyes.

"Are you Lachlan?"

The man looked from her to Ailith. "I ... I'm sorry, who are you?"

Caitriona smiled. "I'm Caitriona, but you can just call me Cait."

ÄTBËNAS EXISTED AS A FULLY SELF-SUFFICIENT TOWN. WHILE settled within the Mazgate Dominion, it had no ties to any king or steward. It was a town of peace and magic, where those most powerful worked to hone their gifts or taught others how to work their own. Lachlan had been at Ätbënas since he was a babe, at first for protection after Queen Onora married Malcolm, but then because of the explosive talent he inherited from her.

While Lachlan was befuddled upon Caitriona's appearance, he was welcoming, as was the rest of the community. It wasn't uncommon for a few people to travel through seeking help or guidance from the fae elders of the community, and children excelling in magic regularly joined the community to hone their talents. Despite it being a hidden town, word leaked out to those who needed it most and a few small homes were kept near the waters specifically for visitors, and they were quickly offered one to fit them all.

"Thank you for agreeing to speak with us," Caitriona said as they entered the guest house with Lachlan following close behind and an elder dressed in gray coming along as well. Everyone spread into the living room, dropping their packs to the ground before turning. All eyes were on the destined king.

"If you're coming to announce my mother's death," Lachlan began, his voice soft and quiet. The elder placed a hand on Lachlan's shoulder. "I already know. That—that's what you walked in on. It was a ceremony singing her soul to rest."

"Your mother was wonderful," Ceenear began, her gray eyes passionate and sincere. "We're so greatly sorry for her loss. She has so many mourning her departure."

"You knew her?" Lachlan asked. The party collectively paused before looking at one another. The elder's lips pressed together.

"I mean ... she ..." Ceenear began to stutter.

Raum shook his head and lowered into a chair. "She was our *queen*."

Lachlan blinked. Slowly, he studied them with obvious confusion. His softness and quiet manners reminded Ailith of Caitriona and she could feel herself soften to him.

"Lachlan," Caitriona began. "Do you know who your mother was?"

Lachlan stepped back, his hand running over his chin before dropping. "She brought me here when I was young and visited a few times when I was a child. In recent years it's been harder. We've spoken through speaking stones and the occasional letter, but it's been more infrequent. I knew she had enemies and wanted to keep me distant and separate from her life. But she never told me much. She only ever asked me about my own. She wanted me here to hone my skills with magic. I never knew ..."

The room fell quiet again. Ceenear and Raum looked to Caitriona who gave a small shrug.

"I think you should begin," she said softly, stepping away and taking a seat beside Ailith.

"Your mother ..." Raum began only to pause. "Actually, you should take a seat."

Lachlan's eyes widened.

"Listen to him, Lachlan," the elder said, his voice deep. Lachlan turned, accepting the empty seat next to Ailith. His robes smelt of pine and cedar as he settled beside her.

"Your mother was from Invarlwen. You've heard of it?" Raum started and after Lachlan's nod, continued. "Well, she was the queen there until her death—which we're greatly sorry for. She was a kind, fair ruler and Invarlwen never saw blood or harm while she was on the throne. She wasn't meant to rule; her brother was king first. That's when you were born, during his reign. From what we've been told, you lived with her until her brother decided she would wed Malcolm from

Norkasserf, beyond the sea. Upon the declaration of her marriage, you disappeared. No one knew where you went beside a few of her closest confidants."

Lachlan leaned back; his face filled with doubt.

"As much as I want to say this isn't true, for your safety," the elder cut in, drawing Lachlan's attentive gaze to him, "what they're saying *is* true. Your mother is—was—queen."

Raum nodded before continuing, "The king died shortly after your mother wed Malcolm. And now, years later, we've lost her as well. Malcolm and your mother had a son, Shad, and the two men declared Invarlwen theirs to rule.

"Niveem of Ulla Syrmin respected your mother greatly. She oversaw one of the mountain peaks of Invarlwen. When your mother passed, she admitted you were taken here to Ätbënas for your learning and safety. Your location wasn't known by Malcolm because of his behavior. He's always been a greedy bastard, ruthless and cruel. Rumor has it his son is just the same, if not worse. Many wonder if he's Onora's child because he's received nothing of your mother. No kindness, no gentleness, just hardness and bloodlust. So, it's with particular concern that when Malcolm claimed himself king and Shad his heir, he also declared war upon Wimleigh Queendom."

"Wimleigh Queendom, despite the past two generations, has turned a new leaf," Caitriona said as she leaned forward to look Lachlan directly in his eyes. "Two rulers outlawed magic. They ostracized those with it and murdered the rest. But there's a new ruler, Queen Greer, and she's tossed aside all their hateful rhetoric. She's trying to lead the queendom to a new age where magic users and those without can live in respected harmony rather than viewing each other as a threat."

"Malcolm declared the war upon Wimleigh Queendom to wipe out any existence of the royal line and to rid the queendom of people without magic," Ceenear added. "He's only continuing the misunderstanding but from a new perspective. We fear such a war will bring destruction to many more than just the two lands. We hope to stop it."

"And you've all come here for ... what?" Lachlan asked. "I've no use for battles and wars. My only ties to Invarlwen are gone. Why have you come to me with all of this?"

"Because you're the rightful king," Ceenear explained. Lachlan leaned back into his seat as if strength was depleting.

"And because my sister wants to ensure you're placed upon the throne," Caitriona added, drawing Lachlan's gaze to her. She smiled weakly and lowered her gaze. "My sister's Queen Greer. I've come on her behalf to see if you're willing to help."

Lachlan stared at her before shifting in his chair, his hand brushing over his chin again then moving through his strawberry blond hair. He glanced at the elder whose expression remained stoic. The older fae would provide no guidance on this but waited for Lachlan's response. Lachlan returned his attention to the group.

"I appreciate your effort and am honored by your presence, princess," he began, "but my answer is no."

AILITH FINGERED THE SELECTION OF ARROWS IN ÄTBËNAS'S little shop. While Ätbënas made the majority of their own supplies and grew their own food, they made a little money selling merchandise to travelers before they descended back into the Northern Wood. Fiana stood beside her, eyeing the arrow Ailith looked at. It was coated in an elixir that would cause it to explode with fire upon hitting a mark.

"What do you think they'll do now?" Fiana wondered aloud, drawing Ailith's attention. The shopkeeper behind the counter placed more arrows into the holder as another person entered. The shopkeeper drifted away to talk to the newcomer and Fiana turned fully to Ailith.

"Since Lachlan said he won't help?" Ailith asked, placing the arrow back in its holder and turned to prepared potions.

Fiana nodded.

"I don't know. I imagine they're figuring it out now. Cait said she was going to message Greer to let her know Lachlan doesn't want to go, but I don't know if they've given up hope yet."

"What do you think Queen Greer is going to do without Lachlan?"

Fiana leaned her hip against the display. Behind her, the shopkeeper left and another took their place behind the counter. A shift change, Ailith assumed. Fiana continued, "From what I heard back there, you all hoped to put Lachlan on the fae throne and, I don't know, make some type of a lasting tie with the kingdom. What's she going to do without him?"

Ailith swallowed, she thought of her family; she thought of Barden and all his patient, careful lessons. She considered Barden's father, what little interaction she had with Shaw, and how he would be the first to defend Wimleigh Queendom. In the end, no matter the politics, it was their home and they would fight to save it, and Ailith knew she would too. Even if it was a losing battle—the power of magic was too much. "We fight back and hope Greer and Wimleigh Queendom survive."

Fiana studied Ailith for a moment before giving a nod and stepping away from the display. "I'd say you're a fool, that you won't win against a bunch of powerful magic-making fae, but I can see you already realize that."

Ailith sighed. Fiana clapped her hand on Ailith's shoulder, giving it a squeeze. "I'll see you back at the guest house."

Alone now, beside the shopkeeper, Ailith relaxed her shoulders and raised her wrist to her lips, biting casually at the cuff of her sleeve as she lifted a vial and studied the inscription on the paper tied to the neck. *A potion for protection, good for a day.* Perhaps she could buy enough for the entire group to make it through the woods towards home.

"Miss?" the shopkeeper called. "Miss? Can I help you with anything?"

Ailith shook her head, placing the potion back on the counter. Everyone else could handle themselves in the woods, *she* was the problem. The creatures were attracted to *her*. Her lack of power was so painful in that moment, doubled by the disappointment of Lachlan's answer, she couldn't help but foresee the future battle ending in blood and loss primarily on their side.

"You look like you're searching for hope," the shopkeeper continued. Ailith offered the person a smile. He was a boy, just old enough to join the guard if they were in Braewick.

"I suppose I am."

The boy looked out the doorway conspiratorially before returning his gaze to Ailith. He was shorter than her with large gray eyes and dark hair, his ears funny and jagged as if the tops were scarred.

"We have items, you know," he began with a whisper. "Special things we keep behind the counter. They're expensive but they might help you."

Ailith stepped closer and glanced out the door as well. People of Ätbënas were busy in the streets now, a stark contrast to when they arrived. Everyone had a role and rotated through their assigned tasks through the day amongst the practice of their magical gifts, but none seemed interested in the shop.

"What are these special items?" Ailith asked, half to encourage the boy and half out of curiosity.

The boy smiled and reached behind the counter, pulling free a plate with three pieces of jewelry on it. A gold ring with a red stone, a gold bracelet with black stones inlaid, and a gold necklace with a green stone hanging from it.

"Oh, those are pretty." Ailith smiled.

The boy grinned. "They all have magical properties. The ring is for wealth, the bracelet for finding love, and the necklace for protection."

Ailith leaned forward, pretending to inspect all the pieces but particularly interested in the necklace. Protection was what she needed, if only to not be hurt so easily by the creatures that attacked. "How much are these?"

"One hundred gold each," the boy replied seriously. Ailith grimaced, putting on a show. She knew full well a necklace typically cost more than a hundred gold, but who was she to tell them?

"You know, I'd like that necklace," Ailith responded. "And three of the arrows that catch fire."

The child grinned and before Ailith pulled out her coin purse, he dropped the necklace into her palm. "Certainly. Would you like to wear the necklace now?"

The gold felt unnaturally light, and yet weighted and tingling in her hand, as if abuzz with magic. She was never one for jewelry, but she couldn't help but put the jewelry on right away and tuck it under her shirt. "Should I feel anything?"

The boy grinned.

"Oh, no, it doesn't work like that," he replied. "But you'll find protection where you previously did not."

Ailith thanked him and turned to leave; not recalling she requested the arrows nor that she hadn't paid. But the boy let her go with a self-satisfied smirk before receding into the shadows where he came.

CHAPTER EIGHTEEN

Caitriona

Already the morning sun held heat, but the northern sea blew in a constant coolness that combated the sun's attempt to scorch. Lachlan stood at the river's edge where the fae elder who confirmed his ancestry pointed him out.

"I completely understand your hesitancy," Caitriona attempted. "I've no experience in fighting and while I've begun training, I doubt I'm suitable for war. We aren't expecting you to battle either. We only want to have you on our side, to hopefully convince some of the people of Invarlwen to abandon Malcolm's plans and side with us so when we win, you can take your rightful place as king."

Lachlan shook his head. He wasn't wearing the green robe he wore the day before, but gray pants and a simple linen shirt. He appeared at ease, if a little sad, and Caitriona hoped meeting him in such a pleasant environment would soften him to her explanation, but he wasn't having it.

"I know how to fight," Lachlan replied. "We train here. Not just with magic but fighting with arms. So that isn't the problem necessarily ... well I suppose it is. I've never taken a life before and I don't particularly have any desire to start."

"Very few people who are thrust into war have the desire to take lives," Caitriona continued. "But we're fighting a man who *does* want to do that. He wants to take lives and make people suffer."

"Like you've suffered?" Lachlan asked. Caitriona leaned back and Lachlan immediately blushed. "I'm sorry, I don't say that accusingly. I meant it as a point. I've heard of you and your story; a princess cursed to become a dragon and attack her own home. That she was left with permanent scars."

Caitriona stepped before Lachlan.

"A man like Malcolm did this to me," she whispered, tears threatening to fall from her golden eyes. She never spoke about the curse so plainly. "He was made into that man because of my father. My father was a man like Malcolm. He made so many people suffer, so many people die, all because of fear and greed. It's the same thing with Malcolm but you, Lachlan, you can help us stop this. You can help end this cycle."

Lachlan's lips parted, his head shook and Caitriona knew it was pointless.

"I'm sorry," he repeated. "I'm sorry I just ... I can't. I'm not a prince. I'm not a king. I'm Lachlan. I study magic, I can turn into an eagle, I like to sing, and I care for the children most mornings. But I'm nothing big, nothing threatening. I wasn't raised to rule a kingdom as I assume your sister was. I can't turn into a dragon like you."

"I can't turn into a dragon," Caitriona whispered. "At least ... well, I don't know. I haven't tried. I'm afraid to."

Turning from Lachlan, Caitriona stepped to the riverside and pushed a small rock into the water with her toe. A ripple formed but quickly disappeared from the force of moving water. The gravel stirred behind her under Lachlan's footfall as he approached to stand beside her.

"I'm sorry," he repeated as he overlooked the water rushing toward the sea. "Your sister sounds like a good ruler. Like she has everything in focus and will protect her people at all costs."

"She is. She's a wonderful ruler. And she'd guide you, she'd teach you, but she wouldn't force your hand in anything. She wouldn't pressure you."

"She sounds ... wonderful." Lachlan's voice was sad, and Caitriona wanted to snap at him. What right did he have to be sad? He was dooming them all. But she immediately chastised herself for her anger. She understood Lachlan probably better than anyone else, because she was also hidden away for most of her life. She also didn't want to wield her power. Greer understood that about Caitriona, and she would about Lachlan too. He only needed to see that.

"You'd like Greer if you met her," Caitriona sighed. "But there's no convincing you, is there?"

Lachlan looked down at Caitriona, offering a half smile filled with sorrow. "I'm sorry, princess, but no. My place is here."

There wasn't much that could make Caitriona's mood worse. They left a few hours later, diving back into the torturous woods with growls and hisses lingering in the darkened shade. All seemed relatively glum. Caitriona used Ceenear's speaking stone to convey the news of Lachlan's refusal to Isla. Raum attempted to contact Lumia again to no avail and while he strived to remain cheerful, between laughter and smiles Caitriona saw his brow furrow with worry. It was weeks since he last spoke to Lumia and the weight of the silence was obviously hanging over him.

Ailith and Fiana were the only two who seemed bright with energy as they led the charge through the ferns.

"It'll be fine, Cait," Ailith said as they settled for their evening meal in a small clearing with the sky a fading blue above. "We'll figure this out and beat Malcolm."

"I hope you're right." Caitriona plopped down glumly onto her sleeping mat and hugged her knees to her chest. "I didn't realize how hopeful I was for Lachlan's help until he said he wouldn't give it to us."

Ailith eased to the ground beside her, pushing her shoulder into Caitriona's and kissing her cheek.

"Don't worry about it," Ailith continued. "What's the point of worrying right now? Things could change. Let's just make it back to Braewick."

A chattering of teeth interrupted them and the group froze. Fiana stood with her bag of salt, halfway through circling the camp.

"Shades," she stated. Everyone reached for their blades as a scent of rotten leaves consumed the space.

The shades snapped, separating into shadow before materializing within the half-formed circle and Ailith let out a cry of rage. Caitriona spun on her heel as she gathered fire in her hands born from thought and the energy within her. She prepared to launch it at the shades, but Ailith stabbed her sword into the beast, making it screech in pain before it collapsed into rotten meat, matted hair and bitter ooze. Kicking at the corpse to pull her sword free, she turned toward Caitriona and smiled.

"It's fine, I've got this."

Another shade rushed forward. Ailith twisted, Barden's blade swinging with the honed technique she achieved in the last year of constant training with the elder guard. It slashed through the shade's throat, the beast's head coming loose and falling to the side as its body crumbled to the ground.

Caitriona stared, the flames in her hands flickering out. Ailith truly gained skill since joining the royal guard. It was something she always had but needed guidance to perfect. Ailith turned from the body and moved onto the next shade Ceenear was fighting and killed it without hesitation, leaving Caitriona stunned. Ailith was emotionless, something that Caitriona didn't know Ailith as, and it left Caitriona frozen with her mouth gaping.

The remaining shades were disposed of by the others. An artful dance of blades and rotting carcass once moving and now still. Six total. Most went for Ailith directly and she killed them all except one Raum brought down.

"I'll be glad to never see this damned forest again," Raum growled as he cleaned his blade.

Fiana snorted and stuck her dagger back into its holster. "Are you saying you don't want to become a hunter?"

"Never!" Raum laughed. "Let me return to the mist. I prefer watching people get lost in it and going to save them."

Caitriona approached Ailith, a question on her tongue, ready to spill forth as Fiana and Raum joked further when the hum of the forest suddenly silenced. Fiana held out a hand and looked to the skies.

"I don't like that."

Caitriona looked around her, even the air seemed to have gone still. "Do you know what's going on?"

"Something big's coming," Fiana whispered and as if on demand, the trees began to breathe. Waves of air pushed over the forest floor followed by a sudden cry that made Caitriona go rigid.

She knew the scream, not due to her childhood, not from her death, but from her curse. She made the same sound from the bottom of her throat as it curled upward and spilled forth, with fire raining down upon the castle—her home.

"A dragon," Caitriona whispered.

Through the clearing, a gold dragon flew. The wind from its wings pressed the trees toward the earth and caused their limbs to snap and break. Leaves and twigs cascaded around them. The dragon roared again, vibrating the very earth, before another familiar sound grumbled in the depths of its throat—the churn of flame spilling forth from its mouth. Caitriona stumbled backward, keeping her eyes on the dragon through the canopy break. The spray of fire was directed to the northwest, far from them, but the scent of sulfur still reached the group.

"*Oh*," Caitriona murmured, her knees growing weak as she sunk to the ground. Her nails were thick claws and the scales on her shoulder spread down her arms. She squeezed her eyes closed. The dragon inside of her was wild.

Let me free, let me protect them, it begged. It felt like her entire body was threatened by the dragon's presence, like instinct was taking over and urged her to rise to the challenge the creature in the air possessed. Like dogs in the castle howling when they heard wolves in the valley hills.

Her very skin crawled. It itched, as if readying to split and stretch. Her tongue held fire, her throat filled with smoke, and a small moan escaped her lips when hands touched her shoulder. They moved upward to cup her face and Caitriona opened her eyes.

Ailith knelt before her, her brown eyes wide and her thumbs made circles upon Caitriona's cheeks.

"Change if you have to." Ailith's voice was quiet, but her tone was sincere. "I'll be here all the same. But know we're safe. The dragon didn't set fire to our area of the woods. We're okay."

The scent of burning wood leaking through the trees said otherwise, but it didn't increase and the flame couldn't be seen. Whatever it struck with its flame was far away from them.

The rush of wind from the dragon's wings eased off, the forest calmed, and sounds returned. Ailith remained before Caitriona, not looking anywhere else but at her face and Caitriona found herself locked in her human gaze as she reminded herself over and over she was human too.

No one moved, frozen in their places until evening birds sang again. The dragon never turned back; it never made another round overhead. Wherever it was headed, it wasn't to where they were, at least not at that moment.

"The fire isn't too close," Fiana stated as she looked into the darkening woods. She picked up her bag of salt and worked on the circle of protection again. Ailith kept her eyes locked on Caitriona's, her thumb still rubbing along Caitriona's cheek.

"We're okay," she whispered and at last, Caitriona felt herself relax. The itching of her skin receded and when she looked at her hands, she found her fingers normal and her nails short.

"We can still stay here?" Ceenear asked, her eyes still directed toward the sky.

Fiana shrugged. "We're just as likely to be attacked by a dragon if we move as we are if we stay."

Caitriona turned; her brow furrowed.

Please, let me fly. Let me ensure the dragon doesn't return.

Caitriona ignored it once more, burying it deep into her belly.

She wasn't a dragon.

She would *never* be a dragon again.

"Hey." Ailith's hands remained on Caitriona's. "Are you alright?"

"Oh, yes," Caitriona replied, returning to her senses with a dawning realization. Ailith seemed fine. The girl who still had nightmares during thunderstorms because they reminded her of the dragon attack had one fly overhead and she comforted *Caitriona*, completely unaffected by what should have triggered her anxiety. "Are you?"

Ailith looked at the sky and dropped her hands to her lap. Caitriona's cheeks felt cold from the loss of Ailith's touch.

"I've seen better dragons than that one," she teased, knocking her shoulder into Caitriona's. "But really, I'm okay. We're safe, that's all that matters."

They bedded down for the night and Fiana willingly allowed Ailith to take first watch. As everyone fell to sleep, Caitriona found herself still awake. Rolling to her side, she looked at the back of the guard. Ailith sat on the ground with her bow in hand, scanning the forest quietly.

"You know," she said softly, not bothering to turn toward Caitriona. "I packed extra clothing in my bag for you."

This drew Caitriona from her mat. She wrapped her summer cloak around her shoulders and curled her feet beneath her. "Extra for me?"

Ailith twisted to meet Caitriona's gaze. "In case you ever need to change into your dragon self. I brought extra clothing so you have something to put on when you change back. Just ... just so you know. I didn't like keeping that from you."

She didn't know how to feel. Slightly irritated, a little embarrassed, but also comforted.

"Thank you, Ailith," Caitriona whispered with a small, secretive smile. She'd never need the clothing. She'd fight the dragon back like she did hours before, but the effort Ailith put into caring for Caitriona shone through all the same.

"Go to sleep, princess," Ailith said. She smiled and for a moment Caitriona was back on the valley ridge, the first night of their traveling two years prior, a memory etched in her mind for eternity. Caitriona's smile broadened.

Closing her eyes to the world, the scent of wood smoke still in the air and her core warm from the proximity of the beast resting within her, she found herself slipping into a dream where she took to the skies and flew as a dragon once more.

CHAPTER NINETEEN

Greer

Royal guards bordered the edge of the wood surrounding the Elder Tree. They circled the great expanse of the canopy cover to ensure privacy and safety for Greer as she arrived at the tree's base. Barden stood beside her, his hand on the hilt of his sword as he gazed over the lush landscape around them.

"So, it *is* damaged." Greer knelt to the ground; her knees pressed into the moist earth while she ran her fingers over the roots. The thick, gnarled wood stood the test of time, but it seemed it was no match for the quake.

The trunk was so large, it would take a handful of adults to encircle it entirely, fingertip to fingertip, and yet it now stood all the broader as a deep crack split the tree at its center. The break began at its base, beneath the dirt before spreading upward. From the crack, wide enough an adult could squeeze through, a reddish-brown sap dripped. Greer leaned back on her heels and rested her elbows on her knees.

"I don't know how we can fix this. Tie the tree together and hope it closes the crack? I wonder if this type of break will kill the tree." Greer let out a gush of air tinged with stress. "That's the last thing we need. People will riot if the tree is dying."

"Perhaps the fruit growers will know," Barden murmured, his back to her as he scanned the woods.

It was risky being beyond the castle walls. Isla, Maeve—whatever her name was—continued trying to contact her friends in Ulla Syrmin with no success and from what she could scry, it appeared King Malcolm was gathering supporters for his cause with rapid success. Sitting in the forest outside the castle walls was dangerous, but with citizens enraged over the quakes and blaming it entirely on magic, Greer was desperate to do something her citizens would find joy in. Something to raise their hopes.

When reports came that the beloved Elder Tree was damaged, she felt like they were truly facing an uphill battle. The tree was a symbol of peace and hope since it was the maker of all life that existed in the world. But it faced its share of threats frequently in the last few years. First when Caitriona's dragon form crashed into it and broke a part off, and now this. Greer gathered guards so she could see the tree herself. She didn't want to rely on messengers and simple reports.

Barden remained quiet beside her; eyes scanning for threats despite additional guards standing further off and out of sight. Other than his occasional commentary or replies to Greer, he wasn't talkative. He hadn't been since Greer collapsed on the parapet walk with another spell of panic as the death bringers swarmed the city. Other guards came to her rescue, finding her before Barden had a chance. He had been trapped by the hustle of injured people and guards aiding them beneath the curtain wall; by the time he reached Greer, she was coming out of the spell. Sweaty, exhausted, and embarrassed. He was distant and cool ever since.

Now at the quiet of the tree, its lofty branches being something that brought peace to many—including Greer—his quiet became a solid thing. A mass expanding over the forest and weighing down on Greer's brain. There were many unspoken words filling the air, words that were Barden's and she only needed him to speak but his silence persisted.

It drove Greer insane.

"I'm sorry, Barden," Greer blurted. The guard startled and turned on his heel, looking at her with confusion. As if he didn't understand, as if he didn't know.

"What are you talking about?"

Greer shook her head as she climbed to her feet. She hated the burn of embarrassment and misunderstanding. She hated her behavior and her expression of emotion. But bravery came in many forms and facing their strange interaction was nothing but brave. "I feel like I've done something wrong. You've been distant since the quake."

"The quake was two days ago."

"Three," Greer corrected. Barden's lips pressed into a line.

Greer dropped her head back, the Elder Tree's branches spread overhead and she wished for aid. "I know. There's just ... I've felt there's been a shift with you. A shift between *us*. I fear I've upset you."

She looked at Barden and for a moment, felt her fears confirmed as his brow wrinkled and his expression grew serious. He shook his head and stepped closer.

"Greer, you nearly fainted outside the gatehouse. I was stuck down there with those screaming idiots and those damned birds, and I couldn't get to you in time. It scared me, is all. I just ..."

He let out a puff of air and stepped back, turning toward the rest of the small forest again. Greer moved after him and reached for his arm; the solid muscle of his bicep met her fingers.

"I'm fine though. Completely recovered. And you were doing what you needed to for the people."

"I *see* you're fine, we're here, aren't we?" Barden snapped and immediately squeezed his eyes closed. His fingers rose to pinch the bridge of his nose. "I'm sorry. I'm out of line and shouldn't give you such a tone. Forgive me."

Greer studied him silently for a moment. Not allowing him the reassurance of a quick answer.

"Barden, what's going on?"

His tongue darted over his lower lip, and his blue eyes in the shadows of the tree grew dark, fierce and upset.

"I want to ask the same of you." He looked over her face, his gaze lingering on her lips. "What's going on? Ever since your father died there's something off. I know, I know you've suffered a great loss and I've tried to be empathetic of it all. Particularly with what happened with my own father. I understand now how great a loss it is. That your parent who was there every day in the expanse of your life is suddenly gone, no longer a part of it, no longer a witness to your existence. I *understand* that pain. But you've never been like this before. You've never had these spells of panic. You feel more distant to me than ever before. I used to be able to read you, to know what bothered you, and I can't right now. All I know is I want to fix this and I'm at a loss of how I can."

Greer's shoulders dropped and closed her eyes for a moment. "I don't think there *is* any way to fix it."

"But you admit something is going on?" Barden asked, his voice quiet, serious.

Greer opened her eyes. "I think I'm losing my mind. I don't know what I'm doing as queen. I thought permitting magic would win me favor and I was an idiot not to see how many people have always supported my father. I mean, we knew, *I* knew, but I overlooked it all.

"I was blinded by the need to ensure Caitriona was accepted and things were done right. My father always ridiculed me for how much I adored Caitriona. You know that. He thought it was my greatest weakness, that I wanted to ensure her happiness. But it wasn't just her. I thought of all the people we saw on our various campaigns, the people killed because my father wanted magic gone. I thought I'd save others like them if I made it legal, but instead I've created an expansive divide in my kingdom. There're groups of people who hate my family, who hate me, who are reporting their neighbors and claiming they've been cursed or magic was done to them against their will. I have a city of hateful people who tattle at every opportunity. And my father was right, my desire to make Caitriona happy—to ensure she was accepted—has led us to this."

"But you're missing all the quiet people," Barden said quickly, grabbing hold of Greer's shoulders and making her face him fully. "You're missing the people like my family and every guard who attended my father's funeral. You're missing all those people we saw on our travels because they're out there and we're stuck here at the castle. Do not fall victim to the belief that a few very loud voices make up the majority of opinion."

He leaned forward, his eyes wide. "And never regret your love for your sister. It made you selfless. And that's a characteristic your father lacked in abundance."

Greer's eyes flooded with tears. She clenched her jaw and swallowed, trying to force her emotions back. But the cracks were there, her mask was breaking, and she couldn't hold back anymore.

"But there's more than that," she whispered and Barden's tight grasp on Greer's shoulders lightened.

"What?"

"I haven't spoken to anyone fully about what happened with my father after he died." Greer almost felt him there, standing over her shoulder ready to bark orders. She could smell his scent in the breeze, of sweat and stale beer and hot metal in the sunshine. Of bitterness, loathing, and the need for control.

Murderer, he hissed in her ear. His breath hot and wet against her skin, the scent foul. Greer rubbed her arms as if to chase off a chill and shifted on her feet with discomfort as she fought the urge to look over her shoulder. She wasn't sure if she wanted the confirmation that he wasn't there. What's worse, she was fearful he *would* be.

"I fear he's haunting me, and I understand if he is. I killed him and my only regret is how I've felt ever since. My regret is that I have none, that I wish I'd done it sooner. I regret we suffered under him for so many years. Not just the kingdom, but my family. Caitriona. My mother. They suffered. I regret knowing we all would've been better off if I just plunged a knife into his chest when I turned eighteen and hadn't waited nearly ten years before doing the job."

Barden's hands shifted as he gently rubbed her arms with the palms of his hands. "Greer—"

"No, let me finish," Greer replied, putting a hand on Barden's chest and feeling his heart drumming beneath her palm. "The night of the vigil of the heir, I sat in that room, locked inside with his corpse, and I just ignored him. I didn't want to learn anything. But a few hours into my vigil, I heard the call for death. That damn chirp. The *die, die, die.*"

"A death bringer?"

Greer nodded. "It was in the room, sitting in the rafters, the first I've seen since he killed the cage full of them."

Killer, her father spat.

"I watched it flutter about the room before it descended to my father's body. It landed on his face and I didn't move. It pecked his eyes and pried at his mouth. I still didn't move. It ate my father's soul and I allowed it to. Not once did I try to stop it. His soul was this wisp of shadow, this dark thing that somehow felt like my father. Like every awful emotion he ever brought out was made up in that cluster of particles.

"The bird pulled it from his mouth and swallowed it whole like it was a worm. I watched it all and when the bird was done, I got to my feet and let it out the window. Even in death, I'm still punishing him for the awful man he was and yes, we can list his crimes, we can detail how awful he was, but the fact is … what does it make me? What does this make me when I killed my own father and I didn't mourn him, and I let his soul get devoured by a damned bird? How am I any better than him if all this death is happening around us and we are about to plunge fully into war?"

Greer stopped and realized she was shaking. Her heart fluttered and quaked in her chest so often but this was all encompassing. Her hand quivered as she wiped her eye, the emotions long withheld finally being acknowledged and set free.

Barden lifted his hands and cupped her cheeks as he bent forward, meeting her eye to eye as he had in Stormhaven weeks before. "Greer Gablaigh. You're *nothing* like your father but you need to let that fear live in you, let it guide you so you never *become* anything like him. He could've benefitted from feeling fear and sadness, he may have been a better person if he cared. Do not convince yourself to be numb. It's emotion that keeps us human, but you also need to not let it own you."

If it ate my soul, why am I still here? Why am I tethered to you, daughter? Cearny smelt like rotten leaves and late autumn death. From the corner of Greer's eye, she saw him looking more deteriorated. He was rotting; like he was dying again. Hopefully he wouldn't haunt her for much longer.

The feel of Barden's hands on her made her brave. The honesty of the situation felt like enough of a reprieve that she wanted to tell him more.

"Sometimes, I think I hear—"

"Your highness?" A guard's voice called, interrupting the last of Greer's confession. Greer stared at Barden. His thumb moved circles over her cheek before he pulled away and turned toward Paul who pushed through the brush and into sight. "Your highness. Barden. I have a report from the castle."

"What's wrong?" Greer slipped her mask back into place and stepped around Barden. Back straight, face blank, hands gently knit together before her. The queen once more.

Paul looked between them and his expression made Greer suspect she would be fighting off rising panic soon, then he confirmed her suspicions.

"The witch woman spoke to your sister. She said Lachlan, the rightful heir to Invarlwen, refused to join Caitriona and your fight against the fae."

CHAPTER TWENTY

Caitriona

Caitriona looked like herself. Her true self. The one she pictured in her mind's eye, the person she was her whole life until she was forced into something else, and it made her happy despite that everything else felt awful.

The painful effect of May's potion overcame her just before they left the Northern Wood. Through the early morning mist, the sun was slow to reach the trees. They woke early and traveled through the last bit of woods towards the city grounds. Dew was heavy on the ground, a sign that summer was turning a corner and beginning its journey toward its end. The wetness soaked through their boots and left the air moist, yet cool. The heat of the summer day had yet to arrive, another sign that the latter half of summer was drifting further toward autumn like a leaf on a slow-moving stream.

When they entered the world of Avorkaz, freeing themselves of constant attacks and stalking creatures, Caitriona expected to breathe a sigh of relief yet movement on the outskirts of the city that wasn't present before kept her breath in her chest.

Fiana paused, holding up her hand to still the party.

"Something's off." Fiana crossed her arms and watched people move quickly from house to house. Toward the little homes where the hunters lived, there were multiple people with weapons and other gear similar to Fiana lingering outside. They stood in a circle talking—a stark contrast to their appearance when they originally came to hire a hunter.

"Stay by the trees." Fiana looked at the four of them. Her brow furrowed as she looked at the two groups. "I'm going to find out what's going on."

Caitriona and Ceenear exchanged looks as Raum watched Fiana walk away. "Something's changed about her."

Ailith stepped forward, looking after Fiana. "What do you mean?"

"Remember, my gifts only work from a distance," Raum reminded her. "I can see the intentions and soul of a person from far away. When we first met Fiana, she was only interested in making a profit. But now she's colored with concern."

Fiana greeted the other hunters in a friendly way and nodded as they spoke. At one point, the group turned toward Caitriona's party with interest as Fiana stepped away with one hunter. A large man, tall and thick, who oozed strength but had a calm and welcoming face followed her to the party.

"This is my friend, Samuel," Fiana introduced as they neared the group. "He knows what's going on."

The man looked them over and spoke before anyone had a chance to introduce themselves. "Fiana said none of you are the dragon that came through yesterday. But there's talk in the city that the dragon was from Wimleigh Queendom. Specifically, that it's the princess being sent on behalf of Queen Greer."

Caitriona's eyes widened. Ailith's expression turned dark, her protective nature taking hold. "Did the dragon do anything?"

"We saw fire coming from the north and received messages from a hunter's raven from the woods near Ätbënas's border. The dragon set fire to the town."

Caitriona thought of Lachlan, the children he cared for, and the elders who came by the guest house in the evening with food. The world felt like it was rushing past her. Caitriona pressed her fingers to her temples, feeling the base where her horns normally were, and squeezed her eyes closed for a moment.

"Are there—" She felt like she could cry. All those people gone. "Are there any survivors?"

Samuel shrugged. "The hunter hasn't sent any additional messages since he shared that the town was attacked. He remained in the woods and headed there with others to help. We've tried to speak to him through stones but haven't received a response."

"And the city thinks Wimleigh Queendom's princess was the dragon? That she's behind the attack?" Ailith asked.

Samuel nodded, looking away from Ailith after meeting her harsh gaze. Instead, he settled his sights on Caitriona. "Hergrew said Princess Caitriona passed through a few days ago and hired a hunter to go to Ätbënas. Hergrew thinks Caitriona attacked due to his refusal to help Wimleigh with their war."

Caitriona stepped back, the ground feeling uneven under her feet. She felt lost to the world and as if the dragon within her would take over to propel her forward. Ailith shifted to slip her hand around Caitriona's waist. Caitriona couldn't follow the discussion as the rushing of blood and her rapid heartbeat grew too loud, but she focused on the guard and slowly, sound returned.

"You need to leave the city immediately," Samuel continued. "I trust Fiana, perhaps Hergrew will too. If she says Caitriona wasn't the dragon then I believe her, but people are scared and defensive. They worry Avorkaz is next and I doubt any will question your group if they realize who you are."

"How ..." Caitriona dropped her hands. "How do we leave without being caught?"

Fiana smiled. "With a band of hunters."

Fiana and Samuel retrieved the group's horses from the stable while the rest hid in Fiana's home. The plan was hastily made, but there was no time to figure out the finer details or consider better alternatives. They would ride together. The hunters on the outside of the circle with Caitriona's party inside. They'd dress in hunter clothes—vests made from hides with sewn pockets full of spells and tricks. They wouldn't look at or speak to anyone. They only had to make it out of the city gates because the city, and Hergrew, assumed they were in the Northern Wood.

Caitriona and Ailith still appeared fae with what remained of their potions and Ceenear used her gifts to appear human. Fiana, educated on potion use, created a third to change Raum's appearance. His brown hair turned white, his eyes a light blue, and his ears shrunk into curved, human arches.

"White hair," Raum murmured as he inspected his reflection in a looking glass. Caitriona felt her heart twinge by the sad expression Raum wore. His hair was something similar to Lumia's and the absence of the third fae who was by their side when they visited the fae queendom felt like a thing made physical. A heaviness of weight and with the taste of tears.

"I mean, I can give you a potion to make you turn into a half human dog if you'd like," Fiana said, crossing her arms over her chest.

"No," Raum laughed, but it was a sad, forced sound. "It's just that this hair reminds me of someone."

As they continued to wait for the hunters to gather, they attempted once more to reach Niveem or Lumia, finding no one willing to answer the speaking stone. The look on Raum's face as they put the stone away made Caitriona's aching heart all the worse.

"Maybe Isla can figure out a way to contact her when we get back to Braewick," Caitriona offered as she gently patted Raum's back.

"I don't even know what I'll say if we were able to speak. I miss her? I'm sorry? We were arguing frequently before I went through the mist. Things have been strained. That tension left behind makes this all the worse."

Caitriona frowned but said nothing else. The couple, to her understanding, were together for years, but this was the first she heard of there being tension.

With their clothing packed and hunter vests on, the group took to their horses and began the slow progression around Avorkaz to the southern gates. The hunters commanded the roadway, their jobs and talent well known and leaving people to step aside and allow passage without word.

"We'll make it out of the city this afternoon," Samuel said when they began. "You only need to be quiet and follow us."

On Onyx, Ailith rode beside Caitriona with a sour expression.

Waiting until there were few people on the road, Caitriona reached to the side, grasping Ailith's hand and forcing a small smile.

"Remember what you told me?" Caitriona said softly. "What's the point of worrying now? We have to wait until we have something to worry about."

She needed to remind herself this as much as Ailith. Because she *was* worried, she was scared, and she was sad. All the kind people of Ätbënas possibly lost ... including Lachlan. She wouldn't tell her sister until they were back at the castle. This wasn't something to share through a speaking stone.

As Samuel said, they passed the city gates in the afternoon and continued moving south past Greenbriar until the homes turned to farms.

"We'll stop here," Samuel announced. "I think you're well enough to continue without Avorkaz guards coming upon you."

"Thank you for aiding us. On behalf of Wimleigh Queendom, I'm grateful."

Samuel nodded his head as he urged his horse to separate from the group and turn around.

"Stay safe." Samuel smiled. "Good luck with your war."

The hunters moved away yet Fiana lingered. Ceenear touched Fiana's shoulder and smiled. "You've helped us more than we can say."

"Yes, I have." Fiana grinned with self-knowing. "I was thinking though ... if Ätbënas is destroyed, I doubt I'll be doing as much passage through the northern woods. So, perhaps I'll continue with your lot."

Caitriona felt a flash of hope warm her cheeks. "You want to join us?"

Fiana shrugged and brushed her dark hair over her shoulder.

"I knew the people in Ätbënas. I've visited it enough. If King Malcolm's sending dragons to destroy the village—which is the only thing I can think actually happened since it just happened to be a *gold* dragon and a very fitting blame on your queendom—I'd rather help if I can. It might be a losing battle, but maybe it's not. Still, I know my monsters and King Malcolm sounds like he might be the biggest monster of them all. Let me join you."

"We aren't going to pay you more than what we agreed to for taking us through the Northern Wood," Caitriona replied, trying to school her face to be serious. "But we'll feed you and pay for your lodging and provide you with any spell ingredients you need."

Fiana smiled. "It sounds like a plan. Now where to? Let's get a move on so I can kill the bastard that destroyed that town."

CHAPTER TWENTY-ONE

Róisín

Ten Years Prior

Greer rode out at dawn and Róisín made sure to stand on the parapet walk with Caitriona at her side to wave goodbye. Her eldest daughter was a girl of sixteen; bright eyed and eager for the world, and Róisín was certain she would make a great queen. For years, as Cearny kept Greer on a tight leash and as far from Róisín as possible, Róisín worried Cearny would poison the girl's mind. She kept a careful eye on the girl, as much as she could, through reliable servants who would report to Róisín weekly on Greer's behavior and adventures. When Greer was permitted around her, Róisín kept a frosty appearance and ensured the girl didn't get too close. She didn't want the king to see, she didn't want him to view their relationship as a threat. At least at this distance, she still saw her daughter daily—even if their interactions were brief and without much weight—and knew what was going on in her life, even if she wasn't as involved as she wished.

At twelve, the girl joined the royal guard and Róisín watched from the royal corridor windows as Greer practiced. She failed again and again, but Shaw offered his hand and worked with her to slowly improve her skill. During the first day of dueling practice, she was paired with

Shaw's eldest son Barden. The boy was a few years her senior and allowed the princess to win. Even from within the castle, unable to hear what was said, Róisín could tell Shaw gave his son an earful because when they dueled again, Greer ended up toppling head over heels in the dirt. There would be no easy victories for the princess of Wimleigh.

It took a year for Greer to win one of their duels and Róisín fought hard to not break into a grin when Greer discussed her accomplishment over dinner that night.

But she was proud, so painfully proud of her golden girl. Yet so desperately scared as she watched the princess ride through the main gate of the castle and down the center road of Braewick City. Greer beamed in the early morning light as she rode beside Barden. The two had an unbreakable bond and with Barden named the heir's top guard just before they departed, it seemed to become even tighter.

"He's looking at her funny again," Caitriona murmured as she peeked over the edge of the wall. "He's always doing that."

"Who, darling?" Róisín asked, reaching down to brush her fingers over Caitriona's red hair.

"Barden." Caitriona pointed over the edge. Róisín pushed Caitriona's hand back.

"You mustn't do that, Caitriona," Róisín said. "Your father doesn't want you spotted by the people below."

"How come?" Caitriona chirped, turning on her heel to her mother. While only ten years old, she was nearly Róisín's twin, only with a rounder face than Róisín ever had due to having decent meals her entire life and not sharing with a house full of other hungry orphans. When Caitriona was born and Róisín saw the swathe of red hair on her head, panic built in her chest as the babe was placed on her belly. She didn't immediately embrace the infant, didn't nurse her, but instead ran her fingers over the ridge of Caitriona's ears to ensure she hadn't inherited the fae points. So not quite her twin, but close.

"He feels it's for your safety," Róisín replied, the ongoing lie she told Caitriona and others who asked for years when, in fact, Cearny said under no circumstances would the youngest princess be perceived by anyone beyond the castle. He felt the less they knew about the girl who came back from the dead, the better. Her worth was only when she came of age and he could sell her off in marriage. Róisín wished to the Elder Tree daily that Caitriona would never know.

The girl pressed her lips into a line, considering this answer before turning back to the wall and peeking over. Greer's horse slowed and she turned on her saddle, her gaze rising to the castle's curtain walls.

Róisín lifted a hand, waving goodbye, and before she could stop her, Caitriona pushed herself up and waved as well. It wasn't until Caitriona appeared that Greer grinned, waving her arm wildly before turning back on her saddle and continuing forward. Caitriona just as quickly dropped down and sighed.

"I wish I could go with her."

Róisín frowned, her heart strings tugging as she brushed a strand of hair from Caitriona's face.

"Someday you'll do so much more than what you have within the castle," Róisín reassured her. She turned to the street below, her heart full as Greer brightened from the sight of Caitriona.

The princess's mother wolf personality remained despite Cearny keeping Greer's schedule quite full. Any opportunity she had, she slipped into Caitriona's room and Róisín would find the two whispering together under blankets. Some nights, when Róisín checked on Caitriona before going to bed herself, she found Greer and Caitriona sleeping together in the same bed, curled up around each other with pictures drawn by quill and dolls between them. Despite the age difference of six years, despite the wedge Cearny tried to drive between them, they were tethered to one another and it was a point of pride Róisín had that she had nothing to do with.

"You never answered my question," Caitriona said as Róisín turned away from the scene after Greer rode out of sight. The little girl skipped after her.

"What question?" Róisín asked, spotting one of Cearny's guards studying her. She frowned at the man and he turned away.

"Why does Barden look at Greer like that? Like he's hungry."

Róisín pressed her lips together, attempting to smother a laugh. "I doubt you'll understand anytime soon, but someday you will."

They entered the castle and turned toward the halls where their rooms were, the king and his guards nowhere in sight. "But if you promise to keep a secret, I'll tell you."

"Oh," Caitriona whispered, her blue eyes bright and curious. "Oh, I promise, Mother. Please tell me!"

Róisín dropped to her knees and held her hands up to shield her mouth from any passersby. "I think Barden likes Greer much more than as a friend."

Caitriona nearly grew two inches with budding excitement. "Oh, how romantic!" She knit her fingers together and spun on her foot. "So maybe one day they'll get married and they'll rule the kingdom together!"

Róisín raised her brows as she got back to her feet and began walking down the hall again. "Perhaps, if your father decides that."

The blur of red hair disappeared from Róisín's side and the queen paused, turning to find Caitriona standing still, her brow wrinkled with confusion.

"Why would father have to decide that?"

"Because he's the king, and he decides who your sister will marry. He may pick a prince from another land, but perhaps he'll pick Barden. The spouse of the monarch doesn't always have to be royal."

"Were you royal?" Caitriona asked, an annoying habit of hers which Róisín wished would go away. The girl was determined to learn as much as she could about Róisín's family despite that the queen dutifully kept her mouth shut since she baked Cearny the poisoned hand pie.

"Not at all," Róisín replied, choosing honesty for just this once. It could have been a scandal when she married Cearny, but she had the hearts of the people at that point, she had their favor. While Caermythlin was in on the lie of their love, word of it traveled beyond the small town rapidly and most of the kingdom knew about her relationship with Cearny before she was even engaged to him. Donal couldn't deny the story either, how his family saved the poor orphan girl from the magical village, it was too much to pass on and Róisín was too blind to see.

This little note of honesty was enough for Caitriona, at least for the moment as she took to skipping down the hall again. Even now Róisín saw magic churning under Caitriona's skin. It was the magic that brought her back to life, but also demanded something else, and not a day went by that Róisín didn't wonder what the curse truly was.

When would it rise and take over? What would she do when it happened? How would she save her daughter? Kayl said something about a creature Cearny took pride in killing. Cearny found joy in killing many creatures but in particular the dragon that took Caitriona's life.

A dragon.

But Caitriona's personality was nothing like a dragon. If anything, it was Greer she suspected would turn into one. She could never get close enough to Greer to see if darkness churned under Greer as well. But she often wondered if it was her eldest destined to devour the king. Perhaps she would devour Róisín too, if she was lucky.

Her town was gone, the magic users she knew dead and the one she knew that still lived set the curse. Donal banned magic from the city, but Cearny made it such a crime there was no hope Róisín would find any magic users to help her children. Shaw was the only person she knew who was familiar with the old ways, and it became abundantly clear some years before he wouldn't endanger his family. Róisín had come across the man in the gardens once more and asked him what he knew of curses.

"Enough that I don't toy with them." Shaw glanced at the castle windows. "Enough to know that in this very element, asking such questions could get us both killed. Respectfully, my queen, be careful who you ask such questions to. There are many others who work for your husband who will not be kind."

And so Róisín continued doing the only thing she felt capable of: tending to her youngest daughter. The discarded, magical child her father wanted nothing to do with. The child Róisín was allowed to interact with, to watch grow and thrive. All the easier to keep an eye on the liquid gold that seemed to pump through her veins as Róisín waited to see if it would rise to the surface.

CHAPTER TWENTY-TWO

GREER

The city found peace for a brief period. The fires from the quake died and what buildings were damaged would be fixed with the aid of the crown. The injured were cared for and healed miraculously fast with the administration of magical herbs and supplements; an admission that brought forth plenty of opinions but in the end, many had a change of heart and, at the very least, appreciated how magic came to their aid. The city's blacksmiths worked around the clock to create more blades, shields, and arrow tips; and royal and city guards rushed their students through training. There was no hiding it anymore, war was coming, and the people of the city only waited for the official decree.

They were never fools, though some said they were for so readily leaning into the politics of Cearny or Greer, fighting amongst their families over which side was right and wholeheartedly standing by their opinions, but that was human nature.

"Tell me," Greer began one evening in the dining hall. She invited Rowan and Barden's sisters to dine with her, along with Ailith's parents and their caretaker. "You all have ties to the city; you all interact with the townspeople. If you're comfortable, will you share what you've heard from them all?"

"What are you looking to know, dear?" Cari asked, looking up and smiling kindly. The spectacles she received from the palace healers made her eyes extraordinarily large; similar to an all-seeing owl, but paired with her sweet smile, it made Greer appreciate Ailith's mother all the more.

Greer looked around the table. Her mother sat regally at the far end and Barden stood by the door with his hand on the hilt of his sword, not joining the meal despite Greer's invitation. Since they spoke at the Elder Tree, he was nothing but studious and serious before others, but in the darkened places of the castle halls there was something else that seemed secret between them. Hands brushing and lasting looks that left Greer hungry for more while Barden remained frustratingly professional.

"I suppose …" Greer trailed off and immediately looked at her mother, silently pleading for her to find the words lost to her.

Róisín balled up a cloth napkin in her hand and dropped it on the table. "My daughter hopes to have insight into what people think is going on. Both your families know we're preparing for war, and while you all understand such internal discussions must not occur outside the castle walls, you're all permitted into the city. We know you visit it; we know you run errands and stop in with friends. Have you heard citizens discussing the possibility of war?"

"I wouldn't say they're discussing the *possibility*," Holly, one of Barden's sisters said with a small snort of laughter. She leaned back in her chair and crossed her arms over her chest. Beyond, Barden frowned. Holly always cut to the chase and never minced words; she was Greer's favorite of the bunch. "Everyone suspects we're about to descend into chaos at any moment. They can hear the blacksmiths working, they have family and friends who aren't answering questions when asked and are working longer hours than usual. They see the gates being closed when usually they're open. It's pretty clear what's going on. The problem is that they haven't heard from the crown about it. And there are … *opinions* regarding that."

"Yes," Gwen added, her eyes bright and eager. She seemed dazzled since stepping inside the castle. While she escorted Ailith's parents to ceremonies Ailith partook in since becoming a royal guard, a meal within the castle walls was something entirely new. "From what I hear, people are confused the royal household has said nothing. The fact there hasn't been a formal announcement has led everyone to doubt their own eyes. The signs are there, they see war is coming based on the preparations alone, but the silence from the castle's made some confused and others, well, angry."

"As Holly said, they've noticed the uptick in weapons being made," Taren said quietly, looking at his hands. "The city carpenters are wondering if they'll be called to make wagons to carry men. They've wondered if they'll have to create stakes for battle. Seamstresses and fabric makers in the city are wondering if they'll be expected to make additional uniforms. All are wondering and waiting for information.

"Queen Greer, if you're asking if citizens know war is coming, the answer's yes. Abundantly so. But they wait to hear more details from *you*."

Greer looked at her mother. For all the distance they had while Cearny was alive, they were now consistently paired together. Her feelings for her mother were complicated at best. She wouldn't admit it, but she needed her. Even though the years of distance between them still stung. But she needed her mother's reassurance. She couldn't deny not being yelled at or threatened by her parent was substantially a better way to build a relationship than her experience with her father, too. Greer appreciated her advice. Now was no different.

"Fear is one of the greatest threats to a queendom." Róisín knit her hands together and rested her chin on them. "Greer, I understand you want Invarlwen surprised that we know their plans, but there comes a moment where that element of surprise may endanger others. It's time to tell the city what we're up against."

The attention of everyone in the room fell on Greer. Her throat tightened and her heartbeat quickened. Her eyes moved over the table and settled on Barden standing at the doorway, his gaze on her as well.

"Fine." She looked at the two families before her. "I'm grateful you all could join me tonight and answer my questions. So please, enjoy your meals, because tomorrow the entire city will be different. Tomorrow I'll declare war."

Greer stood at the window overlooking the city in the crown's hall where her office and room sat separate from the family bedrooms.

The sun set hours before and the full moon provided a glowing light highlighting many buildings brightened by lit fires and lanterns. Even the hall was brighter with each sconce lit. But for all the world it was silent. After her guests finished their meals, Róisín saw them off while Barden escorted them to their homes, allowing Greer a moment of silence as she requested her other guards to give her space. Town criers were sent to the city to announce the requested presence of citizens at the castle gates the following day when Greer would speak to them all and announce the impending war. The city was unsettled and by morning light their suspicions would be confirmed. She dreaded it.

Greer's forehead touched the glass and she sighed from the coolness against her skin. The exhaustion of the last few weeks made her eyes tired, playing games with her vision as the lights of the southern tip of the city began winking out one by one. Greer lifted her head, blinking hard before looking again.

The late hour, surely, she thought. *What a strange coincidence that the southern neighborhood blew out their candles and went to sleep at the same time. But stranger things have happened, of course.*

But there was no denying that the disappearance of lights increased as a shadow fell over the southern portion of the city like a cloud passing over the full moon.

Glancing upward, the moon still shone, the stars its audience, and the sky clear. But upon the city, darkness tripped over itself, stumbling to fall over each building, and plunging each street into its blind grasp. Calling it darkness seemed inappropriate, a bland descriptor as it was something more akin to an absence of light. As if all familiarity of the city structures were immediately winked from existence. The vanishing light increased, moving rapidly forward to the castle and devouring every light in its path. Greer stumbled backwards, remembering she sent her guards off, and she was truly alone.

"Guards?" she yelled, hoping one was close enough to respond but knowing there wasn't enough time for one to hear and aid her. There likely wasn't even enough time to notify the guards on the castle's parapet walk. Throwing open a window, she leaned outward to try anyway. "Guards! The shadows!"

Screams echoed off the stone walls of the city, funneling through the streets and into the guard yard of the inner ward. The wave of darkness rose, coming closer and taking with it building after building. Down below, guards stumbled from their homes, looking upward to the sky while those on duty and stationed on the walls shouted. It was all confusing action. Weapons at the ready but to attack what? The gloom was there, licking the castle walls and pulling itself over stone. The city beyond was gone, only inky black remained with the sky filled with stars above.

It seemed the shadow paused for a moment, considering the castle grounds before rushing forward in a torrent to wrap itself around guards and funnel into their mouths and down their throats. It silenced their cries before their bodies slipped out of the light and disappeared from Greer's view.

Greer slammed the window closed. The glass panes rattled in their holds as she fell away. Would the window keep back the gloom? But what is glass to a lack of light? A door opened and Etta, her elderly nursemaid who they kept on staff despite having no children to tend to any longer because they loved her so deeply, rushed forward with panic in her eyes.

"The shadows are possessing people. They're taking the light!" Etta crashed into Greer who grasped the older woman's arms. "My child, we have to get you to safety!"

But the gloom knew no doors. It did not care about human structures. It thrived on the existence of walls and roof, and Greer was poignantly in the midst of both. Through the hall, torches winked out one by one, beginning at each end and growing as dark as pitch as the wave moved closer.

"Get behind me," Greer instructed as she stepped before Etta and pulled free her sword, raising it and preparing to strike, although she didn't think blades had any weight when it came to darkness.

"Your grace, we should *go*," Etta begged, her little hand grabbing Greer's arm before growing still.

Etta let in a long, sucking sound and Greer turned as the gloom wrapped its tendrils around her head before pressing into her nose, her mouth and eyes then tugging her backward. Etta vanished from sight and into darkness's embrace. A cry echoed in the hall and Greer realized it was she who was crying out.

The last torch winked out and what etchings of substance, the lines of the hall and walls ebbed from existence.

Greer stood very, very still. Her body felt like a tree, resolute and unmoving, her feet rooted her to the spot. Her breaths rattled in her chest as she gripped her sword. There was no sound, no breathing, no footfall. The silence itself was a thing made of terror, expanding to press against her and fill her whole.

"*Greer*," a voice said from behind, its breath cold against her neck, like ice particles knitting itself into every pore of her skin.

Greer spun but only faced more darkness. The voice returned, this time filling the space and coming from all directions. Its speaker the darkness itself.

"*Let it be known, my father is a kind ruler, and with that in mind, I give you a warning, Queen Greer Gablaigh of Wimleigh Queendom.*"

Matches. Greer had matches in her pocket.

Fumbling, she tugged them free but dropped the box as she pulled a stick out and struck toward where she believed to be the wall. Over and over, it scraped against the rough stone until it sparked to life, giving meager light to detail Greer's body and trembling hands, but nothing else. Darkness—she was in a pit of it. Swallowed entirely and existing from within its bowels.

"*Blood will spill for your crimes against the fae and magic alike. You have until summer's end to prepare.*"

The flicker of the match was so small and quickly fading while Greer's panic grew.

Two months. There were barely two months until the start of autumn.

"*I look forward to meeting you with my blade, Greer Gablaigh.*"

Shad, Malcolm's son, somehow made into darkness itself. A sigh bounced off surfaces unseen and drenched Greer's skin, then the gloom shifted as if deciding not to leave. A shadow escaped its hold, becoming something solid with eyes of dim, smoking light like the full moon seen through fog. Greer's blade swung forward, the light of the match catching the glint of its metal as it swept through the figure. It dispersed, fading into the dark.

"*But I can't help myself if the opportunity arises ... I wonder what it will feel like to choke the life from your body through this form that I've been given ...*"

Greer swung the sword again and backed against the wall. The match dropped and flickered from the floor.

"*A precursor to our meeting ...*"

Pressing along the wall, she reached for a door handle but only found cold emptiness as the figure made of smoke and darkness leaned in. It seized Greer, wrapping freezing fingers around her neck and held her still. As it squeezed, the pressure made her gasp. Greer choked, attempting to bat off the shadow that was capable of pressing its shadowed fingers into the skin of her throat, and yet she couldn't hold onto it nor hit it with her sword. It swung through empty air and her fingers were lost, falling through the shadow's body and only feeling cold.

The shadowed Shad crept forward, its mouth parting as it seemed to take in her desperate breaths. Her vision swam, making the shadowed figure blend into the dark around her, but another noise echoed from the silent dark. A scrape of heavy wood against stone until a burst of light exploded, making the hall brighter than day. Shad shrieked back, his fingers pulled away and left Greer falling to her knees. The light swept forward and there was a scream, similar to the voice that spoke before, and all at once the shadow creature, as well as the darkness, disappeared.

Greer held her hands over her eyes and didn't move until she felt the pressure of a warm, living hand on her shoulder. Isla bent before her, offering her a hand to stand. Beyond Isla stood Róisín, resolute with a flaming blade in her hand. Her eyes glowed green from a light from within, similar to how Caitriona's glowed when she made fire. "How did you ...?"

"A magic pall that snuffed out all the light," Isla explained, tucking Greer's hair behind her ear and laying a gentle hand on Greer's shoulder as she guided her to stand. "And only magic light can destroy it."

THE GLOOM, AS PEOPLE OF THE CASTLE NAMED IT, RECEDED. Etta was found collapsed on the hall's floor but recovered. The cries in the night from frightened townspeople diminished, but Greer still felt her heart in her throat, pounding rapidly like a frightened bird trapped in a cage. Through the darkness the gloom brought and the declaration of war that was shouted from the mouths of people overtaken by it, an unease lingered. No one felt safe, but no one wanted to leave their homes to seek additional safety.

Greer drifted from room to room, looking for something of importance, and tried desperately to recall what she should do next. The guards were stationed at the walls—what little good they could do to fight mist and shadow that bent around blades and steel without being pierced—and the doors to the castle itself locked. She felt untethered as she drifted, calming skittish servants who jumped at the dwindling darkness in the corner of doorways, and called for additional candles and lanterns to be lit.

"We'll fill every inch of this space with light. Use every candle, every torch." Greer rubbed her neck; it was tender where Shad had touched her and as she passed a looking glass, red fingerprints already showed on her neck that would likely bruise with time. She tugged at the collar of her shirt in a poor attempt to cover the area. "I suspect they won't return. The message was quite clear. But a little extra light ... that may do us all good until morning."

At last, she entered her room. It was void of light. The darkness spread over the room and buried into every surface, immediately shifting Greer's awareness to a heightened point. Movement in the shadows caught her attention and ignited a spark of feeling in her neck.

She reached to her waist and pulled her dagger free; gripping it in her hand, she spun towards the wall and used her free hand to push the being against the stone surface. Her knife tip met the hollow of the figure's throat, the metal flashing dully in the low light. Greer internally rejoiced that the figure was of substance and not something she couldn't touch.

"Now isn't the time to sneak in shadows," she hissed. Narrowing her gaze, she tried to make out the details of their face.

"Is it sneaking if I've been welcomed here before?" Barden's voice came out in a breath, his body stiff beneath Greer's heightened rage. She froze, her knife still pressed to Barden's throat.

"Barden?" Her heart raced and thumped against her ribs while her eyes grew used to the darkness, something she wasn't able to do with the gloom before, and his familiar face came into focus. He looked down at Greer and remained very still. His auburn hair was loose and an errant curl hung over his forehead and into his eyes. Greer fought the urge to brush it from his face.

"Will you release me? Or do you want to continue pinning me to the wall?" Barden growled. His eyes held no anger, yet they were heated in a different way that Greer wanted to greet. Greer saw it before in moments during practice duels. She witnessed it during nights when they traveled for the crown while they camped beneath the stars, the rest of the men having fallen asleep, and only she and Barden were left awake by the dwindling campfire. It was there most recently in every private interaction. The garden before the quake, the Elder Tree just before. Something hungry that hadn't been fulfilled, a look drew Greer's pulse to the surface and blood to her cheeks.

"Why would you come into my dark room after the gloom attacked?" she asked, immediately hating that her voice softened to a whisper. Barden blinked then breathed in, his chest rising. He swallowed and the tip of the blade rose and fell against his throat.

"Why would *you* walk into a dark room after the gloom attacked?" he asked, his voice still gruff, and in that moment Greer knew she was undone.

"You should be with your family," Greer offered, an attempt to delay what she knew was inevitable. She saw this coming, dreamt of it even, but did such a good job denying it all. She had a purpose to this life, the very reason she was born, and she couldn't allow distraction.

But the fact remained that she was distracted for years by the static of close proximity and constant knowing of his presence. She gave so much of herself for duty, why couldn't she have one thing that was entirely her choosing? Was it so bad to be selfish just this once?

"They're safe." Still unmoving under her hold and the point of her knife, he licked his lips and his gaze shifted, looking down to her mouth and back to her eyes. "I was with them when it happened, but they know my loyalty remains tied to the safety of my queen."

Greer pressed her lips together, clenching her jaw as his chest rose and fell beneath her hand. There was a war brewing. She didn't have time for matters of the heart. She didn't have time to do anything for herself. "I have other guards."

"But none are as good as me," Barden said softly. His hands moved cautiously to her hips, and he shifted forward, pressing against the knife. Greer's heart thrilled. "None are as tied to you as I."

Greer realized he felt it too. It was obvious, there was no need for light in the darkened room for it to be abundantly clear. Something shifted between them when Shaw died. Something when they stood side by side before the drowning dukes and watched his body disappear beneath the dark water. The change continued, the invisible ties between them growing taut, and now the world seemed ready to crumble around them and Greer wanted comfort, support, and she only wanted it from one person.

"We very well may not live to see the end of the year." Greer's dagger lowered slowly, the tip of the blade trailing down his throat, and her eyes focused on the bead of blood forming where Barden leaned into the tip.

"Then all the more reason—" Barden breathed, leaning closer and against the blade. Greer pulled the knife away, her hand dropping to her side and the dagger loose in her grasp. Greer was stock still, her joints locked in place, unwilling to step away, but in fact tied to the spot. Tied to him. His eyes narrowed as his hand moved, fingers brushing against the sore spots of her neck. Gently there and gone again. "What ...?"

"The message from the king, or I suppose, his son. The shadow attempted to choke me."

Barden's eyes darkened, a muscle tightening along his jaw.

"I'll kill him myself," he whispered. "The bastard. I'll drive a blade into his ribs."

"Someday soon, I'm sure," Greer replied. Her blade clattered to the floor, forgotten as her hand lifted to touch Barden's cheek. Her nails scraped lightly over the stubble there, the pads of her fingers felt the warmth of his skin humming with life. A finger lifted, touching that taunting curl as she gently pushed it back from his face. "But I don't want to talk about that now."

She was starved and quick to pull Barden's face down so his lips finally met hers. He groaned, just as hungry as she, as his hands moved along her ribs. As they began to make drunken turns toward her bed, Greer pulled at the shoulders of his shirt. She was a creature unleashed, descending upon the feast of him.

His hands returned her administrations with strength and insistency, yet still gentle and cautious. Each touch a silent agreement, a call and response asking what Greer wanted and offering a willingness to stop if she deemed it necessary. They explored one another in ways that were always denied.

Oh, how she dreamt of this. The moment she met him when she entered training, the instantaneous desire to kiss him. As they grew older, her feelings matured, her cravings grew. The thrill of sleeping outside beneath the expanse of the universe, together in fields, left her dreams rich with the imagined taste and feel of him, and she found her dreams weren't quite right because reality was far better.

Their lips barely parted until he lifted her. Her legs wrapped about his waist as he stumbled closer to her bed. Still unmade, just as she liked it. They collapsed onto the soft sheets as his hands tugged at the ties of her dress.

"These damned gowns," Greer gasped. She pulled away from Barden's lips with a hungry grin as she jerked at the fabric, desperate to take it off. Twisting on Barden's lap, she tried to undo her ties but growled with frustration. "We need a knife."

Barden shifted and drew a knife from his thigh. He ran his hand over Greer's shoulder, encouraging her to turn before slipping the blade under the ties, snapping each one to finally release Greer from the fabric and pressure on her ribs. Together they took apart the pieces of her gown. Together their eager hands grasped Barden's shirt and pulled it over his head, then tugged at his pants to discard them to the floor. Greer pushed Barden onto her bed and climbed on top of him.

He lay beneath her, grinning broadly. She reached forward and captured Barden's large hands, before pushing them down above his head. She bent forward, her breasts brushing over his chest, as her lips sought his. Letting go of his hands, she settled, pressing herself against the hardness of him and prolonging the moment to join together as his fingers ran over the temporary indents in her soft skin from her corset.

They held still. It was a marvel to finally find one another together in that place. Mutual desires and hopes solidifying while the world around them crumbled.

"Greer," Barden whispered, "I wanted to tell you—"

"No." Greer ran her hands down his chest as she drank in the sight of him. The moonlight outside cast him in a silver blue. His hair was sprawled against the blankets, his toned chest rising and falling underneath her hand, and she wanted to paint the image into her mind. "I don't want you to tell me anything."

"I've wanted to tell you this for years—"

"I know." She leaned forward and kissed along his jaw, her lips coming close to his ear. What if the words ended the moment? What if the ghost of her father heard them and snapped them away, broke them, and made her lose this precious thing? "I know and I've felt the same. Always. Say it when we've won the war."

Barden's hands wrapped around her naked torso, holding her tight before he rolled them over.

"Whatever you say my queen. Now ..." He kissed her fully on the lips before pulling away and running his hands down her body. Fingers passed over the buds of her nipples, drifted over her thighs, and parted her knees. Slowly, he knelt beside the bed, his gaze bright in the shadows as his fingers dropped between her legs, and his smile grew devilish and hungry. "Let me serve you."

CHAPTER TWENTY-THREE

Ailith

They camped in a field for the night, not wanting to threaten May and Declan's peace by returning to their home. Ailith sent Crowley to the skies to ensure no Avorkazian soldiers followed before they settled. As the hunters predicted, they were safe.

They built a fire to make their evening meal before allowing it to die as they bedded down in the tall grass. The grass held the heat of the day, and their skin burned from the sun, uncomfortable and heated all on its own. The night air, while still warm, felt comforting and they could sleep with ease on their sleep pads with only their light blankets.

Ailith laid beside Caitriona whose eyes were to the night sky. The dying campfire highlighted her cheeks and red hair. Ailith's stomach churned with emotion. Rage that the blame for the loss of Ätbënas was placed on Caitriona and determination to return to Braewick as quickly as possible so they could set off and destroy the fae king. Sometimes her upset became so great that everything became foggy and distant, or perhaps it was the heat of the day.

The fae king repeatedly reminded her of Cearny, but this time in a different form. Why did men always hold such fear to what they misunderstood? Why couldn't they look at it with curiosity and wonder? Instead, it was something to destroy or conquer.

"Are you alright?" Caitriona whispered, facing Ailith. The dying firelight reflected off her eyes, flashing orbs similar to beasts in the wood when torchlight caught their gaze. It was a change Caitriona didn't seem to know of. Something that startled Ailith every time, but she kept it to herself. Even the potion didn't take away that change. Even magic couldn't hide the fact that the dragon was beneath the surface. "You've been sighing like something's upsetting you."

Ailith curled her arm under her ear. "Just thinking of Malcolm and Cearny."

"Ah."

"Sorry." Ailith's fingers lightly traced Caitriona's cheek. That morning, they took more of the potion before escaping the woods, but it would wear off soon.

Ailith would never tell Caitriona she missed the red-headed girl she first met. She *did* miss her, a great deal. But it was less about the princess's appearance and more about who Caitriona was before. Before the curse took hold of Caitriona, she loved herself and her smiles were easier to come by. Afterward, particularly when Caitriona learned she burned Ailith and left her scarred, Ailith had to coax Caitriona out of hiding, and convince her she wanted to be near her. That was when Ailith noticed the first poisonous influence of Caitriona's self-hatred, how it colored Caitriona's movements and dimmed her joy. Now her self-disgust was so pungent it filled every room she entered.

"It's alright," Caitriona replied, lifting her own hand to brush back Ailith's hair from her face. She smiled. "Your little fae ears are cute."

Ailith laughed. "They stick out from my hair. It's a little annoying."

Caitriona's smile dimmed as her fingers ran along the ridges of Ailith's ear. The red in Caitriona's hair began to fade and return to gold. Her blue eyes turned green, then gold as well, just as when the curse took more hold of the princess nearly two years before. And slowly, the points of four horns slipped from the skin of her scalp to curl outward. The potion ran out; they were back to their normal selves.

"Well." Caitriona sounded sad. "We haven't any use for the potion anymore."

"Cait." Ailith scooted closer and pressed her palm against Caitriona's cheek. "I wish you saw how beautiful you are. I know you hate what the curse left behind but you're still you and you're still gorgeous."

Caitriona frowned and pulled away, sitting upright to hug her legs. "You don't have to say that."

"I'll say it daily until it finally sinks in," Ailith reasoned as she sat up. "I know Kayl took so much from you. He changed you against your will and it's a damnable thing. But don't let him win. Don't let him get away with that. Use what you were given, use it as a strength."

"I'm trying."

"I know," Ailith said quickly, grabbing hold of Caitriona's hand and pressing it against her chest. "I know, I see it. You've begun making fire again and I'm so proud. But I know the dragon's also trying to push forth and you've pushed it back. I've felt the heat rise on your skin; I've seen the look in your eye. I'm not saying to become a dragon today, but maybe someday you should try. Keep your mind open to the idea, okay? And if you ever decide to do it, I'll be there with you."

"I'm afraid I won't come back," Caitriona whispered. "I'm afraid if I let the dragon out, it'll just do what it wants like the first time. I'm afraid if I do come back to being human again, that I'll look even more like a dragon. I'll be even more of a misshapen thing. I'll have a tail or pointed teeth."

"And I'll love you all the same."

Caitriona pressed her lips into a thin line and looked at Ailith. They were cast in moonlight, the fire finally fell to embers, and fireflies lit the tall grass around them like stars drifting down. It would be romantic without the backdrop of Raum snoring.

Viewing the self-doubt on Caitriona's face, the pain it caused her, hit Ailith with an overwhelming urge to protect her at all costs. She failed to stop the curse, something she thought she forgave herself of. With the summer night around them and war brewing on the horizon, she realized she wouldn't hesitate this time. She'd kill anyone who threatened her and do so with pride.

"Plus," Ailith continued. "I think you have more control over the dragon than you realize. That first time you were forced into it, but Isla said what happens after a curse is complete doesn't necessarily follow any course of rights and wrongs. I think you can make of it as you will. I think you'll be yourself when you're a dragon, but you won't know if you don't try."

Caitriona blinked, her gaze becoming far away for a moment. Whenever they discussed her appearance, it sucked Caitriona's energy away. Self-disgust was an exhausting thing to carry.

"You should get some sleep," Ailith said, leaning forward to kiss Caitriona. Caitriona responded with eagerness and pressed into Ailith's kiss. Ailith savored the moment, humming as Caitriona's hands moved through Ailith's hair and down her neck, alighting her skin with sparks of eagerness. But Caitriona pulled her lips away and left Ailith wanting more. Her golden brow knit as her fingers pulled the metal chain out from beneath Ailith's shirt.

"What's this?"

"Oh. It's something I bought from Ätbënas. It's supposed to give us protection." Ailith reached beneath her shirt and pulled the simple necklace with the green gem hanging from it fully out. She shrugged. "I don't know if it's doing any good but now, I sort of want to cherish it, you know? It was a nice little town. It was peaceful."

She thought of the boy with the big eyes and the elders who offered them the guest house. They could be dead now. The heat of anger welled in her gut at the thought of it. It wasn't just Caitriona she'd kill for; she'd do it for them too.

"That's a nice keepsake." Caitriona studied her, but Ailith couldn't read her expression.

"We should both rest," Caitriona continued, leaning forward to give Ailith a quick kiss. "We have a lot more traveling to do tomorrow."

THEY TRAVELED A DAY AND A HALF UNTIL REACHING THE Umberfend outpost. It stood like a beacon in the summer heat. While the Northern Wood was cool and moist, everywhere else sat in the heat of late summer. Riding in the full sun for the entirety of the day left the group bitter and annoyed.

"Should we pile into one room?" Ceenear asked. "Stick together for safety? I worry that with the dragon attack people are more sensitive to Cait's appearance."

"I'll stay with her," Ailith said. As they traveled further and the heat grew, Ailith found her irritation growing too. Everything annoyed her and the conversation pushed her to an edge. Her tone came out nasty and she found she didn't quite care. They did just fine when they stayed at the outpost before with each to their own rooms. "Do you think she's not safe with me?"

Ceenear blinked and leaned back. "No, no of course not."

"Then we can stay in separate rooms like we did before," Ailith replied as she continued riding, ignoring the pointed looks everyone gave one another. She just wanted to get to the post, wash off and lay down on a bed rather than a mat in the grass.

As the days passed, she found her determination to keep Caitriona safe grew. She was hired to protect her once before and when Greer told her to travel with Caitriona this time, she intended to do it all again. But she was still nursing her wounded ego when she was arrested in Avorkaz and attacked over and over in the wood. Her heart broke in two when she remembered the cut on Caitriona's arm caused by her flailing sword. Even *she* was a danger to Caitriona.

When she killed the shades in the forest, not allowing any to come between her and Caitriona, she felt she finally proved her worth. She wasn't about to let that go. She'd prove she could protect Caitriona in their own room without the constant supervision of the two fae or the hunter.

"I'll request a few rooms," Ceenear offered as they arrived at the outpost. She looked at Ailith and there was something cool in her expression that Ailith didn't try to read. "I'll make sure you're with Cait, Ailith."

"Good."

"Are you alright?" Caitriona caught Ailith's arm as they got down from their horses. "You seem bothered by something."

"I'm fine." Ailith flashed a smile. "Don't worry about me. Go with them, I'll get the horses untacked in the barn."

Caitriona nodded but didn't move. She watched Ailith in a way that made her all the more irritated, they all did.

"Is no one going to remove their bags?" Ailith snapped, sending everyone to pull their items free from the backs of the horses. Their startled reaction, their quick movements and the way they now seemed to avoid bumping into Ailith whilst exchanging looks immediately made her apologetic. The situation was becoming messy.

"Sorry. Go on, get the rooms and maybe some food. I'll see you all in a bit."

Already they filed into the outpost and the scent of the evening meal hung thick in the air. As her group took their items and brought them into the inn, Ailith waited, watching as they went. Once alone, tension eased from her shoulders. The heat was obviously getting to her and she'd have a round of apologies to make after she cooled off and drank some water.

"Come along, Onyx." Ailith led him over the roadway to the stable. One by one, she took each horse and settled them into their own stalls. She paid the stall hand as he walked out to grab his evening meal, then passed through to dole out oats and water to the horses.

"I'll leave some nuts out on the windowsill of our room, Crowley." Ailith pulled a nut from her pack and tossed it to the black crow that hopped along the grass and pecked the ground. "I'll call for you. But go cool off in a tree for now, the air's probably moving further off the ground."

She didn't have to tell the crow twice. He flapped his wings and took to the sky, gliding to the large tree that grew beside the outpost. Alone in the stable, Ailith relaxed. It was hot and sticky there too, but with the sun setting, the heat finally began to lift and cooler air crept in.

"We'll be home soon," she whispered to Onyx as she brushed his mane. "And you can rest a little before our next big adventure."

The floorboards above the hay loft creaked and Ailith went still. Men's voices argued and Ailith crept toward the ladder to the loft, listening intently for what they said.

"I'm telling you," a man said, "that's her."

"And what do you plan to do about it?" another replied, his voice more nasal than the first. "So, what if the princess is at the outpost? Remember when the queen used to come here? Before she became queen?"

"Things were different then," the first man said, his voice low and clear. "The crown made sense back then. Not any of this ridiculous allowance for magic. Not any of this insanity. We weren't under threat of war."

"We were *in* a war back then," the nasal one replied as Ailith gripped the ladder and slowly climbed. She peeked over the edge of the loft floor. There were only the two men she heard, standing toward the end of the stall against a wall of hay.

"That was by the decision of the king. No country felt they could declare war on us and now look where we're at. We're going to be attacked and by none other than a bunch of magic-wielding fae."

"And what does the princess have to do with any of this?"

"She's one of them," the man hissed. "She's half dragon. She can make magic. She'll likely turn on the queen herself. We need to make it a point to remove the kingdom of these magic users and ensure the kingdom doesn't go into the hands of her kind. We need to send a strong enough message to the queen that magic makers are *not* welcome here. Maybe then she'll have a better following willing to fight the fae. She just has to learn to ban magic again, she has to learn it's what the people want."

"You're saying to kill the princess?" the nasal one asked, his voice quiet, and for a moment neither spoke and Ailith held her breath.

The man with the deeper voice who was taller and older with carved wrinkles over his spotted face nodded. "We'll do it tonight. Her entire team's exhausted; did you see them when they arrived? And they were talking about getting separate rooms. It'll be easy. We'll force our way in and kill her in her sleep."

Ailith felt a surge of adrenaline. She squeezed the edge of the floor with one hand, pulling herself upward and through the hole. Her other hand went for her sword still on her waist. She moved quickly and quietly, clearing the edge of the loft and pausing behind a hay bale to inspect if the men had any weapons.

They were oblivious. They kept discussing killing Caitriona as if they were discussing trapping and killing a rabbit for dinner.

They were distracted. Their voices muffled Ailith's slow approach.

They would answer to her. Because she wasn't going to let anyone harm Caitriona.

She wouldn't allow anyone to spread such falsehoods. Caitriona would never turn on Greer; how dare they even consider such a thing. And Ailith wanted to know if there were more. More men like this who crept in the shadows discussing the downfall of a young woman who had nothing but good intentions in her heart.

But they were all like that, weren't they? Every man with an ounce of power Ailith came across in the last two years was. Men who only turned to strength, rage, and blood to combat what they deemed frightening. Men who were afraid of women.

Men who didn't realize women could have internal rage as well.

They would learn.

CHAPTER TWENTY-FOUR

CAITRIONA

After they separated near the entrance of the outpost, Ailith was gone for almost an hour. Wringing her hands until she finally sat, Caitriona's gaze returned again and again to the door leading out of the barkeep's private room.

"Maybe she's calming down," Raum reasoned as he sat beside Caitriona. "She was in an awful mood. She probably decided to take her time with the horses and return with a better mindset."

And she did, coming to the room later with water in her hair and fresh clothing adorning her sun kissed body. She offered a sheepish smile.

"I'm sorry for being snappy." She slipped into a chair; her eyes downcast as she tugged at the edge of her shirt sleeve. "I think everything that's happened, plus the heat, set me off."

"Did you bathe?" Raum laughed.

Ailith rolled her eyes. "I poured a bucket of water from the well over my head. It's what snapped me out of the bad mood."

The air felt substantially lighter as they ate dinner and departed to their rooms.

"I think I'll just go to bed." Ailith moved a chair under the door handle and laid out her weapons as she had each time they stayed at the outpost. "I'm exhausted."

"It's been a lot," Caitriona replied as she pulled off her boots from the edge of the bed. She busied herself with her end of day routine but kept a cautious eye on Ailith. "Maybe an early night will do us all some good."

"That's my thought exactly," Ailith replied, kissing Caitriona on the top of her head, her lips a brief warmth between Caitriona's horns before she stepped away and pulled her clothing off, save for her undergarments and the necklace. She fell asleep the moment her head hit the pillow without another word, without even a second touch to Caitriona, and left the princess alone in the center of the room. It was unusual but the exhaustion of the day hung on Caitriona as well and she crawled into bed, pushing her concerns aside in favor of sleep.

Thunder woke Caitriona hours later. Its rumbling strength made the entire outpost shake and lightning brought the room into vivid detail for a span of a second with each explosion of light. Caitriona rolled to her side and touched Ailith's arm, readying herself for one of Ailith's night terrors. When the dragon attacked while they were children, the lasting impression on Ailith came in the form of blinding terror during thunderstorms. In their time together, Caitriona grew used to Ailith's obvious fear, preparing to comfort her when she'd wake from the storms as they came.

But Ailith didn't wake.

The storm raged; the rain beat against the glass of the window with such intensity Caitriona was sure it would break. The trees outside bent and thrashed in tantrum to the gusts of wind. Caitriona ran her hand down Ailith's arm, over the rippled flesh of her scars, but Ailith continued to sleep. She didn't stir or flinch from the shaking thunder.

Odd. But Ailith was increasingly odd.

Caitriona looked at the winding clock on the wall and realized it was just prior to dawn. Seeing the hour, she slipped from bed to wash her face. Preparing for the final part of their journey towards home, she braided her hair and wiped her limbs down with a damp cloth with the weight of the future on her mind. They were a day's ride from Braewick

City and would arrive after sunset. Soon enough, she'd be with Greer and tell her the dreadful news about the attack and likelihood of Lachlan's death. In just a matter of hours, she'd make her sister's day all the worse.

Lightning struck again and the room lit, but outside, a warm light remained, flickering and casting shadows against the ceiling. Caitriona dropped the cloth into the wash basin and slipped a new shirt on before she crept toward the window to gaze past the tree beyond to the stable yard. Men gathered and spoke to one another, pointing at the stables despite the rain, and turned their attention to one man as he stepped out, shaking his head and gesturing behind him.

"Ailith?" Caitriona whispered from her spot near the window. "Ailith, wake up."

The guard didn't move. Draped in shadows, she continued to sleep. Caitriona reached for a match, striking it to light the lantern on the bedside table. It cast a small glowing circle that plunged Ailith further into darkness.

"*Ailith*," Caitriona repeated, crawling onto the bed and shaking Ailith's shoulders. Ailith rolled onto her back, her eyes dark when she first opened them, but seeming to brighten as she woke.

"What's wrong?" Thunder boomed and Ailith jumped. "Did I sleep through a storm?"

"That and possibly more," Caitriona replied as she glanced over her shoulder toward the light of the men's torches glowing outside. "There's something going on. I don't know if we should be on our guard."

Ailith sat upward, looking toward the window for a moment before crawling to the end of the bed. She pressed a hand against the glass, unaffected by the lightning and thunder. "What're they doing?"

"I don't know," Caitriona whispered, pressing her hand to Ailith's shoulder to look around her. "I can't tell."

"I'm going to wake the others." Ailith turned from the window and moved toward her clothing. "Stay here and lock the door behind me. I'll knock when I come back."

"Do you think it's something dangerous?"

Ailith tugged on her pants and slipped into her shoes. "I suppose we'll find out. I really hope we don't have to climb out a window and sneak off after a storm again."

Caitriona couldn't help the small laugh despite her unease. She hugged herself at the window, looking at the scene below as Ailith went into the hall. The guard was gone for only a few minutes before returning.

"Fiana's going to request breakfast brought to our rooms," Ailith said as she closed the door and locked it. "The kitchen's already working, so she'll see what information she can get downstairs. We'll get ready to go, eat, then try to retrieve our horses."

Caitriona finished dressing as Ailith packed their materials, glancing uneasily out the window repeatedly despite the unchanging scene. The storm moved on and daylight brought out the gray highlights of the world.

A knock sent Ailith pulling out her dagger from the holder she kept on her thigh. She peeked out the door before opening it fully.

"Well, we need to leave," Fiana announced as she stepped in the room. She wore her hunter garb of riding pants, a white shirt and vest. Her hair was pulled back into a ponytail and despite the early hour, she seemed fully awake. "There's a lot of men sniffing around for information and gossip, and I swear, they're worse than hungry wolves. The first scent of blood and they don't think straight."

"What happened?" Caitriona asked as she tied her boots.

"The stable hand found dead bodies in the hay loft. Sounds pretty gruesome. I already told Ceenear and Raum to get their things. Let's stick together when we go." Fiana stepped out of the room then paused and turned back. "Ailith, can I talk to you for a second?"

"Yes, of course." Ailith dropped her pack on the bed and followed Fiana out the door. Left in the room alone, Caitriona turned to her pack for a second before thinking again and pressing her ear against the door.

"They had a note," Fiana said. "We need to get out of here and do so as quietly as we can."

"Who had a note?" Ailith asked.

"The dead bodies in the loft. One had a note crumpled in his hand. It said '*the loft at sunset, the horned beast.*'"

There was a hiss and a pause. "You think they planned to hurt Cait?"

"I assume so," Fiana continued. "But it doesn't answer who killed them in the first place. You didn't see anyone at the stalls last night, did you?"

The floorboard outside the door creaked as one of them shifted on foot, making Caitriona jump back. Having heard enough, she returned to her bag and finished packing.

"There's only a few drops left of May's potion. It isn't enough to last the full day, but it can get us out of here," Ailith announced as she returned to the room. "Just for a little more discretion."

Despite that Ailith was sweet and kind to Caitriona, the growing irritation she had, the short temper, all made Caitriona hyper-aware of Ailith's every movement and comment. Caitriona looked Ailith over, watching as the guard pulled on the clothing she wore the evening before and gathered her weapons. When Caitriona didn't answer, Ailith looked at her and Caitriona stood a little taller. She smiled. "Yes, that sounds like a good plan."

As they readied to go, each sipping their potions to change their appearance, Raum paused over his.

"It's the white hair, isn't it?" Caitriona asked and the fae guard frowned. Her heart ached for her friends. Lumia was kind to Caitriona while she was in the fae queendom, but it was abundantly clear Raum viewed the pale fae like a flower facing the sun. As the days passed, dread filled Caitriona whole over what happened to the fae woman.

"I'm worried. Lumia and I rarely go a week without speaking to one another. But we haven't spoken since Niveem told us about Onora. I told you we've been arguing more frequently. She's always been headstrong, but we often complimented each other with our opinions. Lately, not so much. Now with this silence there's something wrong with it and this potion reminds me of that."

"Oh, just *take the potion*," Ailith sighed as she pushed her own potion bottle into her bag. She looked at Raum, scowling. "We get it, you miss her but wasting time making a new potion so you don't think of your lover isn't helping any of us. You're right, things are weird. They probably aren't great. Maybe something happened to Lumia. Maybe she was taken or killed, but what good is wasting *our* time nitpicking over potions when we could already be on the road heading towards Greer? There's a *war* brewing, Raum."

All stared, their mouths at varying stages of hanging open. Caitriona swallowed back the distaste of Ailith's comment. Ailith groaned and rolled her eyes. "Let's just get a move on, please?"

"It's alright," Fiana whispered after Ailith stormed from the room. "I just need to add chamomile to the mixture, and it'll make your hair blonde. Will that work?"

Raum stared at the door Ailith left from, his brow wrinkled with thought. Blinking, he looked at Fiana as if he just realized she was standing there. "Yes, that'd be great. Thank you."

They slipped out as the sun fully rose. Raum and Ceenear retrieved the horses while Ailith and Caitriona stood with Fiana.

"How do you think we should get home?" Ailith asked, shifting her pack onto her back. "We can take the main road south of here, straight into Braewick Valley, but do you think that'll be dangerous?"

"I'd avoid it if possible. I don't know if there's any forest roads we can take but ..." Fiana trailed off. "I don't know ... it feels safer."

Caitriona said nothing. No one told her what was found on the men, so she pretended not to know. Looking at the growing hills to the west that eventually led into Braewick Valley, an idea struck her. "There's an old farming road this far north. If we go straight towards the trees to the west, we'll have to backtrack slightly, but the road should still be there. Greer used it a few times when she traveled and wanted to avoid the main roads and I've noted it on maps I've drawn. It goes toward the farmlands north of Braewick City. We can cut straight down from there. I don't know how much safer it'll be, but we'll avoid the main roads."

"That could work," Ailith said as Ceenear and Raum walked out with their horses. "Will it add a lot of time to getting home?"

Caitriona took a slow breath; this was the part she didn't like. "Probably another day or two, depending on how quickly we move and if we avoid any issues."

Ailith *tsked* her tongue and dragged the toe of her boot in the dirt. "I don't like that."

"It may be the best option though. We can always send your crow ahead to tell Greer about Lachlan," Fiana suggested and Caitriona shook her head.

"No, Lachlan possibly being dead is something I need to tell her directly. I can't destroy her hopes for aid in a letter. If the path toward home seems to be taking too long, we can send Crowley ahead just to let her know we're on our way, but I can't mention Lachlan. Not yet."

The pathway to the farmlands was overgrown, and without complete familiarity of it, they moved slowly. Ailith sent Crowley to the skies to scout the roadway and he flew in lazy circles overhead indicating the direction to go. Everyone rode silently, the horses snuffing and stomping across the ground the only sound.

Ceenear and Ailith led the party this time, with Caitriona behind them, and Raum and Fiana took the rear to ensure her safety. There were no obvious threats, but something crept into Caitriona's mind that she couldn't quite free herself from, yet she wasn't ready to admit.

Ailith's mood hadn't lightened as they rode, and their first night sleeping on the hillside of the valley ridge was awkward and quiet for all. The following day, the unease spread to the rest of the party as they reached the valley's crest and moved toward the northern farmlands.

"We should reach Braewick tomorrow." Caitriona investigated the dip of the land. Lights winked in the dying day from little farmhouses throughout the lush land and Caitriona felt there was a sense of ease she was lacking. She was so close to home, why didn't she feel comforted?

Turning back to the camp she smiled at the two fae and the hunter sitting before the fire. "I can't express how much it means to me that you three have helped us—"

Ailith stepped from the tree line with a dead rabbit in her grasp and Caitriona lifted her gaze and froze. Expanding from Ailith's chest like tendrils of smoke was a darkness; fizzling and electric it spread over Ailith's body and surrounded her head.

When Caitriona recovered in Ulla Syrmin, Niveem worked with Caitriona to understand when she witnessed magic at work—it was one of the lasting impressions from the curse that stayed with Caitriona—and while magic often looked like glittering dew in sunlight, she saw it a time or two appear like this blackened wave filled with sharpness and bite.

With her breath tight in her chest, Caitriona looked away, and her gaze met Raum's, whose brows rose slightly. He glanced at Ailith and again at Caitriona questioningly. Caitriona frowned and slowly lifted her finger to her lips.

She pretended things were normal; sitting beside Ailith as if nothing was amiss, kissing her cheek and whispering goodnight despite the darkness that was swarming Ailith's head like a colony of bees. Ailith seemed exhausted again and didn't volunteer to keep watch as the previous nights.

"Sleep," Caitriona encouraged her. "We have four people who can do watches. Not everyone has to take one. You're exhausted and we don't know what Greer has planned for you when we get back. Just rest for now."

And that's exactly what she did. Ailith fell into a deep sleep almost instantly, snoring slightly as she lay on her back beside the fire, and leaving Caitriona and the others watching her with building dread.

"What's wrong with her?" Fiana asked. "I don't know her very well, but she was a lot nicer when we met than she's been the last few days."

"This harshness isn't like her. I'm not sure what's happening but it isn't good," Caitriona whispered before glancing at Ailith once more.

"Perhaps we should move a little bit away from her for some privacy? Although I don't think she'll wake," Ceenear suggested. They settled apart from her, but still in view, huddled close together as they considered the human guard.

"She's been nasty," Raum added. "And she's never been like this. She's more caring. And then this evening ..."

"There's magic at work," Caitriona explained to Fiana and Ceenear. "I can see it on her. When we took the potions, she was bathed in magic, but since they've run out there's something new. This dark magic. It's not good."

"Her aura's different," Raum continued. "We've been so close to her these last few days I haven't had the distance to see her aura at all, but when she came out of the woods her aura became clear. It's normally light pink, but now it's diluted and barely visible. There's a shadow to it and this sense of wrongness from it that isn't entirely coming from *her*."

"Do you think she's cursed?" Ceenear looked toward Ailith with a frown.

Raum shook his head. "The true aura will still show, but you'll see a darkness at the center, like a bad spot. It's how Caitriona looked when I first met her. But Ailith's different. The darkness covers her, it's taking over the pink color and drowning it out."

They fell silent and Caitriona slipped into guilt. She should have noticed sooner and caught onto what was going on. She flipped backward through the past days, trying to recall each instance where something felt off, until it became clear.

"When the shades attacked the last time in the Northern Wood, it was strange. She always doubted using her blades and while she's certainly gotten more skillful with plenty of practice, she's never been someone to seek out killing something else. But with the shades, she went for them rather than waiting for them to come to her.

"And that was after we left Ätbënas. She told me when she was in Ätbënas she got a necklace to help protect us. Do you think it could be that?"

Fiana looked at the two fae and leaned forward. "She got it from Ätbënas?"

"Yes, from the little shop."

"I was with her at the shop. Nothing seemed amiss and they aren't the type of people to place curses or poisons in their items."

Ailith stirred and the group fell silent again.

"I think that's enough talk for now," Ceenear said as she scooted forward on the stone she was sitting on and got to her feet. "Whatever's going on, we should get our sleep while we can and figure it out tomorrow. If she acts strange again, we corner her. Fiana, can your protective circles work on people?"

"It can work on whatever I decide we need protection from. I'll make sure my supplies are ready." Fiana stood and stretched her arms over her head. Dropping them down and straightening her shirt she looked at Caitriona and gave a half smile. "We'll figure it out. Don't worry."

Settled beside Ailith for the night, Caitriona watched her breathe, realizing she had never been one to *not* worry, and she wasn't about to start now.

CHAPTER TWENTY-FIVE

RÓISÍN

Nearly Seven Years Prior

"Where's Father?" Greer burst through the door like a whirlwind in winter, her anger like snowflakes swirling with insistence to coat all surfaces and force enemies to cower against its chill. Her blonde hair, normally in place and pulled back, was half loose from its bun. Strands bordered her face and stuck to her sweaty brow. Her cheeks were flushed, riding gloves still covered her hands and her boots were caked in remnants of the horse stalls. "*Where is he?*"

"Are you injured? What's going on?" Róisín dropped her spoon, her shock keeping the rising panic quiet and her movements slow as her mind raced forward with a million scenarios as to why her eldest stood before her. "Why are you here?"

"Because I have to see my father."

Róisín had just begun a late dinner after tucking Caitriona into bed. The day was nearly done. The guards by the door looked uneasily between the two royals but remained at attention, waiting, and surely listening. Róisín rose but remained at the table.

"I don't know where he is. I met with dressmakers and attended the dedication ceremony for the fountain in the city. I've just returned. He isn't in the war room or his office?"

"No. I went there first." Her eldest daughter's lip curled back in a snarl, eyes flashing with rage; it was unfortunate that Greer looked so like her father, but in manner she often was similar to Róisín—except when she was angry. Then she was fully her father's daughter, his near equal match.

"Greer ..." She had to be careful, her daughter was like a captured beast, ready to attack if she sensed any danger. Though Róisín wasn't quite sure what she would perceive as a danger. "You aren't meant to be here ... you were sent to the fields."

"*Exactly*. He sent me to the fields. He sent me there and now I'm here and I *need to talk to him*."

After Caitriona's magical return to life ten years prior and Cearny admitting he knew Róisín had magic, the two kept apart as much as possible whilst performing a dizzying dance of separation. To the staff and people of the kingdom, they were honorable to one another because they attended necessary functions together, but in reality they kept far apart. What Cearny did on a day-to-day schedule was beyond Róisín's knowledge. She only had an inkling of Cearny's activities through gossip or scheduled interactions before the public eye.

"Come, we'll find him together." Róisín extended her hand as she stepped from the table. Greer turned on her heel and disappeared into the hall leaving Róisín's hand empty.

Whatever this was, it wasn't good.

Greer left for the Avorkaz battlefields a week prior. She was due to be there, leading a charge, and likely wouldn't have been home for another fortnight at least. Róisín hated it. She hated to see her child leave for war with a tense pressure on her shoulders and heart that she may never see her again. Beside that quaking fear, she ached from the knowledge that with every call to arms Cearny made for her daughter, it was another instance Greer became more like him. Another battle, another witness to the death of magic, another moment Greer followed Cearny's orders and mirrored his decisions.

Greer stood a few feet outside Róisín's room, a near specter with her rage as she waited for her mother. Her jaw set as she turned toward the king's wing, not waiting any longer for Róisín to catch up.

"Greer, we'll do this together," Róisín called. Her guards followed like shadows, the metallic rub of their swords against their sides a rhythmic sound as they walked. "But you need to tell me what's wrong so I can help."

Greer's fury wafted off her and reminded Róisín of Kayl when they were younger with a bitter pain. His emotions could coat a room just like Greer.

"I don't need your help," Greer said as she marched with her hands in fists. But Greer's step hesitated, her next words coming out soft. "Not in that way."

"Then tell me what happened, please," Róisín continued as attendants opened the doors to the king's hall and held them back for the pair to pass. Distantly, Róisín could hear Cearny's laugh from his office and the hairs rose on the back of her neck. Wherever he was, he had returned in the time it took for Greer to find her. She avoided him so much and now she was following Greer who was sure to burst through his door unannounced, certain to bring on his ire, and if it wasn't for the love she had for Greer, the clear fact her daughter needed her, she would rather run the other way. "Are you hurt? Injured?"

"Not physically," Greer chirped as she predictably walked straight to Cearny's door and thrust the heavy doors open without hesitation. The room beyond was brightly lit with a multitude of candles. Cearny sat at his desk with a scattering of lords arranged at his side who often whispered in his ear. They all held goblets as an attendant finished pouring wine.

"Father."

They stared, clearly surprised by Greer's appearance, while the guards at the door stepped aside to allow the heir's entrance. The attendant placed the bottle of wine on Cearny's table and darted for the door.

Róisín approached at a slower pace and allowed the attendant to leave. He was smart to do so.

She took her position in the doorway of Cearny's room, not wanting to enter the place if she could avoid it. Uneasily, she caught the eye of other attendants who waited near the entrance between the king's wing and the family's hall. Nodding, they propped the doors open. A quick escape from Cearny if necessary.

"Greer," Cearny rumbled, drawing Róisín's attention back to the room. His eyes narrowed on his daughter, but he maintained a smile for the good of the lords. "My heir, what's brought you back to the castle? I believe your orders were to the Avorkaz battlefields."

"They were." Greer's words were stunted, jagged things split between sharp teeth. Róisín was certain her daughter could spit venom if she tried. "I was there and now I've returned because I needed to speak to you. I have a question, a very important one."

"You couldn't have sent a squire?" Cearny laughed, glancing at the lords who chuckled with him. They followed like mirrors to his emotional demands, reflecting any reaction he had.

Greer straightened her posture, standing taller than her twenty years allowed. "I think this is best asked by me and without your lords present."

Cearny's bristled eyebrow rose. They were so alike, two stubborn people who would bite down on what they desired and not let go. They would be unstoppable if Greer followed Cearny's command. But this heavily felt like the opposite. The way her daughter quivered, her hands fists, reminded Róisín immediately of Greer as a toddler when she outright refused to follow directions.

Róisín wasn't privy to the goings on of the Avorkaz war, only that it was happening and never in the favor of their kingdom. Standing behind Greer, Róisín couldn't see her daughter's expression, but she imagined it well enough based on her tone. Her comment held a warning and Cearny would be wise to listen.

He leaned back in his chair and looked at his lords. "They are part of all my plans, they help guide me, and so, they stay."

Cearny was never very smart.

Greer's head tilted to the side and Róisín could hear the smile on her breath as she spoke, her tone warm and smooth, yet sharp. "I want to know if you gave the order to murder Avorkazians who approached our men for aid."

Róisín grew still, wishing she could blend into the doorframe and become part of the wood. It would be safer than standing there, a physical being that could be marked by Cearny's wrath that was sure to brew beyond the flash in his eyes Greer's words instantly caused.

"Gentlemen, my lords," Cearny sighed, the tail end of a laugh attempting to bubble up but only half-heartedly. "Would you excuse me? I need to speak with my heir."

"Explain to me why I reached the battlefield and within a day, upon us approaching a village, your men began hacking at innocent citizens?" Greer snapped, stepping closer to Cearny's desk. The lords, already making their way out of the room, paused and turned their attention to their king.

Cearny stared at Greer for a breath. He blinked, seemingly remembering his lords still stood there. His rage turned to them as his face grew red and his eyes bulged. "Get. Out."

They rushed, a river of robes, clanking swords that never saw battle, and bobbing heads for their queen as they passed through the door. Puppets, all of them.

"You too."

Róisín turned back to the room and found Cearny looking at her. She felt the spark of nerves spread across her body like lightning crawling across a summer sky.

"She stays," Greer replied, her voice low as she looked over her shoulder at her mother. "She has a right to know."

Róisín looked at her husband. It felt like another lifetime when she was able to gaze at him and feel power and control. A lifetime ago when she felt she had a chance, that perhaps they could find love and work together to better the world. Now she was only a shadow. A remnant of the girl who came to the castle, a figure standing in the back who quickly bent under Cearny's decisions because it was better to obey than to invite trouble. It was better to listen and be as distant as possible than to cause his anger to rise. When it did, the tidal wave of his temper always turned into threats towards the livelihood of her youngest child. He grasped her greatest fears and tossed out the threats with regularity. But in this, she felt emboldened by her first born's bravery.

"I stay." She took a small, determined step further into the room.

The smallest smile curled along Greer's lips before she returned her attention to her father. "I reached the battlefield and the following day we moved towards one of the villages. We were meant to reconnoiter the village and decide our next move, at least that was my decree. I wanted to see what advances we could muster and if we had any success in the battles preceding my arrival. And yet, when I arrived, your men began to slaughter people."

Cearny stared at Greer, his face blank, yet irritation radiated off him. Slowly, he lifted his goblet and sipped his wine. "Yes?"

Greer's shoulders dropped. "Why were they slaughtering people? You've poisoned the crops of Avorkaz, you've poisoned the river, these people were starving and sick. They came to us begging for help, promising allegiance, and the response was to kill them?"

Caressing the goblet between his hands, Cearny investigated its contents and sighed. He seemed bored and it enraged Róisín. How could he face his daughter who was obviously distraught with so little emotion? "That's what I ordered them to do, yes."

"They were *my* men, *mine* to control," Greer hissed. "I told them to stop and they didn't."

"Because they're *my* men, Greer. You're only the heir right now and you forget your place. You aren't queen, not yet, not for a long time. They're mine. They follow *my* rules."

Greer's chest heaved and she remained quiet for a moment. Her tongue darted over her lips and her throat bobbed. "It was an entire village, Father. They killed the entire village. Men, women, children, the elderly. All are dead. All gone."

"We had to send a message. What good is this battle if we cannot make Avorkaz understand that they're beneath us, that they're weak and must be controlled?"

"What good is this battle if all the people are dead? What are you after, Father? Control of a city empty of people? What is the point of all of this if you're going to kill them all? They were asking for help; they were willing to do anything for safety and health."

"Because the town was filled with magic makers." Cearny lifted the goblet, his eyes rose and shifted away from Greer to meet Róisín's gaze. "We aren't going to welcome that filth into our kingdom ever again."

Greer's strike was quick. Her hand swung out, a flash of her palm as she lurched close to the desk. The goblet flew from Cearny's hand and bounced off the wine bottle. It hit the stone wall with a clatter and wine sprayed across the white paint like splattering blood. The wine bottle tipped to its side and poured its contents on the desk, Cearny's paperwork, and the king himself. Róisín couldn't help but gasp.

"This is beyond what little decency exists in war. This is too far, Father, and I won't do it. I won't partake in this behavior. I won't fight your battle."

Cearny stared at his desk, the wine spreading to coat the papers in deep red—the closest he came to anything resembling spilt blood in years. Too often he stayed at the castle, only leaving to seek out new areas to attempt to conquer or give a heartened speech to battle-weary guards.

Greer lifted her hand once more, the intent to slap her father clear, and with a pain in Róisín's chest, she realized this was something learned. Róisín never raised a hand to her children, but the same likely wasn't true for Cearny.

As he lifted his gaze, Róisín rushed forward to Greer and stilled her daughter's raised hand. Greer's hand quivered with fury, stiff at first from the connection to her mother but slowly, gratefully, it relaxed.

When Greer spoke again, her voice was low, a barely-held whisper as if to speak any louder would undo her. "I refuse to partake in your battle of blood. I'll go to other fields, I'll do presentations in kingdoms, meet with princes, and travel the land for you, but I will no longer go to Avorkaz or anywhere near there. And I refuse to allow you to schedule my own men, the heir's royal guard, to battle there anymore. They're mine, they obey my word, and I'll not have you step over that boundary, *Father*."

"Who do you think you are to command me?" Cearny shook droplets of wine off his hand before getting to his feet. He towered over both Róisín and Greer. Róisín shrunk backward, but Greer's hand gripped hers, holding her mother to the spot beside her.

"Your heir. The future queen of Wimleigh. Your only hope to continue our family line."

"I could easily dispose of you. We have a spare."

"Don't speak as if Caitriona means anything to you, Father," Greer said. Her voice was low with rage simmering under her tongue. "You can't even say her name. You only refer to her as a spare. We all know. It's been obvious for years. You haven't cared for her since the dragon attack, and you'd rather die than let her rule this kingdom. Let's be honest with one another, I'm your only hope, and you know that."

Cearny was silent. Róisín looked between the two with large eyes. The crash of panicked desire to flee the scene and abundant pride in her daughter battled within her chest, her breaths rapid. Two stubborn rulers who held opposing opinions would be the end of Cearny if he could open his eyes wide enough to realize the signs before him.

Years before Róisín spoke like Greer. She was rarely one to back down from a verbal fight when she was young, but it was quickly taken from her, the words of rage and quick commentary zapped from her very soul when she came to the castle. She became someone secretive who battled Cearny in silent ways because it was the safest option. Greer hadn't learned that lesson yet, apparently.

"I'll do as you say in all things but Avorkaz," Greer continued, her grip still tight on Róisín's hand. "But in that, I'm done. I refuse. If you want that horror to continue, it will not be through me. Do you understand?"

The silence was like a looming storm, darkening every surface and giving a sense of uncertain doom. Cearny's eyes moved over his office, studying the surfaces and eventually finding their way to Róisín. His brows furrowed. "I understand," he replied, but kept his gaze locked on Róisín.

"Good. All of my men traveled back from Avorkaz with me and have returned to their homes per my command. Since we've had this discussion, I'm going to retire for the night and allow you the opportunity to see what use you'll have of me since my schedule has rapidly become open. Goodnight, Father."

Greer's hand released Róisín's as she turned and walked from the room. Cearny continued glowering at Róisín, nearly locking her into place if it weren't for the sound of her eldest receding. Her soul was perpetually tied to her children and where they went, she would follow.

Turning on her heel, she left Cearny's office and followed Greer back to the family wing. She ran forward, gripping her skirts in her sweaty hands as she rushed to catch up. "Greer, are you alright?"

"I don't understand how you married him," Greer hissed, her anger still evident and now turning on her mother. "His cruelty expands beyond our family and destroys the lives of strangers, innocents. It's abominable."

Róisín came to a stop. She had this coming for her, she knew it. A mother couldn't remove herself from her child's life and leave her to the controlling attention of her father without the expectation of facing the ugly toll at some point. She didn't know what to say other than what flitted through her head for years. "I'm sorry."

Greer shook her head. "I don't want to hear it, honestly. It's done, there's nothing that can change it all."

"Ree?" A voice came from further down the hall. Caitriona peeked around her bedroom door, her blue eyes large, her red hair a tangle of locks around her rumpled nightgown. Her pale skin was marked with blemishes as womanhood just began to descend upon the thirteen-year-old. "I heard a crash, is everything alright? What are you doing here?"

And just like that, the fight left Greer. The young woman visibly deflated, a sigh escaped her lips as she let go of her frustrations, and a smile showed on her face.

"I'm home early." She moved forward, her arms held outward. "Would you like me to sleep over?"

Caitriona smiled; the same gleaming sun similar to her sister's. They were both so bright when they were happy. The perpetual flames of Róisín's heart. "Yes!"

"But look at me, I'm a mess and tracking dirt through the halls. I'll change and come join you. Get in bed, Cait. I'll be there shortly."

Caitriona didn't need to be told twice before she returned to her room, not once noticing her mother standing in the hallway. Greer slowed her movement when Caitriona's door clicked closed and turned back to her mother.

"You should go back to your room, Mother." The light in her voice was gone, the reserved and angry woman returned. "You'll likely not want to cross Father's path for some time."

There was no use hiding it all. "I suspect you're right. Goodnight, Greer."

Greer only nodded to her in reply, yet neither moved.

"Greer," Róisín attempted. She ran her tongue over her teeth and looked about the hall, her unease making it hard to greet Greer's gaze. "You did well. I want you to know that."

Greer was still, her breath held in her chest and her eyes stared at a spot on the ground. Rubbing her lips together, Róisín bowed her head and turned toward her own rooms, unable to stay any longer. She was certain Greer would be alright. She'd be safe and when she was queen, she'd rule justly; Róisín only hoped that day would come soon.

CHAPTER TWENTY-SIX

CAITRIONA

The roadway curved down the valley ridge at an angle, propelling them closer to Braewick City while remaining within the confines of the steep valley hillside. Below, farmland lush with summer growth spread out in a patchwork of various greens in tidy rows. There were berry and fruit fields along the border, and farmers worked hard to harvest late summer crops toward the south while autumnal crops grew in thick rows towards the north where the sunshine would still reach as it came lower on the horizon. Even in the quiet morning, Caitriona spotted wagons ladened with produce moving along the central pathway toward the city for markets and the castle.

Despite the peaceful start to the day, everyone tried their best not to antagonize Ailith, yet she was still foul all the same. Ailith woke first, her movement stirring Caitriona from her own rest, and while Ailith already made breakfast for them all—something Caitriona was grateful for—she still lurked around the camp with annoyance radiating off her.

Caitriona saw Ailith overcome by emotion before, she saw her annoyed from time to time, but the constant edge in her voice left even Caitriona keeping her distance. She opted to settle with her morning meal on a rock ledge where she could look at the farmland. Soon they would be home and hopefully Ailith could get some rest and cheer up. But Ailith's mood seemed determined to make their travel feel double the length.

"Come on," Ailith declared, waking those who still slept just after sunrise. "Now's not the time to get lazy. We have to go; we have to move."

"We *are* moving," Raum growled, unable to hold back much longer. Caitriona twisted from her perch and shot him a look of warning. Reacting to Ailith's mood was *not* the plan..

Luckily, Ailith was oblivious and continued her rumbles. "This ridiculous road already added an extra day of travel. We should've continued along the marsh. If anyone bothered us we could've just killed them." Ailith shook out her sleeping mat and began rolling it up.

"We should stop early for lunch," Ceenear suggested, causing Ailith to grumble further. Ceenear's shoulders dropped as she turned to Ailith. She looked pleading, her brows arched and her head tilted slightly to the side, and when she spoke her voice was soft. Gentle. As if not to upset an animal. "I'm just thinking if we have to scavenge for anything and if we eat well enough, we can just push through to the city for the remainder of the day."

"I'll hunt for something now then. Animals aren't as active by midday, it's too hot. I'll carry the carcass until we break for a meal. Cait, I need you to tie my bags to Onyx." Ailith sighed as she carried her supplies and hoisted it onto Onyx's saddle to tie it off. She took his reins and stepped forward, shoving them into Caitriona's hand before stomping into the forest. All looked at one another before tying their horses to nearby trees.

"We were about to leave," Fiana murmured, letting her head fall back with an exasperated sigh as the rest of the group watched Ailith disappear.

"She's not thinking straight." Caitriona watched Ailith in the shadows of the trees before their shade enveloped her fully while she half-heartedly tied Ailith's supplies to Onyx. The horse turned his head toward her and butted against Caitriona's shoulder. She pet his soft, warm nose and sighed. Her heart felt ready to break as she made excuses for Ailith while simultaneously feeling embarrassed by her behavior.

Raum looked towards the woods while tying his horse to a tree. "I feel like, if this is going to happen, we should do it soon."

"Be on the lookout for her approach," Ceenear forewarned. "Take another look at her. See if magic's still on her, if her aura's dimmed, and if it is, we'll do it."

As the sun climbed, the heat stuck to them like an unwanted smock. Moments dragged by as the sun reached its highest point in the sky, the morning now lost while Ailith remained in the woods. The sun bore down, pressing their patience and they shifted to the shade to continue to wait. Caitriona felt sweat pinprick along her brow and gather by her horns.

"Should we look for her?" Fiana asked, but a crash from the woods answered before anyone else could.

Ailith stepped forward, her body lurching unnaturally. From her chest spilled the darkness, wrapping around her like cloth. It circled her arms, draped over her legs, and curled over her head before settling into her temples. Raum and Caitriona rose to their feet.

"I see you've been waiting for me," Ailith sneered. She wasn't holding anything, no kill for the midday meal. Dirt was smeared across her face, and her hair was pulled from her ponytail as if she got caught in a bush.

"Ailith," Caitriona stepped forward, but there was still considerable distance between Ailith and the rest. "We're worried about you."

Ailith avoided eye contact with Caitriona entirely as if hurt or embarrassed as she walked forward with uneven footsteps and a sway to her body.

Months ago, after celebrating Greer's birthday, Ailith got deliciously drunk. Caitriona led her to her room, holding Ailith up as she stumbled and lurched, walking as if the world was tilting sideways and ready to throw her off. She moved similarly now, but the revelry present months ago was absent, as was the joy of celebration. This was different, this was unnatural.

Ailith's lips curled back as she sneered. The hatred in her eyes an expression Caitriona never saw on Ailith's face before. It scared her.

"You're teaming up against me. You're all a danger; you're all a threat." She reached to her side and drew the sword Barden gifted her.

The metal shown in the sunshine as her gaze landed on Caitriona. She shook her head. "Even you? I *love* you; I just want to protect you. I want to protect *all* of you and you're turning on me."

"Ailith, we're not." Raum held his hands up. Side-stepping closer. "We don't know what's going on but something's off."

Ailith grew still for a breath before swinging her sword back over her head. She released a desperate scream before running toward Ceenear who stood closest to her. Ceenear jumped back with ease and pulled her own short sword free with a fluid movement. She blocked Ailith's blade but her expression conveyed her shock.

"Grab hold of her!" Raum yelled, reaching to his belt and pulling his own sword out. He charged forward, meeting Ailith's blade with his own.

Before the curse, when they first entered Ulla Syrmin, Ailith trained with Raum. Caitriona caught sight of them one evening and the duel was vastly uneven with Raum easily overwhelming Ailith over and over. But something changed. Time, training, and whatever was possessing Ailith made her a fiercer fighter, a relentless one.

"Is there anything you can do to slow her down?" Caitriona asked as she spun towards Fiana. "Do you have anything? Quickly!"

Fiana reached into her pockets, dumping supplies as she scrambled through her items. She prepared to trap Ailith with a salt mixture but not to stop her from fighting. An oversight they couldn't worry about now.

Pulling free a powder, Fiana held it up. "Got it!"

She ran forward, dodging a blade and nearly being stabbed by Raum in the process. Moving on skilled feet, she ducked another swinging blade before blowing the powder into Ailith's face, causing her to stumble backward instantly and lose her fighting stance.

Raum lashed out, knocking Ailith's sword from her hand. It spun across the stone outcrop. "Quickly! Grab her!"

Fiana pulled Ailith's arms behind her and pinned her hands with her grasp as Ceenear moved in to disarm Ailith; all that was left was her dagger strapped to her thigh that was quickly pulled and tossed aside.

Caitriona moved forward, her breaths coming fast despite that she hadn't been involved in the near melee.

Ailith thrashed against her hold, attempting to fight Fiana while Raum made quick work of a rope. Caitriona came closer, her movements slow and cautious. Stepping before Ailith with tears filling her eyes, she cupped Ailith's face in her palms, stilling her head although Ailith at first tried to bite. "*Ailith* we're trying to *help you*."

"*Let me go*," Ailith hissed as she struggled against the bindings. The darkness poured from her chest. It crawled up Ailith's neck and over her cheeks before seeping into her eyes. Her pupils widened and the darkness engulfed her eyes until they were black orbs.

Caitriona's breath caught in her throat. Her frightened face reflected in Ailith's black gaze. Ailith smiled, spit dripping from her lips as she tilted her forehead closer to press against Caitriona's.

"I killed them." Ailith whispered. Her voice came out differently, higher and shrill. Mad. Possessed. "Those people at the inn? I killed them both. They wanted to kill you, Cait. They wanted to cut the horns from your head, they wanted to have them as trophies. I heard them say that.

"So, I crawled into the hay loft, snuck behind them, and cut their hands from their bodies. But that wasn't enough, I was still hungry. I cut their tongues from their mouths too. I watched their lives seep out and I filled myself *whole* on their deaths." Ailith lost her strength, her body growing heavy as she leaned forward. Her lips brushed against Caitriona's cheek as the necklace tumbled out from the confines of her shirt to dangle over her chest.

"The necklace." Caitriona looked at Raum as she cupped Ailith's head in her hands. "The necklace she got from Ätbënas."

"The shades in the woods weren't enough," Ailith continued as if Caitriona hadn't spoken. "But I had to do it, I had to protect you."

Raum grabbed hold of the chain and pulled. "Enough of this." The metal snapped and Raum threw it, sending the necklace clattering across the rocky ground until it came to rest a few feet away where the sun glinted off the green stone innocently.

Ailith stopped her rambling. Each breath was slow and deep as her jaw hung open. The darkness in her eyes began to recede and her weight sagged further. As her eyes slowly returned to their brown, they were filled with pure terror.

"I'm ... I'm," she repeated before her eyes rolled back and she slumped into Caitriona's waiting arms.

Ailith rested on her mat with her hands tied behind her back. Her sword, dagger and bow sat on the other side of the campsite. Caitriona remained alongside her friends while they watched Ailith sleep.

"What do we do now?" Fiana asked. She gathered her supplies that she dropped in the chaos, organizing them on a boulder before slipping each into the little pockets that decorated her vest.

"Try and figure out what was going on with this?" Raum lifted the necklace, the green stone hanging from it. "Is it something Greer can use? Is it something more people may have?"

"We should break it." Fiana looked at the necklace with disgust.

"You think?" Raum turned to her and Fiana shrugged.

"Honestly, I'm more familiar with magic potions and beasts. I don't know about magical items. If you're hoping to have someone inspect it or Greer to use it ... I suppose breaking it isn't the best idea. I don't know."

Caitriona buried her face in her hands. She had been on the brink of tears since Ailith came from the woods. Her nervous system was spent, and she felt exhaustion down to her very core. How did their bad situation just get worse? The loss of Lachlan and now Ailith possessed? With Ailith unconscious before them and a mysterious necklace in hand, she felt all her strength deplete.

"We'll figure this out," Ceenear said softly; her hand rested on Caitriona's shoulder with reassurance.

Caitriona sniffed. She wiped away warm tears that escaped her eyes and wiped her fingers on her pants. "I'm just thinking of what she said about those men, how she murdered them."

"We don't know if it's true. She could've been lying." Ceenear smiled and she began to rub Caitriona's back.

"Uh, actually ..." Fiana chimed in. She shifted with discomfort.

"When I found out about the deaths, I heard something about their hands missing, although not the rest ..."

"She came to dinner wet," Raum said as he rubbed the edge of his chin. He looked as badly as Caitriona felt. Beside Caitriona, Raum was the one with the closest relationship to Ailith. "She must've washed the blood off herself."

Caitriona looked at Onyx who stood resolutely tied to a tree. Ailith's bags remained on his back and the sight sparked an idea. Standing on shaky legs, Caitriona crossed the open rockface to the pack. Hesitating for a moment, the reality of the situation like a snake about to strike, she opened the flap and dumped Ailith's belongings onto the ground. She barely stifled her sob.

There, beside clothing that belonged to Caitriona—the clothing Ailith packed in case Caitriona turned into a dragon—was the shirt and pants Ailith wore when they arrived at the outpost. Balled up, it was still clear the fabric was covered with the brown stain of old blood.

"How could she?" Caitriona whispered.

"Because *she* didn't," Ceenear reassured. She stood and brushed past Caitriona to pick up the bloody clothing. "She would never do something like that. Not in her right mind."

Ceenear threw the ball of clothing into the remnants of the fire they had the night before. Squatting beside it, she began to rekindle the fire and leaned back on her heels as she waited for the clothing to catch. "That wasn't her, Caitriona. That was whatever came from that necklace."

"That's what's confusing me." Fiana leaned forward and plucked the necklace from Raum's hand. She turned it over, inspecting the jewel and chain. "This isn't like Ätbënas either. This isn't something they would do. There's something off about all of this."

"Well, it wouldn't be the first time something was off." Raum sighed. "We're dealing with Malcolm, and I suspect he's tied to this necklace somehow."

"He did know where to send the dragon," Caitriona murmured. "He ensured it was gold so the blame could be pinned on me. He must have known I was near Avorkaz."

"And just in case you weren't captured in Avorkaz, this necklace could provide another threat in the form of your own guard turning against you." Raum crossed his arms over his chest and frowned at Ailith who still lay still on the ground.

"No." Caitriona shook her head. "I mean, you're partially right. But all of this, all that Ailith did, every step of the way was to protect me. She said this necklace was to bring us protection. *Us*. I thought it meant all of us in the group, but perhaps it was just meant for her and me. She snapped any time she perceived a threat of someone coming between us. She demanded the room for just the two of us. She killed the shades and those men. Whatever this necklace did, it preyed on her desire to protect."

Fiana frowned at the necklace and sat it on the stone beside her supplies. She wiped her hands on her pants as if the mere touch of the jewelry against her skin brought grime. "Well then, now we just have to figure out if removing it was all we had to do to save Ailith, or if we're walking with something that might poison all of us with time."

CHAPTER TWENTY-SEVEN

GREER

"You need to look over the books," Róisín insisted, not for the first time. Greer rolled her eyes and let her head fall forward. She was sitting at her dressing table, braiding her long hair to pin to the top of her head and out of her face since the day's temperatures had risen to an uncomfortable level from the morning. She was hoping for a moment of quiet while she fixed her hair, but her mother had other plans. While she never had much interest in feminine wardrobes, she loved having long hair, even if it was often in her face and a nuisance in the summer months.

She found a new appreciation for it in recent days over the darkness of night when Barden slipped into her room, wrapping it around his hand and tugging it tight to make her arch her neck so he could kiss her throat over the fading bruises there.

All her romps with visiting princes and dignitaries were passionless, quick, and left little to be desired. She felt she had little experience to bring to Barden. But where she lacked expertise, he made up for it with delicate attention to detail.

During all their time apart, he spent his chances with women as opportunities to refine his love making. As if he practiced, prepared and waited just for that moment, and the moment after, and the many more since the two finally joined together. He taught her, guided her, and while part of Greer was now fulfilled, she also was hungrier than ever. Any free moment she sought him out. In dark halls, secret places, and through the summer night. They collided together, drawn like magic, and moments apart left Greer daydreaming and itching to rake her nails down his chest and taste him on her tongue.

She was recounting their escapades when her mother burst through the door. She now stood beyond Greer's shoulder with her hands on her hips, her eyes fierce as she stared at her eldest daughter and waited for a satisfactory response.

"We just got the books yesterday evening," Greer replied with disinterest. "There's no need to rush to read history books when we have to prepare for a war and have a city full of people in a panic over the announcement."

"Gil'dathon sent those books per your request. They even sent along the books they previously weren't willing to part with due to the war. The war we're about to enter with *magic makers*. They might contain useful information." Róisín stepped closer. "Come, please. I'll go through the books as well. We can ask Isla to join us."

"The both of you are alright then?" Greer asked as she straightened and continued working on her hair. She barely interacted with the old witch, other than when Isla found Greer in the hall when the gloom attacked. Greer was busy, and it seemed Isla kept herself busy as well. The old woman had a tight schedule of interacting with magic healers they gathered and pulling Róisín into meetings to discuss and practice the magic her mother had apparently always possessed; magic that was more substantial than hiding the slight point of her ears.

Greer paused and met Róisín's gaze through the looking glass. "You and Isla worked well together with the gloom."

"She knew what had to be done but she's not as strong as she once was." Róisín frowned and turned. She crossed the floor to Greer's bed which remained unmade with wrinkled sheets. "She's teaching what she can but she's conserving her energy for any possible attack."

Greer curled the braid around her head, pinning it in place before getting to her feet and turning to her wardrobe. Since the announcement of the impending war, people didn't know what to do with themselves. Some wanted to flee, but there was nowhere to flee to. Most were trying to gather provisions and secure structures in case Malcolm's men broke through the city wall.

"And you knew her before all this?" Greer let her voice sound bored and uninterested, but secretly she hoped it compelled her mother to confess her history. Little by little, she learned more about her, and she wanted to know just how close she was to Isla long ago.

Róisín laughed. "She tried teaching me how to use what magic I have, which isn't much, mind you. Just party tricks, really, minor things. But it was just after my mother died and I was sent to Caermythlin. I was furious she wasn't my mother and deep in mourning. I outright refused her aid. Kayl took to her like a flame when he came to the orphanage. She taught him once a week. At first, we walked together to her home. Eventually, his lessons grew too long and I grew bored so I let him go by himself."

"It's a shame. You and Kayl were so close and then he cursed your *child*." Greer didn't hold back the bitterness to her tongue. "Now we're dealing with all of *this*." She waved at the air, indicating everything around them before pulling pants and a tunic from her wardrobe. If they were going to wage a war, she had no need for dresses, but then again, she sought out any excuse not to wear one.

"It is," Róisín said quietly. Blinking, she circled the bed and lifted something from the floor. "Is this ...?"

Greer felt her cheeks grow hot at the sight of Barden's belt. They weren't necessarily hiding their romance but her mother pointedly seeing signs of their activities was a line they never crossed.

"I'll take that." She plucked it from her mother's hand, avoiding her knowing look. Changing into a comfortable wardrobe would have to wait; she desperately needed to drag her mother out of the room before she could ask more questions. "You said you wanted to look at the books, didn't you? Come along, Mother, let's not waste our time."

Gil'dathon kept their word, digging up what books remained in the city and copying others they didn't want to part with to send to Braewick for Greer's consumption.

"How's your father?" Róisín asked Callan as they stepped into the library with Isla following along behind.

"Good, thank you for asking," Callan replied, pushing the wire-lined glasses up his nose. "There's a great number of books. I placed them on the large table by the windows, but we can relocate them."

"Thank you, Callan." Greer flashed a smile at the young man before turning down the library aisle with Isla and her mother following close behind.

The table was covered in texts and scrolls. Each laid side by side, waiting for their consumption, and rapidly the trio of women dispersed to read.

"What exactly do you think these books hold?" Greer murmured with thinly veiled annoyance as she flipped through the pages of a dusty, large volume. She thought of the ever-growing list of things she needed to do. Checking the progress of new weaponry, visiting those recovering from injuries from the quake, looking over the battlements ...

"Greer," Róisín warned.

"Mother, I feel I should do something more productive with my time." Greer shifted on her seat, the wooden chair uncomfortable and the bodice of her dress pinching her ribs. "Yes, I wanted these books but that was prior to all this chaos. They'll serve us wonderfully, I'm sure, but I don't know if we're capable of finding any useful information in their pages. Our land is regrettably low on magic makers."

"You have us," Isla spoke up. "I don't know what your mother told you but she's quick with relearning her magic, even after so many years of not using it. We might find something, even if it's small, that could help us going forward."

Greer turned to the book before her. She lifted the heavy cover and frowned as dust puffed upwards. Once focused, time passed quickly and they moved rapidly through the material. Luckily most had detailed tables of contents and were placed aside due to being full of history lessons and few on magic, but some spouted information about magic and the creatures of the earth, requiring deeper reading.

Meals were brought to the library and Greer remained despite her mind often wandering elsewhere. Caitriona and Ailith would be home within a few days, which felt right and reassuring. Isla and her mother had magic, granted, but Greer hoped Caitriona would pull free from the fear of her own and lend aid.

Then there was Barden, flitting into her mind and making her cheeks blush as she stared at the pages before her. He was her one consistency in life that brought her joy and relief, and the last handful of days finally provided her a reprieve from the haunting thoughts of her father and how she was ruining everything.

Lazily, Greer flipped open a new book, glancing at the front page and reading the inscription before sitting upright. "This one's about the Elder Tree."

"Keep it," Isla grumbled, her eyes still glued to the pages of what she read. "Might be useful."

Greer leaned forward, running her finger over the faded dialogue before flipping through the book. "There're spells. There's magic in here, too. There's—wait, *there's magic in the tree!*"

Isla and Róisín were drawn from their reading. Books forgotten, they circled Greer and leaned in, looking over the chapter Greer flipped to.

"I knew there was something about that blasted tree," Isla laughed. "I knew there were stories of its magic beyond creating the universe."

"'*Elder Tree: a creator of life, and from the sap of the tree, it can provide all it did upon the creation of the world,*'" Róisín read under a drawing of the tree itself. She flipped the page and clapped her hands. "Look! '*Gathering the sap and administering it to the recently deceased whose body is whole will bring them back to life healed and well, thereby giving the life the Elder Tree gave in the world's creation.*'"

"Giving the life it gave in the world's creation," Greer repeated with a smile. "You gathered sap from the tree when Caitriona broke it."

"I thought she crushed the tree and it would die. I assumed the citizens would riot and hoped they wouldn't if they had some piece of the tree that they previously didn't have access to. And if that was pointless, I figured we could use the sap for sweets. That it would prove useful." Róisín rested her chin into her pale palm.

Greer shook her head, her excitement building. "Mother, there was sap coming from the breaks in the tree after the quake. We already have a few buckets harvested from before, we need to get more. We'll put it in bottles and leave them with the healers. This may give us an advantage during battle."

Róisín's green eyes brightened. She smiled and grabbed Greer's shoulders, gripping them hard.

"Not all's lost," Róisín whispered, kissing Greer's cheek. "Do you want to spread the good news or shall I?"

Greer looked out the windows of the library at the glorious sunny day and the birds flitting in the breeze. There wouldn't be many more opportunities for moments of light happiness and she felt selfish. "I'll go and gather people to get sap."

She was out the door before Róisín and Isla settled with their books, running down the hall with her skirts gathered in her hands and the fabric flowing behind her, and a smile on her face as she considered what lay before her. Her sister would be home soon, as well as two fae who had magic and talent and knowledge of the very people they would fight against. Ailith would be there too who was sure to help convince Caitriona of the need for her own powers. The sun was bright enough to chase any shadows away, the temperature perhaps not as oppressive as she thought, and they had magic sap from a magic tree.

Greer grinned from the feeling within her. Something she hadn't quite felt in the last few years, not since she found Caitriona's body amongst the broken pieces of the Elder Tree after her transformation. It was nestled in her chest, growing warm, stretching its wings and spreading.

As she stepped into the guard yard and spotted Barden running drills with other guards, he turned to her and smiled. The thing in her chest burst, swallowing her whole in the most uplifting way. As she ran toward him, excited to share the news, she realized it was the feeling of hope.

CHAPTER TWENTY-EIGHT

Ailith

She was in the woods holding her bow as she scanned the growth for a squirrel or rabbit. Crowley flew overhead, cawing intermittently as she struggled to focus. It was hard to focus as of late. She felt off, grumpy, and on edge. Like the weight of travel and the queendom's events led her to the brink. She was standing on the ledge of a mental cliff, teetering, her arms flailing as she attempted not to fall over and into a crevice of all her negative emotions; every feeling no person in their right mind enjoyed experiencing. Ailith lowered her bow and rubbed her temple. Every day the feeling worsened. Then came a voice.

I need you to protect yourself.

The voice rose from the depths of Ailith and she froze in place. Eyes wide, she stared before her, listening intently to the voice that was not hers.

They're on to you. They'll hurt you, they could hurt her.

Ailith spun, confusion coating her movements as she searched for the maker of the voice. Surely it wasn't from within her mind, surely this was something out in the open. But the woods stood empty.

Think of those men who wanted to kill her, the voice came again and Ailith saw a flash of the stables.

Independently, she didn't remember much of that evening. She brought the horses to the stable, washed off at the well, then changed in her room before joining the others for dinner. But there was an expanse of time that was in the dark, now thrust forward with clarity.

She used her sword to hack off the men's hands.

She used her dagger to cut their tongues.

She wrote a hasty message filled with words she hadn't thought of. Penned by her hand yet spoken by another.

All of it, every motion, was not her own.

Right?

"Oh," Ailith gasped, falling to her knees. Her knee landed on a rock and distantly she felt pain, but it was nothing compared to the remorse coating her. She lifted her hands to her chest as tears fell from her eyes. How could she harm them? How could she take their lives? How could she be so cruel?

But they did mean harm, the voice came again. *You remember it don't you? The one knew who she was. The one who wanted to send a message to the queen ...*

"That was only one of them," Ailith cried, "the other didn't want to."

It doesn't matter, they're gone now, the voice continued with a sigh. *But I need more. More blood, more power, whatever I can get.*

"I'm not going to give it to you," Ailith hissed, plunging her hand under her shirt and pulling the necklace free. She felt the weight of it twisting around her body, plunging into her heart and brain like ice spreading along the glass of her veins. "You're what made me kill the shades. You're what made me kill those men."

You're only half right. All I did was bring forth your inner thoughts and the actions you are capable of. But see, I need it. Magic fills me most but when there is none, I've found I can feast off blood, life, energy, and emotion. What stronger emotion exists than rage? What greater source of energy than the draining of life and blood? I need their soup to sup upon. It was you who served me my helping.

"No." Ailith wept, twisting the necklace to the clasp and fighting to unhook it. "Find someone else, whoever you are."

No, no. I was commanded to do this, I was forced to follow through.

My hunger's too great and my power has weakened my control, and I can't let you do that, the voice came, pressing darkness into Ailith's mind and making everything go black.

When she next registered her surroundings, Ailith's skull pounded like a drum and the light of the sun made her cringe. She opened her eyes and discovered she lay upon her sleeping pad, her hands tied tightly together behind her back. Moaning, she tried to sit up but only rolled onto her side. Footsteps approached, followed by firm hands pulling her fully upright into a seated position. Opening her eyes, she found Raum looking down at her with a scowl.

Her memories were murky, shadowed things barely viewable, and when she tried to speak all that came out was vomit she spilled onto the stony ground.

"I know you're angry with her, but you need to help her," Caitriona said, her voice growing close. Soft hands brushed back Ailith's hair, gently keeping it from her face as she continued to empty the contents of her stomach.

The shadows in her mind drifted away to reveal memories of everyone circling her and Caitriona's face before hers, full of tears as she pulled Ailith's necklace free. But why?

"What happened?" Ailith asked. Caitriona's hands ran down Ailith's shoulders, helping her adjust as Raum handed her a skein of water.

"Drink this," Caitriona's voice was soft, calming, and Ailith obeyed. She recalled commotion, yelling, and the clash of swords. It came back, scene after dreadful scene.

She fought Raum, she wanted to kill him. But that didn't seem right, because Raum was her friend. There was the lingering sense of needing to protect Caitriona and Ailith looked to the two of them, squatting side by side beside Ailith. Raum obviously wasn't the threat Ailith remembered him to be.

"I'm confused. I have memories that are half formed. It's like they're covered under soot," she whispered and Caitriona's expression broke down. Tears filled her golden eyes and slipped over the curve of her cheeks.

"A lot's gone on in the past few hours," Raum admitted, his

expression still serious and guarded. She tried to trace her steps backwards.

"The necklace," Ailith said miserably. "There's something wrong with the necklace."

"Yeah, we figured that out," Raum said as he got to his feet. "Do you remember any of it?"

"Unfortunately, it's coming back to me."

Raum ran his hand through his hair. "I'm going to take a walk and see what your aura reads."

Raum pushed to his feet, leaving Ailith alone with Ceenear. Fiana stood near, keeping an uneasy eye on her. Caitriona shifted closer, her hand resting on Ailith's thigh, but like the others she had a look of confusion, distrust, and hurt. Ailith leaned back slightly; was this what predators felt like when they were captured? Did bears feel this mix of fear and distrust? Did wyverns feel guarded? Surely they didn't feel the acidic taste of guilt on their tongues.

"I'm sorry," Ailith said, but it sounded like she was pleading. "I did awful things. I did such terrible things."

"That wasn't *you*," Caitriona replied. She brushed Ailith's hair back and began to tie it away from her face. "I don't know who it was exactly, but it wasn't you."

"She looks like herself," Raum called as he came out from the woods. He looked at Ailith and his expression softened. "Your aura was strange but it's back to the color it used to be."

"So, it *was* the necklace," Ceenear said.

"It doesn't make sense," Fiana said, pulling her hand away from her face. "This isn't like the people of Ätbënas. They don't do this."

"Ailith, where did you get the necklace?"

"From Ätbënas," Ailith replied. "In that little shop you and I were at. Remember there was a change in the shift? A boy came to work. He offered me a selection of jewelry with magical properties. I chose the necklace; it was supposed to bring protection. I thought if I protected myself, I'd be better able to protect others. I figured it'd be good since I kept being a magnet to the creatures in the Northern Wood."

Fiana shook her head. "There wasn't anyone who came in. There wasn't a shift change."

"No," Ailith bore down. "There was a boy. He came in. You were *there*."

Fiana stared at Ailith, her dark brows furrowing. "Ailith, I swear to you, no one came in. The shopkeeper wrapped up for the day. They said they were closing. I left and you said you were going to buy arrows."

Ailith stared, racking her mind over the encounter in Ätbënas. She remembered the boy with such clarity, his oddly shaped ears and his large, impressionable eyes. Ailith's eyes went wide. "The ears ..."

"What?" Caitriona turned towards her.

Ailith looked at Caitriona, the memory of that night in Beaslig returning.

For months after Caitriona turned into a dragon, Ailith had nightmares. Watching Caitriona's body racked with pain, her skin splitting, her arms and legs extending as blood coated her. It was horrific and Caitriona's painful screams haunted her even still. But there was more to that night, so much more. Kayl told them what Cearny did to his village and what Kayl did in retaliation. But not just what was done to the village, but what happened to *him*.

"The boy in the shop, his ears were funny and I realize what it was now. They were cut, like the points were cut off, like Kayl's ears."

Caitriona breathed slowly. "Do you think the boy was Kayl?"

"I don't know what I think anymore," Ailith said with a sad laugh. "Is it even possible? That it could've been him?"

"He has a great deal of power," Ceenear offered. "He was one of the most gifted magic makers of this time, comparable to Niveem, if not greater. I'm sure he could've shape-shifted to a version of his younger self."

"Kayl's pointed ears were cut off years ago," Ailith explained. "If he shape-shifted now, wouldn't he be able to make his ears appear normal?"

Ceenear looked to the sky for a moment before shaking her head. "I'm not sure. If he's becoming an unbound, he may not have the strength to maintain full change. Being an unbound ... it doesn't follow a straight course of expectation. You weaken and feed off magic. You still have your own magic but what you can and can't do depends on how much magic it takes. If you're losing your power, if you're weak or falling towards darkness, bits of yourself will seep out. It's entirely possible he had enough magic to make himself appear as a child, but not enough control to change his ears."

"So, Kayl could've given you the necklace." Caitriona looked towards the jewelry where it sat upon a stone. The hot air stirred and far off, a cry of a bird sounded. "But why?"

"We should bring it to Isla," Raum suggested. "Put it in a saddle bag and don't wear the damn thing. Maybe she'll figure out what's going on with it."

"Do I still need to be tied?" Ailith asked. "I mean, I completely understand if you want to keep me tied up but if I don't have to be ..."

Caitriona looked at Ailith then Raum. "I don't see any more magic on her either."

"She, for all intents and purposes, is back to normal," Ceenear added.

Raum frowned and studied Ailith. She felt her heart could break into pieces, the betrayal of trust, even if she hadn't been in control of her actions, marring their relationship. She suspected it would be some time before he looked at her the same as before, with trust. "You don't get to touch any of your weapons. Not 'til we get back to Braewick and Isla looks you over."

"That's fair," Ailith replied with a nod. "Take them away. Do whatever you have to do with me."

Raum hesitated for a moment before moving forward and began to undo the ties of the rope. "I'm glad you understand."

"I'd do the same thing to you," Ailith replied as she rubbed her wrists. Caitriona leaned forward, slipping her arms around Ailith and hugging her tight.

"You scared me," she whispered into Ailith's ear, making Ailith's heart lurch and her cheeks grow pink with shame. "But I'm glad to have you back."

"I'm sorry," Ailith replied, returning the hug. "I'm sorry I scared you. I won't do it again."

A crackling came from a nearby tree, drawing their attention to Crowley who perched nearby. Arching his neck, he let out a loud caw and Ailith frowned.

"That's his warning cry," she said. "Something's coming."

Caitriona grew rigid in Ailith's embrace and Ailith pulled away. No one gave her weapons back yet. She swung around and spotted them on Onyx. Too far away to get them now as everyone reached for their weapons and she stood powerless, her hands empty. They shifted on their feet, making a loose circle. Ailith stood between Caitriona and Fiana. Crowley cried again and there was the scream of a large bird in the air, closer now, responding. Crowley flapped his wings and looked to the sky, cawing once more.

Turning to follow his line of sight, Ailith gasped. "Everyone, look!"

At first the eagle appeared close by, but as it flew down, Ailith realized it wasn't close at all, it was simply large. Its powerful reddish-gold wings expanded wide as it rushed lower from the sky, the cry from its beak loud again.

Everyone stumbled backwards as the eagle landed on the stone outcrop. Raum withdrew his sword and Fiana her bow. The eagle stumbled forward, its claws grasping at the ground as it moved, its body shifting with each step. Feathers fell like a down pillow being cut, its wings bending unnaturally and curling forward. Shoulders appeared while its legs expanded, and suddenly a man stood before them, gasping for air.

He wore pants, boots, and a light shirt. His sunset-colored hair hung in his face and he pushed it from his eyes with a hand whose fingers still separated and lost feathers.

Ailith stared with her jaw hanging at the heir to Invarlwen. Lachlan, at long last, had joined them.

"*You're alive?*" Caitriona whispered. Raum lowered his sword and Fiana dropped her bow.

"We thought you were dead," Fiana murmured.

He looked exhausted, his face damp with sweat. "I wasn't sure if you returned to Braewick already, so I've been flying along every southern path for days looking for you. Ätbënas is ruined."

"We know," Ceenear said. "We heard about the dragon attack."

"It's why we thought you were dead," Fiana deadpanned.

Lachlan nodded, taking a breath. "It burned half the village. The dragon was foolish, exhausted. Those of us who survived brought it down. We killed it. And when it died it became something else. A fae. Someone made into a dragon."

Ailith looked at Caitriona who stood very still, her mouth working to get words out for a moment before she managed to speak. "Did you know this fae person?"

Lachlan shook his head. "We thought it was bewitched or cursed. Forced to change, like yourself."

"And you know it wasn't me?" Caitriona asked.

"Of course. I knew it when it arrived. It didn't have the same horns as you. But the village ..."

"I'm so sorry."

Lachlan closed his mouth, his jaw set. He nodded before continuing, "Princess, do you think the offer still stands? Can I help your sister?"

"Of course."

Lachlan stepped closer; his watercolor eyes narrowed. His voice shook with emotion not yet conveyed in his expression. "I believe the dragon was Malcolm's."

Ailith immediately felt it: the rage, the heartbreak, and the unfairness of it all.

"He killed children. That was one of the buildings lost. A schoolhouse full of children and he tried to pin the blame on you. If he's willing to do that, I can't fathom the lengths he'll go to get what he wants. I don't understand any of the politics of what it takes to be a king, but I know that I fear what he'll do if he gains more power. I know that I want to prevent this from happening again."

"We'll help you." Caitriona stepped forward. "My sister will guide you; she'll make sure you're fine and she'll fight for the greater good."

Lachlan nodded; his eyes growing red from tears. He hastily wiped his eyes, then grew still, his face paling noticeably as he looked toward the ground. "Where did you get that from?"

All followed his gaze to the necklace still sitting on the stone.

"Oh." Raum picked it up. "We believe this possesses the wearer and were about to bag it."

"Don't touch it," Lachlan hissed, slapping the necklace from Raum's hand. It tumbled through the air and fell to the ground, sliding to a stop behind Caitriona where it twinkled innocently in the light. "Do you realize what that is?"

"I just said ..." Raum began.

"Do you recognize it?" Ceenear asked.

"That necklace is known in older books, accurately detailed, as something that captures a soul," Lachlan began to explain. "It can entrap an unbound, providing the unbound a tether to this world while the unbound's body falls apart. It allows them to still use their magic without wasting as much of their energy keeping their form together."

"Kayl!" Ailith spat. "That bastard. It *was* him at the shop. He was the one getting in my head. He was talking about becoming an unbound before the curse began."

"What do we do with it?" Raum asked, gesturing at the necklace. "We were going to bring it to Isla, she's a powerful magic maker like you. Is that safe?"

Ailith looked at the necklace behind Caitriona and felt the earth shift beneath her feet. The same confused feeling rose as when she wore it. Shaking her head, her mind muddled and grew uncertain of what she saw. Upon a second look, it was true. The dark smoke crept out, leaking from the necklace like a thick ooze. It curled forward, tendrils spreading as if searching for something. Time slowed and Ailith forced herself forward, moving with sluggish speed. Everything was a crawl, distant and unmoored, impossible to obtain.

Raum still spoke, yet his voice slowed as the darkness spread upward, reaching desperately towards Caitriona. Its tendrils curled around her hands and slipped past her ribs to embrace her chest. Ailith couldn't move any faster. Throwing herself forward, she crashed her body against Caitriona's to knock her away.

But Fiana moved too, having caught Ailith's sudden movement quicker than the rest. Too slow to pick up her bow, but quick enough to reach forward, she attempted to catch Ailith. A flicker of a thought flashed through Ailith's mind, a recognition that Fiana thought Ailith was a threat, attacking Caitriona, and planning to hurt her.

From the moment Ailith agreed to take Caitriona out of Braewick City two years prior, she meant to protect her. She wanted to save her, to let her live and thrive and love. She did so with her whole heart and it didn't stop now.

The most selfless decisions are ones done with action and very little thought. This decision came so swiftly that in a moment she pushed forward and reached to knock Caitriona away from the tendrils of Kayl's unbound powers. But in her place, the shadowed, ghostly fingers grasped hold of Ailith and Fiana instead.

In Caitriona's place, the seeping darkness choked Fiana and Ailith. The darkened grasp pulled both women—the two without any magic of their own—backward and into the green gem. They vanished from sight as the gem grew dark and dull while time spun ever forward.

CHAPTER TWENTY-NINE

Róisín

Nearly Two Years Prior

For the second time, Róisín sat beside her sleeping daughter. Caitriona lay unmoving and unaware of the world as she was lost in the exhaustion of magic. The toddler who was brought back to life was now fully grown, a young woman of eighteen, but Róisín found it painful to look at her youngest daughter now.

Gone was her red hair and in its place was gold that looked as if it could be melted down and fashioned into a crown. Her skin was badly damaged by wounds from arrows her own father shot into her torso. They were bloody, but clean, and hopefully would heal without issue. And her shoulders, her shoulders that were once covered with only freckles, now glimmered in candlelight from the sheen of her scales. All of this would be something they could hide from the scrutinizing view of the public, but it was Caitriona's horns that worried Róisín most. She never had the type of magic to change the appearance of other people; even covering the points of her own ears was a stretch for Róisín's abilities, but Caitriona's horns were too large and prominent for any little magic to hide away.

When Caitriona was found in her human form after the curse

completed, Greer and the guard she hired—Ailith, the very woman whose absence from the city had Cearny frothing at the mouth with rage—carried her to the castle with bits of each of their clothing covering Caitriona's modesty.

"You can't bring her here!" Róisín had hissed, stopping the two from moving any further. "Do you realize what your father will do? If you want her to live, you need to get her away from the castle immediately!"

"*Mother*," Greer snapped as Ailith looked between the two with brows raised. "He's *dead*. Father's dead. She's safe. *We're* safe."

Róisín didn't believe it until Greer dragged her to where guards gathered, and a healer worked desperately to bring the king back to life.

"I told you, he's dead," Greer said before vanishing through a door. Róisín frowned at the emptiness in Greer's voice but couldn't deny that she felt a strange twist in her gut. A mixture of relief to finally be on the other side of her marriage, and sadness for the years wasted in the midst of her failure. She meant to convince Cearny magic wasn't a threat, and when that failed she meant to kill him. She did neither, yet her daughter accomplished the task, something Kayl brought forth into the world, and Róisín wished was done by her own hand.

Now after the appropriate mourning period, Cearny would be buried the next day and it wasn't until Greer disappeared behind the closing doors of the prayer room, locked in with her father's body for the night, did Róisín believe Cearny was truly dead and wouldn't come crawling back.

"Your poor sister." Róisín leaned forward and grasped Caitriona's hand. "I hate this tradition, you know. The Vigil of the Heirs. I think it's downright horrid. To think, you lose your parent and then you must sit with their body the night before their burial to learn from their corpse. The only lesson any of the Gablaigh monarchs learned from the corpses of the previous kings was to slowly go insane. Now your sister's trapped following the same tradition."

She knew Caitriona wouldn't stir or respond and continued after a brief pause. "I don't believe she'll go insane though. That's not what I'm saying. Your sister, she's different, stronger, better.

"When your grandfather died, your father attended his vigil with a whiskey barrel. He got so drunk he vomited off the carriage as we rode to your grandfather's burial place, the fool. I regret you never had a proper father, but I don't regret that he's dead."

She fell quiet again. So much of her existence in the castle was just that, her thoughts leaking out only for silence to greet her. But there was no one to stop her now. For the first time in thirty years, she felt free and knew magic would be legal. Greer declared as much before Caitriona's sleeping body the night of Cearny's death and she believed Greer would stick to her word.

Looking across to the hearth where a roaring fire battled the wintery chill, Róisín considered her options. Caitriona was asleep like after the first dragon attack, Greer was locked away in a room, and the castle was tightly guarded. If there was a moment for her to step back into magic, the moment was now, and there was one person she wished to see.

It was quick work despite the years since she last performed the ritual. Her hands and feet moved to places she hadn't allowed herself to think of while Cearny grew more and more erratic and dangerous. Going to her room, Róisín climbed atop a chest and reached to the top of the curtains hanging heavily by her windows. Sewn behind the fabric was a little pouch she created years before, filled with eyebright flowers she gathered and kept to dry.

Returning to Caitriona's room and running a hand over her sleeping daughter's cheek, she bolted the door before settling before the fireplace. All in all, the castle was quiet, staff were in mourning and Caitriona's healers sent off to their families per Róisín's request. There was no one to interrupt her.

"Show me what I don't know," she requested the smoke, "and show me what happened to Kayl."

Her lungs filled with the smoke from the burning eyebright flowers, choking her thoroughly and thrusting her far and away. She coughed while the bedroom grew dark. The air cleared as stars appeared one by one overhead, the moon too. The heat of the fire dissipated and was replaced by a damp chill. She was on her feet and standing in a clearing, the ground packed dirt with stone benches nestled into bushes bordering the circle she stood within. Beyond, the trees were bare and a dusting of snow lay over fallen leaves in spaces the sun mustn't show during daylight hours. Mountain peaks were hinted over the tree line, their snow glittering under the moonlight.

A man stepped from the bushes, pale, thin, and not much taller than Róisín herself with mouse-brown hair and ears pointed skyward. He sniffed, rubbing the tip of his nose before plunging his hands in his pants' pockets as he moved around the circle. He turned and looked outward beyond the tree line.

"So, you've come crawling home, and for what?" the man asked, his accent different than any Róisín heard before. His back straightened before he turned on his heel toward Róisín.

Róisín's eyes widened. She stepped back and through a form that solidified before her. The man looked at this person, not her. Róisín sighed.

"What do you want?"

"I come asking for safety, and a place to rest."

Róisín recognized the voice with a shock to her system. Kayl, the very figure she passed through, sounded like a version of himself heard through fabric and distance. Muffled and far away. But it hadn't prepared Róisín for the sight of him.

It was fifteen years since she last saw her old friend—if she could even call him that anymore—and while she expected him to have aged, what she found came as a shock all the same. She moved across the space, her eyes locked on his figure as she studied him with shock. He was sickly thin, his skin a grayish pale. What remained of his dark hair was thinned out, his head relatively bald and the hair retained moved lazily from the chilly breeze.

But what was most frightening was the gathering shadows around his form, the way the hollows of his cheeks seemed cold and dark, the glossy sheen of his eyes, and how the moonlight leaned away from him. He was a man eternally drenched in the shadows he created; he was becoming a shadow himself.

"Unbound," Róisín whispered, and Kayl's eyes twitched as if he heard her, which wasn't possible. This spell left her a ghost, something lingering on the edge of life, unable to interact with the material world.

"Did your plans go sour, Kayl?" The man sat upon one of the stone benches. He crossed a leg and leaned back for a second before seeming unsatisfied and getting to his feet again to approach Kayl.

In Kayl's youth, with health, he would have stood taller than this man. But now he was a shriveled thing, hunched forward and clutching his cloak about his body. The man frowned as he looked him over. "The curse was activated, hmm? A gold dragon was spotted to the west, flying over the mountains, and by the looks of you, I assume the curse pulled from your core. You're more and more an unbound each day."

"She survived," Kayl began, "the princess—both princesses, actually. But the king of Wimleigh Kingdom is dead by his daughter's hand, as I set forth. I'm weakened though. Let me live out my days here."

"And not use the last of your powers?" the man laughed, taking a spinning step away. "You're one of the most gifted magic makers in Vissenore and you want to simply—what—waste away? The unbound don't want that. They want to feast on the spirit of more lives, they want to taste the flow of magic."

Kayl shuttered, his arms slipping around himself as he looked away. The shadows grew, clawing their way up his body to curl over his shoulders like a cloak. "I still want that but I ... I shouldn't. What I've done is unforgivable. I didn't see clearly when I set that curse. I was blind with emotion and I made a foolish choice. I thought it was the right one all these years until I saw that girl begin to break."

"A threat is still there." The man pointed outward beyond the mountain peaks. "Do you think they'll allow this transgression to go without notice? Do you think they'll not care? You've only made us a target by coming here, by being a magic maker yourself."

"I'm sorry ..." Kayl murmured, his form rocked slightly while shadows licked his cheek and nibbled at his ears. The top of his ears had healed in jagged lines where they once ended in points. Róisín outstretched her hand as if to touch them.

Oh, what horrors her former friend saw. What horrors she brought upon him without intention.

"No, we'll find a way to make this work." The man began pacing, his hands in his pocket, one foot kicking forward, then the next in a lazy dance. "I may not have magic but I understand how it works and I've read enough about your kind. I see the state you're in, you're weak, you can't travel any further. You're using all your energy to keep your body together, to keep it from dispersing. You need to sup on the lives of others, and I need you to do magic for *me*. You want to do something that actually matters? Something beyond cursing a child? Then listen."

He turned, moving quickly and stopping before Kayl. Leaning forward, a breath from Kayl's face, he reached for Kayl's hand which seemed too thin. The bones obvious under his skin and his blue veins showing through. "I have someone for you to gain your strength from but in return, you'll be mine to command."

"Someone ..." Kayl began, his voice weak, his eyes hungry.

The man held up his wrist, showing glittering metal lined with stones. "Do you feel the power in this?" He pulled the collar of his shirt down, exposing a necklace. "What about the magic of this? They're all enchanted with her power; a gift to me, her *powerless* husband. As if she pities me."

The shadows reached forward toward the man and moved along the jewelry until they touched the man's skin and turned away, not finding what they wanted. He lacked magic for them to feed off, just as he said.

Kayl swayed; his eyes unfocused as the shadows he was sinking into searched endlessly for something to feast from. His tongue moved across his broken, dry lips and he blinked with heavy eyelids. "Some*thing* to feed me?"

The man grinned and withdrew a necklace with a green stone glittering from its center from his pocket. "All you have to do is pour yourself into this amulet. It'll keep you safe and when I give it to my wife, it'll pull her gifts from her body."

Kayl took in a shuddering breath, his eyes locked on the gem as the man passed it into Kayl's hand.

"Think about it. I'll give you a minute." The man stepped back, his smile large and vicious. All Kayl was to him was prey, powerful prey.

But Kayl didn't notice the man's predetermined success. He stared into the amulet, his lips moving as he whispered, "Something to feed ... something to feed ..."

"Kayl," Róisín warned. The man drifted beyond the bushes, leaving them alone. "Kayl please don't do this. That man will use the last of your abilities. He'll wring you out. Kayl, you need to let yourself go."

Kayl's lips grew still and his hand lowered, but his eyes, shadowed and glossy, rose to meet Róisín's. Slowly, he smiled and his eyes grew moist.

"*Róisín* ..." he whispered and she stilled. "It felt good for only a moment when I realized the curse was unleashed. But as I left and saw your daughter collapsing under what I cursed her to be, I realized my error. I realized my stupidity. I realized how far off track I've gone. I cursed a child; I cursed *your* child. I'm sorry, Róisín, I'm sorry. But I'm so hungry.

"Sometimes I wish I could stop this. I wish I could undo this. I wish I was done, but I'm not ... *I can't* ... I can't be done yet. My hunger's so great it's nearly all I think of, it *becomes* all I can think of. Hunger is what I am. I'm sorry ... I'm sorry for it all."

He turned, his eyes hazed and searching but not locking in on her. "Róisín, I need you to do something for me. Look to the tree. Look to the tree to make it stop. And maybe someday I'll meet you here again, beyond the material world. I wish that, at least. Wishes are powerful things. You'll find me here; I don't know if I'll ever leave."

He collapsed, becoming a heap of darkened cloth that sunk into the green gem of the necklace now discarded on the ground. Róisín woke on the floor of her daughter's room with bile in her throat and tears yet again in her eyes.

CHAPTER THIRTY

CAITRIONA

It happened so quickly. Caitriona, at first, couldn't comprehend what occurred. She was on her side, her hands scratched raw from falling against the stone outcrop. The cries from Fiana and Ailith suddenly cut off but echoed in her head.

Rolling to her back, she looked before her and only found Raum, Ceenear, and Lachlan. All three looked at the necklace on the ground; Raum and Ceenear looked shocked while Lachlan appeared serious.

"Ailith?" Caitriona whispered as she pushed herself upright. Her voice cracked from fear.

Crowley was panicked. Cawing repeatedly and bouncing from branch to branch, the corvid wouldn't still. He took to the air, swooping over them as if trying to attack, only to circle and fly back to his branch.

"Ailith?"

"It was the necklace," Raum whispered, pointing toward the jewelry.

"Ailith?" Caitriona's tone grew in volume.

"They disappeared into the necklace. Fiana and Ailith both."

"It'll take each of us if given the chance. It can be used as a portal,"

Lachlan hissed. He pushed between Raum and Ceenear and grabbed hold of Ailith's dagger. "You have to be rid of it. We need to break it."

Caitriona stared at Lachlan, Ailith's dagger held high, and felt herself lean forward, her hand outstretched as she screamed for the fae prince to stop. It was pointless, she was too slow, the dagger's blade came down and gave the gem a deadly kiss. The once glittering stone shattered and broke apart.

"No," Caitriona cried. "No, Ailith's in there! Fiana's in there!"

"If the unbound's taking people, they aren't in there." Lachlan stepped back from the broken necklace. "That gem served as a home for the unbound and now it's lost, but if it had the strength to reach out and grasp hold of living, human bodies, they aren't in there. Such gems can't hold people but they can continue to take."

"Where are they then?" Caitriona asked, staring at Lachlan and waiting for an answer. "Lachlan, where *are* they?"

He pulled his gaze from the shattered gem and looked at Caitriona, his face sympathetic.

"I'm sorry, princess." Lachlan dropped Ailith's dagger and stepped forward, offering Caitriona a hand. "I don't know where they've gone. I assume, wherever the unbound calls home."

Caitriona looked at the broken stone and felt a hollowness in her chest. Even the dragon, so quick to react to the world around her and express rage when Caitriona was threatened, mocked or teased, sat in silence, waiting to see her decision. Turning to Lachlan, she accepted his hand and allowed him to help her to her feet. Crowley grew quiet but still puffed his chest and feathers with obvious displeasure from his tree nearby.

Wiping her eyes with the back of her hand, she picked up Ailith's dagger and felt its weight. "What do we do now? How do we get them back?"

"I'm not sure," Lachlan said softly. Ceenear stepped beside Caitriona and placed a hand on her shoulder.

"We'll figure it out," she reassured her, but even Caitriona saw the doubt in the fae's eyes.

"What do you think he was trying to do?"

"Who?" Lachlan asked. "Do you know who the unbound is?"

Caitriona looked at the fae prince and felt sorry for him. He lost his home, his people, and had so little knowledge of the great expanse of everything going on or what would happen soon. "Kayl. The person who cursed me."

Lachlan's shoulders dropped. "I can't claim to know his mind, but I saw the tendrils of his making just as everything happened. It appeared he was stretching towards you, just before Ailith pushed you from his reach."

Caitriona clenched her jaw, a new wave of tears rising to her eyes. Turning away, she took determined steps to Ailith's belongings and slipped the dagger back in its holder. Opening her bag, she shoved the dagger inside then stilled. On top of the clothing was Caitriona's shirt Ailith stole and kept secret, in case Caitriona decided to accept her dragon side and turn. Running her fingers over the stitching of the collar, Caitriona realized Ailith had chosen something simple that would never be missed. The care and foresight made her decision easy to make.

"Enough of this," Caitriona whispered. The dragon in her belly lifted its head in wonder and flushed with hope. She turned to the others. "We have what we traveled for, don't we? We need to get back to Braewick and do so immediately, and we have the means."

They looked to one another and Ceenear stepped close. "Cait ..."

Caitriona shook her head and pointed to Raum. "You haven't any gift that allows you to change into something, correct?"

Raum shook his head. "No, you know my gifts."

Caitriona nodded and turned to Ceenear. "And your shapeshifting is that of human proportions, correct? You can look like any fae, any human, but also other humanoids. Fairies, dwarves."

"Yes ..." Ceenear narrowed her brow with question.

"And those forms with wings, can they actually fly? Can they carry the weight of the body?"

Ceenear nodded.

Caitriona turned back to Raum. "I want you to take the horses. Take our supplies, too. Follow this road down into the valley and make haste to Braewick City. There's a northern gate with our guards there. They'll know you're coming."

"Caitriona ..." Raum began, but Caitriona ignored him, turning on her heel and approaching Lachlan.

"I want you to turn into an eagle and follow me to Braewick," she instructed, "and when all this is over and done with, you're going to teach me how to change back to myself and not lose my clothing in the process."

"Cait," Ceenear attempted again, figuring out Caitriona's intentions, "what about the pain? It'll only take a few hours to get back to Braewick. Just a little longer. We can get there today without you having to do that."

Caitriona turned, her eyes returning to Ailith's belongings. Ailith figured it out long before Caitriona was even willing to learn. She knew, but Caitriona preferred to turn away from the truth of the matter. She preferred to cover her eyes and bury her head, unwilling to accept the fact of it all.

"Ceenear, it's like with the potion I took to look fae. It hurt when I changed, when I became something I wasn't. But it didn't hurt to return to what I *am*. I'm not a girl succumbing to a curse anymore. I'm the girl who survived it. I'm as much a human as I am a dragon."

She looked at Raum and Lachlan who stood to the side, confused and silent. "Get going, the both of you. I'll catch up."

Raum gathered what items they pulled from their horses and tied them into place. He pulled the rope he used on Ailith and drew the horses together.

"Remember yourself, Caitriona," Ceenear warned, gripping her hand tightly.

"That's the thing, Ceenear." Caitriona smiled despite her tears. "I think I just did."

Lachlan shook his arms out and discarded his human form as easily as if it were clothing, becoming the gold eagle in a flash before taking to the skies. Ceenear smiled at Caitriona and stepped back, helping Raum to tie the horses together so he could lead them down the trail. Ceenear turned to Ailith's bag and lifted Caitriona's clothing.

"I'll hold onto this and meet you there," she said with a smile as she shortened in size and translucent wings stretched from her back.

"Good," Caitriona replied. "I'll need them."

She stepped away, retreating from the steps they took the day prior to find privacy. Ailith was right all along and so patient in trying to get Caitriona to understand. The dragon was never a separate creature. It was a part of her. Every time it raised its head, every time it flared to protect, it was all Caitriona. She had a lifetime of holding back emotion and refusing to grow into herself and now she was able to release that. The two could co-exist and perhaps she would be rid of the building fire that kept lighting within her. Or maybe it would consume her. She found she wasn't too concerned though.

Stepping out of her skin was easier this time.

Her bones changed in unnatural ways, her fingers bent into claws capable of crushing stone, and teeth lengthened to points capable of snapping bone. In a wave, the hairs on her skin shifted into shimmering scales that covered the expanse of her body. She pulled off her clothing, leaving it torn and tattered on the ground, discarded, forgotten as she stretched her back and turned her face to the sky. Her tail pushed outward, pulling from her spine as her body stretched and grew in size, becoming enormous. Large enough she felt she could swallow the moon and topple mountain peaks. Not once did she find discomfort.

Joy can be found in a willful choice and pain in what is forced. This time, Caitriona found relief. She found herself sighing as the dragon rose within her to embrace her mortal flesh and tuck it aside, to take hold, and become present. Above all, she found herself within its mind and there she was at peace. Because it wasn't a separate mind at all. The dragon wasn't a separate being. It was her all along.

What a wonder, what a *release* to finally accept all versions of oneself.

She was the dragon as much as the dragon was her. Caitriona only had to accept it as such to take to the skies, feel the heat of the day on her scale-covered body, and the fire churning in her stomach ready to be used when she wanted to set it free. Her wings were broad, catching on trees as she stretched them outward and pushed off the earth. Her tail hit the stone as she shifted into the air. The sky surrounded her, the ridges of the valley her border to follow.

She was beautiful. She was strength. She was entirely herself.

Crowley took to the skies, pumping his wings to follow her but rapidly became a black fleck as she picked up speed. Beyond was a gold eagle that she quickly overtook as well. To the south, glinting in the summer sun, was the gray and white stone that made up Braewick City where she would take her place as heir and help decide how they would set forth to get back those taken and win this unwanted war.

CHAPTER THIRTY-ONE

GREER

The last she heard from Caitriona, it was with news that Lachlan refused to join them and they were heading home. Then it was silence for days and each night Greer looked over her maps of the Mazgate Dominion, measuring the distance and calculating how long it would take for them to arrive. They should have returned days before, but they didn't, and Greer was uneasy.

"They could be taking their time. Give it another day, two even, before you get worried," Barden reassured her as they lay in her bed. Curling his hand over her bare shoulder, his fingers moved down her arm before his lips pressed against the side of her neck, alighting her skin with sparking joy. She sighed into his embrace and let her worry subside until they parted. He was likely right, after all. At least, that was what Greer told herself.

Greer busied herself during the day with further tasks, her to-do list being ever present and never shortening. Barden spent hours with the classes of guards and Greer joined him, finding the swing of her blade an excellent way to rid herself of simmering nerves.

Then the bell began to toll. The higher tone, the special one they chose to signify the golden dragon gracing the skies. Training stopped and all froze in place as they listened.

Barden looked at Greer, sweat and hair plastered to his forehead. "Is that?"

She grinned. "I think it is."

An older guard that served with Shaw took over Barden's teachings as they headed to the stables.

"Queen Greer!" Paul yelled, leaning from the stable entrance. "I have your horse saddled and ready."

"Just as we practiced." Greer grinned. The young guard led her mare to the stable yard and helped Greer mount. Greer adjusted herself upon her horse as a servant ran from the castle and offered Greer a bundle of clothing for Caitriona.

As she left the castle grounds with Barden, Paul and other guards following, she glanced at the barricades where larger weapons waited—all precautions she hoped she didn't need.

"There are no rules now," Isla explained only days before. "Caitriona was part of a now completed curse. Kayl made it clear he wanted a dragon within the castle and for the king to die, both objectives were achieved, and so Caitriona was set free. But that dragon's still in her, it's a part of her, and while I can't promise you it'll be Caitriona if she becomes a dragon again, the dragon will not be a mindless weapon set to destroy the castle. It's no longer entwined in the destiny Kayl set forth."

Greer went so far as tying a ribbon to the Elder Tree to put her wish into the world, that if Caitriona became a dragon, she'd retain her sensibilities, hold onto her compassion, and still be Caitriona, just in another form.

They couldn't be certain though, so the weapons remained. Should the dragon attack, the guards would strike her wing, her tail, but never, ever a killing blow.

"I told her to land in the northern fields," Greer told her troop of guards, "on the off chance she became a dragon again. If she does that, we should be comforted to know it's her. If she doesn't, give it a moment, ensure she's getting her bearings, don't attack unless she attacks first."

Farmers pulled to the side of the roadway, their carts heavy with summer harvest, and watched as the party proceeded northward.

"It feels right," Barden admitted. Amongst Barden's fleet of younger sisters, Caitriona had been added to that list. "It feels like we've finally achieved something, that Caitriona's fully recovered from what happened."

"I agree," Greer replied as they slowed to pass into the woods bordering the northern part of the city before the farming fields. "Perhaps this travel was good for her. She finally got it through her head that we love her all the same."

They rode halfway through the woods when the thunderous wind caused by dragon wings bent the trees and sucked away the air. Through the parting of leaves, Greer saw the flash of gold and a large creature's movement above. Despite being further away, the horses grew skittish, knowing a threat was nearby. Refusing to move forward, they reared and thrashed their heads. Greer held up her hand. "Let's dismount and walk the rest of the way. There's no need to worry the horses more than necessary."

With Caitriona's clothing clutched to her chest, they moved up the pathway, the light of the fields blinding as they approached the break in the trees. The summer bugs and birds grew silent. Typically, the woods were full of noises from the creatures both great and small that made their homes amongst the trees and brush. Greer ignored the unusual silence; it was common behavior to grow silent in the face of a dragon.

Beyond, in the recently harvested wheat field, the gold dragon landed, the air gushing as its wings folded. It shook its massive head and its gold scales glittered in the sun before it began to shrink, curling into itself as it sank closer to the ground and vanished from sight. Greer and the guards stopped walking. It was a marvel that none could turn from.

"She did it." Barden made a small smile and his face brightened.

Greer's pride couldn't be hidden and was made all the better by Barden's delight.

"Let's go get her," Greer said. "You all should stand back a bit though, give her privacy. I don't believe she'll be dressed. I can go by myself into the—"

Barden's hand clamped down on Greer's shoulder and she looked up, freezing in place as a figure stepped out from the tree line. They raised a bow and arrow, and the thunk of the bow string sounded across the space. The swish of the arrow passed through the air and rushed directly toward Greer's heart.

She gasped, stepping backward with Caitriona's clothing falling from her hands. She stumbled as Barden pushed her out of the way and placed his body in her place. The arrow struck Barden in the shoulder, making him twist from the force of the hit. A curse slipped under his breath as he touched the arrow shaft briefly before looking up. It hit him in his non-dominant shoulder, a lucky blow allowing him to still fight and wouldn't be a killing wound. Greer breathed.

The rest of the guards rushed forward, their boots picking up the pathway's dry soil, and swords and bows coming out with each forward step. But the figure already let another arrow fly and it hit one of Greer's guard's in the center of his chest; a man named Dwayne who was ten years her senior. He collapsed immediately.

"Hurry! Someone get to Caitriona!" Greer called, drawing forth her own sword. She stepped forward, ready to charge the figure as well but Barden's arm came around her torso, forcing her behind him. He grabbed her arms, pinning her to the spot as she pushed forward again to charge the bowman.

"You can't go running head on into a fight," he whispered, his brow prickled with sweat. "Greer, you're *queen*. You aren't the wild heir anymore. You need to stay behind. Let the people who are trained to protect you do this work."

"*Barden*," Greer growled. "Cait is out there, too!"

"Let your guards take care of it." He ran his fingers down her cheek, a brief movement that conveyed so much more. He turned to Paul who stood nearby, sword out as he stared down the archer. "Go to Caitriona. Make sure it's safe before she comes into the woods."

Greer knew he was right, damn him. She looked over his shoulder at the figure, rapidly becoming surrounded by other guards. Paul gathered Caitriona's dropped clothing and jogged past the cluster toward the field. Two more followed on Paul's heels, their heads turning as they looked for additional threats. Barden's grip lessened, drawing Greer's attention back. The arrow still stood out from his shoulder and his clothing was growing wet with blood. "Are you alright?"

"I'm fine, just an annoying shoulder wound. I can feel it, it's in the flesh of the muscle, it can get fixed once we're back at the castle," he breathed, adrenaline making his cheeks pink and his lips pale. He looked over his shoulder. "They already got him, see? You need to keep your head on, my queen. Don't go running directly into danger. You're no good to anyone if you're dead."

Greer gave a half smile. Some people said Barden worked so well as her right hand because he was talented with a sword and quick to fight and defend. But Greer knew the truth, it was because he was one of very few people on a very short list who could talk her out of her hot-headed decisions.

"Well, since he's apprehended ..." Greer gave Barden a nod before stepping around him and moving forward. She stepped past Dwayne's body; he had a wife in the royal guard who was currently guarding her mother. Greer's heart churned over the awful news she'd have to deliver. At least the arrow hit him square in the chest and took him quickly.

Pointing at two other guards, she nodded toward the tree line. "Spread out, look for more. Someone else, go back to the castle to get a cart and a healer."

In the fields beyond, a giant bird landed, and a person who seemed capable of taking flight as well. In any other circumstance, Greer would stop to marvel, but she only registered the three figures as they approached, all fully dressed. Caitriona, golden in the light of the afternoon, and Ceenear with her bow in hand, along with a man she didn't recognize. Raum and Ailith were missing from the group, which was a distinct thought in Greer's mind swiftly buried by the chaos around her. Paul ran to the trio's side and the other guards loitered on the edge of the field where they scanned for additional threats.

Caitriona lifted her face and paused before approaching more hesitantly. Her gaze on the man who was knocked to his knees and held tight between two guards with more arrows trained toward his head.

Greer crossed over the pressed earth and cuts from wagon wheels, her guards parting to allow her to make way before stopping before the man and angling her sword to press it into his chest if need be.

"Who are you?" Greer hissed as she looked down at the figure. He was a man not much older than her, his clothing dirty, his ears pointed. "Who sent you, fae?"

"I believe you've already been introduced, haven't you?" the man began. "He was gifted the ability to creep into your halls and possess your people. He said it was a delight to touch your flesh and squeeze your throat. He said his pulse still upticks with excitement when he thinks of your desperate breaths. He said he can't wait to do it again."

A chill traveled up Greer's back, the memory of the light-sucking gloom still fresh on her mind while the bruises from Shad still colored her throat.

"Do you have a message from him?" Her voice was stern, all warmth she had with Barden swept aside, and now she was a queen with a sword in hand, sick of the princeling's torment on her city. To the side, Caitriona entered the grove of trees, Ceenear behind her, and a man with copper-blonde hair followed. The fae bowman's eyes flickered toward them with interest, throwing fuel on Greer's rage-filled fire. "Or did you just come here to do something he's too weak to do himself?"

The man smiled. "Oh, I've done exactly what he wanted me to do. You realize, Queen Greer, you were never the true target. Not really."

Caitriona gasped; a sound filled with fright that drew Greer's attention to her sister as panic jolted her core.

"Cait?" she whispered, looking for some other threat she hadn't yet perceived. Caitriona remained on the forest edge but her face was pale with shock, her eyes shimmering with tears as she looked beyond Greer.

"Barden!" Caitriona stepped forward with her hands extended.

Greer spun in the other direction; the action so immediate she hadn't thought to turn, she simply did. Down the pathway in the trees where she just stood, Barden's knees went out and he fell to the forest floor.

"Barden?" Greer's voice was something unfamiliar to her. She left the bowman and ran down the pathway. Her sword dropped from her hand as she collapsed beside Barden.

He lay gasping in the leaves, his eyes trained on the sky above as his hand uselessly reached the arrow sticking out of his shoulder and missed again and again. Greer looked over his body for further wounds she missed but he was whole, *solid*, beside the arrow in his shoulder.

"Barden? *Barden*," Greer repeated, running her hand over his moist face to brush back his hair pointlessly and cup his cheek. She looked at the arrow, hesitating. This wasn't right. The arrow shouldn't have caused him much harm. It was just a shoulder wound.

He said he was fine. He said he wasn't concerned.

But Barden's face rolled to the side and his gaze found Greer's. *This wasn't fine.*

The whites of his eyes were bloodshot and made their blue glow. His lips were pale and speckled with spit. He worked his mouth, trying to form words on his tongue that betrayed him and kept him silent.

"Barden?" The panic held her in place, clutching her throat and heart, and made the world seem unnaturally still around her. "How do I? I don't know what to do, this shouldn't ... *what happened?*"

"I'll help!" a voice called and there was movement drawing near. "I know some medicine, let me look!"

Greer turned toward the approaching figure, her hand going for the sword she dropped feet away—too far to reach—but it was the man who had stood beside Caitriona. He slid to the ground opposite Greer with his strawberry-blonde hair hanging in his face as he pulled Barden's shirt to expose the wound.

"It's Lachlan, Ree. He can help, he can help," Caitriona said from somewhere in the distance, but Greer couldn't focus on her, not now.

She stared at the quick-moving hands of the man before her as Lachlan wiped Barden's shoulder and drew still. He ran his fingers over the arrow sticking out, slick with something greasy, and rubbed it between his fingers, lifting them to his nose and sniffing. His gaze rose to Greer's, eyes wide as he met her look, and Greer knew. She knew in his expression it was the worst of her fears.

"Save him?" Greer pleaded, trying to reason with something she knew was impossible but would not yet acknowledge. She was a queen, was she not? She could demand anything she saw fit. And in this, she demanded life. "It's just a shoulder wound. This shouldn't be happening, he said he was fine. He said he was ..."

Lachlan shook his head and gestured at the arrow.

"It's coated in sap." He wiped his fingers on his pants leg and the grease came away black on his trousers.

"What does that mean?" Caitriona asked.

"It's sap from an Elder Tree. There's no—I'm sorry—there's no saving him."

Greer shook her head repeatedly, grasping Barden's hand that twitched in hers with a fine vibration he seemed unable to control. His hand was so cold, like ice found on a warm spring day, unnatural to the surroundings, and unfamiliar for someone who was meant to be alive and filled with the heat of pumping blood.

"No, that's not how it works," Greer whispered. She didn't recognize her own voice. It was quaking, weak, and filled with something feral and broken. They were words spoken by another version of her, a version she was going to leave behind. The person she would always see as the person she was *before* as she slowly became the person she was *after*. "The sap brings people *back* to life. It doesn't kill them."

Lachlan shook his head. "It does the reversal once and only once. The dead come to life and the living die. There's no undoing it, there's no saving—"

"You *need* to save him," Greer insisted, staring at Lachlan through tear-filled eyes that gave him an underwater quality. She wanted to grab hold of him, shake his shoulders, beg at his feet, weep all the tears in the world against his chest. This stranger she waited for who was going to be the answer to all her problems. All of them. "*You need to.*"

A sound drew her attention down. Barden stared at her as if seeing her for the first time. His eyes were filled with wonderment, the corner of his pale lips curling slightly as he tried to smile. He was oblivious to the conversation around him; already shifting further from Greer onto a path she could not follow. Greer's grip tightened on his hand, unwilling to let him leave her behind. But oh, his hands were cold. His palm clammy. His touch not right.

This wasn't right. Barden was always a force, always strong, always bigger and brighter in the world than Greer ever hoped to be. He was solid, he was power, he was heart, and now he was reduced to something weak and shaking on the forest floor. His body quaked from a wound that should have been a simple fix, a simple thing to care for.

He said he was fine.

From his shoulder, his veins turned black, spreading rapidly along his collarbone and up his neck before spilling over his cheeks and reaching toward his eyes. Lachlan was yelling for herbs and supplies. Ceenear was running into the bushes. Caitriona sat beside them as Lachlan's hands moved to the arrow and pressed down on Barden's shoulder as he tried to pull it free.

Barden's lips moved repeatedly, a whisper of words still working their way out. Greer stretched out her legs, pressing her belly to the earth to get closer to him, to lay with him like they laid together that morning.

"It's all right Barden, you don't have to speak," she whispered, squeezing his hand. His free hand touched her hair, fingers pulling away strands from her scalp without trying, the movement clumsy and uncontrolled.

Lachlan worked across from her, cleaning the wound and pressing chewed herbs into it. He seemed to yell at guards, but Greer couldn't hear him, she couldn't follow what he was saying. Even Caitriona moved to Barden's head now, her hands touching Greer's shoulder gently, but they were all distant. All these people around her. Her sister, the guards, Lachlan, Ceenear. They existed in some other realm while the only person to exist beside her and hold Greer's full attention lay on the ground.

Barden's lips kept moving with repetition, and Greer crept forward, leaning her ear down. His lips brushed over the curve of her earlobe, light and bittersweet all at once. Almost like a kiss. The words she held out on, the one thing she didn't want to hear.

"Not until we win the war," Greer said. "Not until we—"

He stared at her, his lips still. The shaking breaths ceased as the black veins successfully covered his face and leaked into his eyes, leaving them empty, foggy, and unliving. Greer stared for a moment, feeling Caitriona's arms come around her. Lachlan grew still, his hands still over Barden's shoulder but his eyes studied Greer.

Waiting, he was waiting to see what she would say, what she would do.

The forest was silent. The birds, the bugs, all gone. Still gone. Or perhaps they were there, waiting, watching, just as Lachlan was, knowing what would come next. The band of guards were still, all present but three. Two dead on the ground and one missing, Greer realized distantly. Ailith, where was Ailith?

Everything watched. Everything waited. All but a slow, gurgling from behind Greer, bubbling up and outward into a laugh. Greer plummeted back to her body, suddenly present and full of pain.

She let go of Barden's hand, her heart ripping from her own chest to lay on the ground beside him where it could bleed out. At least, that's what she felt it was doing as she got to her feet and turned toward the fae bowman. Walking forward, she lifted her sword, taking it in both hands as she came closer to the man who continued laughing, the corners of his eyes crinkled and tears filled them with glee. The guards holding him reacted to her movements. Stepping aside, they held his arms tight.

She quickly swung her sword with all her heartbreak and rage lent into her strength to send it through the man's neck with ease. It cut his laugh off with a gurgle of spurting blood, his head fell to the forest floor with a dull thunk before rolling to the feet of a guard. Yet no one moved, save for the two who held the bowman still. They let go of his body, allowing it to fall to the dirt where blood poured into the earth.

Greer dropped her sword. Stumbling backwards before turning towards Barden.

The woman she had been when she stood there previously solidified into the person she was *before*. She was in the realm of *after*. Like any other moment similar to this, she hadn't known it when she experienced it and that was the bitterness of it all. Mere minutes passed but it was done. The last time she held his hand and he squeezed back was over. The last time he admonished her, the last time he smiled, the last time he said ...

And when she sunk to the ground beside him once more, his final words were already spoken and left to live as an echo in the hollowness of her chest. His final words something only *she* heard, left to be cherished and protected from others. A special gift no one else could have.

She lay upon the ground, curling her body against his, and placed her cheek to his chest. She wanted to pull the earth over them both, to bury herself beside him.

She rested her head there just that morning, hearing the strong vibration of his heart. He had laughed, some joke passed between them, and his laughter echoed in his chest where stillness now grew, stretching to her, spreading, echoing. The hollowness within her expanded as well, so large it could engulf the world of all feeling. He wasn't there, it was only a shell, his life already gone when it had *just been there*.

It all became a series of justs: he was *just* alive, *just* speaking, *just* training, *just* walking, *just* ...

Reverberating through her skull and everything within her, his final words, his long-withheld feelings she was an idiot to ignore. She lied to herself, saying she didn't want it. All that time wasted when it was there, *right there* within reach. The thing she *always* desired and was too stubborn to enjoy, too focused on duty to reach for—the one craving that was within arm's reach. She committed his voice to her heart, lest her memory forget.

His final breath, his final words, repeated with dying strength and the final beatings of his heart, going on forever and ever:

My Love,
My Love,
My Love.

EPILOGUE

GREER

Each day attacked Greer's hollow body. The blows rang dull and vibrated through. Each day the separation between before and after grew. It was a place she had no desire to be in but was dragged forward with bloodied knees and wounded heart all the same. Each day drew her closer to the true end, the end she didn't want to have, but was unable to give consent to. Her power as queen only went so far.

Barden was laid out in the castle's mourning hall. While it was a grander location, there was no other place Greer wanted him to be and gratefully his mother Rowan appreciated the offer. As the sun settled beyond the valley for its night's rest, a large crowd gathered for the rites. The four men who carried Shaw to his grave now stood at the corners of the dais where Barden's body was placed upon a sheet with flowers, marsh fruit, and herbs.

Greer stood behind Rowan, wearing colors of green and black, which was appropriate for the burial they were about to perform. She remained straight backed and kept her face blank as she watched the room fill. Caitriona and her mother stood to the side, and Raum and Ceenear beyond, along with Lachlan. The half-fae prince's gaze met

Greer's and she looked away. She couldn't, *wouldn't*, be able to meet his eye. Not now. She needed time.

Lachlan tried all he could but the fact of the matter remained the same. The sap of the Elder Tree could revive someone who died, yes. But the books they read left out a critical detail, it also could kill someone who was already healthy. All that was necessary was the mix of blood with the sap and dutifully done by dipping the arrow into the sap itself. Greer hadn't thought twice when the guard Dwayne fell from the arrow to his heart, but upon inspection, they discovered it hadn't gone directly there. The sap was close enough to enter his bloodstream and spread quickly, taking his life immediately. While with Barden, it took longer because of its placement. The result was always going to be the same. Even giving Barden another dose of the sap would have done nothing. It all was a one-use trick. Good to kill or bring to life once and nothing else.

Lachlan knew from his lessons in Ätbënas. He tried to explain it, but he still obeyed Greer and made attempt after attempt to bring Barden back until Caitriona pulled Greer away from Barden's body. Night was falling and guards had arrived with a cart and sheet to carry Barden home.

Greer had fallen into the oblivion of exhaustion some time near morning, and woke with Caitriona in her bed, her sister's arms wrapped tightly around Greer even in sleep. She attempted to continue plans, reading documents, looking at maps but found herself staring. She had no idea how much time passed. Her mind couldn't stay focused.

The terror of that day made memories of Barden in those final moments confusing and fuzzy. Did she want to remember them? Her last moments with him? Did she want to remember how he fell, weak and hurt; of how he faded away before she could do anything? Did she want to remember how she couldn't save him? But if she forgot, she would be letting go of his voice, so small and soft and declaring all that his heart kept.

Rowan instructed her on the funeral proceedings, teaching her the songs and promising to take her hand and lead her through. So, Greer stood back, overseeing the start of it all, her eyes settling on Barden's face.

He remained pale, his veins still black, but they forced his eyes to close. They dressed him in his armor, cleaned his hair and brushed it back, and Greer found herself wishing she could see his eyes one more time. But even that was taken and rendered impossible. The magic of the sap left them veined orbs.

Rowan stepped forward and slowly began to sing, the guttural song rose into her throat and curled into an echoing hollow sound that released the loss into the air. Her voice floated through the crowd; it ricocheted over the walls of the mourning room and leaked into the halls of the castle to silence all who heard it. Her keening continued, repeating the verse, and she reached behind to grasp Greer's hand, pulling the queen forward to stand beside her.

Barden's sisters looked at Greer, and Holly smiled through her tears. Beyond in the crowd of faces stood Ailith's parents. Seeing their pale, heartbroken expressions was a dagger to her heart. Their daughter was lost and yet they found themselves there to show their respects for the man who trained Ailith.

Isla lingered in the back, glimpses of her smaller form came and went through the shifting of people in the crowded room. Greer hadn't spoken to the witch, but she saw the look on the old woman's face when she found out that sap could kill someone just as easily as it could make them live. A look of shock and then immediate sorrow, shadowed by concern.

Greer pulled her gaze from the crowd and took in a deep breath, feeling her lungs expand and her heart ache as if it were filled with glass and cutting her to pieces from within. She closed her eyes and forced the song out. Curling through her throat and on her tongue, the lyrics coated the room with her heartbreak and sorrow.

They sang as Barden's body was lifted and carried from the room. Greer clung to Rowan and she to her as they followed. The keening spilled forward, exploded through the castle doors, and followed them down the stairs to the waiting carts. His body was placed gently, the flowers, fruit, and greenery draped over him, and Greer climbed onto the cart as she had only weeks before, the place beside her where Barden sat feeling physically painful to be empty.

They moved through the city, down the curving streets and towards the valley hills. People gathered this time, lining the sidewalks and taking off their caps, silent despite there being so many who watched as they passed by. Three carts held those who meant the most to Barden. His mother, his sisters, Greer, Caitriona, and an empty seat where Ailith should have sat. Beyond were the guards. The city guards were called to help with the castle as too many royal guards requested to attend the ceremony, and the winding procession lasted long after Barden's body passed.

The road to the marsh flickered with fireflies, twinkling on and off as they passed, unbothered by the lives of humans and the death of lovers. The marsh stretched out ahead, the steady glow not from fireflies, but the eyes of waiting dukes.

Arriving there, Greer was quick to get off the cart. Moving toward where Barden rested she grabbed a corner of the sheet he was carried on.

"My Queen, we can do that," one of the men murmured. Greer didn't care to notice who.

"I'm fine, I can carry his weight," Greer replied, not budging from her place. Rowan began singing, her voice mournful and splashing over the landscape.

"I'll help too," Caitriona said softly, stepping beside Greer and taking hold of another corner. Before the curse, Greer would have chased her off. Caitriona always wanted to help, but she hadn't the strength. Yet the magic retained from the curse and Caitriona's own determination made her strong and more capable than even Greer realized. Magic was powerful, too powerful in many ways, but she hadn't the energy to refuse her sister this. Caitriona smiled, although it didn't reach her eyes. "If Ailith was here, she'd help too."

Greer nodded. She wished Ailith was there, if only to know what occurred to her. If they were ever able to find the guard again, if they could save her from wherever she was taken, Greer hated that she would have to relive the day Barden was lost. She would have to see Ailith mourn and process the death while everyone else had likely moved on. Then again, Ailith would have company in her mourning. Greer couldn't fathom there being a point where it didn't hurt.

The men who carried Barden took the other two corners, the last two followed close behind to help if necessary. They walked into the water of the marsh. The coolness of it traveled up the skirts of Greer's dress and filled her shoes. The group paused and Greer swallowed, feeling the familiar tightness in her throat that she would no longer be able to breathe if she didn't move past her anxieties. Perhaps they could drown her with him.

"Greer," Caitriona whispered, returning Greer to herself to realize all had let go of the corners of the fabric, all but her. She dropped the cloth and stood still as the others left the water. Caitriona touched Greer's arm as she passed, giving it a reassuring squeeze as she stepped onto the shore.

Alone now, Barden's sinking body the only thing between Greer and the dukes who drew close, she looked at them with quiet fury. How dare these creatures live out the rest of their lives with the person who was taken from her too soon. How could they ever begin to understand what was lost when all they lived for was to capture fools near the water's edge and possibly, if they so found it honorable, to rise and fight in long forgotten battles.

Behind Greer, others sang, their voices rising to the stars and washing over Greer whose feet sunk into the silt. She reached to her side and pulled Barden's heavy sword free. It was made to fit his grasp which was greater than Greer's, and she looked at the etchings of the handle one final time. Simple curls of metal, entwining together then separating at the ends. She was so deep in her grief she felt pain from the design, and wished the curls remained entwined.

Stepping to Barden's body, she laid the sword upon him. An offering for the dukes, a sign to know he was taken too soon and would join their ranks if they saw fit. The dukes waited only a few feet away, their glittering eyes watched her steadily as they whispered in trickles and drips.

The water slowly rose to cover Barden's face as his body sank. Greer swallowed and stepped back with the weight of the universe pressing in.

The singers quieted and Rowan sang one lonely key as Greer stepped further onto the land, giving the dukes their space. Then silence descended. Greer knew it was time. The final step.

She sang, her pronunciation of the words Rowan taught her poor, but she sang. Her voice clear as a bell, rising ever louder. Nearly the same message Barden gave for Shaw only a few weeks prior now was hers to give on his behalf. Similar but different, the message was clear: *he is my love, I give him to you, please take him into your ranks.*

Her song ceased and the dukes slipped forward, circling Barden's body and gently taking the sword before one duke rose above the rest.

He appeared more solid than the others, more alive. He only just joined; the waters hadn't worked their way through him fully but the change was still apparent. He was meant to rest eternally but for this, he would rise again.

He stood before Greer with too sharp teeth and claw-like hands, the webbing between his fingers clear as he reached forward despite the low light. A duke through and through, but he took Barden into his arms as if he were a babe, cradling him to his chest as he gazed down upon him. Barden, his son.

Shaw lifted his gaze. His eyes were unblinking, beside the cloudy membrane that had grown over them. Greer returned his stare without flinching.

"Take care of him, please."

Shaw lifted his chin, a silent declaration of understanding, then lowered beneath the water clutching Barden's body against his own. He disappeared below the dark surface, leaving Greer on the marsh edge as alone as she felt she would be for the remainder of time.

Footsteps approached, and a hand touched her shoulder.

"Come, Greer," her mother whispered. There was a quiver in her voice *not* from unshed tears. The woman was never prone to them. No, this was from barely withheld anger. "Let's go home. You must rest; there's a war to win and an unworthy prince whose blood you must spill."

COMING SOON!

Grief is a crown she cannot take off—and war waits for no mourning. Vanquished, book three of The Elder Tree Trilogy, releasing January 2026

ACKNOWLEDGMENTS

I am beyond grateful to have *Diminished* brought into the world. While *Tarnished* was the book I yearned for as a teen and young adult, *Diminished* is the book of my heart, and reflects so many of my struggles that I know others have experienced as well. In particular, it's my love letter to queer youths and those who suffer with anxiety disorders. To young queer readers, I hope you know you're special, unique, and there are people in the world who accept and love you for exactly who you are —even if you haven't met those people yet.

To get this book into your hands, it passed through the hands of Jean and Staci first who continue to champion my story. I thank you both for being patient with me as I didn't want to commit to a trilogy until I knew the final book was figured out. I'm also grateful to the creative team behind the visuals of *Diminished*: Luxury Banshee, Olesya, Michelle, Dewi, and Diana.

My beta readers of *Diminished*, you're all amazing and I'm sorry for the torment I put you through (except I'm not, but you already know that). Meredith, Christine, Josie, Teagan, Taylor, and Andrew, thanks for enduring the emotional onslaught.

Ali, thank you for jumping in to help me develop the continuation of this story when I was not yet finished with *Tarnished*, and far and away from a publishing deal. You did so much for this story, from helping me figure out the title to finding ways to make everything hurt a little more. Of course, there's my elementals too: Christine, Courtney and Kassidy. You three empowered me so much as I worked on this book. You helped me through so many emotions and your cheering was such a positive influence as I juggled this novel and so much more. You all taught me the true power of girlhood and I am grateful to have you in my life.

This story is deeply entwined with my emotions. It was exhausting to write, but also therapeutic and fulfilling. Róisín's orphanhood is based loosely on that of my grandmother's whose subsequent sternness could be viewed as uncaring, but she loved deeply. The mental path Caitriona travels is deeply familiar to me as I navigated entering adulthood with my disabilities coming forward and not recognizing myself anymore. I often felt I had nothing to live for, and I'm so grateful I was wrong. Greer's anxiety and panic attacks were written from my personal experience with the generalized anxiety disorder I've endured for more than a decade. My anxiety attacks often felt like being haunted by darkness, and with time I received help to keep that darkness at bay. I'm grateful to my medical team, including therapists of both the mental and physical varieties—Alisa, Diana, and Corey—for helping me recognize those feelings for what they are.

I have such amazing support in my life as I write, but also as I've focused on both my career, and mental and physical health. Thank you to my parents and my in-laws. You've all been receptive, patient, and willing to both embrace and learn the various life changes that have been thrust upon me. To my spouse, your support and love means the world and I'd be lost without it.

For my little boy, you are my heart thrust from my body to live and breathe and grow and learn beyond me. How wonderful it is to know you. How grateful I am to have your love and support. Know that if ever you find you don't recognize your heart, I'll be there to remind you.

www.ingramcontent.com/pod-product-compliance
Lightning Source LLC
LaVergne TN
LVHW040140190825
819011LV00012B/21/J